luca

EDEN SUMMERS

1

PENNY

My heels tap along the floorboards as I make my way down the shadowed hall of my new temporary home.

It's nice here. Quiet.

I no longer need to constantly straddle fight or flight. There are no monsters knocking at the door. Only the haunting thoughts of my past to interrupt the peace.

I enter the living room, the warm lights illuminating the man waiting for me on the sofa.

Luca Hart.

He's my savior. My protector. An undefeatable force who rescued me from a life of sexual slavery.

His mouth kicks in a subtle grin, the coaxing tease of lips making me wish I could return the gesture with equal measure.

"You look nice." His gaze treks my body, from my face to my toes and all the way back again.

Normally, that sort of admiration would make me shudder, but the shiver wracking my body stems from something inquisitive. Something more aligned with anticipation.

He has a way of bleaching my past to make me feel clean, despite my mind's determination to do the opposite.

"Thank you." I lower my focus to take in the beautiful dress clinging to my waist, the shiny satin, the polished shoes. This isn't an outfit I'd usually enjoy wearing. In fact, it's something I would despise after the years being forced into exquisite attire by my puppet master, but Luca makes everything easier.

He pushes to his feet, all tall, broad and handsome, his black suit tailored to perfection. "Are you ready to leave?" He stops before me, his lingering gaze intense, yet somehow kind.

"Yes. I just need—"

A burst of noise assaults my ears. Glass rains to the floor from the French doors across the other side of the room.

Luca's smile vanishes. His body jolts in slow motion.

Everything slows—my mind, my movements, and my comprehension. What's happening?

"Luca?" I reach for him and that's when I see it—the blood. The approaching death.

A lake of deep crimson seeps out from beneath his jacket, the crisp white of his shirt transforming before my eyes.

Snapshots of a similar injury assail me.

Chloe was shot like this. *Exactly* like this. One minute, she was alive. The next, she was dead.

Please, *no*. Not again.

The world snaps back to match the hammering pace of my heart. "Tell me what to do."

Blood splutters from his lips as he stands immobile, his eyes blinking without focus.

Fear consumes me, pummeling me with sickening heartache. I grasp his arm, clutching tight, but he doesn't respond. "*Luca.*"

I don't know what to do. I'm lost. Helpless.

Those demons usually kept at bay rush back to attack me. They taunt me about losing my protector. They cackle about my approaching demise.

I'm nothing without him. I won't survive. I don't want to.

"Luca, *please*."

He slips from my grip, falling to the tile, his head hitting with a reverberating thwack.

"Oh, God, *no*." I collapse beside him, smothering his wound, trying to stem the blood even though it gushes through my fingers. "Don't leave me."

He stares at me. Gurgles. Chokes.

"No." I beg. "Don't do this. Stay with me."

"There's no use."

I freeze at the familiar voice coming from the other side of the room. The icy chill of horror slithers through my veins. I don't want to raise my eyes, but there he is, standing before the French doors.

Robert—the man I was promised to like an object, and now he's here to claim me.

But it can't be real.

He's meant to be dead.

I scamper to my feet, blood dripping from my fingers, bile rising up my throat. "No."

"Penny." He starts toward me, one slow step after another, his voice getting louder and louder. "Penny."

"No." I prepare to run toward him. To kill him with my bare hands for taking Luca from me. But my legs won't move. "You should've shot me," I scream. "Why didn't you shoot me?"

He smirks, chilling my veins. "*Penny.*"

I startle and shoot upright in bed. I gasp for breath, as I cling to the soft sheets, my body coated in a sticky layer of sweat.

Every night, it's the same. One nightmare after another. One death that follows the next.

It's either my brother, Sebastian, my protector, Luca, my parents, or one of the many women I lost while living beneath the roof of a sex traffickers' mansion.

I've witnessed everyone I care about being taken from me. Always by the same man. The same ghost.

Yet, I'm never the one to die.

I know why, too.

It's because I don't fear death. If anything, I continue to crave it.

What frightens me is the loss of those I care about. That's the true taunt of the nightly demons. I'm constantly reminded I still have so much to lose. That this freedom is only a mirage.

I shudder out a shaky breath and wipe my hands down my face.

I hate this.

Every day starts with horror, and every night begins with dread. There's no escape.

I've been safe for days now, cocooned in the protection of Luca's inner suburban home in Portland.

I suck in a deep breath, forcing calm, and let it out slowly.

Sunlight bathes the room, letting me know it's morning and I no longer need to battle for rest.

Because that's all I've been doing. Battling.

I fight to pretend I'm doing okay. I scramble to create some kind of normalcy in a world entirely unfamiliar to me. It's like I've been thrown into a melee of mental torment. My thoughts are my shackles now. This head of mine is a prison.

I never imagined freedom would be like this.

Painful.

Suffocating.

Now I know better.

I slide from the bed, drag my feet to the adjoining bathroom to take a shower, then dress and make my way through the house.

The hall is exactly like it was in my dream. Shadowed and empty. The living room is a carbon copy, too, those French doors tormenting me from my peripheral vision.

I attempt to distract myself by pulling pans from drawers and food from the fridge, like I have every morning since I've been in this sanctuary.

I cook. I eat. I clean.

And when Luca walks into the open living area, his hair mussed from sleep, his hazel eyes lazily blinking, I breathe a sigh of relief at the visual confirmation that my nightmare was nothing more than a cruel joke of my subconscious.

There's no suit this time. Only a black T-shirt and stone-washed jeans, the casual attire suiting him perfectly.

"Morning." He rakes a hand over his skull and winces when his fingers brush the slowly healing injury above his ear. He'd been shot while saving me, the bullet grazing his head, and there's not a moment when I'm not entirely aware of what he could've lost.

"Morning." I turn to the far wall of the kitchen and flick on the coffee machine. "I only finished cooking breakfast a little while ago. Your omelet should still be warm, but you might want to give it a few seconds in the microwave."

"I'm sure it's fine."

There's the slide of a plate behind me. The clink of cutlery. Then the low grumble of a man who appreciates a home-cooked meal. "This is good."

"I'm glad you like it." I pull two mugs from a head-high cupboard. "Strong coffee this morning?"

"Always."

I press buttons on the coffee machine, the tingle of his attention resting at the back of my neck as the sweet gurgle of liquid heaven fills the silence.

"What are your plans for today?" he asks.

I stiffen, hating this rerun conversation. "The same as yesterday, I guess."

"You should go out. Get some fresh air. We could even catch a movie."

I shake my head and pull the filled mugs from the machine. "Not today."

As much as it pains me to trap him here when he refuses to leave the house without me, I'm simply not ready to face the outside world. I don't want to be in the open, waiting to be found. Not by the police, my family, or Luther Torian's men. Right here is where I want to stay until I can figure out an alternative.

"You should leave, though." I turn and slide his mug toward him, seated at the opposite side of the island counter. "I can stay on my own."

He forks a mouthful of egg into his mouth, his reprimanding eyes holding mine as he chews. "No."

"You've shown me how safe the house is." The security system is state of the art. Video cameras. Door and window alarms.

"I'm not leaving you." His tone is final. *Lethal*. I wish I wasn't comforted by his stringent protection. "If you're adamant about staying, at least let me set up the phone so you can call your friends. You haven't spoken to them since Greece."

I disguise the pang of guilt with a fake smile. "Not today. They need more time to focus on getting their story straight so they can return home."

"Penny." My name is a warning. A barely growled admonishment as his jaw ticks. "One phone call—"

"Not today, Luca."

I hate his disappointment. It tears at me. But I'm not ready to speak to my sisters. I know it's hard for him to understand. Hell, it's hard for *me* to understand. This time last week, those women were my life. My everything. Along with Tobias—my captor's son. The little boy I helped raise.

It's clear, though, that I need to keep my distance. The only thing I can bring to their lives at the moment is negativity. And I won't risk my bad attitude rubbing off on them.

"Fine. Have it your way." He wipes the back of his hand over his mouth, brushing away any stray remains of his breakfast. "I guess staying home and chilling out is at the top of our agenda."

"Chilling out?" I scoff. "Do you even know how? You spend hours in your exercise room punishing your body as if you're preparing for Armageddon."

"Like you can talk. You flitter around the house all day, cooking, cleaning, doing laundry. It's like you're my fucking slav —" He stops mid-sentence, his chin hitching. "*Shit*."

A slow burn creeps up my neck, my shame undoubtedly visible in the color of my skin. It's not the word that bothers me. I've been called a slave more times than anyone could count. What hurts is his reaction. His embarrassment. Over me.

He cringes. "I didn't mean—"

"Forget it." I fight harder to keep my smile in place. "You know it doesn't bother me."

He sighs and glides a rough hand over his forehead. "I need more fucking sleep."

"Yeah." I grab a cloth from the sink and begin wiping down the counter. "I agree. You go to bed too late."

He huffs out a faint chuckle. "Again, you're not the best point of reference. I'm pretty sure you get less sleep than I do."

I keep wiping, determined to remain busy as he continues to eye me like a bug under a microscope. He knows too much about me. Horrific details. Lies, too. He was told I enjoyed the torture Luther put me through. That I loved everything those monsters inflicted.

I hate him having that information. I hate even more that he might believe the slander.

"You're having nightmares, aren't you?" he asks.

"No." The denial slips out easily. "I'm getting a lot of sleep. I'm doing really well."

I don't want him wasting his time worrying about me. Not when I'm already a grade-A burden. He was never meant to bring

6

me back to the States. He wanted to stay in the Greek Islands and help take down the sex trafficking operation.

Instead, he's here. Stuck with me, while doing his best not to show his resentment.

That's why I cook. Why I clean. Why I paste on a smile whenever he's around and pretend I'm climbing back on my feet.

I won't cause any more trouble than I already have.

"Sure you are." He forks another mouthful and scrutinizes me as he chews. I'm sure he sees through my fake facade, but until he calls me on it, I'll maintain this charade.

I'm content in his sanctuary even though the irony hasn't been lost on me.

I fought so hard to escape Luther's house only to mentally trap myself within another. I spent years trying to liberate myself from one man—now I'm racked with fear that the guy before me will cut me loose at any given moment.

It's a complete shift in situation. Yet the sense of being trapped is the same.

"Why are you looking at me like that?" I place down the cloth and reach for my coffee, attempting to shield my face. "I swear you keep scrutinizing me, hoping to find some hidden issue that isn't there."

"Penny, you know I—"

The doorbell rings, startling me. The jostle of my arms sends a splash of coffee over the lip of my mug.

"Don't panic." He places his fork on the counter. "I'm expecting someone."

My heart sinks, the painfully squeezing organ dropping to my stomach as I wipe up the liquid spill.

"Is it that woman again?" The question flies from my lips unbidden.

I shouldn't have asked. I've deliberately kept my curiosity to myself, not wanting to pry. Yet the lack of knowledge has plagued me.

"Yes." He glides off the stool and when I raise my gaze to his, those eyes have gentled, as if he's trying to soften a blow. "Do you want to meet her?"

"No."

She's come here every day for the past three days. They talk for hours, murmuring in low tones over unending cups of coffee. It's clear they're close. Or at least, they want to be. I'm certain my lingering company is the only thing keeping them apart.

That's one of the reasons I hide when she arrives. I haven't even met her, choosing instead to remain in my room, or in the secluded spot I've claimed on the back deck.

I've tried hard not to pry about the woman who keeps him company even though I get a sinking sensation whenever she arrives.

"I'll leave you in privacy." I keep clinging to my mug as I walk around the counter. "I'll be in the backyard."

I wish I could remain by his side. That I was whole enough to be a normal person, conversing and laughing whenever company arrived. Once, I even tried to imagine what it would be like to live here long-term. Like a wife. Just me and Luca. No outside world. No fears.

But those fantasies are for normal people. Unbroken women.

I'm nothing if not entirely damaged.

My only choice is to tread lightly and lessen the burden on a man who never wanted me here. I need to pretend I'm invisible and make sure I don't provoke any unwanted reactions.

Just like I did when I was a slave.

2

LUCA

The doorbell rings again as Penny creeps onto the back deck, closing the door gently behind her.

"Fuck." I wipe a rough hand over the back of my neck, entirely out of my element. I don't know what I'm meant to do with her. I've given her space. I haven't pushed. But, goddamnit, all I've wanted to do is shove her into facing reality. She can't heal when she continues to ignore her past.

"*Luca*," Sarah shouts from the front yard. "Are you home?"

"I'm coming." I stalk down the hall and yank open the front door to find her scowling, a clump of filled shopping bags hanging from her hands.

"What the hell took so long?" She slams her haul at my chest, making me struggle to grasp the bags as she maneuvers around me to enter the house. "The least you could do is open the damn door when you're treating me like your little errand bitch."

I wrangle the straps of the bags into one hand and kick the door closed. "And the least you could do is have some fucking patience when it's barely nine o'clock."

I follow after her, but continue down the hall when she diverts to the open living area. I take the bags to my room, doing a quick search of the contents after I dump them on the bed. The self-help books I asked her to pick up are all there. The titles on trauma and PTSD wait for a time when Penny will be ready to read them. There're more clothes in there, too.

9

I keep buying shit in an attempt to help her... then can't bring myself to hand them over.

She's not ready for my input.

She has a process for dealing with her pain, and I have no right to mess with it.

I've gotta be patient—a fucking saint—while I watch her suffer.

I leave the bags in a pile on the mattress and return to Sarah in the kitchen, her hands already clasping a filled coffee mug.

My filled coffee mug.

"You know that's mine, right?" I stalk for the cupboards to retrieve another mug.

She shrugs. "Yeah, I know. But things always taste better when they're taken from someone you don't like."

Great. She's in one of *those* moods. The combative, poking, prodding type which does my head in.

"So, how is she today?" She cocks her hip against the counter. "Any change?"

"Nope." I play with the coffee machine, pressing buttons until it grumbles to life. "She's exactly the same, pretending life is peachy when clearly it isn't."

"Have you given her any of the things I've brought over? The clothes? The books?"

"I gave her the cell." I wait until my mug is filled, then walk around the island counter to reclaim my stool. "She didn't even bother to open the box. It's still sitting there. Untouched." I jerk my head toward the plastic-wrapped package on the dining table. "Every day I offer to set the phone up for her, but she doesn't want it. She has no interest in speaking to her friends. She says she's not ready. Which might be a good thing seeing as though I'm struggling to get in contact with Benji."

My brother was left in charge of taking care of the other women rescued from Luther's mansion. The three of them—Abi, Lilly and Nina—will remain with him until he's certain they've got their stories straight. Unfortunately, their freedom comes with a price. None of them can breathe a word about their time held captive.

"He's out of range." Sarah speaks through a slurp of my dregs. "Apparently, he's taken them to a cabin away from civilization."

"Says who?" I've been kept in the dark since returning to Portland—the isolation being partly my fault because I'm still pissed off at Torian for sending me home. But mainly because I want to keep Penny away from any unwanted external triggers.

"Layla. She said she spoke to her husband a few days ago and that he's trying not to pull his hair out. According to him, all the women do is cry."

Yeah, that sounds like my brother. Benji wasn't born with patience. Or common sense.

"Well, if you speak to her again, can you tell her I want him to call me? Even though Penny says she's not ready to talk, I want the information on hand in case she changes her mind."

"Sure. But have you actually asked her why she doesn't want to get in contact?" Sarah takes another gulp from her mug, then places it in the sink. "It could be something simple."

"I'm not pushing her." It's not my place even though I have to battle my instincts to do the opposite on the daily. "She speaks to the kid occasionally. Whenever he calls my phone, she picks up. But the conversations are brief. From what I've overheard, she stays on the line long enough to determine he's doing okay. Then she makes an excuse to end the chat. And she never asks to call him in return."

"She's distancing herself."

"No shit." I roll my eyes. "But from what? That woman is a fucking mystery to me. Is she distancing herself from the trauma? Or is it deeper than that? Is she trying to place space between those she loves because she still fears she's going to lose them?"

"Have you asked her?"

No. I try not to ask much of anything. "It's not my business."

She raises her brows, unimpressed. "I think you've earned the right to ask a few questions. Does she seem scared?"

"Yes, she's freaked, despite doing her best to act otherwise. She likes to paste on this fucking sweet smile and pretend she's fine." If only I couldn't see right through it. Her lips might lie, but those eyes never do. I see the pain she harbors.

"How do you know she's pretending? She might actually be healing. Maybe that smile is for real."

I pull my cell from the back pocket of my jeans and scroll to the app for the outside security cameras.

"Does this look like healing to you?" I swipe to the video feed of the backyard. She's sitting a few yards from one of the cameras, her face a picture of sorrow, her eyes dull as she stares blankly at the ground a few feet in front of her. "Look. She's fucking dead inside. She sits like that every minute she's not around me. Then as soon as I walk into view she switches to Mary freakin' Poppins."

Sarah leans into me, her attention on the screen. "Why is it that Torian's men have a thing with breaching the privacy of women? Does she know you're spying on her?"

"She *should*. I went through the house security with her when we first got here. But now she acts oblivious. I don't know if she forgot or if she's too numb to care. I don't even know if she remembers who you are because the vibe I got from her a few minutes ago felt…"

I'm not sure what it felt like. It was odd. Uncomfortable.

"Felt like what?" Sarah steps back, frowning at me.

"I don't know. It was like she thought she was intruding."

"On us?" Her voice holds a tone of incredulity. "As in, she thought we wanted privacy? Just the two of us."

"Yeah. Maybe."

She straightens, standing taller. "I hope you set her straight."

"I didn't get a chance. Someone kept ringing the fucking—"

"I come here for her, Luca. Not you." She scowls. "And for her to even assume—for *anyone* to assume…" She shudders. "You're so far from my type it isn't funny."

"You think I don't know that? *Jesus*. You're no dream boat yourself."

She gives a snake of a smile. "Hunter would disagree."

"Hunter's judgment is questionable. The guy's a walking, talking—"

"Choose your description wisely, my friend. I'd hate to have to hurt you."

"You mean to say you can hurt me more than this painful conversation?" I huff out a derisive laugh. "That would be quite a feat."

"You know I've got skills. But we're diverting off topic. What are you going to do about Penny?"

I slump against the counter, my forearms resting on the marble. "I don't know. I don't want to push her. Yet she lies through her teeth about how well she's coping. She just finished telling me she's sleeping well, and less than an hour ago I had to shout her

12

name three times to wake her from whatever nightmare had her screaming the house down."

"She lies even though you woke her?"

"I don't think she knows I've been waking her. I don't enter her room. I yell from down the hall."

"Christ, Luca, you're such a pussy. Why don't you take charge? Demand change."

My hibernating anger awakens, the warmth in my veins heating. Sarah thinks I don't want to take charge? Like I don't fight every day against the instinct to take control and dictate how Penny should face her recovery?

I want more than anything to drag her out of the darkness. To shake some life into her. But she's so fucking temperamental. She hasn't grieved for those she's lost. She hasn't cried. Not even once. Which makes me fucking petrified I'll push only to break her beyond salvation.

"I'm done with this conversation." I slide from my stool. "It's time for you to leave."

"No, not today. I'm not going to let you block me from her anymore. Enough is enough. Forcing her to speak to me isn't going to kill her."

"You're not pushing her," I snarl.

"And you're not her keeper."

Like hell I'm not. Her keeper is *exactly* what I am.

Her savior.

Her protector.

Her whatever-the-hell-she-needs.

"Luca, you're meant to be watching her temporarily. To get her on her feet so she can return home."

"She doesn't want to go home," I grate through clenched teeth. "And if she wanted to speak to you she wouldn't have spent the last two days hiding in her room while you were here. Or fled to the back deck this morning. She's made it clear she doesn't want company."

"No, she's made it clear she wants to hide, and that's not how you recover from trauma."

"You're not a—"

"I'm done arguing." She starts for the French doors. "I'm going to let her know I've been coming here for her. *Nobody* else."

My pulse detonates, triggering the migraine I've held at bay all morning.

"Wait," I growl, stalking after her. "Stop." I'm about to grab her arm and yank her backward when she pauses and looks at me with a raised brow.

"What?"

"If you do anything to upset her, I'll…"

The grin is slow to curve her lips, taunting my threat. "You'll what?"

I grind my teeth harder, determined not to give her the fight she wants. "I promised myself I wouldn't push her. And so far, I've succeeded. I've let her do her own thing even though it kills me to watch her suffer. So don't you dare go out there and stir trouble."

"Me? Stir trouble?" She clasps a hand to her chest, her sarcastic look of offense taking a second to fade into something more serious. "Give me credit. I'm not a heartless bitch all the time."

"Says who?"

She scoffs. "I get it, okay? You care about her. You're protective. Even a little obsessive. Believe me, I don't want to do anything to poke that bear."

She doesn't understand. Doesn't get it.

I'm skating on thin ice here, barely managing my threadbare restraint when it comes to Penny. She's far more fragile than she was when I rescued her. Back in Greece she'd had fire in her belly. There'd been unending grit and determination, which I'd thought would see her through to a remarkable recovery.

That all changed the minute we stepped onto the private jet and began our return stateside.

The fight vanished. The determination and grit disappeared.

The woman who I was certain would grasp her newfound freedom with both hands turned into a quiet, timid ghost, too frightened to even leave the house.

"Don't worry, Luca." Sarah steps closer and claps me lightly on the cheek, taunting the pain in my head. "You know I have experience with trauma. I'm not going to do anything to make her life harder."

She reaches for the door and opens the barrier wide, the cool air sweeping inside. But she doesn't step onto the deck. She waits, letting me take the lead.

"Be civilized," I mutter under my breath as I walk around her, then farther along the length of the house to the place where Penny hides.

She's seated on one of my wooden chairs, her coffee mug cradled in both hands, a blanket tucked around the legs cuddled up at her side.

She pastes on that fake smile at the sight of me, the bright expression still not reaching her eyes. But when Sarah steps around to stand at my side, Penny stiffens, her face falling lax in a sudden show of apprehension.

"Penny, this is Sarah." I hike a thumb at the annoyance to my left. "She thought it was time you two finally met."

Sarah inches forward. "It's great to meet you. I've been coming over for the last few days in the hopes we could talk, but the big protective bear didn't want me near you until you were ready." She shrugs. "Today I pulled rank."

"Hi." Penny glances between us, apprehension, or maybe confusion, remaining heavy in her tight lips.

"You remember me talking about Sarah, right?" I walk closer to grab the seat beside her and pull it backward a few feet before sitting my ass down. "She's Hunter's fiancé."

A spark of understanding widens her eyes. "Oh. I vaguely remember… I just didn't realize…" She shakes her head, her brow pinched. "The last days in Greece are a blur."

"You spoke about me?" Sarah's voice is filled with unwarranted ego as she leans back against the deck railing. "I'm not sure if I want to know what was said."

Penny's cheeks blush. They actually fucking blush. All pink and sweet and shy. I wouldn't have picked her as a timid woman, but maybe that's who she really is beneath all the layers of damage.

"Okay, now I'm curious." Sarah chuckles. "What did he tell you?"

Penny glances from Sarah to me, then back again. "Nothing. They were a few brief words in the middle of madness. I can't really remember."

Yes, she can. I can see it in the way her gaze briefly flicks to mine. The unease. The concern.

"I told her the two of you have a lot in common." I lean back, faking relaxation in the hopes it will let her know there's nothing to worry about. "And that I thought you both might get along."

"What's with the rabid blush then?" Sarah asks.

I shoot her a glare, warning her to stop pushing. "I think that might stem from my off-the-cuff comment about you being the type to slit a throat with a smile on your face."

Her laughter returns. "Nice intro, Luca. Now her look of trepidation makes sense."

"No, it's not trepidation," Penny blurts. "I'm just..." She shrugs, shrinks into herself, then sighs. "I guess I'm still a little shell-shocked. It's been a whirlwind."

"That's understandable. As long as you know I'm here for you. Not *him*." Sarah whacks me on the chest. "I've been coming over with bags of gifts the big guy has demanded I buy for you. The least he could do is introduce us, right?"

Shit.

Sarah knows I've been holding back on giving those gifts. Why would she tell her about them? I don't think I'm even ready to hand them over. Not when some of the items are fucking idiotic.

"I was waiting for her to be ready," I mutter.

"You don't have to worry about me." Penny's expression fills with regret. "The last thing I want to do is be more of a burden."

"You're not a burden," Sarah cuts in. "You're part of the family. And we look after our own. Fiercely...well, maybe not as fiercely as Luca, but he's special, in a mentally unhinged kind of way."

Penny's lips lift. Her pleasure at my ridicule is slight, but beautiful.

So fucking beautiful.

"Tell me more about this unhingement," she says. "Us mentally challenged people need to stick together."

I know she's only trying to be a part of the conversation, and yeah, I chuckle to encourage more of her involvement. But Jesus, I hate her being down on herself. It makes me want to shake her even more.

"Well, that's my cue to leave." I grab the armrests, waiting for a protest from Penny to keep me in place. "If you're going to talk about me I'd prefer you do it behind my back."

Her eyes flash. Her lips part.

"Good. Go." Sarah shoos me with a wave of her hand. "It's time for some girl talk."

I remain poised to move, waiting, wordlessly demanding Penny to ask for help.

Just tell me to slay.

Ask me to protect you.

"Go on," Sarah demands. "Get going."

I pause for one more second. Two. But when Pen doesn't speak, I give up.

"You sure know how to make a guy feel special." I push from my seat and shoot a warning look at Sarah. "Be nice."

She snaps her teeth at me before stealing my chair. "Run along, soldier."

3

PENNY

Luca walks away, and the whole time I wish he wasn't leaving me alone with her. I don't know this woman. I don't think I want to. There's a hardness in her eyes that unsettles me. A bitterness. And I'm unsure if it's aimed at me personally.

"Do you like it here?" she asks as soon as the French door closes behind him.

I continue to cradle the coffee mug in my hands and shift my focus to the backyard. It's simplistic. Fresh-cut lawn. A few shrubs. Two billowing trees. It's completely different to the perfectly manicured gardens of the hell I previously lived in, and for that I'm thankful.

"Yes." I appreciate being welcomed into Luca's home. But I hate being *here*. In my own skin. Cloaked in irrational emotion. Haunted by thoughts.

"You're not uncomfortable? You wouldn't prefer to be somewhere else?"

"No." The truth is, there is nowhere else. I have nowhere to go. Nowhere to belong.

"And what about Luca? Is he treating you well?"

I nod and begin to resent the manners instilled in me as a child that make it impossible to ignore her. I'm too tired for this conversation.

"Are you sure? He said yesterday that you've been cooking and cleaning. Is that out of obligation? Is he making you do those things?"

My narrowed gaze snaps to her. "No, of course not. He's been nothing but kind to me."

"So he hasn't implied you need to carry your weight? Or maybe return his hospitality with a sexual favor or two?"

I shove to my feet, the blanket falling from my waist to land on the wooden deck. "Not at all." My tone is harsh. Adamant. "He's been perfect." *Too* perfect. Especially for a man burdened by my presence.

"Okay. Good." She nods and indicates my chair with a wave of her hand. "Please sit. I meant no offense. I'm just doing my job."

"Your job?" It's her duty to question the man who saved me? The person who took a bullet to the head, risking his life to rescue a complete stranger? "And who gave you this job?"

She blinks back at me, those hard features softening. That's when the puzzle pieces fall into place with a deafening click. She's not here for me. She's here for my brother.

"Sebastian," I whisper. "This interrogation was requested by him."

"I was asked to keep an eye on you."

"Well, you can report back and let him know I'm fine. Luca has gone above and beyond to keep me happy."

Her lips tweak, her grin sly. "To be honest, I think that's what he's more worried about."

Again, it takes a second for comprehension to dawn, but when it does my cheeks heat at the innuendo. I glance away, my skin prickling.

"Please," she repeats. "Sit."

I don't want to. I'd love nothing more than to walk away. If only I wasn't certain it would cause a scene Luca would have to deal with.

"I had no doubt he would do right by you," she murmurs as I reluctantly slump into my seat. "He's a great guy. And from the sound of it, you already know that. But your brother is—"

"I don't want to talk about my brother." I still can't go there. Can't picture him remaining in the Greek islands, slaying my demons at the risk of his own safety. I need it all to be over. To fast forward through this chasm filled with worry for people I wish I didn't love.

"He cares about you."

I glance back at her in confusion. "Who does? My brother?"

"Yes, Decker," she clarifies. "But Luca, Hunter, Torian, and Keira, too. You're family, and we always take care of our own."

My insides scream at me to deny her. I'm not one of them. I don't want any association with my torturer's family.

I also want to make her well aware I can take care of myself. I had for years while in a situation far more dire than this. I've lived through the worst life has to give. Yet I can't honestly say I'm capable of anything anymore. I've lost the will to fight. I'm not sure how to find strength.

"So, what's the plan?" she asks. "When are you going to see your parents?"

I sigh. "Is this another question from my brother? Is there a list I need to get through so you'll leave me alone?"

"No. The interrogation is actually for your benefit. I assume you don't want to stay with Luca forever."

She assumes wrong. I have no desire to leave.

"You really do like staying here." She states as fact. As if she's finally beginning to understand the truth of my comfort. "If you're comfortable in your surroundings, why aren't you opening up to Luca? Let him in. Clearly you don't want to talk to me, and I get it —I'm an acquired taste. But you need to speak to someone. It isn't healthy to keep the past bottled."

How does she know I've kept it bottled? Unless Luca told her. Vented to her.

"Believe me," she continues. "You have to let it out before it eats you alive."

She has no idea.

There's no way anyone could understand what I've been through. Not a shrink. Not even the other women who accompanied me in Luther's cage. And definitely not this woman.

"Your thoughts are loud." She gives a brief smirk. "And yes, you're right. I have no concept of what you must have gone through. But I know about monumental loss. And utter helplessness. Not to mention the cloying anger and suffocating grief that come afterward." She holds my gaze, never letting go.

"Those types of situations change you irrevocably, no matter how much you want to return to the person you once were. So ask Luca for help. Trust him. You never know—the guy might have something smart to say for once."

I huff out a laugh. If only the humor could stick around for longer than a heartbeat. "I'm sorry for your loss."

She inclines her head. "And I'm deeply sorry for yours. My point, though, is that you're going to get through this. Despite everything I endured at a young age, I found my calling. And I swear on the graves of those I love that you will find yours, too. You only need to be willing to work for it."

"I'm willing to work. I just..." I close my eyes and turn my head away.

I don't believe anything will change. How can I when I'm free —completely unshackled and unbound—yet I feel more trapped than ever before?

More helpless.

Hopeless.

Broken.

Something is wrong with me, and I'm scared I'll never be able to fix it.

"Your mind builds on what you feed it," she murmurs. "And you would have so much pity and fear that it's only natural to gorge on what you know. But that's not how you heal. You can't beat him until you turn the tables and take control."

Him.

Luther Torian.

The man who continues to torment my thoughts from beyond the grave.

"Your brother will hate me saying this," she adds, "but trust in Luca. He's a great guy. And from what I've seen and heard, he's willing to do anything for you."

"He's burdened to do everything for me," I correct, squeezing my eyes tighter. "He doesn't even want to be here."

"Really?"

When she doesn't elaborate, I look at her, finding her brows raised in question.

"Penny, do you really think a guy like that, all strong, determined, protective, and annoyingly stubborn would do

21

anything he didn't want to do?" Her brows remain hiked. "He *wants* to be here. He *wants* to help you. Otherwise he would've hightailed it long ago, dumping your ass on my doorstep as he went."

"He's honorable. He wouldn't—"

"Make all the excuses you want. But like I said, if you feed yourself that negative bullshit, it's going to eat away at you. Use Luca while you've got him. What do you have to lose?"

His respect.

His sanctuary.

She gives me a pointed look. "What did I say about the negative shit? Your eyes seriously speak volumes. Maybe that's something you can work on, too." She winks at me and pushes from her seat. "Now, before I completely outstay my welcome, I'm going to leave. I'd like to come back tomorrow, though."

"For another highly motivational pep talk?" I ask. "Or to continue spying for my brother?"

She laughs. "Look at you letting down your guard to be a comedian. But just so you know, I'll totally be back for both. Now go find Luca and talk to him."

"About what?"

"Whatever comes to mind."

She walks for the door, leaving me to deal with the emotional whiplash as she disappears inside. One minute I'm content in my isolation, appreciating the distance Luca has given me—the next I'm thinking about where he is and if I should listen to her advice.

Since returning to the States, I've become increasingly indecisive. Almost constantly manic. Calm on the outside, a whole bunch of crazy on the inside.

In captivity, I'd only had the option to fight. Strategy was all that ran through my mind.

Now there's no need to battle physically, so my brain wants to make it a mental challenge.

I'm hammered with thoughts. Memories. Fears.

The voices in my head are a looped recording filled with panic and shame. And I can't quieten them. I've tried. They multiply no matter what I do. Despite how fortunate I am.

It's as if piranhas are constantly nipping at my ankles, eager for the taste of my suffering.

22

My mind doesn't want me to heal.

I sigh, entirely weary.

I want him to help. I want it more than anything. But talking to him means I'll become more of a burden. It will also wake him up to the reality that I'm not the person he saved in Greece. I'm not a fighter. Only a failure.

I still yearn to be rescued.

I swallow over the lump forming at the back of my throat and force myself to walk inside.

The house is peacefully quiet. Sarah must have left, allowing the comfort of normalcy to gently spread its wings around me.

It's back to being me and Luca. The way I like it.

If only there wasn't this new pressure slowly bearing down on me. The ability to recover seems entirely out of reach.

But what if she's right? What if he can help?

The sooner I get back on my feet, the sooner he can be unburdened from my annoyances.

My stomach churns as I make my way toward the rustle of paper down the hall. My nerves build when I realize he's in his room. In unchartered territory. Yet my feet move of their own volition, taking me to his threshold, the door slightly ajar.

He's near the huge bed, his back facing me as he rifles through a myriad of paper bags spread across the mattress. Some are crumpled and empty, the contents seeming to be the mass of material piled in front of him.

I take another step and the door hinges squeak in protest.

Shit.

Luca stiffens, his spine snapping ramrod. "Did Sarah leave?"

I wince. "Yeah."

"Did she go of her own free will or did you kick her out?" He turns to face me, a lock of hair falling over his forehead to tease his eye.

"I'd never kick someone out of your house."

"Why not? Don't be polite on my account. When it comes to her, you've got free rein as far as I'm concerned."

I know he's joking, attempting to make light of an awkward situation. Again, I'm appreciative. "Did you know she was coming around so she could report back to Sebastian?"

"I gathered as much. I don't blame him, either."

"But you speak to him, right? I've heard you talking on the phone."

He nods. "At least once a day. But it's no secret he doesn't trust me with your welfare. He's keeping tabs the best way he can."

I wince, wishing the way my brother kept tabs didn't add more of a burden. "Thank you, Luca."

"What for?"

"For having her over every day, knowing she was spying, yet keeping her on a leash. I know this can't be easy for you."

"Can't be easy? Are you kidding?" He waves me away and returns his attention to the mess on the bed. "You treat me like a king. All that cooking and cleaning. I haven't done laundry once since we got here."

"It's the least I can do."

He shoots a warning look over his shoulder. "Do we really have to have this conversation again? You know I don't want you lifting a finger."

"It keeps me busy." I bite my lip, hesitant to expose my vulnerabilities. "My hands and my mind."

"Well, I'll buy you a gaming console. You can button bash for a while instead of getting cleaner's elbow."

"No, thank you. I'm not a gamer." I take another step, the intoxicating earthy smell of his aftershave sinking into my lungs. It's everywhere. In every breath. "What are you doing?" I continue to the bed and focus on the mess covering the mattress.

"Tidying up crap I had lying around." He begins shoving things into bags, his movements agitated.

Something has changed. Something's made him uncomfortable.

"I've overstepped." My thoughts become words. "I'm sorry. I shouldn't have intruded on your private space."

"You haven't." He keeps shoving, shoving, shoving the items of clothing. "Give me a second and I'll have this all bagged up."

No, I've definitely triggered his annoyance. I can see it in the way his usually graceful moves have become jerky.

I retreat a step, preparing to leave.

"Penny, I'm serious. Don't go." He meets my gaze, his intense eyes holding mine. Demanding. "You've barely sought me out since we got here. Don't leave me now."

I don't want to. It seems like I've reached some sort of

24

threshold by walking into his room. But... "Why does it feel like I've done something wrong?"

"You haven't. It's me." He waves a hand at the items scattered over the bed. "I'm the one making it feel weird in here."

"Why?"

He straightens, sucking in a frustrated breath. "I don't know."

"Are these things sentimental?" I lower my focus to the bags. "Do they belong to a girlfriend? Or an ex? Is that why—"

"No. I bought all this for you."

I tense.

Freeze.

The only movement I feel is the rampant beat of my heart.

The reminder of the gifts Sarah mentioned comes back to bite me. I do a frantic visual search of the items scattered in front of us, trying to understand where his discomfort could stem from.

"I blame the concussion." He snickers. "I went on a crazy bender, buying shit I thought you might need... or like... or whatever. I dunno. It was a stupid idea." He grabs the two bags closest to him and walks around me to carry them to the corner of the room. "I'll get rid of them."

"Why?" It's my curiosity talking. My fear, too. *Always* my fear. I want to know what he thinks my needs look like. "What did you buy?"

"Nothing you're going to want. Like I said, it was stupid."

"Please let me look." I tentatively move forward, keeping my gaze on him as I grab the closest bag.

"It's not a big deal." He shrugs. "Just keep in mind I wasn't thinking straight."

The contents of the first bag make my cheeks heat—tampons, pads, a heat pack.

I wish I knew how to react, but emotion overwhelms me. There's appreciation, guilt, and shame. Always shame.

I reach for another bag and pull out the material contents to expose a casual, full-length dress, the pattern pretty with light pinks and shades of cream. Those emotions intensify. The exact same ones—appreciation, guilt, then shame.

My throat tightens as I reach for a third, finding more clothes. More dresses.

By the fourth and fifth bags dread begins to take over, the ickiness coating my skin.

"I told you it was stupid." He slumps onto the mattress near the head of the bed. "I'll give them to a local charity."

I want to tell him not to. That maybe one day these items will become useful. But that's a lie. "Luca, I wish…" The words clog in my throat.

"What is it?" He frowns, pushing to his feet to take a step toward me.

"No. Stop." I raise a hand, unable to handle closer proximity when my mental demons are overwhelming me. "I'm beyond thankful for you. And this." I swing out an arm to indicate the gifts. "But you're right. I can't use any of it."

He nods, pretending to understand.

He doesn't. How could he?

"The pads and tampons…" I rub my knuckles over my sternum in an attempt to ease the building pressure beneath. "I don't need them. Luther made sure of that."

He snaps rigid, his nostrils flaring. "Why? What did he—"

I shake my head, trying to stifle whatever he thinks that monster did to me. "He made sure there were no inconveniences—that's all. I have a birth control implant. It's temporary. I'll have to get it removed."

"I'll take you to a clinic. We can make an appointment for today."

I nod and smile the best I can. "Thank you. But I'm not ready."

Going to a doctor means touching. Poking. Prodding. An internal exam. And the outside world. It's too much.

"You tell me as soon as you're ready, shorty. You hear me?" His words are filled with venom. Fiercely protective. "Snap your fingers and I'll be all over it."

"I will. Thank you." I swallow. Nod some more. "Then there's the dresses… I can't wear them. Luther always forced us to—"

"I know." He cuts me off. "I remembered too late and I'm sorry. That's why I didn't want you seeing any of this. When we first arrived, I made the fucked-up assumption that you kept wearing the baggy clothes you ordered online because of a sizing issue. But it's deliberate, isn't it?"

My heart squeezes. My lungs and stomach, too. "Yes."

"See? I fucked up. I'm not the best woman whisperer, but I assume you already knew that."

I huff out a laugh at his charming self-deprecation. He's too good to be true, which scares me a little. I know who this man is. *What* he is—a criminal, a murderer. It's the heart of gold that sets him apart from the family he works for.

"You're doing just fine." I back away, hoping the distance will stop my chest from humming.

"You're walking out on me?" He glances at me from the corner of his eye, disappointment heavy in his voice. "Are we finished with this conversation already?"

"No." I keep walking until I reach the far side of the room, then lower myself to the carpet and sit facing him. "The opposite actually. I'm getting comfortable."

He juts his chin in subtle acknowledgement, but those eyes speak of relief. He's happy I'm stepping out of my comfort zone. He's pleased with me, and I both hate and love the sense of accomplishment it inspires. "I'm trying, Luca. I'll admit I'm not doing as well as I've led you to believe."

"Really?" His mouth lifts, subtle and sarcastic. "You haven't led me to believe you're doing well at all, shorty. I know you're struggling. You're not sleeping well either, are you?"

"No."

"Nightmares?"

I nod.

"I've woken you a few times," he admits. "I'm not sure if it helped though."

My throat restricts. My cheeks heat. "You've woken me?"

"Don't worry; I didn't disturb your privacy. All I did was call your name from my room, or the hall if you were determined not to wake up."

The heat increases, the fear disappearing as embarrassment takes hold. "But how did you know I was having nightmares?"

"You cry out. You've called my name a time or two, as well, which speaks volumes of the horrors you must be enduring." He shoots me a sly grin. "But all jokes aside, the first time I heard you I thought you needed my help. That something serious had happened. But once I reached your door, you were yelling for your brother, and then at Robert."

The humiliation increases, scarring me. I break our gaze, unable to look him in the eye when my burden on him continues to grow.

"If you're interested, there might be something in one of these bags to help you sleep better."

I shake my head. "I don't want to be sedated."

"No, not sedatives. After your first few restless nights, I did some googling. There's an air diffuser around here somewhere. It's got some type of oil that's meant to help. It's a lavender blend or something."

This is ridiculous. Seriously, ridiculous.

This man, with his cold calculation and criminal ties, is googling sleep aids and buying air diffusers. It's enough to make a delirious laugh bubble in my chest.

He narrows his gaze on me. "Did I say something funny?"

I stop fighting and let loose with an embarrassed chuckle. "You're this big, tough, aggressive bad guy. I never would've imagined the words 'lavender blend' coming from your mouth."

His grin stops my pulse.

So many men have grinned at me. Leered. Ogled. So many that I never thought I'd appreciate the beauty of a male's face again. I thought I'd always find their interest threatening. But when Luca smiles at me, the routine spike of apprehension fades into a strange sense of accomplishment.

"Laugh all you like," he drawls. "I'm only going to get more stir crazy the longer I'm stuck inside these four walls."

And there goes my happiness.

Poof. Gone.

"I know you're not ready to get out of here," he adds. "But how would you feel about writing a list of goals and attempting to take on one at a time?"

I glance down at my fingers tangled in my lap. I don't feel good at the prospect, not good at all, even though the uncharacteristic sweetness is appreciated.

I want to stay within my comfort bubble. Unhappy, unhealthy, yet cozy in the familiar surroundings. "Can we leave this for a few days?"

"I don't think we can. It's time to start moving forward." There's an edge of authority to his tone. "These goals can be small or big—you decide. And we only need to work toward achieving one a day."

"We?" I raise my gaze, my self-loathing growing at the determination in his expression.

"I'm in this for the long haul. We can do it together."

I return my attention to my hands and pick at the quick of my thumb. Truth is, I hate disappointing him. I have ever since the first day we met. And now a lifetime of events have passed between us. He rescued me, risked his life to save me. He deserves better than my resistance. I should be giving him my full compliance. If only it didn't feel like launching myself into a complete free fall.

"Which leads me to my hidden motivation." He pushes to his feet and walks toward me, towering above me with an outstretched hand. "I'm hoping the first task on your list might be to help me out."

"Help you out how?" I pause, not eager to place my hand in his. Part of my reluctance is due to my past. There's more than that, though. I don't fear him hurting me. My hesitation stems from something different. Something I can't pinpoint.

When I finally give in, sliding my palm against his, I hold my breath.

His warm, calloused fingers grip mine. Tight. Strong. He pulls me effortlessly to my feet, making me shiver.

"Don't look so scared." He drops his hold and takes a step back. "You stitched my head in Greece. I'm only hoping you'll work your magic to help take those suckers out."

4

LUCA

SHE FOLLOWS ME TO THE KITCHEN WHERE I GRAB A NOTEPAD, PEN, AND a chair, then continue into the main bathroom. The blade, antiseptic, tweezers, and pile of tissues I attempted to use yesterday are still spread out on the counter as if waiting for the torture to begin.

Just like in Greece, when I hadn't been able to see the injury on the side of my head to stitch the wound, I now can't remove the cotton firmly embedded in my skin. And I've left it too long for the removal, not wanting to ask Sarah for help and also not feeling comfortable pushing Penny. But she's given me an inch. Maybe it's time to strive for a mile.

I place the chair down in front of the basin and meet her gaze through the room-length mirror. "Are you still happy to do this?"

"Of course." She nods. "Sit."

I take my place on the chair, sitting tall. I'm determined not to let her nearness get to me. Not under my skin or in my head. It feels like a lifetime since I opened my mouth in Greece and let the stupidity of flirtation burst out. But my attraction hasn't wavered. If anything, it's intensified.

Seeing her all helpless and meek taunts me into protecting her. And that baggy sweater and the loose sweatpants do nothing to temper my memory of her perfect thighs, slim waist, and perky tits.

She's a siren.

An intense trigger to my temptation.

She walks around me, moving to the injured side of my head, her eyes gentle as she takes in the healing wound. "It looks like you've been taking good care of it."

"Haven't taken much care at all. I attribute any awesomeness to the nurse who stitched me up. She did a remarkable job."

A smile teases her lips. "I appreciate the praise. I'm also thankful you don't have the ability to see the error of your words. The stitching resembles a hack job at best."

"I'm not a pretty boy. I don't care what it looks like as long as the risk of infection is gone."

She reaches out, her fingers lightly brushing through the shortened lengths of hair around the wound, inspiring goose bumps to blanket my arms. "Your skin has started to heal over the thread. It might feel uncomfortable when I pull it out."

I can smell her.

Actually, I can smell *me* on *her*, which is fucking worse. She must be using my shampoo. Even though I've placed five years' worth of flower-scented products in her bathroom.

"Do your worst." I swallow over the unwanted build of lust. "As long as you don't leave anything behind, I'm good."

She nods and grabs the blade and tweezers, dousing them in antiseptic, then returns to her position at my side. "Tell me if I'm hurting you."

She is.

The agonizing discomfort of her proximity is fucking killing me. The curiosity surrounding her use of my shampoo is a thorn in my side, too. Why does she want to smell like me?

She leans in, those fingers resting against my scalp as her breathing brushes my skin.

She's everywhere—in my lungs, in my head, forever in every room of this fucking house. And of course, my dick doesn't want to miss out on the admiration. It twinges to life as I clench my jaw, hard, determined to keep my libido in check.

Her first nick of the blade is tentative. So goddamn gentle and feather-light.

"Don't hold back, shorty. You're going to have to be more firm than that if you don't want to spend all day staring at my skull."

Her mouth kicks into a smile, but she doesn't change her tender

31

style as she uses tweezers to gently pick at the cotton.

It's nice to see her smiling. *Really* smiling. Not the fake-ass, untruthful curve of lips she likes to placate me with.

I can't pull my attention from her as she works in silence, using the blade before tugging out a tiny strand of thread to place on the counter.

Bit by bit she removes the cotton, her breath a constant caress against my temple, her fingers an ongoing tease.

"Why don't we start making that list?" I wait until she leans back to look at me before I grab the notepad and pen from the counter. "What small steps could you take to help kickstart your recovery?"

She winces. Shrugs. "I don't know. Hasn't stepping out of my comfort zone to open up to you been a big enough achievement for today?"

"Definitely. But this is for tomorrow, and the day after. Just one at a time, Pen. That's all I'm askin'."

Her sigh is slight, barely audible as she leans in and tugs another piece of thread from my skull. "I don't know. I guess having the guts to call my sisters could be on the list. Or messaging my brother to tell him how I'm doing so Sarah doesn't have to keep spying."

I write both down in bullet points. "Anything else?"

She shakes her head. "I honestly don't feel capable of achieving anything else. Not even those things I just told you. Having a list is only going to add more pressure and increase the sense of failure."

She's not a failure. Not even close.

"What if I write some ideas down?" I ask.

"Write all you like, but you need to be aware your understanding of who I am and what I'm capable of is completely warped. This is going to be too hard."

No, it's not. And my perception isn't warped. If anything, I'm the only one who knows the real Penny and what she's truly able to achieve. I've seen her at her worst. This person beside me is merely a shadow of the remarkable woman waiting to break free. "Trust me."

There's another sigh. Another brush of painfully gentle fingers. "I do," she whispers. "It's the fear of disappointing you that makes this harder."

32

I don't know what part of her admission surprises me most—the trust I never thought I'd receive or the sweet way she wants to impress me. Both have an unwanted effect on my dick.

"You're not going to disappoint me." I scribble on the notepad, adding more tasks to the list. "We only need to focus on one goal a day. If you achieve it, that's great. If you don't, we can try something else."

She refocuses on her task, raising the blade to my wound, not acknowledging my words. She tugs at the stitches, placing more and more cotton on the counter.

I get that she hates being here—hates me pushing—but maybe Sarah is right. I can't watch her wallow. If this tactic doesn't work I'll try something else. And if that doesn't help, I'll find another way. I'm not giving up on her.

I keep writing as she tends to my head, the two of us working in comfortable silence until she gives a final tug to the embedded cotton, then leans real fucking close to inspect her handiwork. "You're doing a lot of writing."

"I've got a lot of ideas."

She sidesteps, the blade and tweezers dumped in the sink before she rests against the counter to stare at me. "Well, don't keep me waiting. What are these great ideas of yours?"

"You sure you're ready?" I ask. "This is going to change your life."

She crosses her arms over her chest, plumping her breasts beneath the heavy sweater. "You're well aware I'm not ready at all. So hurry up and get this over with."

I chuckle, appreciating her underlying spite a little too much. "Okay. Number one."

She straightens, as if preparing for torture.

"Watch a movie with me."

I didn't think it possible, but she stiffens further, her brows furrowing. "Watch a movie?"

"Yep. As simple as that. Sit your ass on the sofa and chill out to mindless television. It's better than the isolation of your room or the deck."

Those brows rise for long seconds before she says, "Okay. I can give it a try."

"Number two—teach me how you do laundry."

33

Her smile creeps back into the conversation, her brows knitting. "Laundry? Really?"

"Really. I've been a grown man who takes pride in washing his own shit for over ten years now, but my clothes have never smelled as good or felt as soft as they have since you've worked your magic."

She rolls her eyes. "It's called fabric softener, Luca."

"I don't have fabric softener."

"Yeah, you do. I found it in the back of one of your laundry cupboards. It's probably old enough to burn holes through your shirts, but obviously it's doing the trick."

"Obviously." I mimic her eye roll. "Number three—exercise."

She sucks in a subtle breath and I pause, waiting for the stereotypical female retaliation.

It's clear she doesn't need to lose weight. Her body is on point. What she requires is the shift in brain function.

"Right." Instead of a protest, she nods and breaks eye contact to focus on the tiled floor.

"Don't get huffy on me," I warn. "I'd never comment on your body in a negative way. Not only because it's fucking rude, but because you're stunning. With or without the small village supply of material covering you at any given time."

I wait for a smile that doesn't appear and mentally berate myself for not prefacing my suggestion. "Exercise lowers cortisol, which is a stress hormone, while helping to increase endorphins. In your case, working out is about mood and mental health—not anything to do with appearance."

"I get it." She nods. "You don't have to explain."

"Yeah, I do. I can already see you creeping back into that shell of yours and it's pissing me off."

Making her feel like shit has a reciprocal effect. The only bonus is my resulting limp dick.

"Sorry," she mutters. *Murmurs.*

Fuck.

I hold in the need to growl in frustration. "Number four—read a self-help book. Number five—meditate. Number six—go for a walk. Number seven—get plastered."

She doesn't respond, just keeps her attention on the floor.

"Penny?" We've come so far this morning. From no words to

34

heavy conversation and even physical contact. I'd thought I was receiving the jackpot of recovery. Turns out it was only a slight detour. "You still don't like the idea of a list, do you?"

"No, it's not that." She pushes from the counter. "Your ideas are great. I actually like them."

"But?"

"No buts." She gives me a placating smile. "You make it sound too easy, that's all."

"I've got no misconceptions about how hard this is going to be. Despite whatever warped perceptions you think I have, I know you're trudging through hell at the moment." I push to stand, the notepad hanging idle in my grip. "This list is only an attempt to get you to live a little."

"I'm living, Luca."

"That's where you're wrong. And the sooner you realize, the easier this will be. You deserve more than this limbo. And I'm here to help. I'm not going anywhere. *You're* not going anywhere. We're stuck together for now. So share the load, because it's sure as shit harder for me to watch you struggle from the sidelines than it will be at your side."

Her eyes turn somber, the wrinkle stretching across her forehead burrowing deep.

"I'm only asking you to try. I have no other expectations." I hold out the notepad for her to take. "But, come on, Pen. Aren't you at least a little excited to try and get out of your funk?"

"It's not a fun—"

"You know what I mean." I don't want to give her struggle a toxic label, whether it's depression or PTSD. All that shit has negative connotations. "Aren't you the slightest bit interested in doing something different?"

She grabs the notepad and raises her other hand, cinching her thumb and pointer finger so they're a breath apart. "A little."

Good.

Fucking fantastic.

A little is all I need. For now. "What do you say if we keep the momentum going and cross an afternoon session of movie watching off the list?"

Her smile is subtle, the slightest curve of tempting lips as she lets out an exaggerated sigh. "What did you have in mind?"

5

LUCA

We ticked the movie off the list without a hitch.

I don't care if she fell asleep before the dramatic climax to have a two-hour power nap. If anything, I count it as a victory that she felt comfortable enough to sleep in the same room. Her rest was peaceful, too.

No nightmares.

No murmured cries for help.

The next day we moved on to the laundry. And props to her for giving it her all as she talked down to me, slow and demeaning, with her instructions on how to unscrew the lid to the fabric softener and pour the contents into the allocated tube of the washing machine.

Day by day, hour by hour, she starts to open up. Gradually. The lessening of her fear is incremental. But it's there. That's all that matters.

"So, what do you have in store for me today, GI Joe?" She enters the doorway to my weights room, hands on hips, the baggy sleeves of her sweater scrunched at her elbows.

She's lighter today. Brighter. Her eyes have a healthy glow.

And even though her nightmares haven't disappeared, at least our new routine of a daily movie session has ensured she's getting a nap during the daylight hours. The time she now spends reading might be doing the trick to distract some of her negative thoughts, too.

"I want you to go for a basic run." I keep pushing out my muscle-up reps, dragging myself over the bar again and again.

"Basic run?" She steps into the room, moving toward the treadmill with trepidation. "Define basic."

"I want you to run a mile." I drop to the floor and shake out the burn in my arms. "Without stopping."

"That doesn't seem so bad. A mile isn't far."

"It is if you're not used to running. Hell, even a couple hundred yards can be difficult on the body if you haven't exercised in a while."

She climbs onto the machine and attaches the safety clip to her sweater as I approach the side of the conveyor.

She presses buttons, placing the starting pace high. Far too high for a beginner.

"You might want to dial it back a notch. You can work up to a fast pace over time. Today is about getting through the mile however possible. I don't care if you have to granny shuffle over the finish line."

"Granny shuffle? Where's all that faith you're supposed to have in me?"

"I've got faith. I just don't want you falling on that pretty face right out of the gate."

She huffs. "Fine. I'll start with a light jog." She presses buttons again, turning on the machine, the conveyor slowly sliding into gear. "Do you have any music?"

"Yeah." I return to the chin-up bar and grab my cell from the floor. "What's your preference?"

"I don't mind." She undoes her ponytail, her stride flawless as she refastens it higher and tighter. "Whatever you usually listen to will be fine."

I start my workout playlist, the intense beat of Slipknot's "Duality" filling the room.

I try to concentrate on my reps as she runs. I clasp the chin-up bar. Do another set of muscle-ups. But my attention keeps drifting to her. Her stride. Her ease.

She increases the pace, pushing harder, moving faster. I don't hear her panted breath over the music. Instead, I feel it. The heavy lift of her chest. The distinct purse of her mouth. Each step acts like a cattle prod to my libido.

"You're fit." I pull myself over the bar and pause, waiting for her response. "Why didn't you mention it when we were discussing the list?"

She presses the treadmill dashboard again, creeping the pace higher. "I didn't think you'd want to know the intricate details of how Luther liked his women in peak condition."

She's right. That information isn't welcomed. In fact, my anger spikes, the reminder of her captor spurring me to push out an additional two reps of pure frustration before falling to the floor.

I slump onto the bench press, watching her, *amazed* by her.

Tightness enters my chest and it has nothing to do with exercise and a whole hell of a lot to do with things I shouldn't be thinking about.

She decreases the pace for long enough to remove her sweater and throw it to the floor. Then she's back running again, her oversized T-shirt billowing at her hips. It's not enough to stop the display of her bouncing tits. Or to hide the hardness of her nipples pressing against the thin material.

It's times like this where I wish it had escaped my attention that she didn't have any underwear in yesterday's load of laundry. She has no visible panty line either. And maybe I'm daydreaming or living in a fucked-up fantasy, but I don't think she's been wearing underwear at all. Not now, and not since returning stateside.

Fuck me for being the prick who noticed.

I shove to my feet, needing an additional set of reps to drag my attention away from something that will get me killed. Something that's a fucking dick move to even think about.

She deserves better.

Decker trusted me with her protection. He didn't give me an all-access pass to ogle his sister.

I drag myself up and over the bar, punishing myself, pushing so fucking hard my arms scream in protest. And still I can't stop the imagery taking over my mind. Can't drag my fucking gaze away.

She's completely oblivious. She keeps running, surpassing the mile marker to plow straight ahead.

There's never been a more remarkable woman. More powerful. More inspirational.

I'm caught up admiring the perfection until I finally gain the restraint to drag my attention away. I stare out the window in front of her, wishing I had the power to give her a better life. To solve her problems.

I'm stuck in the daydream of making her smile... until my gaze catches on her reflection in the glass, those dark eyes staring back at me.

Shit.

I force myself not to look away and announce the wicked shit filling my head. And I try even harder not to readjust my cock. To put the fucker back in his place—into deep, dark confinement far away from her, all while she keeps staring, keeps undoing me.

"That's enough for today." I release the bar and drop to my feet. "You don't want to push yourself too hard when I'm going to make you come back tomorrow."

Fucking tomorrow—the necessary vicious routine that will help her, and slowly kill me.

"Yes, boss." She thumps a hand against the treadmill dashboard, making the conveyor stop. "Same time, same place?"

I ignore her sarcasm, too fixated on the nickname she gave me. If only she knew how bossy I could be. How demanding. How dominant.

A man like me isn't meant for a woman like her, no matter how incessant my attraction.

"Same time, same place."

The music cuts off mid song as my cell starts to ring. Torian's name is written across the bright screen while the device vibrates on the floor.

"Are you going to answer that?" She steps off the treadmill and raises the long length of her shirt to wipe the faint hint of moisture from her face, exposing sweat-slicked skin.

"Yeah." I snatch the cell and connect the call. "What's up?"

"How kind of you to finally answer your phone," he drawls. "Does that mean you've stopped holding a grudge over me sending you home?"

"Still holding tight, asshole. What do you want?"

He chuckles, the tone laced with aggression. "I thought you'd appreciate an update."

"I don't need one." I walk from the exercise room, leaving Penny alone, and continue down the hall to shut myself into my bedroom. "Decker calls me on the daily. He's kept me posted on your progress in Greece. Progress I deserved to be a part of."

"And from the progress reports I've received, it sounds like you're coping just fine in your cozy isolation," he counters. "I'm told the role of protector suits you. Maybe a little too well."

Fuck Sarah and her big mouth.

"What do you want, Torian? I've got shit to do."

A lengthy sigh travels down the line. "There are two things. First, I thought Penny would like to know your brother is returning the first of her friends home today."

I pause a beat. "Why are you telling me this? Why didn't Benji call me himself?"

"He's busy. And you told me he struggles to handle his wife, let alone look after three rescued women. He's also been out of range. But the process of returning them home has started, and I assume the information will be a relief to Decker's sister."

I agree. Doesn't mean I'm letting him off the hook for sending me home.

"Okay." I shrug. "I'll let her know. What's the second thing?"

The conversation gains another pause.

Another sigh.

"You're not going to appreciate this news."

I clench my fist, my impatience building. "So spit it out. It's not like you have an issue with pissing me off. If anything, I'm sure you enjoy it."

"It's to do with the kid and Keira."

The kid and Keira.

The kid—meaning Tobias. The son of Penny's captor, and the boy she helped raise. The kid she would claim as her own if she had the choice. And the child who is Torian's half-brother.

I cling tighter to the cell. "What about him?"

"He arrived in Portland a few days ago."

"A few days?" I grate, trying not to let anger consume me on Penny's behalf.

"Yes."

"And you kept it from us, why?"

"Because Tobias has come a long way since the death of his father. He's doing well. But every time he gets on the phone to

40

Penny he loses momentum. She's dragging him down, and it's best if they keep their distance for a while."

I huff out a derisive laugh. "You're a fucking asshole."

"Am I?" he snaps. "Why? For protecting my brother?"

"For having no fucking concern for Penny."

"She's not my problem. She's yours." His usual sense of superiority enters his voice, the dictatorial aggression barely leashed. "I'm telling you out of courtesy and nothing else. It's up to you if you inform her of the situation."

"In that case, thank you," I drawl. "How fucking generous."

"Watch yourself. I've put up with your hostility for long enough. I've also let it slide when you don't answer my calls. But I assure you, my patience is growing thin. I'm doing what's best for everyone. Including Penny. Keeping her away from Tobias might be the push she needs to stop hiding with you when she has a family who would kill to know she's still alive."

"She's making progress," I snarl.

"Not fast enough."

I close my eyes and pinch the bridge of my nose. There's no negotiating with him. He's already made up his mind.

It doesn't matter that he's keeping Tobias from the essential pain of recovery. Finding a way to support and communicate with Penny is part of the process. Torian just wants to make this easier on himself. Less drama. Less theatrics. Less trouble.

I guess I've been doing the same thing. Not wanting to push Penny to leave the house or see a shrink all because I want to shield her from more trauma.

"Fine." I walk for my bedroom door and pull it wide. "Do whatever you think is best. It's too late to stop you anyway." The kid is already here. Probably within a few minutes' drive.

"You're not going to keep railing on me? I expected more of that aggressive, ex-SEAL defiance I've grown to despise."

My defiance has nothing to do with my previous life as a SEAL. If anything, it's the cornerstone that got my ass kicked out. Rebellion and misplaced loyalty have caused me to fall so fucking far from grace that all I seem to have done over the past few years is descend.

"I get it," I mutter. "You're trying to protect Tobias. And I'm going to do the same with Penny. I may have drawn the short straw this time, but I'll deal. I always do."

"It doesn't sound like you're dealing. If anything, I'm hearing a hint of defection. I hope you're not thinking of crossing the fence again."

There's a threat in his words. The most subtle reminder that I'm no longer one of the good guys, whether I like it or not.

"I'm dealing just fine. In fact, I'm even starting to think you were right to send me back," I lie. "I deserve a break. Consider me on vacation until further notice."

6

PENNY

I REMAIN IN THE EXERCISE ROOM, TINKERING WITH PIECES OF equipment, trying to teach myself how to use them while the barely heard mumble of Luca's voice carries from somewhere in the house.

Today's achieved goal has already started to take effect. I feel lighter. The burden of darkness doesn't hinder my vision like it has recently.

I don't know if it's the endorphins or the decrease in cortisol, but the sensation is comforting. Strengthening. The voices in my head have been quietened.

My feelings toward Luca are changing, too. I'm not sure where the subtle shift is leading. Yet I'm eager to get more of the enthusiasm I feel in his presence.

I'd even lost myself while staring at his reflection in the window. I'd been in awe of his power. Both daunted and inspired.

But then our gazes collided, his attention making me transfixed.

Usually male scrutiny chills me to the bone. And for a split second, it had. The routine fear made its presence known. It attacked, hard and fast. Then it flittered away, the withdrawal an exquisite dance as a hesitant curiosity took over.

I began to enjoy the way he watched me. The subtle hint of praise spurred me to run farther. Faster. I wanted more. Even craved it.

"Want me to show you how to use the machine?"

I spin around at the sound of his voice and pretend my heart isn't lodged in my throat. "No, thanks. It's a little out of my league."

"After that effortless run? I disagree." He walks toward me, his stride confident, his posture tight.

Everything about him intrigues me. Especially the secrets hidden behind those hazel eyes. It's the slight hum of attraction that catches me off guard.

I like the look of him. More than that. I like having him near.

After everything I've been through—after all the handsome men whose charming smiles turned into deviant smirks—I should remain as far away from him as possible. I'm sure it's imperative to my healing, despite my body attempting to make me feel otherwise.

"Sit." He juts his chin at the machine in front of me. "I'll walk you through it."

"Seriously, I don't—"

"Just do it." He comes up beside me, tall, broad. An effortless protective presence. "Sit your ass down."

My body obeys without mental consent.

"This is for upper arms," he continues.

I scoff. "I figured as much. I'm not completely ignorant."

He grins, the flash of perfect white teeth increasing the hum in my belly. He leans in, adjusts the weights stacked to my left, then pulls down the dangling bar hanging above my head.

"See how that feels." He hands over the bar. "Keep your core tight and do as many reps as you can."

He steps back to sit on another bench as I pull the weighted bar down below my chin, then raise it again. He doesn't watch me this time. He lowers his gaze to the floor and bends over, resting his elbows on his knees.

There's no comforting smile. No heated gaze. There's nothing. Only a flat line of lips against a blank expression that makes me think he's hiding something.

"Am I doing this right?" I continue to work the bar, my arms wobbling under the unfamiliar exertion.

"Yep." He nods, his gaze briefly raising only to catch on my chest. His face tightens. Hardens. Then he glances away, his jaw ticking.

I can't help following where he looked, my cheeks heating when I see my nipples beading through the thin layer of my shirt.

The bar slides from my grip. The weights clatter onto the stack.

Luca shoots upright, his attention flashing to me as he frowns. "You okay?"

I nod and slump my shoulders, feigning fatigue when what I'm really doing is loosening the material around my chest. "Sorry. I've never done arm weights. I didn't mean to let go of the bar."

I didn't mean to be sexually insensitive either.

It's just that I can't bring myself to wear underwear. Not bras or panties.

I'd dreamed of having those luxuries while I was a slave. I'd always thought I'd love the comforting feel of added layers of clothing after having the option taken away from me. But then I'd come here, and the dreams had come true, only to become another nightmare.

I'd hated the restriction. The suffocation. The itch of something foreign against my skin.

"Don't worry about it." He keeps his chin high, as if determined not to lower his vision. "We can try again tomorrow."

He holds out a hand and waits for me to stand. The offer is forced. There's something different about him. Something has changed since he reentered the room.

His eyes aren't as kind. His shoulders are too stiff. He's on edge, for reasons other than my appearance.

"Who was on the phone?" I ask.

Brief seconds pass as his hand falls to his side, the silence announcing where the shift in his emotion came from.

"Torian," he admits.

"What did he say?"

He sucks in a long breath, his muscled chest rising beneath his shirt.

"Luca, what's wrong?"

He winces. "I don't want to lie to you."

The admission is barely spoken, yet the words penetrate deep. "Tobias... Is he okay? Did something happen?"

"No. Nothing happened to him." He rakes a hand through his hair.

"What about my brother?"

"They're both fine."

I breathe a little easier. "But something's wrong... There's something you can't say..."

He holds my gaze, his expression hardening. "I don't want to keep shit from you. Problem is, wanting to protect you and also tell you the truth isn't possible."

I swallow as a skitter of unease ricochets down my neck. I want to know what he's hiding. I don't want to add to his burden either. "I trust you'll tell me anything I need to know when the time is right."

He huffs out a laugh and shakes his head. "You're not helping."

I hate seeing him struggle. It's strange. I never thought I'd consider or care about a man's feelings after what the opposite sex put me through. Yet here I am, wishing he wasn't battling whatever weight rests on his shoulders. "Luca, you always make the right decision where I'm concerned. I know you only want what's best for me."

"Jesus Christ." He drops back down to the bench, head hung, shoulders slumped. "Tobias is here in Portland."

My heart squeezes. *Tobias.* My beautiful boy.

"He's been here for a few days." He lifts his head to meet my gaze. "Torian thinks it's best if the two of you keep your distance."

That squeeze becomes a burn, incinerating me from the inside out.

There's pain. So much pain. But I knew this would happen. I predicted these people would snatch Tobias out of my life. I knew they would never want a constant reminder of their father's crimes around the child I spent years raising.

I knew...

Only the knowledge didn't prepare me for the consuming reality.

"I appreciate your honesty." I push to my feet and make for the door, needing to escape before my anger shows.

"Penny, wait." He follows. "It's only temporary."

Lies. All lies.

"Once you're back on your feet," he continues, "you two can catch up."

I keep walking, keep striding out the distance to the sanctuary of my room.

"Penny, stop," he demands.

I don't. I reach the bedroom and slam the door behind me.

"Jesus fucking Christ." He speaks through the barrier between us. "This *isn't* permanent. Every time you speak to Toby, he gets depressed. He's not coping with how you're acting, and who can blame him? In Greece, you were a force to be reckoned with. You led him and he looked up to you because of that. Now, whenever you talk to him, it's a two-minute, one-sided conversation. You can't expect him not to be affected by that."

Guilt slams into me. Hard.

He's right. I barely talk to Toby and our conversations are always short. I'm well aware of how toxic I am in this current state. I'd been getting better, though. With Luca's help, I've been improving. I just haven't spoken to Toby recently for him to hear the change. Doesn't stop me from being livid though.

Cole Torian has no right making decisions for Tobias. No right at all. He barely knows the boy.

"Penny?" There's a thump against the door and I picture Luca's heavy fist weighed against the wood. "Talk to me."

"There's nothing to talk about." I collapse onto the bed. "Maybe you're right. He's better off without me."

Another curse drifts from the hall, then he opens the door. "Don't go back to the place you were in a few days ago." His voice is harsh as he glares. "Not when we were finally starting to get a handle on this."

"There is no *we*, Luca. And there is definitely no 'handle on this.'"

"Like hell there isn't." His glare increases. "Quit the pity party. I promise this is temporary. I wouldn't stand for it otherwise."

I look away, my hands clenched into fists. Tobias deserves better. If only these decisions didn't make me feel completely worthless.

"Like I said," I mutter, "I appreciate your honesty."

He sighs and walks forward to crouch at my feet. The strength

47

of his attention calls to me. His energy does, too. "Look at me, shorty."

I don't. I can't.

"Penny," he growls.

I close my eyes, letting the strength of defiance brush my senses before I finally surrender. Denying him is hopeless. I'm hurt and frustrated and mad as hell. Yet, I can't stand the thought of Luca feeling that way toward me. "What?"

"This *is* temporary. You'll see Tobias soon. I promise."

I've never wanted to trust him, but my heart always has. The pained organ finds comfort in his words.

"And there was more to the conversation with Torian," he adds. "It's good news this time. My brother is returning one of your friends to their family today."

"Who?" The question slips out with a shallow wave of relief. "When?"

He shrugs and pushes to his feet. "I don't know. But I can find out."

"No. It doesn't matter. I'm thankful regardless."

He gives a sad smile. "I thought you might be. Do you want me to call Benji so you can speak to them?"

I've yearned to speak to my sisters since we were separated in Greece. The only difference between Tobias and those women is that with them, I've had the strength to keep my distance, knowing I'd be a negative addition to their recovery. They are together. All three of them left the Greek Islands to return home. They had each other's support. They didn't need me hindering their bright future. "No."

"You don't have to use my phone. I can finally set up the new cell I gave you."

"No. It's better if I don't."

He closes his mouth, his lips pressing tighter the longer I remain firm until he says, "I disagree. I'll go get the phone."

"I said *no.*" I slide from the bed. "Torian is right. I'm a negative influence. It's best if we don't speak."

"But they need you."

"They need the *old* me," I grate. "They need the maternal figure who kept them alive. The person who continuously battled for our survival. That's not me anymore."

"Yes, it is. You're—"

"No, Luca. Listen. I'm not that person. I can't help anyone. I can barely help myself."

His eyes harden, the flare of his nostrils feral. "You're not giving up because of him. I won't allow it. This phase is only a brief backward step. A slight hibernation period. It won't last."

"I'm not a goddamn bear."

"You sure?" He scowls. "Because you're acting like one."

It's my turn to grind my teeth and scowl. Fire ignites in my belly. Heat builds in my veins. The instinct to fight awakens in me after being dormant for so long, but I shut it down. I won't let Luther back into my life. He changed me, making me lash out at the first sign of fear. But I don't want to fight anymore. I don't want to be reminded of him every time I'm scared. Or angry. "I said, 'no.'"

"Fine." He turns and starts for the door. "Call them. Don't call them. I don't give a shit. But you're going to get your ass back into the exercise room. I've decided you're not finished for the day."

7

LUCA

I WAS SURPRISED WHEN SHE JOINED ME IN THE EXERCISE ROOM. THE continuous glare and tense muscles were predictable, though. I made her jog another two miles. Then demanded she sit her ass down on the sofa and continue our daily movie routine.

This time she didn't sleep. She kept giving me the silent treatment, her glare cemented in place.

I let it fly because I appreciated seeing her committed to something for once, even if that commitment was her annoyance with me.

I even anticipated the animosity seeping into the following day, but she woke this morning without bitchiness. In fact, she's acting as if nothing happened yesterday. She talked to me over breakfast, went for a run on the treadmill afterward, and has just joined me for a movie at our usual mid-afternoon screening time.

I know she's faking the sudden recovery. Ignoring and bottling all the hurt. But even being able to pretend she's not dying inside takes a level of strength beyond my comprehension. I bet she doesn't realize how incredible she is. How fucking remarkable.

If only she'd finally break down and face her past—completely —then maybe she might start to recover instead of merely providing herself with distractions.

"What movie are we watching today?" she asks from the outstretched recliner.

"We could try the second half of the superhero movie you checked out on two days ago."

I didn't continue watching without her. I changed the channel as soon as she fell asleep. Not that the viewing is anything more than a lullaby. She usually passes out like clockwork within thirty minutes.

Those moments have been the highlight of my existence. Her content face. Her relaxed, slightly parted lips. Her beauty.

Fuck.

I need to get out of this house. Hit the shooting range. Spar the fuck out of a worthy opponent.

But I won't leave her or bring anyone over here she's not comfortable with. I'm stuck in this tempting isolation. My blue balls are the size of gorilla nuts.

I turn on the movie and lie across the sofa, my attention on her from the corner of my eye—the long, dark hair splayed across the recliner as she rests her head back.

I don't focus on the screen as the actors do their thing, blowing up buildings and shooting up shit. I stare at her, fast becoming entranced by how fucking gorgeous she is as those lashes flutter closed.

It's such a sinking feeling of helplessness, watching someone battle an invisible enemy. If she had a physical wound, I could tend to it. I'd make sure any injuries were stitched to perfection. I'd be meticulous in applying new dressings. And when the site healed, I'd make sure she used the very best scar-lightening creams on her delicate skin.

I'd do anything.

Everything.

But she's not struggling with a physical injury. There are no men to hunt down or kill. Her fight is internal. Entirely out of reach.

All I can do is be patient. I've always been good at that.

Until now.

Until *her*.

The vibration of the cell in my back pocket breaks my trance.

I retrieve the device, the preview of a message from Sarah on the screen—*Open your front door, I've just pulled…*

Jesus. She's here.

The bitch had been smart enough to keep her distance after I spoke to Torian. That gossip grapevine is effective in these parts. Too bad she didn't have the smarts to stay away too.

I type back—*Fuck off. Penny is asleep.*

I don't want her here. I'm done letting her report back to Decker. If he wants answers about his sister, he can ask during the daily phone calls I have to endure. I'm not opening the damn door. She can crawl back into the hole she came from.

Instead, I lower the sound on the television, then switch off the movie when my cell vibrates again—*Turn on the news.*

The hairs on my arms rise.

I change the channel, flicking to news station after news station, trying to find something to trigger familiarity, but there's nothing. No reports of drama in the Greek islands or issues back home surrounding Torian's questionable business dealings.

I'm clueless.

What am I searching for?—I send back.

Just open the goddamn door.

I push from the sofa, annoyed, tired, and so far over this shit with Sarah, Decker, and yes, Torian, that it takes a few seconds to recognize the woman's face that flashes on the screen.

The heavy weight of dread takes over.

It's one of Penny's friends. One of the women I helped rescue from the same sex-slave hellhole in Greece. The words beneath her picture state—*Up next: Missing woman dies by suicide.*

Holy shit.

I stare. At the woman. At Penny peacefully sleeping. At the stillness surrounding me that will soon erupt into sorrow.

The cell vibrates again—*Open the fucking door, Luca.*

Fuck.

I stalk from the room, measuring my footfalls so I don't wake the sleeping beauty, and reach the front of the house without taking a breath.

"What the fuck happened?" I ask as I pull the door wide.

Sarah stands there, her face somber. "I don't know. All I got was a call from Torian telling me to get my ass over here to help control the situation."

"I don't need your help controlling anything." I scrub a hand through my hair and try not to panic. "Why didn't he call me?"

"I guess he wanted you to have backup."

"What I need is information."

She shrugs. "I don't have a lot. Torian said Benji had been certain the woman was ready to return home. He'd prepped her the best he could. Made her realize talking about her time in Greece wasn't an option. And set her up with a backstory. Then he dropped her off a few blocks from where her parents live."

"Obviously, he fucked up somewhere," I growl.

"You can't know that. These women are unpredictable. How could they not be after that level of abuse?"

"Then he should've kept her long—"

"Luca?" Penny's voice carries from the living room. "Where are you?"

Jesus fucking Christ. I just need a second. One crystal clear thought. One hint of a plan so I don't make this harder for her.

"At the front of the house. I'll be with you in a minute." I pin Sarah with a scowl and begin closing the door. "I don't need backup. Not from you."

She steps forward, placing her foot at the threshold. "So how are you going to handle this?"

"That's not your concern."

"Luca." Her tone is derisive. Demeaning. "This won't go down well. She's going to lose it."

"No shit." But I've managed worse. A bullet to my head for starters. Not to mention the numerous times Penny has attempted to kill me. I talked her down from those ledges... well, I manhandled her from the cliff a time or two, but I still got the job done.

"So you can handle her tears? Her grief? Her heartbreak?" She raises her brows. "You can be a shoulder for her to cry on?"

"She doesn't cry. Never has."

"And you realize that's unhealthy, right? She needs to let it out."

Yeah, I realize. I realize too fucking much where Penny is concerned.

I pinch the bridge of my nose, squeezing tighter and tighter to stave off the building headache.

"*Luca?*" This time Penny's call is frantic, the tone etched in fear. "*Luca.*"

My heart drops to my gut. "*Fuck*. I left the television on the news."

"Goddamnit." Sarah lunges forward, shoving past me to jog down the hall as I rush to close and lock the door behind her.

The television volume increases as I run after her.

"—*Abigail Foster, a twenty-five-year-old who went missing four months ago,*" the reporter informs the viewers, "*miraculously returned to her family yesterday, only to take her life overnight.*"

I reach the entry to the living room and get hit in the chest at the sight of Penny standing before the recliner, a hand clasped over her mouth as she shakes her head.

The television cuts to a middle-aged woman cradled by the side of a stricken man. "Our baby had only just come home to us," the woman sobs. "Now she's gone." She buries her face in the man's shoulder. "*My baby is gone.*"

The vision returns to the newsroom, the anchor's emotionless face filling the screen. "*Initial reports state Abigail Foster's disappearance was due to a secret elopement. She only returned when the relationship dissolved.*"

"No," Penny seethes, no sorrow or tears in sight. "*No.*"

Sarah reaches for her. "I'm sorry for your loss."

My warrior pulls away, distancing herself from vulnerability. "What's going on?" She turns to me, blinking rapidly as those pleading eyes beg for information. "I don't understand."

"I'm sorry, shorty." I start for her, wishing I had more than useless condolences. "I don't know."

"This isn't happening." There's a wealth of conviction in her voice—so much pained adamance. "Abi wouldn't kill herself."

"I'm so fucking sorry." I don't know what else to say as I raise my hand to brush my fingers along her sweater-covered arm. "I wish there was something I could—"

"She didn't kill herself." She slaps my hand away. "She *wouldn't*. I know her, Luca. There's no way she'd take her own life."

Denial is a bitch. I know from experience.

"What you all went through in Greece was traumatic," Sarah murmurs. "It would affect each of you in different ways."

"Can't you hear me?" Penny snaps. "I *know* her. She would *never* do this."

"Penny." I reach for her again. "It's—"

"No." She shoves by me. "They're wrong."

The continued denial slices through me as she rushes for the hall, disappearing around the corner.

I should go after her. I should do *something*. But I'm still wading in indecision when her bedroom door slams moments later.

"That went well." Sarah turns off the television, the thick silence closing in on me. "What are you going to do now?"

I know what I want to do. It's the same damn thing I've itched to do since the moment we got here—to push her. To force her to face what's going on. To shove her toward tears instead of isolation. She has to stop hiding and finally start grieving.

"For starters, I'm going to call Benji and find out what the fuck he was thinking returning that woman to her family when clearly she was unstable."

"Don't blame Benji. This isn't his fault."

"It isn't?" I raise my brows. "You sure?"

She winces. "Luca, his job was to get them prepped for the questioning that would arise once they returned home. He only had to make sure they were aware of what would happen if they spilled any secrets."

"Well, maybe he made them too aware. Maybe he scared the fuck out of her to the point where she couldn't cope."

"Luca." My name is a warning. "You're too invested in this. It's just a job."

Like hell it is. I'm so far down the emotionally invested path with Penny that there's no going back.

"Thanks for your help, Sarah." I start for the hall, my tone demanding she follow. "But I've got it from here."

"I'm not going anywhere."

"Yes, you are. Get the fuck out."

"No, I'm staying until I know Penny is okay. Unless you plan on physically removing me, you need to get used to having me here."

I swing around, glaring.

I'd have no problem heaving her over my shoulder and dumping her on my front lawn. In fact, I'd appreciate the inevitable cat fight, my climbing blood pressure demanding an outlet. It's her rare expression of panicked concern that makes me pause.

She's worried. Not just for Decker's sake.

Fuck her and her perfectly managed manipulation. Even though I'm well aware she's potentially playing me, I'm struggling to turn away someone who cares for Penny. My battling warrior needs all the support she can get.

Even from a crazy-ass bitch like Sarah.

She holds my gaze, not moving, not backing down.

"At least make yourself useful and start the coffee machine." I continue to glare as I retrieve the cell from my pocket and walk onto the deck to call my brother.

My pulse pounds through my skull with every ring. Once. Twice. When the line connects I grind my teeth, waiting for the muttered greeting from the only member of my family I have left.

"What the fuck is going on?" I demand. "I'm here watching the news and wondering why the hell you didn't call?"

"Excuse me for having my fucking hands full. You've got no idea what it's like with these women."

"So it's true? The news reports have it right?" My nostrils flare as I strangle the deck railing with my free hand. "After days dealing with you, she finally returned home to kill herself?"

"How the hell would I know? I dropped her off and hightailed it out of there. I don't know what happened after that."

"How was she when you dumped her?"

"I didn't *dump* her. She was fine." Frustration tightens his tone. "She was hopeful. Maybe even fucking excited. The other women thought the same, too. Then this happened."

"This can't be completely left field. You had to have a clue."

"Don't judge me," he snaps. "She was *fine*. She was *happy*. She didn't dance a goddamn jig into the dining room every morning, but she was ready to go home. Don't blame me for what happened. This isn't my fault."

It never is.

"You should've called me before you took her back. You should've paid closer attention."

"Fuck you. I did the best I could. You don't know what I've been through. You've got—"

A burst of muted noise from inside steals my attention. A

smothered thud. I swing around to the house, finding Sarah rushing for the hall.

"I've gotta go." I speak over Benji, then disconnect the call and run inside, sliding into the hall as Sarah grabs for the handle of Penny's door. "*Stop*."

She stiffens, glancing over her shoulder to meet my gaze while crashing and banging thunders from inside the bedroom. "Let me go to her."

"No. Back off. Or go home."

"Listen to me." She speaks in a rush. "I have experience with this. I can empathize with her loss." She raises her hands in surrender. "Storming in there, flying by the seat of your pants, will only cause more damage."

Christ.

I don't know how to help. All I have is instinct and that adamant, demanding pulse is telling me to get my ass in there.

"Luca?" she begs. "Do you really want to risk hurting her more than she already is?"

I clench my fists. "You don't know that I will."

"You're a raging bull—face stark, hands clenched, shoulders stiff. You're going to scare her."

Fuck. I try to calm myself, attempting to relax my muscles and breathe deeper.

It's pointless.

I'm mindless over Penny. Mindlessly failing.

Another scream carries from inside the room, a heavy thud following.

"All I'm asking for is ten minutes." Sarah twists the door handle. "I can deal with this."

Maybe she can. Maybe it would've been better for her to manage the recovery from the very first day we returned from Greece. Maybe all I've done is fuck Penny's life even more.

But I can't bring myself to give Sarah permission to take over. All I can do is turn on my heels and stride back where I came from, my pride and a truckload of hostility clogging my fucking throat.

8

PENNY

I THROW THE BEDSIDE LAMP ACROSS THE ROOM, THE SHADE fracturing on impact, the base smashing before it falls to the carpet in fragments.

Abi's gone.

Dead.

It's all my fault.

I left her with a stranger.

I gave up when I should've been protecting her, and now her death doesn't even make sense. She didn't kill herself. She wouldn't.

If the news report featured Lilly maybe I could digest the information. Lil was always the weakest. The one unwilling to fight.

But not Abigail. She had fire in her soul. Determination in her belly. She wouldn't take her life when she'd just returned to her family.

I refuse to believe the lies, my pulse ramping higher the more my mind conjures memories of her parents on the television. Their tears. Their anguish.

I grab the bedside clock and haul it across the room, the weight thunking into the plaster to leave a dent.

The past returns to haunt me. Images of Abi pummel my mind. I can still feel her. Can still smell the sweet vanilla of her shampoo.

I yank out the top drawer of the nightstand and throw that, too, this time releasing a war cry as the projectile leaves my fingers.

The outside mania quietens the voices within. It soothes the rage. Momentarily.

I scream as I throw another drawer. And another.

"Penny?" The door opens, making me pause as Sarah cautiously glances inside. "Can I come in?"

"No," I pant, my chest heaving.

She ignores me, walking forward, her steps cautious as she closes the door behind her.

"Get out." I grab the last drawer in the nightstand and heft it at the wall, the hard *thwack* no longer bringing relief.

"Talk to me." She continues toward me, not stopping until she reaches the side of the bed. "Tell me what you're thinking."

I shake my head, stumbling backward to the window.

I want to tear my hair out. To scratch at my eyes. To claw at my skin. I want anything and everything to take away the violence inside me, the toxicity molding into my DNA.

"What hurts the most?" she asks.

That's the thing—I don't even know. Is this grief? I'm not hurt. I'm livid. The anger is marrow-deep. It accompanies every inhale. Every thought. It's in the past, the present, the future. I'm surrounded by punishment. The shadows creep closer with each heartbeat.

I let Abi down.

I didn't protect her.

I should've done more. For her. For all of them.

"Leave." I turn to the window, my sight focused on Luca's cream fence when my mind sees nothing but Abi. Her face blinks back at me. Her determination. Her strength.

It's all been extinguished.

Snuffed.

"When I lost my family. I couldn't pull myself together because too many emotions were attacking me at once." Sarah walks to the side wall and picks up the battered shell of the lamp. "The weight of it was brutal. And I was convinced nobody else would ever understand. How could they? How could anyone possibly know what it's like to have every loved one taken away? What I should've realized, though, was that I didn't need understanding. I only needed someone to listen."

"That's not what I need." I reach for the curtain, digging my nails into the thick material, tempted to pull the heavy weight from the looming rod.

I don't know what will help me right now, but it's not chitchat.

"I think you're wrong," she states, matter of fact. "I think you're scared of asking for help... scared of opening up to someone. I was like that, too. I didn't truly find my feet until I let Hunter in. He found me through the darkness."

I glare at her, disgusted. She may have been found, but that discovery led her to a life of crime. To a murderous fiancé.

"And I know you said your friend wouldn't kill herself," she continues. "But everyone handles trauma differently. We never truly know—"

"Stop." Her placations stoke the building flames inside me, the suffering increasing through my anger.

"Penny, you should—"

"*Stop*," I snap. "Your situation holds no comparison to mine. You don't know what I want. What I *need*. And you certainly have no fucking understanding of how well I knew Abi. She wasn't a friend. She was my sister. A *real* sister. Not like the crime-riddled family you joined to replace your own."

Her eyes flare. This formidable woman, with her steely determination and threatening demeanor, is taken aback by my words.

"Ouch. That was below the belt." She rubs her sternum as if I punched her. "But I'll allow it. I'm all for lashing out when I'm in pain, too."

I wince, hating myself. Hating her. Hating the whole damn world.

I don't want to lash out. I don't want to fight.

The reaction is beyond my control, the response engrained while living under the roof of a monster. Luther made me this way. Made me learn to attack at the first sign of fear. And I loathe myself for allowing the transformation.

I wasn't aggressive before him. I was gentle and kind once.

Now I'll forever be his slave.

"Oh, God." I suck in a breath, the shackles of my life sentence tightening. "I'm sorry." I swing around to the window. "I shouldn't have said that."

"Don't be. I didn't walk into a room where furniture was being thrown anticipating fluffy conversation and squishy boob hugs. You're entitled to your emotions. If you're angry, let it out. Same goes with the sadness. You can't bottle it up."

She's wrong. I *can* keep it bottled. Luther made it impossible not to learn the skill when he despised vulnerability. And besides, crying would be the end of me. I'd start and never stop.

"I'm a good listener," she adds. "Luca is, too."

I return my attention to the fence, staring mindlessly as I force myself to be calm. "Luca doesn't need to be burdened any more than he already is. I've destroyed enough of his life. And now his home."

"Pfft. The guy didn't have a life to begin with." The mattress squeaks as she makes herself comfortable. "Listen to me. At the moment, you're being pummeled. There's grief, confusion, and fear. There's loneliness, guilt, and longing. And that was before you even heard the news about Abi. Your only choice is to be overwhelmed. But you're going to need to quieten the mass of voices to be able to move on."

"You're wrong. I barely feel any of those things."

Hours ago, she would've been right. I was drowning in all those emotions. Not now though. What's happening in this moment isn't right.

It's different.

I'm different.

"Then what do you feel?"

I can't admit the truth. It's heartless, learning about the loss of a loved one only to feel anger in response. It's not natural. Not normal.

Luther's influence is seeping into me. It seems the more time I spend away from the nightmare of my past, the more I'm dragged back to it.

I'm changing, and not into someone I like.

"You're angry." She releases a breath of a chuckle. "I guess we're more alike than I thought, because that was my greatest struggle, too."

There's the slightest sense of appreciation in knowing my feelings aren't unique. Just not enough to bring comfort.

"Rage tortured me the most," she adds. "For weeks. Probably months. So I chased it down and figured out what it would take to silence the screams."

I glance over my shoulder, meeting her gaze. "How do you silence anger?"

"Revenge," she says simply. "I wanted retribution for what I'd lost. And what was taken from my family. That meant going after the man who destroyed us. I transformed my body into a weapon. I learned every type of combat and defense training you can think of. I did whatever it took to reach my goal."

I believe her. The physical lengths she went to are still evident at first glance. Her arms show defined muscle beneath the feminine facade. There are scars on her skin. There's hardness in her beautiful features.

"I killed those voices. And the man who murdered my family."

A flicker of respect sparks inside me.

I'm happy for her, but it doesn't mean I can do the same. Luther is already dead. Revenge isn't possible.

"I'll help wherever I can. Luca will, too. And there's no hurry. Don't even think about it today. But why don't you talk to the other women you lived with? They might be able to tell you about Abi's final days and help you understand what she was thinking."

I shake my head. Nothing could make me understand.

"If not for insight, do it for support. You can't keep battling on your own." There's another squeak of the bed. More footfalls. "Here."

I turn to her standing a few feet away, her finger tapping her cell screen.

"Talk to them." She passes over the device, a call to *Benji* written on the screen, the connecting tone humming through the loud speaker.

My hand shakes as I reluctantly take the offering. I don't want to speak to Nina and Lilly. Not yet. Not when my betrayal to them is raw. They'll blame me. They *should* blame me. I spent months protecting them only to leave when they needed me the most. Yet I can't bring myself to end the call, the anger inside me begging for salvation.

"Hey, Sare," a man greets. "This isn't a great time."

The voice is shockingly familiar, stunning me speechless. The tone is similar to Luca's. Deep and graveled.

"Sarah?" he asks.

"Benny, I'm here." She raises her voice from behind me. "Penny has the phone. Can you put one of the other women on the line? She needs to speak to them."

My heart pounds, the need to disconnect waging war with the necessity to be soothed.

"Yeah, okay," he mutters. "Give me a minute."

Silence rings in my ears, along with my heavy pulse, while I attempt to talk myself out of hanging up. This doesn't feel right. I just… can't.

Murmurs filter down the line. A scuffle of scraping sounds brush my awareness.

I push the phone toward Sarah. I can't do this.

"Penny?" The syllables are entirely brittle. Yearning and needy.

I close my eyes and stiffen against a surge of guilt.

"Penny?" she repeats, this time frantic.

"She's here," Sarah answers. "She's listening. I think she's finding it hard to speak."

I suck in a breath, dragging air deep into my lungs, praying for strength. All those emotions Sarah mentioned are right there—the guilt, the sorrow. They're banging on the walls of my anger, trying to get in.

"Oh, God, Penny," Nina sobs. "I don't know what happened. Abi was excited to go home. She wanted this so much. It doesn't make sense."

"So it's true?" I whisper. "She's dead."

I need to hear it, just once, from a reliable source. From someone I trust.

"Yes."

I open my eyes and blink away the sear of unshed tears. I can't cry. I won't.

"B-Benji took us there this morning," she stammers. "We watched from the end of the street as the police wheeled her covered body outside."

"She was happy." Lilly speaks softly in the distance. "She

63

wanted to go home. Now I'm starting to think the home she referred to wasn't with her parents."

Bile churns in my stomach, threatening to join the party.

Heaven *was not* home for Abi. She would never mean that.

"Are you both safe?" My tongue protests against the words, making them sluggish.

"We're being looked after," Nina says. "Benji has given us everything we need. I'm just not sure where we go from here. We're in Eugene, in the neighboring suburb to Abi's parents, and were meant to be heading to my family in Gold Beach."

They're close. Within a two-hour car ride.

I could get to them. Help them. Protect them and make certain they're stable enough to be returned to real life.

I could… but I won't.

I'm not a leader anymore. My time as their protector is over.

I can't help anybody in my pathetic state.

"I'm scared," Nina admits. "What if Abi didn't realize how tough things were going to be until she reunited with her parents? What if the reality of returning became too much? The same thing could happen to me."

"It won't." I swallow over the dryness consuming my throat. "You're going to get back on your feet. Build a career. Be happy—"

"But *she* was happy, Penny. How does that disappear in the blink of an eye?"

"I don't know." I bite my lip. "We don't know what went on inside that house."

"What if this never ends?" Lilly sobs. "What if we're always going to suffer?"

Silence follows, and I know they're waiting for a familiar boost of positivity from me. Problem is, I have the same questions. I can't fake optimism for them anymore.

"Look, I've gotta go." I wrap my arm around my belly and squeeze tight. Speaking to them was a mistake. I can't help them. And they can't help me. Not anymore. All this conversation has done is bring more vulnerability. More agonizingly brutal suffering to everyone involved. "If you remember anything call Luca."

Sarah clears her throat. "Penny, you have your—"

I hold up a hand to silence her. I know what she's going to say

—that I have my own phone. That they can contact me directly if all I'd do is let Luca set up the device he bought me.

I don't want that. I can't give my past twenty-four-seven access to me. And if I have the internet constantly within reach I'll succumb to my pained curiosity. I'll search for all the names of the sisters I've lost. I'll suffocate under the weight of the lives they left behind.

I'm not strong enough for that.

Despite all this anger, I'm nothing but goddamn weak.

"Goodbye," I whisper. "I love you."

"We love y—"

I disconnect, unable to listen, and hand the device to Sarah who looks at me with a mix of disapproval and pity.

"That wasn't really talking, now, was it?" She pockets the cell. "I told you, you need to let this out with someone. If not them, then Luca."

"And I've told you, he doesn't need more trouble from me. He's babysitting out of obligation. I'm only here because there was no alternative... Please, just leave me alone."

"He cares about you."

I shake my head, the movement taking too much effort. I'm not even going to argue.

A light tap sounds at the door, and the man of the moment pokes his head into the room, his intense eyes taking in the destruction of the room before settling on me. "Am I interrupting?"

"No. Come in." Sarah walks toward him. Both of them stop at the foot of the bed to stare at me. "Penny and I were just having a conversation about her coming to live with me for a while. I think it's for the best."

"What?" Luca stiffens.

I do the same, completely blindsided.

That was *not* what we discussed. Yet the denial remains caged in my tightening throat, waiting for his relief to show.

"You're no longer obligated to look after her," she continues. "It's my job now."

"Obligated?" His eyes harden. "She's never been a fucking obligation, Sarah. I chose to come back here. With her. If she goes, I go. I'm not leaving her fucking side. Not for a minute."

My emotions swirl, creating a washing machine of confusion and denial. I don't want to believe him. I *don't*. Yet I crave it, too. Oh, God, how I crave.

Sarah cringes. "Luca, we all know you got dumped with the babysitting job. Let me take over. I'm better equipped to look after a woman. We can have a girls' retreat at my place."

"Is that what you want?" His frantic gaze searches mine. "Do you want to leave?"

No. What I want is to make things easier on him. To stop being a nuisance. To take the burden off his shoulders.

"Penny?" He steps closer, his hand reaching out only to fall back to his side. "Do you want to stay with Sarah?"

What I want is to stop being this person that isn't me. To return to who I was before Luther and Greece and violation. I want peace. Normalcy. And more than anything, I want to be whole.

Sarah meets my gaze from over his shoulder, her lips tweaked in conniving satisfaction. "She's a hassle you don't need."

The truth hurts. But there's confusion, too.

Sarah is enjoying this, and I don't know why.

"Shut it," Luca growls, his eyes softening in my direction. "Tell me the truth, shorty. Do you want to get out of here?"

Sarah's smirk grows as she winks at me.

Winks. At. Me.

I struggle to understand the taunt. Then, like a light bulb, my awareness switches on to expose the meaning behind her tactics.

She's created this drama in an attempt to prove me wrong about the burden I've placed on his shoulders. She doesn't want to take me away. She wants me to feel at home.

"Penny?" Luca takes another step.

"I don't know." I swallow, wrapping my arms around my middle. "I don't know what I want."

The corners of his mouth lift in a sad smile. His head inclines the slightest inch in acknowledgement. Then he turns to Sarah, his height increasing as he straightens. "You did this. You messed with her fucking head. You made her question being here."

"Me?" She places a hand to her chest, her eyes wide with feigned offense. "Why would I do that?"

"Get the fuck out." He stalks for the bedroom door, jabbing a finger toward the hall. "And don't come back. I've had enough of your bullshit. Everyone knows I'll protect her with my life. I'm done trying to prove it."

Sarah remains in place, her attention on me, one brow raised as if to say, 'I told you so.'

I guess she did.

I knew Luca would be kind enough to deny wanting me to leave. I never imagined he'd be passionate about me staying. Or furious at anyone attempting to take me away.

"Are you sure this is what you want?" she drawls. "You don't have to stay under this psycho's roof."

"Get. The fuck. Out," he snarls. "*Now.*"

She rolls her eyes and gives another wink. "Okay. Okay. I'm leaving."

9

LUCA

I lead Sarah to the front door, waiting until she's got one foot outside before I slam it on her ass, then lock the deadbolt while she mouths off.

I'm angry. Unjustifiably livid. And entirely fucking blindsided.

One minute, I thought she was helping. The next, she was attempting to steal Penny away.

I lean against the door, my head hung, a pulse ticking beneath my left eye.

Maybe if I hadn't interrupted when I did, Sarah would've been successful. It's not like she doesn't have a point about being better equipped to look after a woman. I don't know how to be the person Penny needs. But I'll be damned if I trust someone else to protect her.

There's no way in hell.

If she leaves, I'll follow.

I shove from the door, needing to get back to her. To stop her from questioning our sanctuary.

She's still standing near the window in her bedroom, her arms around her middle. Every muscle is pulled taut. Despite her stiffness, sorrow seeps from her. Her heartache escapes with every breath even though there are no tears.

She continues to trap her emotions inside. Caging them.

It's time to break them free.

"I'm sorry." I'm drawn to her side, my fingers itching to touch. "I know I keep sayin' that, but I've got nothing else."

She doesn't move. Doesn't react.

"You're going to get through this." I reach for her, stealing the physical connection I crave, my palm sweeping over her shoulder. "I'll get you all the help you need."

"Please don't." She flinches away. "I just want to be left alone."

No.

No more isolation. No more hiding from grief.

My limbs throb with the urge to grab her. Shake her.

She needs to let go. To cry. Not only for Abi, but the parts of her own life that died. Why can't she see that?

"Tell me what you're thinking," I calmly demand.

"That it's not true. That Abi didn't kill herself."

"How do you know?"

"I spoke to my sisters and they agree." She turns to me, her eyes filled with conviction. "They said she'd never do this. That she was excited to get back to her family."

"Okay. So maybe her death was an accident." I reach for her again, her violent shrug away stinging my pride. "But she's gone, shorty. That part you can't deny."

She winces. "Don't."

"I know you loved her. You two went through hell together. She was everything to you, which means there's no way you can get around grieving for her. No matter how hard you try."

She retreats a step. "You don't understand."

"You're right. I can't imagine how hard it is to lose her. You left Greece thinking the nightmare would end, only to have it follow." I inch closer as she backtracks. "And you're too scared to let down your guard to start healing. You're clinging to what you know—the sterility, the anger. You think you need to act the same way you did with Luther in an effort to protect yourself. To fight when you should crumple."

Her lips part as if in shock before a mask of annoyance settles into place. "Stop."

"I'm sorry, shorty, but I can't. It's time for this to sink in. For you to acknowledge what you went through. For you to break down the walls you've built out of fear. There's no peace in denial."

"There's no peace?" she asks. "What peace could I possibly obtain, Luca? What peace have I ever had?"

"Peace is on the other side of acceptance. You need to face what's happened."

"I said, 'stop.'" She makes for the door.

I follow, unable to let this go. "We're not running anymore. Maybe it was suicide. Maybe it was an accident. It doesn't change the fact she's gone."

"*Stop.*" She plants her feet and swings around to shove at my chest. "Stop it." Her eyes blink with unshed tears. "Just stop."

Her agony punches into me, my words injuring us both. But she's so close. The slightest crack forms in her defenses. "Luther's not here anymore. You don't have to keep fighting. Abi's dead, shorty. It's time to grieve."

The tears build, her dark eyes an endless pool of heartache bursting to break free. She shoves me again and again, harder and harder.

"She's not suffering anymore. She's free." I snatch her wrists. Tight. They tremor under my grasp.

Those eyes flare, her panic and fear slam into me.

But I can't let her go.

After all the days of sitting on my ass and letting her find her own way, it's clear I should've acted differently. She needs to be pushed to face reality. I feel it deep down in my bones. She can't move on until she acknowledges her past. Until she lets go of the hold Luther had on her.

"You're safe," I murmur. "He's not here anymore. He can't hurt you."

"Don't do this." She thrashes, attempting to break my hold. "*Let me go.*"

I pull her into my chest, releasing her wrists to wrap my arms around her back. "I'm not hurting you. I never will." I cage her against me as she bucks and pushes, doing her best to escape.

"*Stop,*" she screams. Her loose hair whips my face. Her knee jabs me in the thigh.

She's a wild cat. Sharp movements. Feral ferocity.

I hope I'm not fucking this up.

No.

This is the right thing to do.

The *only* thing.

I hold tighter, increasing her struggle. "I've got you."

"*You're a monster,*" she shrieks, wiggling one arm free. She thumps my chest. Slaps my face. Scratches my cheek.

"No, *he* was—*Luther.*" I take her fury, not letting her hatred penetrate. "*He* hurt you. *He* was the monster. I'd never raise a hand to you, Penny. I'd never do the things he did. You're safe now. I've got you."

She has to let it all out. Every ounce of the pain and suffering. I won't let her go through another day clinging to her abuse.

"Let me have your worst." I loosen my arms, allowing her space to whack harder into me.

"Let me go," she wails, raising her face, her mouth a breath from mine. So pretty. So tortured. "Get your fucking hands off me."

"No."

She strengthens her fight. Beating. Clawing. Bashing. "You fucking bastard." The first tear escapes, the glistening path trekking down her cheek like a break in the most arid drought. "I hate you."

"Hate me all you like. I'm not letting you go until you get this out of your system."

"I *can't* get it out of my system," she screams. "This is me. This is who I am."

"No, Pen, this is who you needed to be when you were around him. You needed to fight. You needed to attack and protect. You don't need to do that now. Not anymore."

"Let me go." She uses both forearms to push at my chest, her unyielding strength fucking admirable. "*Please*, let me go."

"I will, baby. I promise. Once you give in."

"I can't." More tears escape, both eyes drenched in sorrow. She's still fighting, still feral. But her aggression tapers. Her hits lose their ferocity. The clawing and scratching packs less of a sting as she begins to sob. "Please, Luca. I can't be weak. I can't be vulnerable."

My pulse spikes at her fragility, and there's no restraint that could stop me grabbing her chin to force her gaze to mine. "You could never be weak. You hear me? You're stronger than you know. But you need to let your guard down, shorty. It's time to let me help you."

She blinks back at me, one tear following the next, her eyes unfocused as if she's no longer listening.

If only it were that easy for me to switch off to her suffering.

I've been through combat. Killed more men than I can count. I've seen dead children and war zones that resemble nothing but blood and broken limbs. And through it all I detached, needing the sterility to work autonomously.

But not now.

Not with her.

She's stripped me bare. Made me the fucking weak one.

"Why?" she wails, the moisture trail on her cheek becoming the backdrop to a waterfall. "Why couldn't you leave me alone? You should've just left me in that house."

And there it is—her agonizing truth.

It's worse than I thought.

Deeper.

Darker.

This breathtakingly beautiful woman, with her warrior strength and harrowing selflessness, wishes she was back with Luther. Because there's comfort in routine, even in the worst of conditions.

"I should've died in Greece." She hiccups. "Those women should've killed me. They thought I protected them, but I caused them more pain. He punished them because of me. He made me untouchable and in return made them targets." She rambles. Cries. Blubbers. "It's all my fault. I hurt them. I'm responsible."

"No, sweetheart. That was him. All him." I tighten my hold as she crumples. "Don't you dare blame yourself."

"I should've died." She snatches at my shirt, her nails digging into the material. "Why didn't I die?"

I wish I had the answers. I'd give anything to snap my fingers and have this all be over—her suffering, her anguish. I'd trade places with her in a heartbeat. God, how I wish I could. "Thank fuck you didn't. I don't know what I'd do without you."

Her knees weaken, her tears running rampant. She shakes with ragged breaths. Gasps. Fucking shudders as I hold her against me.

"I've got you." I rest my cheek on hers, murmuring in her ear.

72

"I promise I've got you." I vow it on my life. No matter what happens, what she faces, I'll be there for her. "You can trust me."

Her suffering multiplies. Her legs give out. She collapses into me. Weary limbs and malleable flesh. The most perfect surrender.

I cling to her, keeping her against me as her tears soak my shirt.

"W-why would she do this?" she stammers. "Why would Abi give up?"

My heart breaks, a million sharp shards embedding into my ribs. "I don't know."

I haul her into my arms and step around the broken mess on the floor to take her to the bed, sit on the mattress and cradle her in my lap. There's never been a more satisfying feeling than having her settle into me, her head nestled against my shoulder, her fractured breathing teasing my skin.

"Luca?" Her voice is weary, the delicate murmur filling my chest.

"Yeah, sweetheart?"

She sighs, the heave of breath long and punishing. "I'm so tired."

"I know, shorty." Our heads rub as I nod. "I know."

"I just want it all to be over."

I stiffen. Her words are a hint to a clearly defined escape plan that follows where Abi led. And I get it. I understand the impatience to end the hardship. But understanding doesn't mean my throat doesn't tighten at the thought of her following through.

I feel for her. Not only possessive or protective. There's more. So much more that it's clear there's no going back. I've fallen for this woman, with her compiling scars. Her triggers innumerable. Her suffering lifelong.

I want her. I despise myself for even thinking it. But I want her with blinding need.

Mentally.

Emotionally.

Physically.

The instinct to heal her suffering with sex is overwhelming.

It takes all my restraint not to tilt my face into hers and kiss the misery from her lips. To turn her cries into moans. To increase her breathing for reasons of pleasure not more fucking pain.

For a woman who's been violated and tortured, the desire

pumping through me is downright repulsive. And still I can't shut it out.

I want her beneath me. Our limbs intertwined. Our skin covered in sweat.

I need to taste every inch of her. To lick and bite and suck.

Fuck.

I grind my teeth through the building lust, my battle continuing for what feels like hours, the silence only breached by infrequent sniffles and the occasional hiccup.

Maybe she's right. Maybe I am a monster.

10

LUCA

I HELD HER FOR HOURS.

She spoke every now and then, giving brief whispers of insight into her past.

She told me more about Abi. Reflected on what she wished she would've done better during her time held prisoner. She even admitted it felt good to cry.

And later that night as I laid in bed, I'd been pleased with myself. Like a stupid fucking chump over my so-called achievement.

I'd thought pushing her into facing her grief was a great idea. I'd convinced myself she would heal afterward.

But days later, there's still no sign of improvement.

Instead, she no longer pretends to be happy. Those fake smiles that used to annoy me would be a breath of fresh fucking air in comparison to the overwhelming despair continuously plastered on her face.

Puffy red bags are now tattooed under her eyes. She barely eats. And those intermittent moments where she hid in her destruction-filled room have become one long stretch of isolation in between bouts of obsessive cleaning and cooking.

She continues to cry.

Fucking rivers.

Every morning.

I hear her in the shower, the gentle sobs echoing from the bathroom to punish me for what I've done.

I fucked up. I shouldn't have pushed.

I tried making amends with a flower delivery, disguising the offering as a tribute to her grief. In reality, it was a sign of guilt. I've asked, *no*, demanded she watch a movie with me. Exercise with me. Fucking talk to me.

All I get are tears.

From a drought to flash flooding, the deluge still in full flow as Sarah pushes by me at the front door, granting herself access to my house.

"Have you forgotten how to wait for an invitation?" I scowl, locking the deadbolt behind her.

"Have you forgotten how to be polite?" She leads us to the kitchen and makes herself a mug of coffee. "I came when you called. Usually, that requires a thank you."

"Thanks," I grate, not feeling appreciative in the slightest. I wanted her advice, not her company. But beggars can't be choosers.

"Before we do a deep dive on this," she purrs, "I think we should put it in writing that you pleaded for my superior knowledge like a little bitch." She settles into one of the stools at my kitchen counter, sipping from my favorite coffee mug with smug satisfaction.

"Don't start."

She grins. "So we're just going to ignore my superiority?"

I glare, thankful Penny is outside on the deck and not bearing witness to my castration.

"Okay. Fine." Sarah waves me away. "Tell me what's happened since you aggressively forced me from your house the other day."

I clench my molars, breathing deep until I'm no longer tempted to throw her back out the front door. "She hasn't stopped crying," I grate. "I thought forcing her to grieve would help. But this is just a different level of hell."

"It was necessary. You know that."

"Maybe. The question is—where the fuck do I go from here?"

"You need to tell her it's time to move on."

I scoff and slump back against the far counter. "Yeah, okay. No fucking problem. I'll just tell her to get over herself, will I?"

"Yes." She takes another superior sip of coffee. "Normal people have the luxury of grieving for months. Even years. But we're not normal. With our lifestyle, it's not safe to let down our guard for too long. She needs to be aware of that."

"Problem is, she didn't choose this lifestyle, Sarah. It was forced on her."

"It was forced on all of us," she drawls. "Nobody chooses to be here. That's just the way the cards fall. The sooner she gets used to it the better."

I don't want Penny to get used to it. I want her to be saved from it. Sheltered.

"You need to take charge." Sarah lowers her voice. "Push her."

"Pushing her is what led to this mess. Look what the fuck happened."

"You broke her down, soldier. It's time to build her back up."

I wipe a rough hand over my face, not wanting any of this. Not the breaking or the building. I'm not the man for that job. But she's right. I made Penny this way; I can't leave her now.

"I've tried talking to her," I mutter. "I've asked—"

"Don't talk. Don't ask." She screws up her face in disgust. "*Demand*. Assert your authority. Act like a SEAL, not a fucking pussy."

My anger bites, the teeth nipping at my insides. "It's not that easy."

"Why?" She takes another sip of coffee. "Because you like her?"

"Of course I like her. I wouldn't be going through this hell if I didn't."

"No. I mean you *really* like her. Lover boy Luca wants to make babies with Decker's sister."

I push from the counter, my teeth set in a snarl. "Don't joke about shit like that. Not after what she's been through."

"Calm your tits." She looks me up and down, seeming to find me lacking, which only increases my rage. "She's still a woman. And a beautiful one at that. Who knows? Fucking your sad ass might be the best thing for her."

"This was a mistake." I stalk forward and grab her mug. "It's time to leave."

She clings tight to the handle. "Don't steal my coffee, Luca. No man could survive that battle."

I itch to pull out the gun that lives in the back of my waistband. To threaten. To frighten. But I know the tactic won't work on Sarah.

Not today when she's an emotionless black hole.

"Fine. I'll stop, Okay?" She raises a hand in surrender. "Release the mug and nobody gets hurt."

"Bullshit. You don't know how to stop."

"You're right." She smirks. "How 'bout I promise to rein it in a little?"

"I'll still want to kill you."

The consuming frustration won't change until I fix this. I feel like a fucking caveman—all action and aggression. No mental comprehension.

I need fresh air. I need a release.

I need fucking guns and adrenaline and sex.

"Look, I meant what I said before." She tugs the mug from my grip and downs the contents. "You need to build her back up. Make her strong. Teach her how to defend herself. Scare her into action if you have to."

"Scare her? After everything she's already been through?" I grab my phone from the counter and scroll to the surveillance icon, making sure Penny is still seeking sanctuary in the deck chair. "You're a heartless bitch. You know that, right?"

She shrugs. "Put that title on a T-shirt and I'll wear it with pride, because realistically, having my opinion without emotional attachment works in her favor when you're too close to see what's really happening. You're enabling her. There's no way Decker would let his sister get away with this death by melancholy."

"I'm doing my best. He wanted me to treat her right. And I am. I even thought about buying her a goddamn puppy."

Her face turns deadpan. "Do *not* buy her a puppy, you fucking pussy."

"Stop calling me that," I snarl.

"Then stop acting like one. Seriously, who the hell are you, and what have you done with the badass I used to know? Where's the real Luca? Because this right here—" she waves a hand in my direction "—is a fucking pitiful replacement. You're pandering. To a woman. She's never going to be reunited with Tobias in this state. She's never going to be strong enough to return to her family. You need to push her again."

She slides from her stool and smoothes her leather jacket. "And just FYI. Torian came home yesterday, so you're—"

"Why the fuck am I still being kept in the dark?"

"Because I asked him to." She straightens to her full height. "You need all the space you can get. And as I was saying, you're running out of time to fix this. Hunt and Deck are still in Greece tying up loose ends, but they'll be back soon and what do you think will happen then? Decker won't continue letting you make choices for his sister when she's a goddamn mess. So buck up, asshole. Or prepare to stand aside."

I stiffen at the truth in her words. At the looming separation.

I won't let someone else take over Penny's care. Not even if it's her family. Especially when it's not what she wants.

"Handle it, Luca." Sarah grabs her keys and purse from the counter and makes for the hall. "And do *not* buy her a fucking puppy."

She walks herself out. I'm too busy wallowing in self-loathing to follow.

I hate that she's right.

Fucking detest it.

The thought of hurting Penny again makes me livid. But I need to make my move—before it's too late.

And, from the sight of Penny approaching the French doors in my periphery, now is as good a time as any.

"Did she leave?" She steps inside, cautiously looking around.

"Yeah. It's safe."

I receive a half-hearted smile in return, the gorgeousness quickly fading. "Why did she come over this time?"

I could lie. I could blame my upcoming actions on Sarah, too.

"Luca?" She approaches, her brows raised in question, her eyes bloodshot from recent tears. "What did she want?"

"To help."

"With what?" She continues to the fridge, turning her back to me as she grabs a bottle of juice.

"With you. She convinced me of something I didn't want to acknowledge."

Her movements slow while she pours a mouthful of OJ into a clean glass, drinks the contents, then returns the bottle to the fridge without a word.

I wait for her to ask for clarification. But she doesn't, instead placing her glass in the sink before walking toward the hall. She's already predicted what's coming. I swear she already knows.

"Penny," I warn. "Your time's up."

Her posture stiffens, her chin raising an inch in defiance. "Excuse me?" She doesn't turn to face me. Doesn't even glance over her shoulder.

"I said, 'your time is up.' You're not wallowing anymore."

There's no response. Nothing at all, before she continues walking.

"Goddamnit. Don't ignore me." I slam my palm down on the counter, the crack of noise making her jump. "I'm serious. We need to get back to your list."

"My list?" She turns, gradually, her brows pinched as she meets my gaze. "You think watching reruns of the *Fast and the Furious* is going to wipe away my suffering?"

I breathe in her pain, sucking it deep. "We'll create a new list. One that will teach you self-defense and weaponry. More rigorous exercise, too. You're going to start training."

"Exercise is your thing, not mine. I just want to be left alone."

"I've listened to you cry for days. I'm not doing it anymore. If you don't want to exercise, then we'll start on self-defense."

"No." She scowls. "You can't make me."

"I won't leave you defenseless, shorty. This world with the Torians isn't the same as the one you grew up in." I approach her, matching her scowl with my own. "You need to learn to protect yourself."

"I already know how. My time with Luther taught me that."

"Then show me."

Those deep eyes search mine, cautious, annoyed. "I don't need to prove myself to you."

"Then consider it a favor. I worry about you. This will help me sleep at night."

She scoffs. "You don't think, after all my time spent captive, that I didn't learn a thorough understanding of what I'm capable of when pitted against a man?"

I encroach, stopping when we're toe to toe, almost hip to hip. "Then. Show. Me."

Her expression loosens, her agitation changing to bone-weary sorrow. "Tomorrow."

"No. Now. Torian is already in Portland. Your brother will soon follow. If you want to stay here with me, you need to show you're improving, not going fucking backward."

Her lips part, her shock subtle before she shakes her head. "My sister just died. And *you* are the one who pushed me to grieve for her. To grieve for *everything*. Now you expect me to stop?"

"You can grieve all you like. But you need to be learning how to live in this world at the same time."

"Tomorrow," she repeats, swiveling on her heels to make for the hall.

I grab her. I fucking shouldn't, but my fingers latch on to her arm, the throb of connection sliding through me before I realize there's no going back. "Now, Pen."

Her breathing hitches, in fear or shock, I'm not sure. She focuses on where I hold her, where my palm grips the baggy sweater just above her arm, before her eyes finally meet mine. "Get your hand off me." The demand is barely audible, so fragile and weak it only increases my need for action.

I drop my hold and choose to walk into her instead. One foot after the other, intimidating her backward.

"Luca," she warns as she retreats, matching me step for step until she's flush against the wall, her head held high, her breaths increasing.

I know those quickened inhales aren't from lust. I fucking know it. Doesn't stop me feeling the heat in my veins, though.

The rise and fall of her chest. The soft, parted lips. The way those eyes hold mine.

She undoes me. Without words. Without actions. She fucking tears me apart. And there's nothing I can do about it.

"Try to fight me off." I loom over her, deliberately intimidating.

"I don't want to fight you."

"You need to learn. If you have a few tricks up your sleeve—"

"I'll what?" she interrupts. "I'll be able to fight off the next person who tries to abduct me? Is that what you think? Because self-defense won't help when I wasn't attacked, Luc. I was led. Luther talked me into leaving the States. The only thing you can do to help that is give me lessons on stupidity."

"He was a master manipulator. Everyone was fooled by him. Even his own son."

She sighs. "I don't have the energy for this."

"Then show me."

She leans back into the wall, defeat slumping her shoulders. "*Please*." She reaches out, her fingers tangling in my shirt. "I'm just so tired, Luc."

I fucking love the way she says my name. The delicate cadence. The shortened familiarity. And that touch, the one that's entirely gentle, yet packs a goddamn punch.

My mouth dries, and I'm consumed by that feeling again—the one where passion and duty collide.

"We can do this tomorrow," she promises. "I'll work hard to have more energy then."

I ignore her and lean closer. "You need to place a jab just below the sternum—that's where there's minimal muscle to protect vital organs. Or aim for the crotch, eyes—even a stomp to the foot can help."

Her hands continue to tangle in my shirt, tugging, pulling, silently begging as her teeth dig into her lower lip.

I could drown in this version of her. The timidness. The exquisite feminine frailty.

I want to trap her further. Not just against a wall. But in my bed. Under my body. The attraction is so fucking potent it suffocates me.

Whenever I'm close to her like this, I become consumed by her.

"I don't want to do this," she murmurs. "I don't want to hurt you."

"You can't. You couldn't. Don't worry. I've got skills of my own."

She nods, yet those hands don't drop from my shirt. They burrow farther, her fingertips sinking beneath the material to brush my stomach.

Adrenaline rushes through me like a storm. My pulse goes manic. She affects everything. Every inch of me. From my drying mouth to my hardening dick. Then I start trippin', because the little sense I have knows that the timid swipe of tongue she lashes over her lower lip can't be reciprocated desire.

There's no way she can feel the same way I do.

No way her heart is pounding from lust like mine.

It's too soon. I fucking know it. But that rationale doesn't stop me from leaning closer to feel her breath brush my mouth in the most delicate tease.

Her teeth sink deeper into her lower lip. She bats those feminine lashes. Her hands splay, no longer fingertips against my stomach, but full palms, skin to skin.

I want to groan from need. To fucking moan against her mouth as her touch glides around my waist, then to my back.

After weeks wanting her, craving her, I can't fight anymore.

I'm done, and about to claim the luscious prize of her mouth when her arms swoop farther. She snatches the gun from my waistband, snaps it in front of me and jabs the barrel into my stomach. *Hard.*

I don't even have time to react before she raises a taunting brow at me.

"Are those skills good enough for you?" She jabs me again, the metal digging deep.

I should be pissed. Ashamed at the very least. She used my attraction against me like I was a sex-starved pervert. Yet here I am, still a slave to my pulsing dick.

"I can manipulate, too," she murmurs, her beautiful face so fucking close. "I'll never be able to physically defend myself against a man. I know that, Luca, because I've had a lifetime of failed experience. But I can distract and influence sometimes."

Distract and influence?

No. She tempted and seduced.

That damn woman has my cock tied in knots.

"Impressive, Pen. But that gun is loaded. The safety isn't on. One nudge of the trigger and I'm worm bait."

The reality should flatten my libido.

It fucking doesn't.

"Then maybe you should back off and take me at my word when I say I've got skills."

I force out a laugh. "Those so-called skills won't work on everyone." Just pussy-whipped chumps like me. "This manipulative display doesn't change anything. You still need to learn how to defend yourself."

"Do I need to pull the trigger to prove I'm defending myself just fine?"

I chuckle in an attempt to release some of the blinding aggression. God, I want her. Crave her. Fucking *need* her. "Don't kid yourself, shorty. I could get that gun out of your hand in seconds and have you flat on your back in a few more."

"You don't scare me."

"I'm not trying to. But if you don't lower that barrel I'll prove my point." *Christ*, how I want to prove that point. "So either shoot me or prepare for change, because I'm not backing down." I flash her a feral smile. "I'm done playing nice."

11

PENNY

I LET HIM TOUCH ME.

I stand frozen before him, *continuing* to let him touch me.

It's a little daunting. Even somewhat intimidating. But I allow it because the physical contact brings an unfamiliar twist to my stomach. The sensation not loathsome in the slightest.

My pulse hammers, the beat erratic. And my breathing couldn't settle if my life depended on it.

He does something to me, something I don't understand. He has a way of wiping the past from my memory, temporarily covering my scars to transform me into an inexperienced teenager.

It isn't safe to feel like this.

I clear my throat, dislodging the uncomfortable tickle, and lick the dryness from my lips. "Please let me go." Sweat coats my palm, my grip on the gun slipping. "I need to use the bathroom."

He doesn't move. The only acknowledgement of my request is the flaring of his nostrils as his focus narrows on my mouth.

He's a wall of muscle. A large, protective wall I itch to melt into.

"You've got ten minutes." He steps back, giving me space that feels like abandonment. "Then you're getting your ass back here to train."

"Okay." I nod, my heart rampantly beating in my throat. I'll do anything, *say anything*, just to get more breathing room. "Ten minutes."

I start for the hall, only to have him block my path with a flawless sidestep. "Are you forgetting something?" He holds out a hand, palm up. "Gun. Now."

I return the weapon, my fingers accidentally dragging over his, the connection increasing the whirlpool of crazy sensations inside me. I literally scamper for the hall like a skittish dog, then continue to my room. I don't stop my escape until I've locked myself in the adjoining bathroom to stare at myself in the mirror. Panting. Gasping.

I barely recognize the woman reflected back at me.

She's frazzled. Mindless and wild.

For the first time since arriving in Portland, I acknowledge how much my appearance has changed. I was far prettier as a slave. All the visual benefits of the compulsory beauty treatments and hair-styling appointments have since faded. My lashes no longer hold the thick tint. The expensive makeup is no longer a daily requirement. And now I sort of wish they were, because I'm not looking my best for him.

For Luca.

It's ridiculous and pathetic. Downright insane, too. Yet I feel unworthy at the sight of my reflection.

There's no sense to my thoughts. None at all. There's even less sense surrounding the dampness between my thighs, my arousal seeping into the crotch of my sweatpants.

I don't like Luca *that* way. I can't.

I shouldn't like any man.

So why do I crave things I shouldn't be craving?

It's disgusting after everything I've been through. Especially when the fluttering sensations were triggered from a moment filled with menace and danger.

I'd had a gun to his stomach. I'd threatened to kill him. All the while, my hands itched to drag him closer. To pull him into me. Against me.

I'd yearned for his proximity. The closeness that always makes me feel sheltered.

"Goddamnit." I wince through the shame.

Luther did this to me. He's turned me into a mess.

He influences every second of my life, and it's got to stop. I refuse to continue being his slave. I hate myself for allowing him to shape me for this long. For not being able to sleep at night. For the inability to wear underwear. For the fear and the anger and the pain.

I cling tight to the vanity and fight the scream clawing up my throat. I *will not* let that man defeat me. I refuse. He may have won the game with Abi from beyond the grave but he won't regain a tighter hold on me.

"I won't fucking let you," I sneer into the mirror. "You're dead, you son of a bitch. *Fucking dead.* You can't control me now."

I storm from the bathroom, yanking my sweater over my head as I continue to the wardrobe. If Luca thinks self-defense lessons will help me, then so be it. I'll learn. It's not like I enjoy being this broken shred of a woman. I don't want to be useless.

I'm just not sure my shattered pieces can be recycled into something worthwhile.

I strip off my moist sweatpants without daring to look at them. That's when I pause, my hand poised near another oversized outfit when my gaze catches on the only set of figure-hugging yoga pants I mindlessly purchased with Luca's credit card when I first arrived.

I have a closet full of baggy items. But I no longer want to hide in those.

I want to be better. To be whole.

I'm not going to like this. I already hate it. Yet, I drag the stretchy pants from the shelf anyway and don't allow myself to acknowledge an ounce of discomfort as I yank them on.

I ignore the snug fit as the material clings tight to my thighs. And I don't take note of my figure after I drag a tank top from the shelf and pull it on. The inbuilt sports bra is the closest I've come to underwear in a long time.

Everything I wear is constricting. I try to make it embolden me, the taunting restriction working as a reminder of what I've been through. A conniving devil smothered over every inch of my body.

Then I turn on my goddamn heels and trek back to the living room, determined to find a piece of myself in whatever maddening defense lesson Luca has in mind.

If only the look in his eyes didn't lessen my wafer-thin enthusiasm.

I wish I could ignore this, too. The frowned shock at my appearance. The wrinkles of disapproval.

"Something wrong?" I ask over the lump in my throat.

"No. Nothing." His voice is gruff as he pushes the coffee table away from the sofa, creating space in the middle of the room. "Just surprised, that's all. It's been a while since you wore something that didn't resemble a sack."

I take a step back, my skin crawling with the need to hide.

"Get over here," he growls. "Let's get this done."

"If this is such a burden, why are we even doing it?"

"It's not a burden." The growl deepens. "It's—" He stops mid-sentence, his hand rubbing at the back of his neck.

"It's what, Luca?"

"Nothin'. Just get over here."

I bite my lip, not wanting to move, equally despising the warmth that has shifted from between my thighs to pool in my chest.

"*Now*, shorty."

"Okay, you don't need to bark at me." I walk forward, my heart fluttering wilder the closer I get, the furious beat only increasing when I stop a few feet away from him. "What do you want me to do?"

He doesn't meet my gaze as he repositions his stance on the rug, spreading his legs a few inches apart. "I'm going to teach you some basic moves first." He brushes his hands together, his biceps flexing beneath the cuffs of his T-shirt. "When someone's coming at you, you want to be assertive and as loud as possible. Obviously, aim for the groin if you can. That tends to drop a guy like a sack of shit. But if you can't, you can try a hammer punch." He clenches his fist and makes a predictable hammer movement. "Or your elbows. Or the heel of your palm. You want to use—"

"Look, I appreciate what you're trying to do, but I learned these basics in high school. I don't need to go through them again."

"Good." Finally, he meets my gaze. "Practice on me, then."

That rampant heartbeat falters. Stutters. "I don't wa—"

"You don't want to. You don't need to. I've heard it all before. Let's not have this argument again. Just because you think you don't need to learn doesn't mean you shouldn't practice. So throw a swing. Get out some of the built-up aggression you have toward me."

"I don't have built-up aggression toward you."

"The outline of the gun barrel in my stomach says otherwise." He beckons me closer with a jerk of his chin. "Come on. Let me have it."

I sigh and lunge forward, attempting to hit him with a gentle elbow.

"Seriously?" He bats me away. "That's all you've got? What happened to the woman who slapped me across the face in Greece? Or the one who attempted to stab me with a syringe?"

I flinch at the reminder.

Even when I didn't know Luca, I hated hurting him. There was always the slightest sense I was doing something wrong. Like I could see his kind soul through his aggressive and dark demeanor.

"And don't forget the tiger scratches you lashed my chest with the other day," he continues. "My cheek, too."

Oh, God.

My gaze snaps to his face, my hands instinctively reaching for the damage hidden beneath his growing stubble. It's an uncharacteristic move, my yearning for touch feeling shockingly natural. "Is that why you haven't shaved?"

He stiffens, his nostrils flaring. "I didn't think it was a good idea to advertise our fight."

"I'm sorry." My fingertips graze over the rough hair along his jaw, the prickle spreading under my skin. "I shouldn't have lashed out like that."

He doesn't respond, just stares back at me, expression tight, shoulders tighter.

"I didn't mean to hurt you." I trace the fading red line that stretches from his cheekbone to the side of his chin. "I wasn't myself."

"You didn't hurt me." He jerks away, rejecting me with the sudden retreat. "Now, let's get back to business. Throw a swing that would make Rousey proud."

"Rousey?"

"Forget it. Just take a swing. Don't be a wimp."

I launch at him, showing just how un-wimpy I can be. I swing and jab and elbow. One after the other, each move defended and dodged with effortlessness that is both enticing and incredibly annoying.

"Good." He nods in encouragement. "But like I said, be assertive. Don't let an attacker think you're meek."

I grunt with my next hammer punch. Yell with an elbow strike.

"Good... good... good..." He continues to placate me with fluid movements and profound skill. "That's the warrior I know."

I'm no warrior. I can barely keep up with my own punches, my energy almost fully drained.

I step back, panting, and slump over. "I've had enough of these moves. Can you teach me something involving blades or bullets?"

"We'll get to that. But can we kick it up a notch and try a choke hold?"

I remain hunched over, my blood chilling despite the sweat coating my skin.

Flashbacks steal my breath. My focus. Memories clench at my heart.

"Stand up," he instructs. "I'll run through the basics."

I can't straighten.

Here I was demanding more vicious attack strategies and I can't even handle the thought of his first suggestion.

"Come on." He claps me on the shoulder. "It won't take long."

"Just give me a minute." My voice cracks, the gravel coating my throat climbing higher and higher.

"You can rest after this."

"No." I look up at him, his hulking frame looming over me. "I don't think I'm ready."

He raises a brow. "You said the same thing about exercising. Yet it made you feel better, didn't it?"

I shake my head, unable to find the words to explain without increasing my pathetic state of mind.

This triggers vicious memories. Lingering nightmares.

"Don't shake that head at me, shorty." He waves me forward. "Get your ass moving."

My heart pounds beneath tightening ribs. My stomach churns. "Please go slow."

He frowns. "Of course. You'll be fine."

I inch forward, my body acting autonomously because I have no capacity to think. Only panic.

Luca raises his muscled arms, placing his hands delicately around my throat. The graze of calloused skin brings a wave of sickening remembrance. The pressure is barely felt. Featherlight. It steals my breath regardless.

"Are you okay?" His voice provides a temporary distraction, the sound giving me the opportunity to latch onto those deep hazel eyes.

I focus on him. On the familiar comfort. The picture of protection.

I don't want to disappoint him.

I can't let Luther win.

"Yes." Memories continue to haunt me from my mind's eye. The digging, scratching fingers. The choking fear.

I refuse to let panic take over. Each time I face my demons I get one step closer to my reunion with Tobias. If I can't do this for myself, I need to do it for him.

"Breathe through it." Luca's hold remains loose. Even kind. The gentle brush of the pad of his thumb is a coaxing reminder of the here and now. "Tell me how you'd get out of this."

His grip tightens almost imperceptibly. But the restriction increases my panic.

I breathe deeper. Shorter. My oxygen lessens as the flashbacks build in force.

A face so close to my own, twisted in sickening glee.

Pressure—so much pressure.

"Focus, Pen." He strokes his thumb faster. "How would you get out of this hold?"

I swallow and force myself to channel my emotions away from fear. "I don't know." I grab his wrists and attempt to push his arms away.

It's no use. He's too strong.

I raise my knee, my attack on his junk blocked with a swift slide of his thigh.

"That's a good start." He wiggles his arms. "You could put pressure on my wrists in the hopes of bringing me closer. The harder the better. Yank or pull my arms down."

I attempt to do as instructed, not achieving all that much when I'm pitted against a wall of muscle.

"Then what?" he asks.

"I don't know." I grow frustrated, the lingering panic mingling with helplessness. "You're too strong. There's no point."

"Stop sulking," he growls. "There's always a point. Hand-to-hand combat is difficult for everyone. The only winner is the guy whose buddy turns up with a gun. What I'm trying to teach you are ways to buy time. Or enough freedom to run. So go back to basics." He rubs his fingers along the sensitive part of my throat. "What are the best places to attack?"

I can't think. Can't concentrate between the memories and that delicately gentle brush of his thumb. "I don't know."

"Yes, you do. Focus. Don't let the fear take over."

I'm trying. Failing.

"Come on, Pen." He leans in, meeting my gaze at eye level. "You did good when you tried to launch an attack at my dick. But what would you do next? Eyes? Nose? Ears? Remember the basics. The throat is a good target, too, if you can get to it."

"Okay." I nod and go through the motions, gently thrusting and punching and swiping.

"Another option is where you grab my wrist with your left hand, then raise your right arm high and twist your hips toward me. This makes your shoulder act as a barrier, but you're also going to bring your raised arm down with a hard strike at the same time to break the hold against your throat."

I blink rapidly as I try to take in the instructions—raise arm, twist, hard strike.

I run through the steps in slow motion. Gently.

"Good." He nods. "That's real good. Now do it again, but this time properly. Pretend this is real."

His grip increases, the restriction on my throat becoming a living, breathing nightmare.

My pulse goes crazy. My sharp inhales sound like a freight train.

"You've got this, shorty."

I don't think I can.

I can't.

Visions blind me. There's Luther. Robert. Chris. Their hands. Their grip. Their unyielding strength. The black spots. The rush of blood to my head.

"Focus," Luca repeats, the soothing balm of his voice doing nothing to ease my mania.

"No." I yank his wrists, trying to break his hold. "Stop."

"It's okay. Just do it one more time with force."

Monstrous ghosts chuckle in my mind, loving my suffering. There's only the threat of rape. The ongoing torture of my pitiful existence.

"*No*," I repeat. "*Stop*."

He removes his hands, the liberation bringing relief, but not freedom. I still feel trapped in the past. The threat is right there, darkening my vision, making it impossible to get air.

I stumble backward, my throat drying to the point of torturous pain.

"Talk to me." He follows. "What's going on?"

I keep stumbling, keep retreating. There's not enough oxygen. I can't fill my lungs.

"Penny, are you having a panic attack?"

I spin around and stagger for the kitchen. *Water.*

This was all too soon. I'm not ready.

I'll never be ready.

I lunge for the faucet, cupping liquid so I can drink, drink, drink away the mindlessness.

"Tell me what's going on." His hand brushes my shoulder. "Jesus, just talk to me."

I hunch over the counter, sucking in breath after breath. I'm suffocating. About to pass out.

"He choked you." His words aren't a question. "He fucking choked you, and you didn't think to bring it up? Why?"

I sway, my head heavy, my legs weak.

"You should've told me." He grabs my arms, stabilizing me, tugging me toward him. Gently, he guides me to sit on the cool tile, the cabinets at my back. "Why didn't you tell me this was a trigger?"

I shake my head, still feeling the grip around my throat, still seeing Luther's face staring back at me with smug satisfaction. "Everything's a trigger."

"Then tell me everything."

"No." I squeeze my eyes closed. "That's not going to happen." Not only because I'd struggle reliving the intricate details of my imprisonment, but because Luca's demeanor changes whenever we talk about my past. His mood shifts. His posture changes. And even though his aggression isn't directed at me, I still don't appreciate being the cause of his negative energy.

"Did he do it more than once?" he asks.

"Luca..." I sigh to fill the void when words escape me. "Let it go."

"I wish I could," he grates. "How I fucking wish."

He shifts beside me, making me panic—is he finally leaving me, running from my multitude of problems? But when I open my eyes he's still there, his head pressed back against the cabinets, his expression filled with failure as he stares blankly ahead.

Weary silence consumes the few inches between us.

"I'm sorry I can't be the person you want me to be." It feels strange apologizing to him. A month ago, I didn't even know this man. Now he's my world. My recovery and survival. "I wish I was the warrior you think I am, but I'm not."

"I don't give a shit if you're a warrior. I just want to help." His words are growled. Brutal and guttural. "It fucking kills me to watch you go through this on your own. That you won't talk to me."

"Because I hate seeing you angry. Every time I mention him you change."

"Of course I change. Of course I get fucking angry." His eyes narrow. "Don't you understand how much I want to go back in time and kill Luther the way he deserved to be killed? You have no idea how I wish I could've found you sooner. How I'd give anything to have known you beforehand so you never had to suffer in the first place."

"Luca..."

"I'd do anything for you." He holds my gaze, intense and unwavering. "Anything."

The warmth he inspired earlier reignites, the flickering flame shedding light on the darkness within.

I swallow again, my mouth needing moisture.

My clothes become more restrictive. The sports bra tightens around my breasts.

I'm drawn to him. All the strength and protection.

I want to breathe it in, suck it deep. Fill my lungs, my heart, and my weary head.

"You're too good to me," I whisper. "Why?"

He huffs out a harsh laugh. "You've got a short memory. You're still on the floor after I pushed you into a panic attack."

I lean back against the cupboards and sigh. "It's not the only thing you've pushed me into. The good outweighs the bad."

"Like what?"

I shake my head, not wanting to delve into the details of why I had to change clothes. "It doesn't matter."

We fall quiet, nothing but our breathing to pepper the silence.

It's soothing.

Just Luca and I.

No expectations. No pressure.

I could stay here for hours.

"I'm proud of you." He places his hand over mine and gives a light squeeze. "We'll try this again tomorrow. Without the choke hold."

He makes a move to stand and I panic again.

"Don't go." I rush to grip his calloused fingers. "Stay with me a while."

I want the contact. Despite the anxiety and the flashbacks, I want his touch.

I *need* it.

"Okay." He settles back beside me, shoulder to shoulder, one leg stretched out, the other bent. "Are we talking or ignoring each other?"

It's my turn to chuckle. "Does it matter?" I shoot him a glance, getting caught up in eyes that smolder.

Why does he have to be so attractive? He's handsome and savage and beautifully lethal.

Those attributes scared me not so long ago. Attractive men were monsters. *All* men.

Now there's Luca. Visually appealing and soul awakening.

My heart beats harder as my curiosity piques. Will more closeness bring added comfort? Does this delicious ache inside me have the potential to assist my recovery?

"Would you let me try something?" I swallow. "I mean, in an attempt to see if it helps my recovery?"

He frowns. "Of course."

I nod against the surge of invigoration hollowing my stomach and rise onto my knees, turning to face him. I shuffle until my legs touch his thigh, his shoulders stiffening with the contact.

"Everything okay?" he asks. "You look scared."

I am.

No. I'm nervous.

I want to touch him. *Feel* him.

But those moments have always been tainted for me.

Touch has rarely been kind.

Not until Luca.

"I just…" I reach for him, my palm reclaiming its favored position against his stubbled cheek. "I…" I shake away my explanation when he stiffens further. "Do you want me to stop?"

"What are you doing, exactly, shorty?" His voice is low. Roughened.

"I don't know. Does that matter?"

"No." He offers the word simply, but his eyes are cautious. "Do whatever you need."

I have a feeling he'll regret the offer, because what I want to do is tentatively place my lips on his and see if panic overwhelms me.

I lean forward, holding his gaze, barely blinking.

Every part of me thrums. I can't hear through the static ringing in my ears. But I feel safe, protected, his strength luring me in.

I approach to within a few inches when his nostrils flare, the grind of his jaw rippling under my fingertips. He's uncomfortable and still I can't smother my curiosity.

I want to try this one thing for me. Not because I was pushed. Or frightened.

For *me*.

For healing.

"Penny." My name is a warning. "You don't want to do this."

"Yes, I do." I steal the space between us, brushing my mouth over his, the connection jolting through every inch of me despite the exquisite softness of his lips.

I awaken with sensation. With tingles and yearning and light.

Sexuality washes over me. But it's not degrading or demeaning like I predict. There's no fear or disgust.

96

Everything is slow and sweet, his kiss a gentle dance as a growl emanates from his chest.

He frees me, helping me spread my wings to soar while remaining immobile.

Warmth takes over. Building. The blaze burns hottest between my thighs.

I could cry from the relief.

I want to laugh and sob and sing.

Until he jerks away, breaking the heavenly connection with a scowl. "Shit. That shouldn't have happened."

I blink rapidly, entirely dazed. "I'm sor—"

"Don't you dare apologize." He shoves to his feet. "This wasn't your mistake; it was mine."

I wince. "I kissed you, not—"

"You were barely fucking coherent moments ago. You didn't know what you were doing. But I did." He shoves a hand through his hair, his scowl deepening. "I knew, and I didn't stop it."

He's wrong. I knew, too.

Heart, mind and soul, I knew.

"I took advantage." He backtracks, his hand falling to his side. "After everything you've been through, I still took fucking advantage."

"Luca, no." I scramble to my feet. "Please don't walk away from me."

"I'm not." He gives a sad smile. "But you were right. You need space. And time. I'm going to give you both."

12

PENNY

He's been true to his word.

He walked away without looking back and kept me at arm's length.

I'm not sure if it was another ploy, but the unspoken threat of being sent to live with Sebastian was enough encouragement to move my ass out of the pit of despair.

It's not that I don't love my brother. Not that I don't miss him. I'm just not ready to face my old life.

There's still overwhelming agony when I think of loving someone and being loved in return. For unending months, everything I cared about was not only stripped from me but tortured. Brutalized. Murdered.

One by one, my sisters were taken away through my entire stay in Greece. And even after my tormentor was killed, more women were stolen from me.

Chloe died. Abi, too.

It's far easier to keep my vulnerabilities at bay.

So instead of living in fear of being sent to stay with my brother, I focused on my health. Mental and physical. I didn't even dwell on the kiss.

At least not to begin with.

I put my mistake with Luca to the back of my mind and exercised. I ran and used the weight equipment.

I cleaned the destruction from my room and filled the wall

dents, sanding them back to smooth perfection with supplies I found in his shed.

I unpacked the phone he gave me and watched online videos to learn more self-defense moves. I even used his credit card to order more clothes that wouldn't hang off me. I ordered extra underwear, too.

But each hour became lonelier with Luca's avoidance, and the memory of that kiss grew legs to run circles around every thought I had. Especially at night.

I started seeking him out after the first day—exercising at the same time he did, disturbing him when he stayed in his room to watch television.

It became obvious how my strength grew when I was around him. How my smile became easy and my heartbeats quickened.

He feels a change, too. I can see it in the tension coiling itself around him whenever he notices me. In the lingering eyes and three feet of space he keeps between us at all times.

Tonight is different though.

He stalked into the kitchen around dusk, dressed in charcoal jeans and a black shirt, his hair styled to cover his scar.

I place down the self-help book I'm reading, already on edge, as he pulls groceries from the fridge and starts to chop zucchini with heavy strokes of the blade.

I rise from the sofa, hating how he doesn't look at me as I approach to stop on the opposite side of the island counter. "You look nice."

"Thanks." He continues to chop, throwing onion and carrot into a wok. "I scrub up okay."

His appearance is far beyond okay. His demeanor, too.

He's solid strength and exuberant power.

"You're going out?" I hide the hint of unease in my voice. "Am I meant to be going with you?"

"No. I'm flying solo."

I knew this day would come. He couldn't trap himself in here with me forever. I just always envisaged he'd drag me along by his side.

"I know you don't want to leave the house," he continues. "So Hunt and Sarah are on their way over. They'll keep you company while I'm gone."

My stomach hollows. The painful stab of fear slices between my ribs, piercing my heart. The betrayal does, too. "Hunter's back?"

"And your brother. They flew in early this morning." Finally, he meets my gaze, the intensity in his features welcomed and unwanted at the same time. "Decker wants to see you tomorrow, if you're up for it."

I blink through the whiplash.

Everything is changing.

His gaze narrows. "Don't look so worried. You don't have to if you don't want to."

"No, it's not that. It's a shock to know I'll be here without you." *Without your security. Your comfort.*

"I won't be gone long." He chops more vegetables as the wok sizzles. "A few hours at most. And you'll be safe while I'm out."

I hate this. For all the hope the kiss gave me, I wish I could take it back because it's driving him further and further away.

"Is this for work?" I ask. "Now that Hunter and Sebastian are back, does it mean you'll be leaving the house more often?"

"No, not yet." He keeps chopping, those arm muscles working overtime. "I just need to get out of the house, shorty. That's all. I've got things I have to take care of."

He's running. From me.

He walks for the fridge and claims a packet of raw beef strips as the doorbell rings.

"Could you get that?" He glances at me over his shoulder. "It's Sarah."

My heart pangs.

I don't want her here.

I don't want Luca to leave me.

"Pen?" He closes the fridge door and returns to the island counter. "Can you get the door so I don't ruin your dinner?"

I nod, taking slow steps backward. "Sure."

I take off, my head reeling by the time I check the peephole and pull open the door.

"Howdy." Sarah walks inside without invitation.

"Yeah, what she said." Hunt juts his chin at me. "How's things?"

He doesn't wait for an answer as he follows her down the hall, leaving me to lock the door behind them.

I don't want this. *I don't.*

But I'm unsure how to get Luca to stay.

I creep back down the hall, stopping before the entry to the open living area to listen to the murmured conversation.

"Let her do her own thing," Luca says. "Don't crowd her. I won't be gone long."

"You only need two minutes, right?" Hunt asks.

"Very funny. I'll probably be out for a few hours. Three at the most."

"Are you sure this is the right thing to do?" It's Sarah this time, her voice filled with concern. "You don't want to think it over?"

"I'm not thinking about it anymore. This needs to be done."

Dread creeps into my stomach, growing with the blossoming silence.

I enter the room, all eyes turning to me as I pad my bare feet against the cold tile.

"Well, I'm going to make myself at home." Hunter places his keys and wallet on the kitchen counter, then heads for the sofa. "No chick flicks tonight."

"Is that so?" Sarah winks at me and follows after him. "I have a feeling you're going to be outnumbered, big guy."

I ignore them as I return to the island counter, noting the increased tension in Luca's posture as the television blares to life.

Something's wrong. Something that makes it hard for him to look at me.

"Is everything all right?" I keep my voice low, not wanting to be overheard. "I'm worried."

"Don't worry." He gives a half-hearted grin and shovels a scoop of stir-fry into a bowl. "Enjoy the time without me."

I thought I'd feared leaving the house, but the more the minutes tick by, the more I've come to realize that it isn't these four walls. It's Luca. *He's* the sanctuary. "Can't I come with you?"

He bristles, the kind expression vanishing. "Not this time."

"Why?"

He fills another bowl and another, placing them at the far edge of the counter. "Dinner's up," he announces to the room and sidesteps, grabbing forks from the cutlery drawer before handing one over. "There's things I need to do, and I can't have you with me."

"Because it's dangerous?"

He cringes. "No. It's…" He shoves a hand through his hair as Hunter and Sarah approach and grab their dinner. He doesn't speak again until they're resettled on the sofa. "It's just something I have to do on my own. You don't need to stress about it."

He isn't telling the truth.

I've had enough experience with liars to read them well.

When he stalks to the dining table it only proves my point. His gun is on display at the back of his jeans. I know it's always there. He's never without it. But that's to protect me, right? Does he really need a weapon if there's nothing to worry about?

He grabs a jacket from the back of one of the chairs, pulls it on and walks back toward me.

"Make life hell for them, okay?" He stops at my side, his body stiff as he leans in and places a peck at my temple.

The connection startles me.

After days with little communication and an invisible wall of space between us, the delicate kiss is out of place.

No, it's guilt in motion.

"If I'm late, don't wait up."

Without another word he's gone, striding away like a determined soldier about to slay his demons, the front door banging shut moments later.

I'm left hollow, staring at the filled bowl of food as my anxiety grows wings.

I don't know what I'd do if he got hurt. Or worse.

He's been my constant for weeks. My guiding force. My survival.

I can't live without him.

I *can't*.

The separation solidifies all the questions I've had toward my feelings for him. He may not have approved of our first kiss, but I certainly did.

It meant everything to me—hope, strength, new life.

I'm going to tell him, too. When he gets back—*if* he gets back— I'll let him know. I won't be daunted by my feelings anymore.

I'll do what he's always wanted. I'll open up. I'll talk and talk and talk until he's sick of hearing my voice.

"Everything okay, Pen?"

Sarah's question pulls me from my thoughts. She and Hunter are staring at me from the sofa, their movie paused.

"Come over here and have dinner with us." She waves her fork at me. "It's actually really good. Who knew that dirt bag could cook?"

"Thanks, but I'm not hungry."

"What's wrong? What happened?" She kneels on the sofa. "Pen? What's going on?"

"Will he be okay?" I let my fears blurt out. "Is he going to be safe?"

Hunter frowns. "Who? Luca?"

"Yes."

"That dumbass will be fine." He forks food into his mouth. "Even if he's not, an STD or two ain't gonna kill him."

"Don't." Sarah smacks him on the chest, glaring. "That's not what she was talking about."

No, it wasn't. My thoughts weren't on STDs at all.

My mind was nowhere near sex.

"He's joking," she placates me. "You don't need to worry about Luca at all. He'll be home before you know it."

She gives another warning glance to Hunter, the two of them clearly exchanging a silent communication about me. About Luca.

"I don't understand." I steady myself against the counter, my stomach hollowing. "What is he doing exactly?"

"Work," Sarah offers. "Torian needed him to throw his weight around with a local thug. It's nothing major."

"But he told me he wasn't working."

She pauses, seeming lost for words.

"I don't know what the big deal is." Hunter shovels more food into his mouth. "He's going out to get laid. And I'd bet good money he'll only need two minutes. Five if I'm being generous."

The information hits like a backhand, causing a rush of blood to my cheeks. "He has a girlfriend?"

"No." Sarah shakes her head rapidly, as if the fast tempo can wave away my heartache. "He doesn't know the woman. It's just sex. Nothing more."

Nothing more.

I keep repeating those words in my mind, praying they dislodge the sense of betrayal.

"Oh, okay." I paste on a smile and pretend I don't care. That I'm not being torn apart.

I swallow over the tightness strangling my throat. The same throat his gentle hands stroked only days before with comforting reverence.

He's going out to have sex. To be with another woman.

I don't want to picture him that way, I don't, yet the mental images play on a loop.

I imagine his naked body. His perfect muscles. His expression of rapture. I see him giving pleasure to a beautiful woman, one far prettier than I could ever be.

I hear it.

I feel it.

My insides revolt. Twisting. Turning.

I'm going to be sick.

"You okay?" Sarah pushes to her feet. "Do you want to talk?"

"No." I wave her away and start toward the hall. "It's fine. Really. It's none of my business. I'm just going to read for a while."

I measure my pace, one foot after the other, forcing myself not to run for the sanctuary of my room.

The thought of Luca's strong hands on another woman guts me in ways I never imagined. It's not due to disgust over an act that previously sickened me. It's not my damaged past making me nauseous.

Strange as it is, the thought of sex doesn't haunt me. That role is now exclusive to jealousy.

I picture him grinding, thrusting, her head kicked back as she cries out for pleasure I've never felt.

I close myself into my private bathroom, tears pricking my eyes.

I can't stay here. I can't face him once he returns.

Not after that kiss. Not when the burden I've placed upon him was far greater than I ever imagined.

As soon as Hunter returned stateside, Luca left. All this time, he's wanted freedom.

For sex.

Did he conveniently forget I was a whore?

That my purpose was pleasure?

He should've just asked for me to earn my protection. God knows, the only skills I have are when I'm on my back.

I wash my face, the cold chill sweeping away the weakness.

I knew I was a burden to him. I *knew*. And still, he adamantly denied it.

Lied.

My pulse hammers with anger. With the need to fight. But the person I want to battle with isn't here.

I return to my room, slide on a pair of sneakers, scoop my hair into a high pony, and tiptoe back into the open living area. Hunter and Sarah are still watching the movie, the sound loud enough to drown out my approach to the kitchen.

"I should check on her." Sarah pauses the television.

"Why?" Hunter snatches the remote and presses play. "A woman like that isn't going to be cut up over a guy getting laid. I'm sure the last thing she wants to think about is sex."

A woman like that.

A damaged, sexually abused woman.

He's right. Someone like me shouldn't be gutted at the thought of their protector seeking solace with someone else. My thoughts are just another vicious layer of damage.

"She likes him," Sarah replies. "If you would've seen them together over the last week, you'd agree with me. She's smitten. And he can't get away fast enough."

Oh, God.

I clench my stomach as I reach the island counter, holding in a sob.

I'm a joke. A fucking punchline.

All this time I never knew.

I slide my hand over the marble, my palm covering Hunter's keychain and the attached car fob.

I have to face my fear of the outside world and escape this fake environment. I'll take his car. Drive far, far away. Then... I don't know.

I'll think of something. All I know is that I can't stay here.

I drag the treasure toward me, the slightest clink announcing my robbery.

I pause, but it's too late.

The movie stops and Hunter glances over his shoulder. "What are you doing?"

I freeze. Panic. After a lifetime spent lying to protect myself, I'm at a loss for words.

"Penny?" Sarah asks.

I inch my hand behind my hip and shrug. "I thought I felt hungry. But now that food is in front of me I've changed my mind again." I give a chuckle that sounds too brittle. "I might take a shower and have an early night instead."

I slowly retrace my steps toward the hall, not meeting their gazes even though their combined focus burns holes through me.

"Penny," Hunter grates. "Show me your hands."

I flinch, my body's involuntary reaction a glaring red flag as I move closer and closer to the hall.

"Show me your hands," he repeats, his hulking frame rising from the sofa.

My heart lodges in my throat.

"Penny," he warns.

I run.

I don't stop when I hear him curse. I push faster, only pausing to fling open the front door before scampering outside. I sprint across the icy lawn to the huge black suburban parked in the driveway, clicking the buttons on the fob until the indicators flash bright into the fading daylight.

Freedom is within reach. Frightening, isolating freedom.

I yank open the car door as Hunter explodes from the house, Sarah following behind.

"Don't even think about it," he yells.

He's right. The time for thinking is over.

I climb into the tank of a car, tug the door shut, and lock it as both of them barrel toward me.

There's so much panic. I can't think straight through my pounding pulse, my shaking limbs.

It's been years since I sat behind the wheel. Everything is foreign. The push start. My foot on the pedal. I don't even bother to figure out how to move the seat forward in an effort to help me drive properly. There's no time.

I press the button ignition. The engine rumbles to life. Hunt reaches my door, tugging at the handle, banging on the window.

"Open up," he warns. "Get out of my goddamn car."

"Penny, please," Sarah tries to soothe me. "We can talk."

There's no turning back now. Not when Hunter's expression bleeds with anger—fierce eyes and snarled teeth.

I shift the car into reverse and press my foot on the accelerator. The car launches, the movement far more vicious than I anticipated.

I squeal, clutching the wheel tight as the vehicle bounces onto the road.

Both of them run after me, Hunter reaching the passenger side to pound on the window with a closed fist, his eyes promising retaliation.

I should be scared. I've seen that look before. I've had it bear down on me from men who left scars that will never heal. But the fear doesn't breach the betrayal spurring my pulse harder. What Hunter could do to me is nothing in comparison to what Luca has already done.

That pain is far greater. Ten times deeper.

"I'm sorry." I shift into drive and press my foot down, screeching the tires as the car propels forward.

I ignore the thunder of Hunter's fist against the side of the car. I push back the internal voice telling me to stop. I drown out the fear of the outside world that barrels down on me and drive, and drive, and drive, passing unfamiliar streets and houses.

Each mile spurs my pulse higher, makes my thoughts more punishing.

I need to get out of here.

Out of Portland.

Out of Oregon.

All I need now is money... and I know just how to get it.

13

LUCA

"Do you use the dating app often?" The blonde seated before me leans forward, her tits plumped, her ruby lips set in a coy curve.

"No. Never." I look away, focusing on anything but her cleavage as the waitress places our drinks on the table—mine a beer, hers some colorful cocktail covered in fruit.

"You're not much of a talker, are you?" Her knee brushes mine under the table. Once. Twice.

I don't enjoy the connection.

"Not usually." I swipe at my beer and throw back a gulp. "Small talk isn't my thing."

"We don't have to talk. Why don't we skip dinner and get out of here?"

I take another mouthful. Continue to avert my gaze.

I should be jumping at the chance to get laid. That's why I'm here. I can't keep walking around the house drowning in lust, my dick constantly at attention.

Penny worked her way so far under my skin I can't catch a fucking breath through my need to have her.

Banging out the obsession with another woman is the only option. Yet, here I am, sitting before a sure thing, stalling for reasons unknown.

"Okay. I guess we're staying." The woman sips from her straw. "Why don't you tell me about yourself?"

"You first." I hate this. Not just the small talk—the fucking pathetic hesitation.

I should take this woman to the restrooms. Fuck Penny from my system in a filthy bathroom stall. Then get home.

I should.

I just can't bring myself to do it. Not yet. I need to wait until the hum of liquor dulls the doubt.

"Tell me where you work." I throw back another gulp and force myself to meet her gaze. "What do you do for a living, Rebecca?"

"Rachel," she corrects.

Shit.

I'm screwing this up. She'll cut and run soon, and I'll be left to head home and jerk off in the shower every five fucking minutes just to dull the edge while my obsession sleeps in a nearby room.

"Sorry." I raise my beer and glance over my shoulder, wordlessly letting the waitress know I need another drink. "Tell me, Rachel. What do you do for work?"

She's a stunner. Light blue eyes. Short, pixie hair. Blinding smile.

She's bright and chipper. The opposite of my current obsession, which is why I swiped right. There can't be anything to remind me of where I want to be.

"There's nothing super exciting to tell." She sits taller, her knee continuing to rub mine. "I'm a medical receptionist at a clinic a few blocks from here. It isn't a career as such, but it pays the bills. What about you?"

I think about the possible answers I could give. All the crime and destruction. The blood and death. It's a temporary distraction for two point five seconds before my mind scampers back to Penny.

I never should've left her. Not when we hadn't discussed the situation first. She could be scared without me. Fucking petrified. But I'd been desperate. Thoughts of that kiss lash brutal blows at my restraint. I've been beside myself. Itching to get out of my own skin, all because of my need to have her.

"You look like a security guard." The woman fills the silence. "I can see the outline of your muscles through your shirt."

Christ.

I can't even deal with the flirtation. How the hell will I react to her naked?

This was meant to be a hookup. A quick fuck. But I'm the one who couldn't bring myself to meet at a hotel, instead suggesting a dinner date. As if being with someone behind Penny's back was more excusable if I bought the woman a meal first.

Still feels like cheating.

How can it not when she's been everything to me for weeks?

I want her. I'm obsessed with her.

But that ship is never going to sail.

Never. Going to. Sail.

I need to remember that. Fucking tattoo it on my wrist.

I snatch at the beer the waitress places before me and knock it back in one long pull before slamming it down. "Let's get out of here?"

The blonde's face lights up. "Perfect."

I stand, grab my wallet from my jacket pocket, and throw a few bills to the table. Once I get my rocks off I'll be fine. A new fucking man.

The isolation has been killing me. Messing with my head. I'd be bat shit over any woman I'd been trapped with for that long. Anyone would.

And lord knows it doesn't help that Penny is so easy to be around. Or that she's admirably strong. Or so fucking gorgeous.

Being stuck in that house was a ticking time bomb, the impending explosion even more catastrophic after Decker returned home.

Nothing good could come from succumbing to my libido.

Penny doesn't need the confusion. And I don't need to be riddled with bullets by her brother.

Fucking Rebecca is a win–win.

It just feels like a loss, that's all.

I trudge from the bar and head for my car parked out the front. The tap of heels behind me is far from a turn-on. Doesn't matter though. I'm still haunted by the residual hard-on I've been carrying for weeks.

There ain't nothin' going to break my cock's enthusiasm.

"Slow down, honey," the woman purrs. "I can't walk that fast."

I pause a few feet from my vehicle as my cell vibrates from my jacket pocket like a sign to abort this mission. I pull out the device and stare at Hunt's name on the screen.

I shouldn't answer. He's the type to call just for the sake of interrupting a fuck session. I wouldn't be surprised if his sole purpose was to laugh at my expense.

But Penny...

If something is wrong I can't ignore it.

"I need to take this." I glance at my soon-to-be bed buddy and take a few steps away. "I won't be long."

"Sure thing."

I connect the call, turning my back to her as I bark, "What?"

"We've got a problem," Hunt mutters. "A big one."

I keep walking, making sure I'm out of hearing distance. "What sort of problem?"

"Your bitch stole my Chevy."

"Very funny." I remotely unlock my car, letting the woman climb in. "What do you want, Hunt?"

"I'm serious. She snatched my keys from the kitchen counter and took off in my fucking car. I don't know where she is."

I hold my breath, waiting for the punchline. There's gotta be a fucking punchline, because if there isn't—

"Luca?" he snaps. "Are you listening to me?"

"You better be fucking joking." I clench my cell. "Either way, I'm going to kick your ass for—"

"I'm not goddamn joking, you stupid son of a bitch. She lost her shit and took off. You need to get back here. *Now.*"

The line disconnects; my mental function, too.

It takes seconds for me to snap out of the shock, then I'm running for my car, skirting the hood to fling open the driver's door.

"You need to get out." I slide into my seat and start the ignition. "Now."

"Excuse me?" The blonde stares at me, unmoving. "What's going on?"

"You need to get the fuck out of my car," I snarl. "*Now.*"

She balks, her face growing pale as I rev the engine.

"*Now,*" I roar.

She scrambles, frantically unfastening her belt to climb out and slam the door shut. "You're a dick." She speaks into the closed passenger window. "I hope you—"

I shift into gear, pulling the fuck out of there.

Buildings and traffic blur as I drive.

I cut corners, overtake on busy streets, and swerve in and out of traffic. I don't dare to think about what could be happening to Penny until I speed into my driveway, slam on the brakes and launch from the car.

"*What the fuck?*" I storm toward Hunter and Sarah on the front lawn, the moon's glow illuminating Sarah's concern and Hunt's livid anger. "What did you do?"

"I didn't do shit. She was fine." He squares his shoulders as I approach. "One minute she's in her room, the next the fucking klepto is stealing my keys."

"Who else have you called? Which way did she go? Have you checked your car's GPS?" I bark questions at him, my palms sweating.

He raises a brow, his look condescending. "You think I'd have any sort of tracking device on my Chevy with the shit I do on the daily?"

"*Fuck.*" I pace. "Then what have you done? Who have you spoken to?"

"I rang Deck. He's freaked. Torian said he'd make some calls. Both are on their way here so you should probably hide. Her brother is going to kill you."

"Me?" I glare. "I looked after her flawlessly for weeks. Then she spent two seconds with you and decided to run."

"It wasn't us she was running from." Sarah speaks up. "It was you."

"What the fuck does that mean? What the hell did I do?"

"Who gives a shit?" Hunter asks. "She took my car. My ninety fucking thousand-dollar car."

I stop pacing and lunge for him, grabbing the front of his shirt. "She's missing, and all you care about is your fucking car?"

He bares his teeth, his eyes narrowed. "That car is fully customed, asshole."

"Your face is going to be fully customed soon, motherfucker." I shove at his chest and back away before I kill him. "Which way did she go?"

"Why don't you give her a few minutes?" Sarah follows after me. "She might calm down and come home on her own."

"Calm down from what?"

She cringes. "She was asking questions about where you were. Hunter told her the truth."

"The truth?" After weeks with minimal headaches, my brain pounds with an energetic migraine. "*What* did he tell her?"

"That you went out to get laid."

Her answer hits me like a sucker punch.

Penny knows. She knows, and she ran.

"Forgive me for not being aware it was a huge fucking secret." Hunter gives me the bird. "A little insight would've gone a long way."

I'm going to kill him. Slowly. Painfully.

"Decker's here." Sarah jerks her chin toward the road as a car pulls into the curb.

In seconds, Penny's brother is running toward us. "Where is she?"

"I don't know, but I'm going to start searching." I make for the driveway, unwilling to stand here with my dick in my hand. "Don't go anywhere." I shove a finger in Hunter's direction. "Call me as soon as you hear anything."

"How come I get stuck here?"

"Because you've got no fucking ride, you piece of shit."

I climb into my car, gun the engine, and start circling blocks. One after another, after another.

Apart from making the decision to run, Penny's a smart woman. She wouldn't have gone far. I'm pinning my hopes on her remaining close to familiar territory.

But the more blocks I circle, the more I panic.

She could be anywhere. Without a phone. Without money. Without a fucking safe haven.

"Fuck." I smash my palms against the wheel. "Fuck. Fuck. *Fuck.*"

This is my fault.

If I hadn't let her kiss me… If I'd been able to keep my fucking dick in line…

"Where the hell are you, Penny?"

I drive faster, scanning darkened sidewalks and house yards.

If something happens to her I'll never forgive myself.

Never. Fucking. Forgive.

My phone rings. This time, it's Decker.

"What?" I answer.

"I just got a call from Torian. He thinks he found her."

"Where? Is she okay?"

"I don't know. Just get back to the house. He said he'd meet us here."

14

PENNY

I'M LOST.

I don't know what side of the city I'm on. I have no clue which direction leads home.

Home.

God.

That's not what Luca's house is. Not anymore. Not when visions of what he's currently doing assault my mind with every blink.

I should never have relied on him in the first place.

Now I've lost Abi and Chloe. Tobias is no longer in my care. And my protector is gone, choosing to share his body with a stranger.

I'm stupid not to have figured it out earlier. I'd been floating in a dream-like state as we'd kissed, my lips gently pressed to his, while he drew back in revulsion.

He couldn't get away fast enough.

I pull over and shift the car into park on a quiet industrial road, barely able to see through the blur in my vision.

I'm not going to cry again. Those days of tears didn't help anyway.

Grief still weighs me down. My past hasn't changed.

But the pain from Luca intensifies.

I'd wanted him to like me. I'd carelessly thought he had. That his protection was more than a job. That he wasn't like the other men who were only interested in sex.

Boy, was I wrong.

"*Goddammit.*" I pound my fist against my thigh and scream. The piercing sound fills my ears. My head. I keep belting my heart out until there's no voice left to give. Until my lungs are dry and my throat is hoarse.

Then I slump into the leather seat, and become illuminated by the bright lights of a car pulling up behind me.

Shit.

They found me. Already. I haven't even successfully left the city, let alone the state.

Seems I can't do anything right.

I sit up straight, tilt away the rear-view mirror and its blinding reflection, and wait for retaliation. In my peripheral vision, I see a figure approaching the side of the car. A masculine frame that's big and bulky.

I square my shoulders against the threat. I won't let him daunt me. If I want to see Tobias again, I need to get over my outburst and become smarter than the unpredictable person I've been.

When a shadow creeps over the side of my face I drag in a breath and wait for Hunter's demand to get out of his car. Or a growled order from Luca.

I don't get either.

There's only an ominous *tap, tap, tap* against the glass.

If they expect me to apologize they've got another thing coming. I don't care if I stole a car.

I jerk my head toward the window, glaring, only to be met with shadowed eyes staring back at me from beneath a thick ski mask. The *tap, tap, tap* repeats, the noise coming from the barrel of a gun against the glass.

Oh, God.

All the air escapes my lungs on a heave.

Everything stops.

Time.

Movement.

My heart.

I plant my foot on the accelerator, the car roaring to life without movement.

Oh, shit.

I fight to put the gearstick in drive as a mighty *boom* thunders beside me. A circle of splintered glass appears on my window, the integrity still intact.

Holy fuck. He's shooting at me. At bulletproof glass.

I shove the gearstick into place and slam my foot harder, my hands shaking as the wheels spin. I escape in what feels like slow motion, the *tink, tink, tinks* of sound against the car frame continuous until the back of the vehicle jostles, a tire seeming to take a bullet.

"Please, please, please let me get out of here."

I keep my head low and speed through the night. I turn left. Turn right. Turn left. I become more lost in the labyrinth of streets until I finally reach a busy road and get stuck in traffic, heading God knows where, fleeing God knows who.

I wind down my window, unable to see through the bullet impacts, and hyperventilate.

I never should've left the house.

I never should've left Luca. Now all I can think about is returning to him, to his protection, but I don't know how.

I have no phone. And the arduous jostle from the back of the vehicle is getting worse.

If I pull over the shooter could find me. If I don't stop I have no clue what will happen to the car.

A siren squeals behind me. Blue and red illuminate the interior. *The police.*

For a second, there's relief. Sweet, overwhelming relief.

Then reality hits like a nightmare.

I don't have a license or identification. As far as the authorities are concerned, I'm dead. A ghost. And I want to stay that way.

"Oh, my goddamn shit, please help me get out of this." My pulse pounds everywhere—throat, wrists, temples. I break out in a cold sweat, my fear of yet another imprisonment making it impossible to breathe.

I don't want to go back to a cage. I can't attempt a high-speed escape, either. Not on three functioning tires. I wouldn't even know how with four solid treads and a record-breaking sports car.

I reluctantly pull over, the police car mimicking my movements, a male officer lazily climbing from his vehicle.

I can imagine what he's seeing—the flat tire, the dents left from bullets.

"Evenin', ma'am." He stops next to my window, one hand calmly resting at his side, the other placed on his holster. "Do you know why I pulled you over?"

I squint against the brightness of his flashlight, unable to speak.

"Ma'am, did you hear me? I asked if you knew why I pulled you over."

I swipe at my nose to dislodge the building tingle and shake my head. "No, sir."

"Do you realize you only have three tires?" He leans forward to glance inside the car, his gaze trekking over the passenger seat to the floor.

"I-I-I—" I shake my head frantically and puff out an exhale. "I-I'm sorry. I knew I had a problem. I just thought I could make it to a gas station."

"Driving on the rim is going to cause some pretty major damage. You know that, right?"

I keep shaking my head. "I'm not good with cars."

"I gathered." He raises his hand from the holstered gun, holding his palm out to me. "License and registration please."

Bile creeps up my throat, the burning acid bringing tears to my eyes. "That's a funny story." I chuckle, the sound far from humorous. "I had an argument with the person I was staying with and took off without grabbing my purse. I-I don't even have my cell."

I try to think. To come up with a story capable of getting me out of this.

"Do you know Cole Torian?" I ask.

The question is risky. It announces a link to crime and gives this officer more ammunition to interrogate me. But Luther had all the Greek police in his pocket. If Cole works like his father, maybe this man can help me. Then I can finally get back to Luca.

"He's, umm…" I swallow at his narrowing eyes. "A well-known businessman. I just thought if you knew him, you could call him for me."

His hand falls back to his holstered gun. "Ma'am, I'm going to need you to climb out of the vehicle."

"No, *please*, no."

Think. Think. Think.

"Officer, I'm not safe here." I scramble, mentally clawing at the walls of my mind for a way out, each ticking second making his fingers grip tighter on his weapon. "A man was shooting at me." I lean toward my window and poke my head outside to find the fresh dents in the side of the car. "Can you see those marks? Those weren't there fifteen minutes ago. They're from bullets. The damaged tire is, too."

He's not convinced, his steps creeping farther and farther away. "You're telling me this car is bulletproof?"

I don't know. I don't know. *God, I don't know.*

"*Please*, listen to me." I sink back into my seat and start raising my window.

"*Stop*," he barks. "Get out of the vehicle."

"*Please*, just look." I nudge the window an inch higher, the circles of shattered glass now visible in the middle of the thick tint. "Those marks are from bullets."

His brow furrows, the slightest sense of contemplation breaking across his face.

I need to come up with something to bring this home. Something convincing. Something he can't ignore.

"Sir." I lower the window again. "I'm in danger. I've been placed in witness protection. That's why I don't have any identification. But they found me." The lies effortlessly slide from my lips, the instincts I'd honed in Greece finally awakening. "I need to speak to Anissa Fox of the FBI. *Please*. As you can see from the car, my life is at risk. They could come back any second."

He snaps rigid, his attention stalking our surroundings. "What's your name?"

"Penny."

"Surname?"

"Please, officer, if you could just get in contact with Agent Fox she'll know who I am." She has to. She's my only hope. "*Please*. I'm begging you. Just try and get in contact with her. She'll know what to do."

But what if she doesn't?

The only connection I have with the Fed was a brief introduction in Greece. She was there when I was rescued. Yet, I never understood her involvement with Cole in the first place.

119

They told me she was helping to take Luther down, only she hasn't sought me out once since my return to the States. There was no investigation. No welfare check. I don't even know if she lives in Portland.

"Stay in the vehicle." The officer backtracks toward the patrol car. "Don't move. I'll return soon."

I do as instructed, remaining still, barely even blinking as time passes and the contents of my stomach threaten to make an escape.

I sit there forever. The minutes accumulate into a mass of hysteria.

I never should've left the safety of the house and run off like a jealous teenager.

Under Luther's rule, I'd been entirely stringent with my emotions. Now I'm reckless. A complete danger to myself. And others.

It isn't until another car pulls in behind the cop that I pause my silent prayers for salvation.

The woman who opens the driver's door isn't entirely distinguishable through the glare of the patrol car's headlights. She's dressed in a pantsuit, sophisticated and empowered, but thankfully recognizable as the woman I briefly met in Greece.

She greets the officer at his car with a handshake. They chat in lowered voices, glancing toward me every few seconds.

I itch to run to her. To plead my case before anyone else is dragged into this mess. But within moments, the officer is climbing back into his patrol car and the confident woman is striding my way.

"Penny?" Her brows are furrowed, her eyes full of concern as she spares me a glance, then takes in the damage to the car. "What happened?"

"Can you help me?" I ask in a rush. "I need to get out of here."

"Are you hurt?" She leans closer.

"No. I'm fine. But whoever shot at me could be watching. They could be anywhere."

"It's okay. I won't let anything happen to you." She placates me with a raised hand. "Did you know who it was? Did you see them?"

"They were right next to my window. Closer than you are." A

120

sleek black Porsche pulls in front of us as I speak. "But whoever it was wore a ski mask."

My throat tightens at the unfamiliar vehicle. This could be the shooter. The only thing keeping me in place is the agent's unflinching confidence. "Who's that?"

She sighs, stepping closer as she watches the newest addition arrive to this mess. "Cole. The officer called him."

The door to the shiny car opens. The formidable man climbs out and casually walks toward us. Dark suit, dark hair, dark eyes, and an even darker soul buried somewhere beneath. He fills me with dread, the resemblance to his father hitting me hard.

"Anissa." He purrs the greeting, his mouth holding the faintest taunt of a grin. "Nice to see you."

"Cut the crap, Cole. She's scared. I need to take her in for questioning. It's time this was handled by the book."

His expression tightens. "No. You're done here." He jerks a hand at the patrol car, signaling for the officer to leave. "Pretend this never happened."

She scoffs. "This isn't Greece. I'm no longer your toy. And I sure as hell won't go on my merry way when someone is shooting up Portland."

Cole's gaze snaps to mine. "You were shot at?" He doesn't wait for my response as his attention skates over the car, then back to Anissa. "Get out of here," he orders. "We can catch up to discuss this some other time. Preferably over dinner."

"I'm not having dinner with you," she growls. "And I'm not leaving until I'm assured she's going to be safe."

He smiles, the show of teeth more of a snarl. "Then I assure you she will be just fine. If she hadn't stolen a hitman's car none of this would've happened. You and I both know the target on Hunter's back can sometimes outrank mine."

A hitman's car.

Oh, shit, a *fucking hitman's car*.

I hang my head and close my eyes. Of all the things could've slipped my attention, Hunter's notorious criminal reputation shouldn't have been one of them.

The pair continue to bark, one barb after another, the conversation brushing past my ears without sinking past my self-loathing.

I just want to go home.

Not to my parents or my brother, but to the only place I've felt safe in a long time.

I want to be with Luca, even though I'm forcing myself to hate him at the same time.

"Please, Agent Fox." The plea is murmured from my parched mouth. "Just let me go." I open my eyes to meet her gaze. "I can't stay out here."

She frowns at me with concern and confusion. "Are you sure?"

I nod. "Positive."

She sucks in a deep breath and straightens her shoulders. "This can't happen again, Cole. I swear to God I won't keep covering for you."

He chuckles. "Sure you will."

"I'm fucking serious, you smug prick." She reaches into her suit jacket, pulls out a business card and hands it to me. "Call me if you need me. Anytime. Day or night. I'll be happy to help."

I take the offering, brushing my finger over the embossed lettering before placing it in my pocket. "Thank you."

"What about me?" Cole drawls. "Can I call you anytime, day or night?"

She rolls her eyes, not bothering to reply as she starts for her car.

"Come on, Nis. Where's the love?"

"Fuck you, Cole," she yells in the distance.

He laughs, creeping closer to Hunter's car, his attention on her for long seconds until his arm comes to rest on the window ledge.

When his eyes turn to mine the humor is no longer there. No smile. No friendly familiarity. "It's good to see you again, Penny. Although, it would've been appreciated if this were under better circumstances." There's a lingering threat in his tone. An ice-cold sterility that leaves me chilled. "Did you see who shot at you?"

I shake my head and stare out the windshield, no longer able to meet his gaze. This is why I didn't want to leave the house. Because of people like him and feelings like this.

"Maybe next time you'll make a smarter choice about which car you steal."

"There won't be a next time," I whisper.

"Good. Now tell me where were you running to?" His attention raises the hair on my neck, my skin breaking out in goose bumps.

"Anywhere. I just needed to get away."

"From Luca?"

The question stings. The answer punishes me even more. Both leave me speechless.

"I heard he went out tonight," he continues. "Were Hunter and Sarah's arrival the issue or Luca's departure?"

"It doesn't matter." I turn to him, scowling, letting him know this is the end of the discussion. "Can we leave now?"

"Whatever you say." He opens the door and holds out an open palm. "Give me the keys."

I hand them over. "Will the car be okay?"

"Hunter can take care of it." He yanks the door wider. "Let's go."

He leads the way to the Porsche, sliding into the low seat while I hustle fast to get into the safety of the new vehicle.

He pulls from the curb in silence, the murmur of his radio too low to stifle my apprehension as he drives. I know I can handle any punishment he might dish out. Luther was a far more menacing man. But I no longer have the determination I did when I was a slave. The will to fight doesn't embolden me.

"In between now and Luca's house, you need to explain." He shoots me a glance. "I suggest you start soon."

"There's nothing to say. I felt like taking a drive, so I did."

"I don't appreciate secrets." His threatening tone grates on my nerves, annoying the hell out of me as the adrenaline flushes from my system to leave me drained.

"Me either. And I guess Luca feels the same." I give him a faux smile. "That's why he told me you already brought Tobias to Portland and how you plan to keep him from me."

He doesn't react, not physically. There's not even a twinge of guilt in his features. He doesn't care that he's hiding that little boy. "Yes, he returned to live with my sister."

I despise the ease with which he torments me, the same way his father always did. "How is he?"

"Good. Resilient. You'll be able to see him once I know you're stable."

I huff out a laugh and turn my attention to the bright Portland skyline. "Stable? What does that even mean?"

"It means when you're functioning like a normal person and not running away for no reason."

"I had reasons."

"Then tell them to me. I didn't get you out of Greece for the hell of it. I want you to live a good life, Penny."

Lies. All lies.

I don't know the real reason he arranged my rescue, but it certainly wasn't out of kindness.

"This will be the last time I ask," he snarls. "Why did I get a call from Hunter telling me you'd run away?"

I press my lips tight, keeping the truth from him just like he's keeping Tobias from me. But my frustration builds, demanding to be heard. "Because Luca left me to have sex with a stranger."

The awkward silence returns. The seconds tick by in agonizing lethargy. I don't know if he thinks I'm naive or childish. I'm not even sure if he's annoyed I caused this mess over something so trivial. All he does is continue to drive, the side of his mouth curving upward in a condescending smirk.

"Do you enjoy my suffering?" I whisper. "If so, it only confirms you're exactly like your father."

His fingers squeak against the leather as they tighten on the wheel, his knuckles turning white. "I'm nothing like my father. And it's not your suffering I enjoy. It's the karma."

"Whose karma?"

"Your brother's." He glances at me. "For a long while, the thought of Decker with my sister was a very sore spot for me. It still is most days."

"I don't understand."

He huffs out a laugh and returns his attention to the road. "All the resentment I harbored toward my sister's feelings for your brother, all that rage and animosity, is now something he will have to deal with between you and Luca."

"It's not like that. Luca doesn't have feelings for me."

That huff of laughter returns, intensified. "I assure you he has enough to get himself in trouble."

"I disagree. And I think I'd know better, seeing as though I've lived with him for weeks."

But I hadn't known. It was Sarah who'd pointed out Luca's desperation to get away from me.

He shrugs. "Maybe you're right."

He doesn't say another word. There are no placations for my dying heart or offers of support.

I turn away, staring out the window as we pass things I recognize from my escape—the corner store, the house with the red mailbox, then finally, the pretty pink roses from the garden beside Luca's.

My stomach falls as Cole pulls into the drive behind another bulky SUV, our headlights swinging past a grimacing woman and three men standing on the front lawn, none of them happy to see us.

Sarah and Sebastian are the only ones whose expressions hold the slightest tinge of relief.

Hunter is plain mad.

And when my gaze reaches Luca I have to raise my chin and suck in a breath to steal myself against the fury bearing back at me.

"If you don't want to stay here I can make other arrangements," Cole murmurs. "Returning to Portland with Luca was your choice, but you can change your mind at any time and stay with your brother."

"And if I don't like either option?"

"They're all you've got for now."

I should get away. From here. From Luca. But anger at my protector is a better option than the vulnerability I'd face with my brother.

"Can I think about it?"

He kills the ignition. "Take all the time you need."

I steal myself for what's to come and open my door, only to be stopped by a punishing grip capturing my arm.

"There's one more thing." Cole's eyes harden as I glance at him over my shoulder. "I've made sure you're financially taken care of while under Luca's roof. I'm certain you know you can have anything you need if you ask. So if you steal from me again, we're going to have problems. Do you hear me?"

I fight the instinct to lash out, fervently holding myself in check because I don't want to risk Tobias being stripped from me forever. "I told you it won't happen again."

I won't steal a car.

I won't even steal time from Luca.

He inclines his head and releases my wrist. "Then good luck. By the expression on Luca's face you're going to need it."

I shudder and open my door to slide out, keeping my gaze averted from the wall of tumultuous male emotion in front of me. I don't look toward the men on the lawn as I walk around the hood. I don't even chance a sideward glance as I pass.

I head straight for the front of the house, my head high, my shoulders straight.

"You're seriously going to walk by me without so much as a fucking explanation?" Luca demands.

I ignore him, refusing to stop and chat when the heat in my eyes is overwhelming. I won't let him see me cry. Not again. Not over this.

I keep walking, thankful the house is unlocked as I slip inside. But he's hot on my heels, snatching the door as I let it go, slamming the heavy wood closed behind us. "Don't walk away from me."

"Why?" I quicken my stride down the hall. "You did it to me first."

"Jesus Christ." He follows me into my darkened bedroom. "I almost had a fucking stroke worrying about you. The least you can do is explain."

"Leave me alone."

"I know you're angry." His tone softens, slaughtering me with pity. "But, fuck me drunk, Pen, what the hell were you thinking?"

I was thinking he had feelings for me. That I was more than a job.

I turn to him, facing his hostility head-on. With him in front of me, a stranger's kisses lingering on his lips, my humiliation digs deeper, clawing at my mind. "I'm sorry I ruined your night. But I'm safe now; you can get back to what you were doing. Or *who* you were doing."

His eyes flare, shock and wrath beaming back at me. "You think I give a shit about who I was with? You think that's why I'm mad?"

"Yeah, I do." I return his glare. Fury to fury. Madness to mindlessness.

I cared for him so much. Without knowing, without understanding, he'd become my world. And now I don't know how to breathe in the vacuum.

"I think you're pissed because I stole a car. *Wrecked* that car. But more importantly, because I disturbed you on your date." I'm making a fool of myself. I can feel it. The heat in my cheeks is a glaring indication. I'm just thankful the faint glow from the living room is the only illumination through the shadowed surroundings.

He scoffs. "I don't even know where to start with that load of ignorant bullshit."

"Start by telling the truth. Start by acknowledging how worthless you made me feel."

"Excuse me?" His brows pinch in a lethal frown. "*I* made you feel worthless?"

"Yes. Why wouldn't I feel that way when you left to have sex with a stranger when you already have a professional fucking whore living under your roof?" My voice raises with every vehement word.

"What *the fuck* did you just say?"

My cheeks flame hotter, the shame scarring me.

He stalks forward. "Don't you ever talk about yourself that way again."

"Why not?" I stand my ground, trembling in fury. "Fucking is the only job I've had. It's all I've ever been good at. The only thing I've known. Yet, for some reason, I'm not enough for you."

"Stop it," he warns.

"You know it's true. I don't know why you can't admit it. I can do your cooking and cleaning. You can even waste your time watching stupid movies with me, but I'm not good enough to fuck."

"I said, 'stop it,'" he snarls. "I'm not joking."

"You did this," I accuse. "You're the reason I ran, because apparently you can't get away from me fast enough."

I throw Sarah's words at him, hoping he'll finally admit the truth. Or at least stop being angry at me.

The opposite happens.

His jaw tenses. His hands clench. He keeps stalking forward, towering over me until I'm forced to backtrack into the wall.

God, I wish I was scared of him. Even just a little bit. But the intense emotion taking over me is something different. Something starved for attention.

It's hatred.

I hate how much I feel for him.

Hate that he doesn't feel it back.

"You're right. I couldn't get away from you fast enough." He looms over me as I press into the cold plaster, foot to foot, almost nose to nose. "Because you're in my fucking head, Penny. You're under my goddamn skin. I can't help you when I'm like this."

Every inch of me thrums, wanting to attack and succumb in equal measure. "I'm sorry I'm such a burden." I grind my teeth. "But I've been saying that from the start."

"Stop." He growls the word, so close to me. So painfully, agonizingly close his breath brushes my mouth. "You drive me fucking crazy."

He stares at me, the intensity climbing into my chest. Every part of me reacts. My heart. My pulse. Everything except my mind which goes blank.

I'm dumbstruck over what to do, caught speechless under the heavy weight of yearning.

I want too much from this man. His guidance. His attention. I want it all.

"Mindless," he murmurs as he swoops forward, smashing his lips against mine.

I gasp into the kiss, my palms instinctively pushing his chest, my nails digging deep to stop the attack. But as fast as my panic arrives, it flees, allowing a crazy clarity to sink in.

My pushing turns to grabbing. My digging fingers cling. I scramble to find a stronghold to withstand the madness, yet all that remains is warmth and frightening exhilaration.

He punishes me with his mouth, his hands clutching my hips.

I've been forced to kiss before. But I've never kissed like this. Never when my body demanded more connection than the force could provide.

I should hate this. Instead, it feels like home. I revel in his warmth. I succumb to the hard press of his chest against mine and the determined lashing of his tongue.

Then, as forcefully as his kiss arrived, it vanishes.

He retreats. One step after another. Again.

Revulsion consumes him just like it did the last time. I can see it.

I slump back against the wall, my fingers raising to my lips as if the touch will soften the burn. "Did you do that to shut me up?" I ask, breathless.

"For the love of sanity, Penny. You've got no idea what's going on here." He rakes his hands through his hair. "Don't you get it? *This* is why I left."

He stalks back toward me, body tense.

I shrink into the wall, a little nervous. A little scared. But it's not of him. *Never* of Luca. I'm frightened of how much I want him.

"This is exactly why I had to get out of here. Because you're still petrified of me." He shoves his hands against the wall at either side of my head, caging me, the rapid rise and fall of his chest animalistic. "Because all I can think about is wanting you more than my next breath, yet you scamper away from me."

"I don't scamper—"

"Yeah, you do. And you should, because what I want to do to you is far from good, Penny. I want to fuck you within an inch of your life. If I had my way I'd shatter all your progress by taking what I want. What I *need*. So don't for a goddamn second think I want you out of here, because having you near me is all I've wanted from the moment I laid eyes on you."

I suck in a sharp breath. Unblinking. Unmoving.

He chuckles. Grins. Neither are kind. "See? Now do you understand?"

No, I don't. It doesn't make sense.

"You're lying," I whisper.

"No, I lie every time I keep distance between us. All I want is your body on mine. I lie when you go to bed at night and I pretend I don't want you sleeping beside me. I lie every goddamn day pretending I'm not obsessed with you because I know I'm not good enough, gentle enough, fucking calm enough."

He creates a whirlwind of emotion inside me. A tornado I'm stuck in the middle of. "You're not making sense."

He grinds his teeth, his shoulders bunching. "I ran because I can't quit noticing how incredible you are. You might be oblivious to your gorgeousness, but believe me, I'm not. I've had a front-row seat to the recovery of the most beautiful woman I've ever met. I get tortured on the daily by her strength. By her fucking unshakable determination to get up every time she's knocked down. And as fucking perverted as it feels after what you've been through, my dick takes notice, too."

I lean further against the wall, attempting to distance myself from my confusion.

"So forgive me," he snarls, "if I thought it was best to try and take the edge off with a stranger because it's crystal clear I can't have you."

I can't reply. I can't even shake my head. All I can do is swallow over the heat licking my throat.

He holds my gaze for long moments, those eyes narrowed with spite.

I want to pour my heart out to him. To tell him how I feel. But I don't understand it myself.

I don't want sex. The thought of it scares me. But I want him.

I crave his protection. His praise. I want to have him close to me.

He shoves from the wall and turns to stalk away, each step creating a painful chasm between us.

"Please, Luca." I shudder out a breath. "Don't walk away from me again."

He stops, his shoulders slumping. "It's not like I want to. Believe me, it's my only choice."

"Why? Because I'm damaged?"

He tilts his head to look at me. "No, shorty. Because I'm falling in love with you. Because despite how fucking stupid that is—how inappropriate and unreasonable—I love every fucking thing about you. And that shit isn't healthy for either of us."

I pull back, my head hitting the wall, my gasp audible. He doesn't love me. He couldn't. And I'm not sure I want him to anyway.

Love means loss.

It gives power to my invisible enemies, and makes me weak.

But the invigoration… it's euphoric. Tear-inspiring happiness tightens my throat, threatening to suffocate me.

"Finally, you understand." He turns his attention back to the hall and starts walking. "Now you'll know why I'm keeping my distance."

"*No.* Stop" I push away from the wall, my demand adamant. "What if I feel the same way?"

He doesn't speak. Doesn't move.

"What if, Luca?"

I don't know how I feel. I don't know much of anything anymore. But what I do know is that he's my rock. He's the shore to my crashing waves. The steadying ground beneath my tumultuous storm.

"Will you answer me?" Slowly, I approach, each step increasing my exhilaration and vulnerability. "What if I feel the same way about you?" I walk around him to meet those shadowed eyes. My heart hammers in my throat as he remains silent, his mouth set in a straight line. "Please answer me."

"Don't do this, shorty." The plea is barely audible. "The last thing you need to deal with right now is cleaning up the mess once your brother kills me."

A loud knock sounds at the door, the banging thunderous.

"On cue," he drawls. "See? Deck already has a sixth sense for these things."

I reach for Luc, my fingers brushing his in a brief swipe before I lose confidence and drop my arm back to my side. "Sebastian will stay out of this."

"No, he won't. And he shouldn't." He waves a hand between us. "This is never going to happen. It can't."

I whisper out a scoff. "How poetic—the man who rescued me from someone who gave me a lifetime of something I didn't want is denying me the only thing I crave."

"You don't crave me, Pen—"

"Don't tell me what I crave." I step closer and he stiffens. "You have no idea how I feel for you. How I've always felt for you. I never knew it myself until you walked out on me."

"I didn't walk out."

"You did. You left me." This time, I don't falter when I reach for his hand. I grab it tight, entwining our fingers. "With a psychopath and his doting sidekick."

There's a flash of a smirk that quickly fades. "Pen…"

"I need you, Luc." I tug him, attempting to drag him closer. He doesn't budge. "Are you going to make me beg?"

His nostrils flare as I keep tug, tug, tugging.

Finally, he stumbles forward, his foot sliding between mine, and we're chest to chest, hip to hip. A growl rumbles in his throat as those gorgeous lips reclaim my mouth, this time in a kiss that's slow. Controlled. As if he's worried I'll break.

I don't.

I awaken.

I luxuriate in him, shedding another tormented layer of my past while in his arms. He helps me escape my mental anguish with gentle swipes of tongue and a possessive hand at my hip. He makes everything right. Yet, I can't stop hearing the taunting devil on my shoulder. I'm tormented with his treacherous, haunting words.

This bliss won't last.

15

LUCA

ANOTHER HAMMERING OF THE FRONT DOOR REVERBERATES DOWN THE hall.

Fuck.

I pull back to stare down at her, fucking besotted as I cup her face. "If we don't stop, our next milestone will be my funeral."

She nods. "Okay. We stop."

The front door opens, the approaching footfalls siphoning my buzz.

"Shit. He's coming. Stay in here." I make for the hall, finding Torian sauntering toward me.

"Don't have a coronary," he drawls. "I ordered the others to go home. I thought you two could use the time alone." He keeps walking, bypassing Penny's bedroom.

"Right..." I give her a brief placating smile as I close the door and follow him. "That doesn't explain why you're still here."

"We need to talk." He turns into the living room, walks straight for the coffee machine, and starts to make himself a mug. "Could you have picked a more complicated conquest?"

"She's *not* a conquest." I keep my distance for his safety's sake, and rest my ass against the end of the nearby dining table.

"Fine. Fuck buddy. Piece of ass. Whatever you want to call it." He grabs his filled mug and takes a sip.

"It's been a long day, Torian. Don't push me."

He smirks. Slow and demeaning. "I seem to remember you

133

telling me not to stick my dick in dangerous places not too long ago, but I'll save you the reciprocated speech because there are more important things to discuss." He starts toward me, taking the seat at the opposite end of the table. "I didn't inform the others about the shooter yet. I wanted to get answers first."

"What shooter?"

"She didn't tell you? What were you two doing in there if not discussing the harrowing ordeal she just faced?"

"Cut the shit." I grab the chair before me in a death grip. "What shooter?"

"It's best to get the news from her. I barely know the details. What I do know is that she got pulled over by a local traffic cop, mentioned my name in an attempt to get help, and when the officer didn't take the bait, she asked to speak to Agent Anissa Fox of the FBI."

Shit.

I knew back in Greece that telling Penny about Anissa's identity was a bad idea, but I hadn't been able to stop myself.

"How did she know Anissa was a Fed, Luca?" The question is level, no rage, no menace despite both lurking in his gaze.

"I told her. I had no choice. She wouldn't trust me when we were trying to gain the upper hand with Luther. She thought Anissa was a slave, and that we were involved in the trafficking."

He takes another mouthful of coffee, those predator eyes scrutinizing me from over the rim of his mug. "You didn't think to discuss it with me first?"

"I didn't have time. I was in the middle of being attacked with a syringe, and if memory serves, so were you."

"That may be the case, but you've caused complications. I know I don't have to mention how important it is for a man in my position not to be associated with the Feds."

"Maybe you should've thought about that before you stuck your dick in one."

He slams his mug down on the table, the contents splashing over the rim. "Don't fuck with me on this. Anissa is not to be discussed, not even mentioned. Wipe the name from Penny's mind or I'll do it myself."

I grind my teeth. I can't push him too far. This is my life now. He's my general. My family. "I'll make sure she understands."

"Make sure you do," he snarls. "Now there's one more thing we need to discuss before you drag her ass out here. I told you to take care of her financially, yet she still stole from me. Why?"

I scoff. "What could she have possibly stolen?"

"Money. I've got a contact at the bank who's been keeping an eye on my father's accounts. He told me a stack of cash has been withdrawn."

"And you're pointing the finger at Penny? What about your dad's informants? Or your sisters? How do you know they didn't take the money?"

"Because I called them. Neither know how to access the accounts. I also mentioned the issue to Penny, and she didn't deny it."

I straighten, not believing his story. "So she confirmed it?"

"Not exactly. I'm well aware she's not in her right mind at the moment. That's why I need you to discuss it with her. Find out where she keeps the keycard and destroy it."

"It's fucking impossible. She came home from Greece empty-handed."

"Her hands might have been empty, but did you do a cavity search? Or did you save that until you got home?" He winks.

"Fuck you." My nostrils flare as I grip the chair tight enough to make my fingers ache. "I'm not sleeping with her. And I'd bet good money she isn't responsible for touching your father's accounts."

He shrugs. "I'll have proof in the form of security pictures soon enough. I suggest you speak to her before then. Now get her out here; I've got other things to do before the night is over."

I pause a second, unsure if I should be placing Penny in front of his barely leashed mood.

"I'll be civil," he drawls, as if reading my mind. "Just get her out here."

"You better be." I call over my shoulder. "Penny, can you come out here?" I wait for a response that doesn't come. "*Penny*?"

"For your sake, I hope she didn't steal my car this time."

"Very funny." I start for the hall only to be stopped by her walking into the living area.

"You wanted me?" she asks.

Without doubt.

Always.

"Take a seat," Torian instructs. "I need to get details on what happened tonight while they're still clear in your mind."

She glances between the two of us as she approaches, wary yet confident. She takes the seat to my right, sitting tall, her hands placed on the table. "I can't tell you much."

I fling out my chair and sit beside her. "What happened?"

"I drove—"

"Where?" Torian interrupts.

"I don't know. I was just driving, trying to get out of Portland. But I had to pull over."

"Why?" I ask.

She shoots me a pained glance, then returns her attention to Torian. "I wasn't in the best state of mind. So I parked on the side of the road in some sort of industrial area. Not long after, a car came up behind me. I thought it was Luc or Hunter. And because I was still angry, I didn't even look as the man approached. I just waited for someone to order me out from behind the wheel."

"You're sure it was a man?" Torian leans back in his chair, still calm, still unconcerned.

"Yes. The frame was too big for a woman. He came right up to my door and tapped the barrel of a gun against the glass."

Jesus.

Why the fuck didn't she mention this earlier?

"Then what?" I reach for her hand and squeeze her fingers.

"I planted my foot. I tried to get out of there straight away, but the car wasn't in gear. So I panicked, and scrambled for the gearstick. That's when he fired at the glass. By the time I got out of there he'd shot at me four or five times. Twice against the window, a few against the side panels, and at least one in the tire."

I wipe my free hand over my mouth, holding in the string of fear-filled aggression. My migraine pulses between my temples. She never should've been in that situation. I never should've forced her to run.

"Then what happened?" Torian asks.

"I kept driving, even when I lost the tire." Her words accelerate, tumbling faster from those gorgeous lips. "I don't know where I went, but the patrol car eventually caught up with me and pulled me over. I didn't know what to do. I'm not even meant to be alive as far as the government are concerned, so when the officer demanded my ID, I asked if he knew Cole Torian, and when he didn't react I made up a story about being in witness protection."

She looks entirely fragile as she relays the story. Fragile yet solid. Vulnerable and strong. Such contrasting facets that make her all the more mesmerizing.

"You mentioned Anissa, too," Torian grates.

"I had no choice. I didn't want to be arrested."

"It's okay. It's over now." I entwine our fingers, trying to offer more support. "Can you tell us anything else about the shooter? What did he look like? What did he say?"

"He didn't say anything. Just tapped the gun against the window." She shudders, her fingers trembling in mine. "He wore a thick, black ski mask. His entire face was covered, and his eyes were shadowed with the headlights beaming behind him. I couldn't even tell you what color they were because all I wanted to do was get out of there."

"Did you get any details on his car?"

"No." She shakes her head. "I didn't see anything. I'd tilted the rear-view mirror away to stop the glare from his headlights. I have absolutely no information at all. Nothing."

I meet Torian's gaze. "What do you want to do?"

He pushes from his chair. "I'll put out some feelers. We'll find who's responsible. Do you have any requests once I catch the culprit?"

"Yeah. Let me deal with them."

Penny stiffens, but I'm thankful she doesn't deny my revenge. Nothing will stop me from slaughtering the person who tried to take her life.

"I can do that." Torian looms over the table, jutting his chin at our entwined hands. "You might want to keep that under wraps. I don't feel like disposing of another dead body in the near future."

Penny's hand slips out from beneath mine, the retreat frantic, as I glare at Torian. "Thanks for the tip."

He smirks. "I'm nothing if not helpful." He starts for the hall. "If you remember anything, I want to hear it."

I stand and turn to Penny as she rises to her feet. "I'm going to walk him out. Why don't you take a shower?"

She nods, her eyes darting from me to Torian who stalks away. "Have I caused a huge mess?"

"It's okay. There's nothing to worry about." I kiss her quick. Hard. "I won't be long."

I leave her standing there, lengthening my stride to catch up to Torian as he opens the front door and turns to face me.

"Do you know what you're doing with her?" he asks.

"No," I answer honestly. "I've got no fucking clue. The only thing I'm certain of is that I don't want Decker finding out until she's ready."

"Well, he won't hear it from me, but you realize it's written all over your face, right? He's going to take one look at you two together and know straight away. He probably already does, with the way you chased her into the house."

"I've got time. I'd only finished telling him I hadn't laid a hand on her when you pulled into the drive. The way she brutally ignored me when she got out of the car helped, too."

"Seemed like a lovers' tiff to me. But what do I know?" He steps outside, glancing at me over his shoulder. "I've got a hundred dollars that says he figures it out next time he sees you, and that he attempts to take your life with your own gun."

"Thanks for the vote of confidence."

"I didn't say he'd succeed." He keeps walking. "Enjoy the rest of your night. It might be the last you have."

Asshole.

I shut the door, locking it behind him, then make my way back toward Penny's room.

She's in the shower, the water loud through the pipes.

I decide to do the same, turning off the lights and checking the doors, before I shut myself into the bathroom to wash away the events of the day.

I need to scrub off the layers of lust she painted over me, the depth of her touch that makes it hard to concentrate on what's important. All I can think about is that kiss... the way I pinned her against the wall... how she'd only just come home from being fucking shot at.

She would've been filled with adrenaline. Fucking crazed.

Now there's a homicidal shooter on the run and I'm standing here with my dick in my hand.

I'm such an asshole.

I hope she's already gone to bed by the time I wrench off the taps. I don't want to see her again. Not when I know that the second I do, everything will come flooding back—the hunger, the need, the cloying obsession with wanting her to be protected.

But I'm walking from the adjoining bathroom, a towel around my waist, ruffling the water from my hair with my hand when I notice her in the doorway to my bedroom.

Just like I predicted, I'm hit with a tidal wave of shit I shouldn't be thinking, shouldn't be feeling. It doesn't help that she's wearing nothing but an oversized T-shirt, the material hanging loose at mid-thigh, her hair damp over one shoulder.

"How was your shower?" I start for my bedside table and pull open the top drawer to grab a fresh pair of boxers.

"Good." She watches me, her attention never straying as she leans against the doorframe.

"Are you calling it a night? I'm ready to crash like you wouldn't believe."

"I actually hoped to finish our conversation from earlier."

Shit. "It can't wait until morning?" I tug the boxers on underneath my towel. "What else did you want to discuss?"

I don't like her in here. In my room. In such close proximity to my bed. She's too seductive and doesn't even realize it.

"I still have questions." She moves from the doorway, approaching me. "Is that okay?"

I close the drawer harder than necessary. "What sort of questions?"

"I want to know if you slept with her."

I straighten, my muscles tight as I untangle the towel from my waist. "No. I didn't have sex with her."

"Did you kiss her?"

My chest tightens, hating these questions, hating even more that her expression is pained while asking them. "No, Pen. I didn't touch her."

She sucks in a breath, standing taller. "Would you have gone through with it if I hadn't run away?"

This time, my answer doesn't come as quick. I don't want to lie to her. I don't want to hurt her either. Neither option is favorable. "I don't know."

She winces and glances away, focusing across the other side of the room.

"I needed to," I continue. "Didn't mean I wanted to."

"Why?" The question is uttered softly. She's so fragile and fucking innocent. "Why did you need to?"

"You know why, shorty."

"No, I don't." She turns back to me, her brow furrowed. "Is it because you think you're capable of forcing me? Raping me? Is that why you have to let off steam with someone else?"

"What? *No.*"

Fuck.

I drop the towel and cross the room to stand in front of her. "I'm fucking scared of manipulating you without even being aware of it. Hell, I've already done it twice."

"How? You've never manipulated me."

"I did when you kissed me the first time. You were in the middle of a panic attack. It was my job to hold you in check and I fucking failed. I did it again tonight. You would've been flying high on adrenaline when you got home. What happened in your bedroom was a mistake."

"Don't say that." She winces. "Don't even think it, because it makes me sound weak."

"You telling me you're strong, shorty?" I inch closer, unable to refrain from placing a hand on her waist. "Haven't we been having this argument for weeks?"

Her chin hikes up, her eyes narrowing. "I'm strong in some things, smart ass. And you're one of them. Everything else is static."

I chuckle, unsure whether I should be humbled or panicked.

"You make me feel alive, Luca." She places a hand on my chest, nestling her body closer. "I want to feel that way more often."

Panic was the right option. Pure panic.

"I'm glad you feel that way." I step back, well aware any brush of her against my hardening dick will be a bad idea. "But space is a good thing, too. Some pretty crazy shit happened tonight. You need time to let it sink in. You should get to bed and rest on it."

She raises a brow. "Which side?"

"Which side of what?"

"Your bed. Which side am I sleeping on?"

Oh, no.

Oh, *hell no*.

"Tap the fucking brakes, shorty, and back up the truck. You're not sleeping in here."

"But I went through some pretty crazy shit tonight," she mocks me. "I don't want to sleep on my own."

"You're hilarious." I walk for the door, hoping she'll follow. "Come on, get your ass to bed."

She looks at me in defeat. "Luc, please. I want to stay here."

The way she says my name. The sorrow. The plea. When she wraps her arms around her middle in a blatant show of vulnerability I'm entirely done for.

Doesn't she know this is what I've battled all along? That this is where I've wanted her from the first day we met?

In my room.

In my bed.

"It's not a good idea." I strangle the door handle. "Your room is a better option for now."

"I know. But this is what I want. I need it, Luc."

Fuck. I scrub a hand down my face. "You need what, exactly?"

"To be near you. To sleep knowing I'm protected. I'm sick of the nightmares."

She hits me right where it hurts. One sucker punch after another.

"Please," she repeats. "Just for one night to see what it's like."

Once will never be enough. There'll be no going back after those flood gates open. Surely she knows that.

I huff out a growl. "Pick the side you want."

"Thank you." She walks around the bed, moving away from the door. "Is this side okay?"

None of this is okay, and there's not a damn thing I can do about it. I can't bring myself to deny her, though. Or myself. This intimacy is a train wreck waiting to happen.

"Yeah, fine. But you might want to move the gun out from beneath the pillow and stick it under mine."

She doesn't show an ounce of shock as she does as instructed, grabbing the weapon tentatively to slide it across the mattress.

I wait until she's settled, her cheek on my pillow, her long hair spread out behind her before I turn off the light.

I'm not going to get a wink of sleep. Not with her scent on my sheets, her inhales caressing my ears. The hours until sunrise are going to be hell.

I climb into bed in darkness, sticking to the far side of the king-size mattress. There are still two feet of space between us and I'm acutely aware of each millimeter as she sucks in a deep breath and sighs.

"Night, shorty."

"Night."

I stare into inky blackness, completely wired.

I spend my time forcing myself to figure out how we're going to nail the guy who shot at her when we've got no description to go on. I think about the leverage tonight will give me over helping her step out of her comfort zone tomorrow. But I also struggle not to think about this all ending soon.

One way or another, this closeness won't last long.

For her, this is a phase of recovery. She wants me for my protection. Everything else is curiosity. Once Decker finds out, he'll put a stop to it.

Maybe that's what I need, too—for him to find out so at least someone has the balls to end this mess.

"Luc?"

"Yeah?" I mutter.

"Can you move closer? Just so I know you're near."

Jesus. Fuck. "I swear you were sent from the devil to test me." I scoot toward her, each inch made with weighty reluctance.

"No. It's you who were sent from the heavens to get me through my trauma, and this is something I need help with."

To hell with her logic.

I'm the last person who should be considered heaven sent.

If only she knew the things I've done. The people I've killed. And the ones I wanted to slaughter before they got away.

I stop a few inches from her, resting on my side to watch her darkened silhouette, the warmth from her body seeping into the sheets and surrounding me. But we don't touch. I make sure of that. I keep an invisible barrier between us, a firm boundary that she proceeds to shatter to pieces when she shuffles closer, nestling into my chest.

"Relax," she whispers. "I'm not going to hurt you."

If only she knew the pounding ache her proximity provides. I hurt everywhere. My legs. My arms. And no place throbs more than my dick. "Get some sleep."

She releases a weary sigh, resting her face into my chest. "I'm trying."

I feel for her. I always do.

I wish I could clean away her troubles and make her life effortless. Yet it seems staying here has only caused more problems.

I could've lost her tonight, and that fucking scares me. She could've been taken in by the cops. Or murdered. My selfishness almost cost this beautiful woman her life, and I'll never forgive myself.

The guilt is brutal, the pound building in my veins. My thoughts try to convince me she's already gone despite her body being close to mine.

Slowly, I wrap my arm around her waist, just to hold her. To make sure she's still whole. Still real.

I don't know how I'll let go of her in the morning. I'll have to pry my fingers from her soft skin.

"Luc?" Her voice is barely audible.

"Yeah, Pen. What's wrong?"

"I need you to touch me."

I close my eyes and press my lips to her temple. "I am touching you."

She sucks in a breath, her exhale ragged. "No. I need you to touch me the way you were going to touch that other woman."

16

PENNY

He doesn't move. Doesn't speak.

He remains rigid beside me, not breathing.

I pull back to stare into the darkened shadows of his face. "Luca, I need to know that part of me isn't broken. That I'm still a woman."

"Trust me, you're the most exquisite fucking woman there is."

He doesn't understand. I don't expect him to. But this is something I want to know. I *have* to know. I need to determine if the tingles he awakens in me are merely surface deep.

"Please." I place my hand on his chest. "Help me with this."

"I don't think I can be that man, Pen. I'm not a good guy."

The rejection stings. *Really* stings.

"Okay." I turn onto my back. I'm not going to force him into intimacy he doesn't want. Manipulating my way into his bed is bad enough.

"You know I want you." His voice is bleak through the darkness.

Yeah, I know. He wants me, just not the damage that comes with the package. He wants recovered Penny. Mentally stable Penny. "I said it's okay. Don't worry about it."

I lay in silence, my despair growing teeth.

He doesn't shift. I'm not sure if he's fallen asleep or if he's waiting for me to retreat to my own bed. I have no idea what he's thinking at all. I guess it's better that way.

"Why me?" he grates. "Why trust me with something this valuable?"

"What do you mean?"

"Intimacy. It's…" He doesn't continue, not in words, but his hand slides beneath the covers, his fingers raking over the top of my shirt to rest on my stomach.

"The only currency intimacy has with me is pain," I admit. "I've never known anything different. That's why I asked. I was hoping to wipe the slate clean of the bad memories."

"What about before?" His fingertips circle delicate details over my covered abdomen. "There had to be good memories then."

"There was nothing before. No steady boyfriend. No casual hookups. There's only my experience with Luther."

His hand pauses, his shock almost palpable through the seconds of thick silence. "You're a virgin?"

"I'm far from a virgin, Luc. But before Greece, no, I hadn't been with—"

"Greece doesn't count," he growls. "That wasn't sex. That was *nothing* like sex."

Maybe I shouldn't have asked. Maybe he's not the right person despite my body screaming otherwise.

"It doesn't matter. I don't want to talk about it anymore."

He returns to his circle work on my stomach. The gentle sweep of his fingertips is contained to a small space, yet the vibrations filter much farther. I feel the tingles all the way through my chest. Down my legs.

It's nice. Welcomed.

It's exactly what I asked for, just in diluted detail.

He traces my belly button. Swirls intricate patterns along my covered waist. The path he travels grows over long minutes of bliss. No words. No bad memories. Just kindness and what I hope is adoration in the delicate sweep of his touch.

I crave more. So much more I squeeze my legs to soothe the unfamiliar pressure.

My pulse pounds in my ears. In my throat.

I shouldn't want this. But I do.

I want to gorge on the kindness. To never, ever leave this moment.

The swirl of fingertips descends in minute increments, from my abdomen, to my hip, my thigh, then the hem of the T-shirt. When skin meets skin, I suck in a breath, the heated contact far more potent in its perfection.

"Too much?" he asks.

"No. Not at all."

He skims his hand under the shirt, hiking the material gradually as he ascends. There's nothing demeaning about it. Nothing threatening or brutal. It's pure gentleness, the only abrasion coming from the brief scrapes of the calluses on his palm.

My heart hammers the farther he travels along my thigh. The sensations are entirely new. Slow and soft and sweet.

"You're in control," he murmurs. "Tell me to stop whenever you need."

I nod into the darkness, incapable of words.

"Penny, you have to answer me. I won't keep going unless I know you're comfortable."

"I'm comfortable," I pant. "I know how to tell you to stop."

"Good." His touch skims to my inner thigh, the sensitive skin bursting into a valley of goose bumps.

It's remarkable. All the tingles. The burn where his attention doesn't even touch.

The approach to my core is painfully lethargic. He takes his time, learning every inch of me, creeping forward one minute, only to double back. Circling. Grazing. Branding.

By the time he reaches the juncture where leg meets groin I'm a mess of rampant breathing, my throat dry, my core pulsing.

I contemplate telling him to stop.

Ending this now—happy and blissed—is far better than the uncertainty that awaits. I can't get through this without acknowledging my trauma. Can I? Being like this with him can't be that easy. I have to break down soon. It's inevitable. I'm merely waiting for the switch to be flicked.

"Luc…"

"Hmm?" He guides my legs apart with slight pressure, exposing my vulnerabilities.

He doesn't say a word. Doesn't move his body closer to mine. He only continues to circle and swirl. Tease and tempt.

It's nothing like my past.

A completely foreign experience. Strikingly, agonizingly different.

"Nothing." I shake my head and clutch the sheets as he circles my pussy, the lightest glide of two fingertips moving around and around my outer edges.

This is far beyond what I wanted.

It's more passion. More kindness.

I envisaged sterility. Fear. Sorrow.

Yet here I am, tempted to beg for more, my hands itching to clutch him to my chest as his inhales labor.

Tension builds inside me. Sweet, needy tension.

I don't know how to sate the pulse becoming an adamant force deep down in my core. It makes me mindless, all the tingles and bliss.

He continues the circles, gliding closer and closer until he's brushing my pussy lips.

I shudder, anticipation trapping the breath in my lungs.

I don't know what comes next, but I want it. I *need it.*

"Luca?"

"Yeah?" His voice is breathy. Graveled.

"Don't stop."

He groans, his digits parting my folds to slide through slickness. My back arches. My breasts tingle. One finger enters me. Gradually. Agonizingly slowly.

I pant, wanting more as I close my eyes.

But bliss doesn't greet me in the mental darkness. Luther does. His conniving face stares back at me, smirking.

I scramble backward, the claws of panic snatching at me.

"What is it?" Luca asks. "What happened?"

"Turn on the lamp." I scoot to the head of the bed as the light flicks on, my arms around my legs, my knees near my chest. I gasp for breath.

The man who comes into view washes away the fear. He holds the memories at bay with the concern in his expression. The silent promise of protection.

"I took it too far." He covers my legs with the sheet.

"No, not at all. I was loving everything until I closed my eyes."

He winces. "It's okay. There's no rush."

There is to me.

There's now a finish line I want to pass. A victory over past demons I have to claim.

I reach for him, my fingers tentatively gliding over his chest. He sucks in a breath at the connection. Tenses.

"I'm wound tight, shorty."

"Me, too. But I don't want you to stop." I sink back onto the bed, turning onto my side to roll into him. "I need you to keep going." I can't quit here or I may never return.

"Why don't we save this for another day? We're not—"

"Please, Luc."

His nostrils flare, his frustration clear in the heavy exhale. "Whatever you want."

I've seen enough men consumed with lust to recognize the sight before me. He's pained with need. And his restraint is a monumental gift I've never received before.

Men don't hesitate to take from me. They steal and torment and punish.

But not Luc.

This time he guides my thigh to rest on top of his, propping my legs apart. He looks down at me, pussy splayed, wetness dripping.

"Fuck you're beautiful, Pen. So fucking beautiful."

I wilt for him, completely slump into a puddle of adoration. "Please kiss me."

I drag my hand around his neck and pull him close. He groans as our mouths meet, the vibration sinking into my chest.

I lose myself in him. Sucking. Licking. Biting. But most of all, learning. I notice the way he growls when I sink my teeth into his lower lip. I pay attention to the way he deepens the kiss if I inch back.

We smother each other, the passion climbing higher and higher with each sweep of our tongues until his fingers sneak back between my thighs.

I didn't think I could become needier than I was before. I never would've thought desire could be this painful. Or that bliss could be entirely consuming, like the way it is when his fingers slide back inside me.

I dig my nails into his neck. Cling. Claw.

"Oh, God." I gasp.

He resumes his slow torment. His digits glide into my pussy, stroking, then retreating completely. Back and forth. Over and over, delving deeper with each pass.

His breathing increases as he continues to kiss me, scraping me with his stubble.

This man may think he's falling in love with me, but my feelings are certain.

I adore him. Treasure him. *Love* him.

He put his future on the line. His *life*. All for me.

My gratitude will never die.

He slides his fingers farther inside, deeper and deeper, the heel of his palm placing pressure on my clit.

I need more.

So much more.

I grate into him, following his rhythm with my hips. I kiss his shoulder, his jaw, his cheek.

He stiffens further, his chest and arms becoming stone. Still he doesn't take from me. He gives and gives and gives. Not protesting when I dig my nails into his skin. Not backing away when I bite his neck.

"How did I get so lucky?" he growls into my ear. "What the hell did I do to deserve you?"

His adoration triggers something inside me. It breaks open the hardened fear and sets my demons free.

I latch onto his wrist between my thighs, rocking harder, faster, until my world splinters away from the destruction and pain and realigns with peace.

I realign with *him*.

I come undone, my core spasming. Pounding jolts of pleasure blindside me.

My breath is stolen with another kiss. My thoughts, too.

"Keep going, shorty." He speaks against my lips. "Don't fucking stop."

I don't want to. I could stay like this forever.

Thrumming.

Throbbing.

I cling to him, rock, rock, rocking, until the waves of bliss recede and all I'm left with are peppered kisses, depleted energy, and an overwhelming sense of exhilaration.

Wow.

"You're incredible." He holds my gaze as I collapse onto the mattress. "How are you feeling?"

"Breathless," I pant. "Overwhelmed... Happy."

"Good." He places a peck on my temple. "Because I need to leave you for a minute."

I don't want him to go. Not now. Or ever. But I don't protest as he slides from the bed, giving me an unrestricted view of all the scars peppered across his back like confetti.

"I won't be long." He walks to the bathroom door on the far side of the room, latching the lock behind him.

My euphoria rapidly recedes.

I'm almost lonely now.

The shower turns on, and the rapid rush of water falters, then rhythmically sloshes. He's pleasuring himself.

Without me.

I turn cold. Should I have offered him relief? Or maybe he ran so fast because he didn't want the offer at all. Maybe he didn't want to be with someone who could be harboring a wealth of STDs, because no matter how paranoid Luther was about the cleanliness of the women he raped, it doesn't mean I'm not dirty.

Luca hadn't wanted to touch me to begin with. Had barely bridged the space between us before I asked him to turn on the lamp.

"Stop it," I snarl to myself and slide from the bed, unwilling to let the negativity burrow further. Not tonight. Not after what just happened.

I make my way to the bathroom down the hall, distracting myself by using the facilities and freshening up.

I even tidy the vanity cupboards in an attempt to keep the taunting thoughts at bay, but it doesn't help. I question myself, wondering if I moved too fast. If the intimate moment should've been more difficult. If I'm a fraud for not being shattered by a man touching me.

Should I have hated the experience?

Why was it easy for him to bring me pleasure after so much pain?

The thoughts pound through my mind, gaining force, stealing away what bliss I had and replacing it with a cage of mental torture.

A tightening, restricting cell.

Breathing becomes harder, my lungs unable to be filled.

The light thud of approaching footfalls soothes me. Luca is here. Outside the bathroom door. I can feel him as if he's on the other side of the wood, waiting for me to come out.

"You're not okay, are you?" he murmurs through the barrier between us.

His insight draws a sob from my throat. "I'm confused. That's all."

The door creeps open, and I'm forced to step to the side as his stern face of concern bears down on me, authoritative and strong.

"Talk to me," he demands in a gruff growl.

"I don't know what to say."

"Say whatever's in your head. Did I hurt you? Are you scared of me? Did I push you too far?"

"No. It's none of that."

"Then why are you upset?"

"I'm not. I promise. I'm just overwhelmed. Both happy and… I can't explain."

"Self-sabotaging?"

I open my mouth to protest, but pause instead. "What do you mean?"

"I don't know. I just thought that either way, this exploration had to end badly. Either you hated it and felt accordingly. Or you didn't, but your mind and body are so used to feeling like shit that you don't know how to react any other way."

I cock my head, blinking as I hold his gaze.

Maybe that's it.

Maybe that's exactly it.

I want to be happy. The euphoria and bliss were everything in the heat of the moment, then as soon as thoughts had the time to fester, they turned the light to dark. "How did you know?"

He gives a sad smile. "'Cause I'm brilliant."

"No, really. How did you know?"

"Trauma has a lot of shitty bonus prizes that tend to bite you on the ass when you least expect it."

"You know from experience." It's not a question. I can see it in his eyes.

"I know enough. But none of that matters now. Let's get you back to bed."

I want to pry, to learn the parts of him he keeps hidden. I want to know everything there is about this man. "Will you tell me about your experience?"

"Sure. If you stick around long enough." He winks and takes my hand, leading me to the hall. "For now, though, you need to get some rest."

17

LUCA

She settles into her side of the mattress, her silhouette unmoving beside me.

Even in the shadows she's becoming easier to read.

Back in Greece, she hid everything—her thoughts, emotions, reactions. Now it's as if she's a written text, understood and deciphered from the slightest cadence change to her breathing.

"Get over here." I reach for her, dragging her into the middle of the bed.

She lets out a gasp of shock, but there's no protest. She comes willingly, draping her arm over my chest. Maybe her escape attempt was a blessing in disguise. Or it could've been, if she hadn't almost died.

We wouldn't be here otherwise.

She wouldn't be mine.

In my room.

In my arms.

But she's quiet. Too quiet. That isn't a good sign.

"What's on your mind, Pen."

"You're tired," she whispers. "There's all the time in the world to talk tomorrow."

"I don't need sleep. And apparently, neither do you. So spit it out."

She chuckles, subtle and breathy.

It's so fucking good to hear that sound from her. The comfort after all the pain.

"It's nothing." She rakes a finger over my pec, her touch pausing on scars. "I was only thinking that I don't know a whole lot about you."

"You're thinking that *now*? Isn't it a little late to be having cold feet?" I add humor to my tone to hide my apprehension.

I'm all in with this thing between us. Balls to the wall. Heart on my fucking sleeve.

I don't want her second-guessing anything. Let alone me.

"No. It's nothing like that. I was just thinking about all the things I know…"

"And wondering about all the things you don't?"

"Yeah." She nods. "I barely know anything, apart from the way you make me feel and how you like your coffee."

"So ask."

"Okay…" She shuffles beside me, raising on to her elbow. "Where are you from? And how did you end up here? You told me in Greece you used to be a SEAL, but never explained why you aren't anymore. I also want to know more about your brother. And your parents—"

"That's quite a list." I stop her there. Deliberately. "We'll be up until sunrise at this rate."

I don't see her smile. I feel it. There's something in the air that warms with her happiness.

This Penny isn't like the warrior I rescued from a predator. Her edges are softer. She's more woman. Less wild, caged animal.

"I've barely even started." She chuckles again. "How long have you lived here? When was your last relationship? How did you end up working for Torian?"

"My brother." I tread carefully, wanting to get this over with before she nosedives any further into unwanted territory. "I was on a mission overseas when I found out Benji had gotten tied up with the most notorious crime family in Oregon. I dropped everything in the hopes I could pull him out before it was too late."

"But ended up working for them instead? Did they force you? Threaten you?"

"No." Despite her probably wanting a different answer, I tell her, "I'm here by choice."

154

"You gave up being a SEAL to work for Cole Torian?"

"Not exactly. I gave up for the love of my brother. It was a case of leaving my post too often to maintain my role. And the last time was in the middle of an op. But Benji needed me, and he's all I've got. I'd do anything for him. So I acted against instructions not to abandon my post. Even ignored my superior's threats to have me court marshalled."

There's a beat of silence where her hand freezes on my chest. "Weren't you worried?"

"I was more worried for my brother."

There's another pause, then, "Did they go through with their threat to court martial?"

"You bet your ass they did. I was dishonorably discharged."

The only stability I'd ever had in my life was gone. I'd been left with nothing. Nothing but Benji in a fucked-up situation.

"That's a heavy price to pay for being the older sibling."

"I'm not older. My big brother has a few years on me. Doesn't change anything though. It's how it's always been. He gets in trouble, and I try my best to drag him out of it." I place my hands under my head, feigning calm. "Isn't that what family are for?"

"I don't know. It's been a long time since I've had one. I barely remember what it's like anymore." She sucks in a deep breath and sighs. "How about your scars? Are they from your time as a SEAL or from working with Cole?"

I force myself not to flinch as she makes a direct hit on a shitty subject. "That's a long story best saved for another day."

"You don't want to share it with me?"

I don't want to share it with anyone.

Not now. Not ever.

"Does it have something to do with the trauma you mentioned before?" She looms over me. "I'm not pressuring you to spill secrets… I just thought if we had something in common…"

"It's not a conversation I want to have, Pen."

There's a slight tweak to her muscles. A flinch that consumes me with guilt.

"I'm sorry." She rests back onto the bed, stealing away her touch. "I won't ask again."

No, I bet she won't. She's too considerate for that.

I'll just be left to feel like shit for denying her.

155

"I'm getting tired." She rolls away from me to wrestle with her pillow. "Good night, Luc. Thanks for everything."

Fuck me.

Fuck me for pretending all my ducks are in a row when clearly they're not.

Fuck me for forcing her to face her past when I barely attempt to face my own. It's not fair. If only I knew how to function any other way.

"Night, Pen." I reach for her, gently running my fingers through her hair in silent apology. "Wake me if you need me."

"I will."

I lie there for hours, staring at her black outline as she sleeps. I don't know when I pass out, but it feels like seconds before I startle to consciousness, blinking rapidly at the sun beaming around the edge of the curtains.

I groan and reach for the bedside table to grab my cell, but it isn't there. I drag myself to the edge of the mattress to scour the floor, still coming up empty.

Shit.

I'm going to have to get up and search for it. There's no rest for the wicked when I need to find the asshole who shot at Penny.

Despite wanting to lie beside her forever, I can't today.

I slide from bed, swiping my gun from beneath the pillow, and wipe my free hand over the back of my neck, getting caught up in the sight before me.

She's peaceful, her gentle face relaxed, her beautiful lips parted.

The loud bang from the front door steals it all.

She startles, launching upright as the pounding continues.

"Luca, open the goddamn door."

Torian.

Fucking, Torian. That's what woke me.

"Don't panic." I stalk for the dresser, pulling out a pair of sweatpants and a shirt. "I can't find my phone. He'd be having a stroke because he couldn't get hold of me. Go back to sleep."

She reclines onto her elbows. "Are you sure?"

"Positive." I tug my pants on and shove the gun into the back of my waistband. "Everything's fine."

At least I hope so. For all I know, Decker could also be waiting at my door ready to take a dick swab. Or a vital organ.

156

"Sleep." I make for the hall. "I'll wake you when I've made breakfast."

I close the door behind me and stride for the front of the house as the knocking continues. A quick check through the peephole confirms Torian is alone, suit-clad and frowning as he attempts to bang my house down.

"What the fuck?" I pull the door wide.

He scrutinizes me with a raised brow as I tug the shirt over my head. "By the look of the claw marks on your neck, I'd say you had a fun night. I hope it was consensual."

"Fuck you."

He laughs and steps forward, nudging past me to enter the house.

"By all means," I grate. "Make yourself at home."

"You didn't give me much choice. I've been calling for an hour." He leads me back into the living area to take a seat at my dining table where my silenced phone lies in wait, the notification light blinking. "Did you just wake up?"

"Yeah. I was completely out of it." I scrub a hand over my face. "I'm tired as fuck."

"I bet." There's the slightest hint of judgment in his tone, but he doesn't put words to it. He doesn't need to.

"What do you want, Torian? What's so urgent that you couldn't wait until I found my phone?"

He sits back in the chair and shoots a glance to the kitchen. "If I were you, I'd start the coffee machine. You're gonna need it."

"Fine." It's a demand to make him a mug, but I don't give a shit because I *do* need it, likely more than he does. "Are you going to tell me what's going on? Or do I need to play barista first?"

"I'll wait."

"Suit yourself."

He doesn't speak again until I've got two mugs in hand and have taken my seat on the opposite side of the table. "What's got your asshole in a bunch this morning?"

He grabs the mug, takes a mouthful, then meets my gaze. "I told you last night that she stole from me."

Jesus Christ.

"Not this shit again. I haven't discussed it with her." I didn't bring it up because it wasn't the time. It'll never be the time. "I'll pay whatever she owes. Just leave her the fuck alone. She's gone through enough."

"She doesn't owe a dime." He places down the mug and grabs his cell from his suit jacket, pressing buttons before he slides it in front of me.

A pixelated black and white photo spreads across the screen. A stocky guy stands before an ATM, the majority of his head shrouded by his hoodie, sunglasses, and heavy beard.

"I was wrong." He taps the picture. "It was this guy."

"And who the hell is he?"

He shrugs. "No clue. But it's someone close enough to my father to have been trusted with a keycard."

"Someone old school or do you think we have new blood in town?" The niggle of apprehension raises the hair on the back of my neck. Luther always had allies here, even after he fled the country. The last thing we need is unfamiliar men stirring up trouble when nobody knows the kingpin is dead.

"Either is possible. The access to a keycard might be how he paid his local associates. My concern is that a threat from Greece slipped through our fingers and came here to cause trouble, because I've never seen this man before."

"He's unfamiliar to me, too." My apprehension increases. "But you're not here for me, are you? You want Penny to take a look."

"Yeah. I do."

I wipe a hand over my mouth, biting back the need to deny him. "She's sleeping. She needs her rest."

More than that, she deserves a few days of peace to get her head straight after last night. From both the fear and the bliss.

"I'm not waiting." He narrows his eyes. "Either you get her or I will."

I grind my teeth. Fist my mug. It takes every ounce of restraint to take another sip without choking on anger.

If I didn't have the slightest sense of concern over the piece of shit in the photo, I'd fight harder to have her left alone. But instinct tells me this isn't the time to make a stand.

"Give me a few minutes." I walk for my bedroom and ease the door open.

"You're back already?" She stretches, lazily blinking up at me.

158

"Sorry, shorty. I didn't want to wake you again, but Torian wants to see you."

She sits upright, then scoots from the bed. "Why?"

"It's nothing exciting. Just get dressed and meet us in the living room." I don't wait for more questions. I trek back down the hall, stopping at the main bathroom to wash my face in cold water. By the time I'm heading toward the living room, she's right behind me, dressed in jeans and a loose sweater as she pulls her hair into a high pony.

"Morning, Cole." She follows me to the table and takes a seat while I stand beside her.

"Morning." He gives a fake smile. "I don't know if Luca already told you, but this isn't a social visit."

"Okay." She frowns. "What's going on?"

"Last night, I accused you of stealing. I was wrong."

I remain coiled tight, listening to the admission that is far from the apology she deserves.

"It was a man." He taps his cell again, lighting up the screen with the picture on it. "I'm wondering if you recognize him."

"Me?" She glances at me in confusion before settling her attention back on Torian. "Why would I recognize him?"

"No reason. Just covering all my bases." He pushes his phone toward her, letting her frame it in both hands. "The image quality isn't the best."

She stares at the screen, not seeming to show any sign of recognition. At least not until I notice the tremble in her fingers and the lighter shade to her cheeks.

"Pen?" I slide into the seat beside her. "Do you know who it is?"

"Is this a joke?" She looks at me, her face ashen. "Please tell me this is some sick—"

"You recognize him?" Torian asks.

"When was this taken?" Her eyes scream with panic.

"Yesterday afternoon."

I reach for her, but she drops the phone to the table and pushes from her chair, distancing herself as she stands. "Where?"

"At a gas station ATM," Torian answers.

"Where?" She repeats. "*What* gas station? *Which* ATM?"

"The one on the corner of Boulevard and Cheshire. It's a ten-minute drive from here."

A heaved breath shudders from her lips. Followed by another and another, her shoulders trembling with the exhales.

"Penny?" I slowly rise to my feet, not wanting to spook her further. "What's going on?"

"You lied to me," she whispers. "You told me he was dead."

"Who's dead?" Torian's chair scrapes as he stands.

"*Robert*," she yells. "That man in the photo is *Robert*."

"No, shorty." My refusal is adamant as I reach for her. "You're mistaken. It's not him."

"The image is blurry at best." Torian speaks over me. "The guy's face is mostly covered."

She shoves me away, regaining space. "You think I wouldn't recognize a man who tormented me for years? I'd know him anywhere. And yet he was *here*. In *Portland*. A mere ten-minute drive away."

"No…" I reach for her again and she revolts.

"You promised." She backtracks. "You promised he was dead. You promised I was safe."

"You *are*." I follow her. "I would've bet my goddamn life he was dead."

"Instead, you bet mine." She places more space between us, one step after another. "You staked *my* life, Luca."

"I'd never do that."

I don't get it.

I don't fucking understand.

"Pen, calm down," I beg. "You didn't sleep well last night. Why don't you take another look at the photo—"

"I didn't sleep well?" Her eyes plead with me. "You don't believe me?"

I hold up my hands in placation. "I'm just trying to understand what the fuck is happening."

Trying.

Struggling.

I'd been in that room in Greece. I watched as Luther drew his gun and vowed to handle Robert. But we had to leave.

Anissa had been hurt. Scared. In danger.

I heard the gunshot. That blast rang in my fucking ears.

"I need to leave." Penny scrutinizes her surroundings, glancing around the room as if threatened by the furniture, scanning the yard as she retreats step after step toward the hall.

"You're safe," I vow.

"How can you say that? You have no idea what you're up against. You don't even trust me. You think I'm crazy."

"I *do* trust you."

"Then listen to me." The tremble in her hands increases as she glances between me and Cole. "*Please*, Luca, you need to believe me."

"Okay." I keep my arms raised. "I believe you. I promise I believe you. Just stop walking away from me. You don't get to run again."

"I don't know what else to do. I can't stay here. He'll come after me. He won't stop."

"Neither will I. You hear me?" I bridge the space between us and pull her against my chest. I stare at Torian over her shoulder, noting the skepticism heavy in his features. "I won't let anyone near you."

"You don't understand what he's like. He won't give up."

I squeeze her tighter, only to have her scamper from my hold.

A gasp breaches her lips. Her eyes flare. "Last night... oh, my God. That was him."

"Okay, that's enough," Torian warns. "You need to stop jumping to conclusions. Even if by some stretch of the imagination Robert is alive, he'd know Portland isn't a smart place for him to hide."

"He'd never hide." She pulls back. "He'd be here for payback. He's here for *me*. I want a gun, Luca. You need to get me a gun."

I nod. "We'll discuss it later. Right now, we have to make a move. Go pack your things. We're getting out of here."

She doesn't wait for any further instruction. She rushes for the hall, her fear-filled expression haunting me even once she's out of view.

"You don't buy this crazed bullshit, do you?" Torian holds my gaze, his eyes narrowed. "After everything that happened, you still think it's possible that asshole is alive?"

I'm trying to piece together the possibilities. We'd heard the gunshot, but we'd left the room. We didn't physically see Robert dead.

"Did you hear his body hit the floor?" I ask.

"What?"

"Back in Greece. We left the room just as the gunshot was fired." I pace, raking my hands through my hair. "But did you hear his body hit the ground? There would've been a hard clap of his fucking head against the tile. We should've—"

"You're saying you think she's right?" He scoffs.

"What I'm saying is that I can't remember hearing Robert's fucking body hit the floor."

"We had other things on our mind," he grates. "Jesus Christ, Luca. You're thinking with your dick."

No, I'm not thinking at all. I'm panicking. "What if she's right? Are you willing to risk your family? Are you willing to risk Anissa? Because if that prick is still breathing, I'm sure he's going to want revenge for what we did over there."

And he's not the type of psychopath to draw out the torture.

18

PENNY

I clean out my wardrobe, packing my belongings into paper shopping bags while Luca remains in the living room with Cole.

I overhear parts of their aggressive argument.

They mention Anissa. My sisters. And Tobias.

My sweet, sweet Tobias.

I fall to my knees. Helpless.

That little boy is entirely vulnerable. But Robert would never hurt him. Not physically. They were like uncle and nephew. It's the mental threat he poses that I can't ignore.

Robert wouldn't stand for Tobias being taken care of by the people who arranged Luther's murder. And my sisters…oh, God.

Bile climbs up my throat.

Abi.

I knew she would never kill herself. I knew, and Luca didn't believe me. None of them wanted to believe me.

I clutch a hand to the base of my neck and bow my head, begging the contents of my stomach to retreat.

Robert killed Abi. He tried to kill me. Who knows what he will attempt next.

"Pen?" Luca enters the doorway and falls to his knees before me. "Are you okay?"

"I need to get out of here."

He nods. "We're leaving right now."

"Where?"

163

"Torian's house." He hits me with sad eyes. "Don't worry. It's a gated property with heavy surveillance. He's already called in a security team to man the perimeter."

I don't think surveillance will matter. Or security. Nothing will stop Robert getting what he wants. Nothing but death.

"I want that gun, Luca. I need to be able to protect myself."

His brows pinch. It's the slightest cringe of a response.

"Luca?" I sit back on my haunches. "You said you could get me a gun. You promised in Greece."

"You're not going to need it. The house will be protected."

"You're denying me?"

"No." He grabs my hands, tangling our fingers. "I'm telling you it's not necessary. We're taking this seriously, Pen. We're going to cover all our bases, which starts with moving everyone to Torian's house. That includes his sisters, our brothers, Hunter, Sarah, Stella and Tobias. It's not a good idea to have you carrying a gun around those kids."

"Tobias is going to be there? I'm going to see him?"

"Yes. We'll all be living under the same roof for a while, which means it's not smart to have guns in the hands of someone untrained."

"Then train me," I beg. "Nobody will protect Tobias like I will. I'd give my life—"

"And I'd give mine." He speaks over me. "For him. *And* you."

I sit back on my haunches, sliding my hands from his. "But I won't make mistakes."

He pulls away and I steel myself against his pained expression, not letting the guilt sink in.

This morning, I'd woken with a smile. I'd been a different woman. Hope had flown through me. I'd been wholeheartedly adamant my life had turned a corner.

Now that's all gone.

Everything is—the security, the glimpse of positivity.

"I didn't mean that. I just…" I wince.

"I get that you're mad. You have every right to be. But you'll see once we get there that you don't need to protect yourself or anyone else." He rises to his feet and grabs my bags from the bed. "Grab whatever else you need and meet me in the garage. We're leaving as soon as Hunt and Deck get here to escort us."

He strides from the room without a backward glance, the slightest slump to his shoulders the only evidence I kicked him where it hurts.

I didn't want to upset him. That wasn't my intent. It's the insanity building inside me that demands to be heard. There are too many thoughts. Overwhelming questions. A punishing outlook.

I push to my feet, snatch the last of my toiletries from the bathroom, and yank on a comfy pair of Sketchers before following him. I run into Cole in the hall, the two of us walking in tense silence until we reach the garage where Luca shows me to the back of his Suburban.

"You're going to have to lay low." He opens the door and waves a hand for me to get inside. "I don't have all the bells and whistles Hunt's car has. So you need to spread yourself out along the back seat and stay out of view."

"What does that mean?" I climb into the vehicle and swivel to face him.

"It means my car isn't bulletproof." He closes me inside and returns to his conversation with Cole, the two of them murmuring in low tones before Luca skirts the hood to get in the driver's side. "It's time to get down, Pen." He opens the garage with a remote, the mechanical burr slow and ominous.

"What about you?" I meet his gaze in the rear-view and appreciate the lack of deserved hostility. "What's the point of worrying about me when it's just as likely you'll get shot?"

"Nobody is getting shot. It's only a precaution." He makes the Suburban grumble to life and reverses into the bright sunlight. "Now, Pen."

I hesitate, glancing through the side window to see Cole follow us down the drive on foot, the garage door closing in front of us. "Are you sure you're safe?"

"We've practically got a presidential escort. Hunter's going to be in front, with your brother and Torian in the cars behind. We're literally sandwiched between trigger-happy assholes. They won't let anything happen to us."

I look through the back window, confirming the cars are ready and waiting.

They're taking this seriously. Even if they don't believe me, they're at least taking precautions. "Can you let me know if you see anything?"

"I'm not going to see anything. Just lay down and enjoy the ride."

I sigh and stretch along the seat, resting my head on my bent arm as Luca reverses the car onto the street.

We don't talk. I'm left to fidget in silence, nothing but crunching asphalt and traffic in the distance to keep me company for miles.

I try not to let my thoughts wander. I seriously work hard to concentrate because I know the darkness of instability waits in the wings.

All the nightmarish thoughts are there. Hovering. Impatient for their time to strike.

"How much farther?" I raise my head to peek out the side window.

"Stay down. It's only a few more blocks." He turns on the radio, the gentle hum of an unfamiliar song doing nothing to soothe me. "You'll get to see Tobias soon."

I wait for excitement to flood me.

Instead, nervous apprehension weighs heavy in my belly. I love that boy, but I don't know what he's been told over the past weeks. About me. About the deaths of Chloe or Abi. Or if he'll be informed of Robert's presence in Portland.

Our reunion will either be shrouded in secrets or tears. Neither option is comforting.

"Only one more block." Luca makes a turn, then another, still without a care in the world. "We're here."

The car jolts as if we've risen onto a driveway and I cautiously sit as we pass through gates attached to a large brick wall.

The setting is reminiscent of my hell in Greece. It's just another set of gates and walls to lock me inside.

"You'll like it here." Somehow, Luca soothes my thoughts. "It's massive, with enough room for you to hide from anyone you don't want to speak to."

He drives the car around the front of a two-story mansion, the manicured gardens perfectly symmetrical with their trimmed hedges and rose bushes. The neighbors' homes are equally overbearing and ostentatious from the other side of that looming brick wall.

"This is the safest place for you to be right now." He cuts the engine and meets my gaze in the rear-view. "But, if at any time you don't feel comfortable, tell me and I'll fix it."

"Fix it how? You'd get me out of here?"

"I'd figure something out." He opens his door, slides free, then helps me from the car. All the while he cautiously scrutinizes the yard, as if he's taking in every swaying branch and rustling leaf.

We're alone. No other cars. No people in sight.

"I thought you said Sebastian was following us." I beat back panic at our conspicuous position. The boundary walls are large, but the neighbors' houses' are far bigger. What if we're being watched? An itch of unease skates along my arms. "Where are Cole and Hunter?"

"Decker and Hunt kept driving once we reached the gates. They need to help escort everyone here. And Torian went to park around back in the garage. He'll let us in through the front door in a minute."

I nod, only slightly appeased.

My arms break out in goose bumps beneath my sweater. All my hairs stand on end. It's as if I'm in the sights of a well-trained assassin and any sudden movement will end my life.

"You can wait at the front door." Luca jerks his chin toward the house. "I'll get our stuff."

I don't listen. Instead I follow him to the trunk and help to carry my paper bags while he hauls a heavy duffle. It's instinctive to remain by his side, and I suppose it shouldn't be. Not when walls are crashing down around me. I need to find a way to make it on my own. Without reliance.

By the time we reach the front double doors, Cole is there to let us inside.

He leads us down a wide hall, the white tiles immaculate, the walls filled with artwork. It's too similar to Luther's Grecian home. My prison. This place is another picture-perfect house, haunted by criminal activity.

"Separate rooms?" Cole stops before a closed door. "Or together?"

"Separate," I murmur, as Luca says, "Together."

167

Cole raises a brow. "I'll leave you two to come to a decision. Make yourselves at home. But once everyone arrives we need to have a meeting. Don't keep me waiting." He continues down the long hall, back straight, stride confident, and opens another door to disappear inside.

Luca doesn't speak. He stands there, staring where Cole had once been, his jaw tense, his hand wrapped tight around the duffle strap.

"Separate rooms would be better." I break the silence.

"You're sick of sleeping with me already?" He makes for the door in front of me, flings it wide and stalks inside.

"That's not it." I remain in the hall, unwilling to follow. "You said my brother will be here. I don't want him seeing us together."

"Fuck your brother," he grates from inside the room. "I'll tell him I'm sleeping on the floor. I'm not letting you out of my sight."

I cling to my bags, the paper crinkling under my tightening grip. "No, it's best if I stay somewhere else."

He dumps his duffle at the foot of the bed and returns to the doorway, his shoulders stiff. "I get it; you're angry at me. You don't trust me anymore. But distancing yourself isn't going to help."

"*You're* the one who doesn't trust *me*, Luc. You don't believe me."

He steps closer, not stopping until his face is inches from mine. "No, I don't *want* to believe you. There's a difference."

"It sounds the same to me."

"Well, it's not. I believe that you think Robert is still alive. And that he was the shooter last night. But I don't *want* to believe it because that means I fucked up. Not just a little bit, but a whole damn lot. Believing you're right means I risked your life and I'm not sure I can handle that."

"How do you think I feel? You made me believe in fairy tales. You convinced me I was safe. Now I don't know what's real and what isn't. I need to step back and protect myself. *On my own.*"

He reaches for my bags, drags both from my arms to steal them inside. "Everything between us is real." He speaks over his shoulder. "So whatever you need to figure out, you can do it in here."

I sigh and trudge after him, stopping at the threshold. "You can't blame me for questioning my safety, Luc."

He dumps my bags on top of a dark wood dresser, then turns to me. "But you're not just questioning your safety. You're questioning me. You're questioning all the things I've done to protect you. All the time we've spent together. All the things that happened over the past weeks. I'm only asking for you to give me a chance to redeem myself."

I slump against the doorjamb and cross my arms over my chest. "You don't need to redeem anything. I just need space."

"I call bullshit. Last night you pleaded to get in my bed. Now you're pushing me away because I fucked up."

"No, I'm pushing you away because you made it clear last night that you won't let me intrude upon your past despite how much you demand of mine. If anyone has been pushing it was you."

My lips snap shut as his shoulders straighten.

I didn't need to say that. My insecurities are meaningless in comparison to the situation with Robert. Yet I feel better for getting it off my chest. One of the millions of voices in my head has been heard.

"Is that what this is about?" He frowns. "My past isn't a topic either one of us want to discuss."

"I understand, but it doesn't stop me questioning the secrecy. Maybe this is more of that self-sabotage you spoke about." I shrug. "I don't know. All I can say is that I feel isolated from the truth right now. And I'm not sure how to get on top of that when the one person I thought I could trust can be physically near me, yet mentally keep me at arm's length."

19

LUCA

"GET IN HERE," I DEMAND.

Her throat works over a heavy swallow. Her chin hikes the slightest bit in defense.

She's uncomfortable. Unsettled.

We're fuckin' twinsies.

"No." She pushes from the doorjamb and stands tall. "I'll find another room."

"Do I need to carry you over my shoulder?" I start toward her, thankful she scoots inside before I slam the door shut. "So me spilling my past will stop you feeling isolated?"

"That's not what I'm saying... I just—" She throws her hands up in the air. "I don't know. I don't know anything anymore. One minute I'm in your house, in your bed, and I begin to feel happy and optimistic and whole. I started imagining a future that wasn't a waking nightmare. And now we're here and all those daydreams are gone, leaving me to question everything."

She wants my secrets.

My truth.

I guess I owe her that much.

"They're cigarette burns," I admit, each word slicing open old wounds. "The marks all over my body aren't from shrapnel. They're not battle scars. Each and every spot of mutilated skin is from the burned end of a cheap roll of tobacco."

Her face falls. Her lips part.

She stares at me for long moments, thoughts running rampant in those eyes, but no questions come out.

"How's that for un-isolating truth?" I drawl.

She shakes her head, her forehead wrinkled in a wince. "Do I want to know who caused them?"

"Probably not. But I'll tell you anyway." I back away from her, moving to the bed to slump onto the mattress. "The lighter, more frequent ones are from my father. Because he liked to constantly remind me he was an asshole. Those few that are deeper came from my mom. She wasn't as carefree about leaving abusive evidence behind, but when she did, she tended not to hold back."

Pity takes over her beautiful face. Such sickening, unwanted pity.

I can't look at her when she stares at me like that.

I don't want sympathy. I don't even want acknowledgement.

"Obviously, they weren't the best parents," I say through clenched teeth. "But my scars are nothing in comparison to my brother's. He bore the brunt of their abuse."

"That's why you're always helping him?"

"I help him because he helped me for years. He made sure he was the main target whenever my folks went on a rage bender. He kept me alive through childhood and has far more scars to prove it. Mental and physical."

He grew accustomed to fucking up for the sake of saving me. It was his routine for so long the habit followed into adulthood.

"How long did the abuse last?" She approaches, stopping within arm's reach.

"Benji was willing to risk living on the streets for as long as I can remember. He only hung around because I was too much of a chicken shit to leave. But as soon as my seventeenth birthday arrived, I forged my parents' signature and signed up for the Navy. I was out of there and never looked back."

"And Benji? What did he do?"

"Whatever he could to survive. He got a job. Rented a shitty apartment and kept his head above water with the money I sent him each payday." I meet the sickening pity still heavy in her gaze. "Is that enough insight? Do you feel better now?"

"Please don't ask me that." She wraps her arms around her

171

middle. "If I would've known what you were hiding I never would've made demands."

"I didn't tell you, Pen, because I haven't told anyone. Not child services when they came to check on us. Not the few friends I had as a kid. Not a single soul since I left that fucking house and never looked back." I shove from the bed and bridge the distance between us, untangling those arms to place them on my waist. "Nobody knows. I don't even think Benji told his wife."

"I feel horrible." She speaks into my chest. "I never should've said anything."

"It doesn't matter. I'm sure you would've found out soon enough. I can't keep shit from you."

She sinks into me, her cheek to my shoulder, her warm breath on my neck. "Where are your parents now?"

"Don't know. Don't care. As far as I'm concerned, my childhood never existed."

"But from your childhood you became a protector. You became a SEAL—"

"I became a SEAL because it felt good to create havoc for the right reasons. To be someone who was the best of the best instead of a cowering little kid who made his brother take his beatings. They were the first family I ever had."

"And then you lost them…"

"I did." I shrug. "But I gained a new one here. These guys have my back, even though they act like pricks most of the time. This job wasn't a hard transition, even though I never would've guessed it beforehand."

"But you went from doing good to bad."

"Did I?" I pull back to look down at her. "I saved you, after all. Doesn't that make me a little bit good?"

She winces. "Yes. Of course it does. I didn't mean…"

"Killing heartless criminal assholes isn't something I feel guilty about. Sometimes people deserve more than a jail cell. I don't lose sleep thinking about the bodies I've buried."

She stares up at me for long moments of contemplation. No agreement. No response.

"Does knowing more about me make you feel any better, shorty?"

172

She swallows and swipes her tongue over her lower lip, the sight fucking tempting. "I'd be lying if I said no."

"You sure I didn't scare you?"

Her lips pull in a half-hearted smile. "Again, I'd be lying if I said no."

"Okay, I'll make sure to leave the closet open for you to dig through my skeletons. But I think it's too early to chat about the work I do for Cole. I can see you're uncomfortable with it."

Her chuckle is breathy. "Yeah, maybe."

"Okay." I grab her chin, grazing my fingers over her soft skin. "I'll do whatever you want. You only need to ask."

I press my mouth to hers, eating up her faint whimper as she settles against my chest. The connection is soft. Slow. Exactly the opposite of what the blood rushing through my veins demands.

"How are you feeling about last night?" I ask against her lips. "No regrets?"

"None." She deepens the kiss. "Only more curiosity."

I keep the laughter buried in my chest. The agonizing, punishing laughter.

This woman is going to get me killed.

"I think it really helped me," she continues between nuzzling pecks.

It didn't help me one iota.

I'm fucking dying to have her. Dying trying to keep my restraint in check.

She sighs. "Will you—"

The slam of a door cuts her question short and drags us apart. The patter of light rushed footsteps lets me know this moment isn't going to last any longer. The kiddie giggle only confirms it. The unmistakable squeal from my niece sends my dick into hibernation.

"I think the mini stampede means Tobias is here." I drag my hands off her. "You should go say hello."

She glances to the closed door, her lips parting.

"What are you waiting for?" I walk to my duffle, busying myself with pulling out a change of clothes. It's not my business to intrude on her special moment, no matter how much I wish it was. We're not at that stage yet. Maybe we will be one day. Who the

173

fuck knows? But I'm not going to crowd her. "Go on. Enjoy the reunion."

"Thank you."

I don't look back at the sound of her fleeting footsteps. I get dressed, pulling on old jeans and a shirt loose enough to hide the gun buried in my waistband.

I try not to focus on all the fucked-up scenarios potentially waiting for us, but it's hard not to imagine the worst when the hits keep coming.

If Penny's right and Robert is still alive, it's not merely his revenge we need to worry about.

His ability to blow Torian's secrets sky-high is more than a huge fucking dilemma.

None of us will be safe, now or in the future, if news of Luther's arranged murder becomes public knowledge. And if that information is paired with the inside info that Torian was working with Anissa—a Fed—our deaths won't come easily.

In this world, snitches get more than stitches. They get a one-way ticket to unending torture to set a blatant example for anyone else who might want to do the same.

Men will die.

Women, too. Maybe the kids.

I doubt anyone will be spared.

Things would be different if Anissa was dirty. Turning a cop, a Fed, or a government official is worthy of a five-star bonus. But that woman wants to remain clean, meaning we're all as good as fucked if Robert is kicking and decides to expose the truth.

So my days could be numbered, and if that's the case, there's no place I'd rather spend them than by Penny's side, my hands in her hair, my mouth against hers.

I walk from the room toward the noise and find the living area filled with familiar faces—Hunter, Sarah, Torian, Decker, Keira, Layla, and my niece, Stella. All of them watch as Penny kneels on the plush rug in the center of the room, hugging the heck out of Tobias.

Her smile is amazing. Far more brilliant than anything I've encouraged.

Shit. That little fucker makes me jealous.

Her entire face is alight. From her skin to her eyes. Even those lips.

"Long time no see." Hunt comes up beside me, nudging my shoulder with his. "Was she okay after we left last night?"

Torian walks past, snickering, his smirk enough of an answer before he continues to the sofa.

"She was fine," I grate. "*Everything* was fine."

"Everything *except* my car," Hunt clarifies. "But just so you know, Decker ambushed me earlier. He wanted to know why Penny ran yesterday."

I face him, trying to read his expression. "And?"

"And you owe me. I told him I must've made her feel uncomfortable, so she took off. He's buying it for now."

The goodwill doesn't make a lick of sense. Unless Sarah put him up to it. Even then, kindness isn't their style. "Thanks."

He grins. "I'm not looking for kind words, bucko. Like I said, you owe me."

"Great. That's just what I need." I turn back to the room, my glare fading as my niece catches my eye.

"Uncle Luca." Stella runs toward me, her hair bouncing around her shoulders. "I missed you."

I crouch and open my arms, hauling her into a tight hug. "Hey, sweetheart. How are you? I hear you've been looking after Tobias."

She smiles. Nods. "Uh-huh. He's fun. Really smart, too. Mom says he might be starting school with me next week."

"Is that so?" I release her to ruffle her tangled hair. "I'm not sure that's the best idea. How will your teachers handle two Torian brats in the one place?"

"I'm not a brat." She giggles. "Not all the time."

"I think your father would disagree."

"Daddy thinks I'm an angel." She plants a playful punch on my thigh and skips away.

"If that's the case," Hunt mutters, "then her dad is a fuckin' idiot. That girl is the devil."

I chuckle under my breath. He's not wrong. On both counts. "You try telling Benji that."

I return my attention to the reunion. Tobias is enthusiastic with rapid arm movements as he describes the park near Stella's house, then proceeds to recount the names and descriptions of all the friends he's made.

Penny takes it all in. She's parental affection personified. Kind eyes. Energetic nods.

"I've got so much to tell you," Toby rambles. "Oh, I almost forgot." He leans forward, whispering something in her ear.

Her surge of tension is almost unnoticeable. The stiffening of her spine is minute. But I see it. I see everything.

She glances over her shoulder to me, the brief expression of panic quickly hidden under a fake curve of lips. She leans forward, returning a secret message to the boy's ear, then pushes to her feet, rubbing his arms in affection. "Don't fret. There's nothing to worry about."

He nods, his bubbly nature returning as he stares up at her. "What about you? What have you done while you've been here? Have you seen much of Portland? Did you know I'm going to school next week?" He jolts, as if hit with another truckload of questions. "What about the others? Why aren't they here? I want to show Chloe a picture I drew."

She doesn't flinch. Doesn't even falter. Not until she opens her mouth. "They're um…"

"Hey kiddos…" Stella's mom, Layla, interrupts. "Why don't the two of you pick where you want to sleep before the adults steal the best rooms?"

"That's a great idea." Keira waves them toward the hall. "I'll help."

"*Yes*." Stella dashes around her aunt. "Toby, I'll race you."

"No fair. You got a head start." Tobias runs from Penny's side without a backward glance, the two little brats leaving in a whirlwind of excitement.

"I'll keep them occupied as long as I can." Keira gives Penny a sad smile and continues for the hall. "But you might want to come up with a plan. He's been asking about the other women for days now."

Penny hitches her chin at the news.

I want to go to her. To pick her up and make all the shit fade away. And I would… if her brother wasn't in the kitchen watching her like a hawk. Watching *me*, too.

Despite Hunt covering my tracks, I swear Decker is waiting for the opportunity to hang me from the closest shower railing.

"Does Tobias need to be told?" Sarah asks. "Don't you think it's best to keep them in the dark? At least for now?"

"We can talk about it later." Torian stalks to the fridge. "Help yourself to whatever food or drinks you need. It's time to have a meeting while the kids are occupied."

There are nods of agreement, shuffles of feet, food grabbed, and coffee made.

Penny remains in the center of the room, those arms wrapped tight around her middle, desperately trying to self-soothe when I could do a far better job. I can't stand idle anymore. I can't watch her struggle.

I start toward her, seeing her brother take notice from the corner of my eye.

He watches, unmoving as I go to her, stopping a foot away to offer wordless comfort.

Her plea for support is equally silent, the furrow of her brow deepening, her nose scrunching.

"What do you need?" I keep my voice low, almost unheard.

She cringes and bows her head. "You... I just need you."

I don't hesitate.

Fuck her brother.

Fuck what's right.

I step into her, pulling her into my arms, hugging her close to my chest. She doesn't return the embrace—merely stands there. Broken. Battered. Her cheek nestling into my neck.

"I fucking knew it," Decker snarls. "You son of a bitch."

I shoot him a warning glare as Penny remains defeated in my arms.

He's furious, his narrowed eyes promising retribution as he sneers, "Is everyone else watching this shit?" He swings around to take in Hunt and Sarah's lack of reaction.

"I'm seeing it." Sarah takes a bite from an apple, a mug of coffee in her other hand. "I just don't give a shit. Luca's been helping—"

"Get your fucking hands off her." Decker skirts the kitchen counter, coming toward us. "Do it before I do it for you."

"Take a walk, Deck." Hunter strolls forward, blocking his path.

"I'm not walking anywhere."

"Like fuck you aren't," Torian demands. "Walk now or you'll be on your own until you cool down."

Decker curls his hands into fists, his face turning red. "That shit better be platonic," he seethes. "Otherwise you're dead."

"Walk," Torian growls.

"Fuck you." Decker storms from the room, spewing a mouthful of colorful language. The verbal barrage doesn't stop for long moments, the creative threats making Hunt chuckle.

"Has he been watching too much TV?" he asks. "He's overly dramatic."

Torian moves to the fridge and pulls the door wide. "Just wait until he finds out they're sleeping together. You're going to want popcorn for that show."

"Ignore them," I whisper in Penny's ear. "This is how they get their kicks."

A door slams in the distance and laughter murmurs through the room.

They all think this is a joke—Pen's situation, Decker's outrage. Maybe I would too if I was on the other side of the fence. But each quip hits her harder. I feel it in the tension coiling through her.

Hunter glances over his shoulder to us. "If this is the way he reacts to you guys hugging, you might want to rest with one eye open. My man might slit your throat in your sleep."

"We're not fucking," I snap. "Y'all are as bad as he is."

"Those scratches don't lie, buddy. Just wait until he notices them. He's going to snap your spine like a twig."

Penny stiffens, her arms finally weaving around my waist in a protective hug.

"They're just having fun," I whisper. "Don't worry about it."

"Yeah, Pen, don't worry." Sarah chuckles through the placation. "We'll protect Luca. We won't let him get too much of a beating."

Vibrations echo from under my feet, the muted *pop, pop, pops* carrying in perfect rhythm.

"What's that noise?" Penny looks up at me in concern.

"There's a shooting range in the basement. Your brother is letting off steam."

"Or perfecting his aim." Hunt grabs a cookie from the jar on the

178

kitchen counter, shoving it into his mouth to chew with an exaggerated smile. "My guess is the latter."

"That's real funny, asshole." I rub Penny's back, trying to loosen her rigidity. "Seriously, don't worry about your brother. I'll speak to him after he cools down."

Keira reenters the room. "Guys, I don't know how much time we have. Layla will keep the kids occupied as long as she can. But who knows how long the nanny will take to get here on short notice?"

"Okay. Everyone, hurry up." Torian leads the way to the hall at the other end of the living area. "My office. Now."

I give Pen a final squeeze, then step back. "You've gotta be hungry; you didn't eat breakfast." I grab her hand and lead her to the kitchen. "Food? Coffee? Both?"

"A piece of fruit will be enough. My stomach isn't playing nice."

I grab an apple and raise a brow in question.

She nods. "Thanks."

I lob the Granny Smith at her and pour myself a mug of caffeine. Sarah and Hunt help themselves to the fridge. Within minutes we're all in Torian's office, Keira sitting in the middle of an elegant sofa, Sarah and Hunt leaned against opposite armrests, while Penny and I remain standing, side by side.

"So, what's this about one of Luther's men being here in Portland?" Hunt asks. "I thought we took out those fuckers in Greece."

"I thought we did, too." Torian takes a seat behind the large wooden desk, and turns his Mac screen to face us. "Penny, on the other hand, thinks this is Robert. One of my father's nearest and dearest."

The bank ATM image is on display, the poor picture quality magnified with the larger size.

"Looks like a big blur to me." Sarah leans forward, squinting. "How can you be sure?"

"I'm not." Torian swings the screen back to face him. "We're playing it safe. But whoever it is stole from us."

"It's Robert," Penny murmurs. "There's no question."

Everyone looks at her, their expressions differing from mild skepticism to Hunt, who rolls his eyes with blatant disregard.

"How do you want us to go about finding this asshole?" I ask. "It's in our best interests to keep this shit quiet and smoke him out as soon as possible."

Torian nods. "It needs to be fast and unnoticed. So far there have been no whispers about him being in town, which means it's either not him, or he hasn't made his presence known to any of my father's men."

"It's him," Penny repeats. "I swear to God, it's him."

"It's okay." I take a mouthful of coffee and close in behind her, rubbing my free hand along her arm. "Why don't you go spend some time with Tobias while we figure this out?"

"So you can question my sanity without me here?" She swings around to face me, her eyes pleading. "You still don't believe me. You think I'm crazy."

"I believe you." It's the truth. "I trust your judgment."

"Nobody thinks you're crazy," Sarah adds. "We just need to be sure of what we're up against."

"Speak for yourself," Hunt mutters. "She stole my car. If that doesn't scream batshit I don't know what does."

I glare at him. "I'm done with the jokes. If Robert's here, we all need to watch our backs."

"He *is* here." Penny faces Torian. "And my sisters need to be taken care of, too. Who's looking out for them?"

"Benji should already be on his way back. Once he arrives, I'll get him to arrange security."

"He's coming here?" I disguise my annoyance with another mouthful of coffee. "Does that mean all the women are with their families? Why the hell haven't I been updated on this?"

"He's taking the last one home today."

"I can get started on the security arrangements," Keira offers. "That way the other women will be taken care of sooner than later."

Torian shakes his head. "It can wait. We've got more important things to focus on."

"More important things?" Penny seethes. "More important than their lives?"

I dump my mug on a nearby bookshelf and return to my position behind her, placing both hands on her waist. "That's not what he meant."

"Then what did he mean?" She shrugs away from my touch.

"Penny," I warn.

She can't make waves in here.

At my home it's different. She can rail on me all she likes without consequence. But here, Torian will use her anger against her. He'll make her regret the outburst.

"No, let her speak." He leans back in his chair. "If she wants to criticize how I've saved her and her friends, by all means, let her continue."

She doesn't reply. Not immediately. She stands tall against his taunt, the tension seeping from her tight shoulders. "I'm sorry if I seem ungrateful." She enunciates the words slowly. "I have nothing but appreciation for what you've done."

She pauses, the silence growing uncomfortable.

"But?" he drawls.

"But one of my sisters was murdered moments after leaving Benji's care. And it's now clear Robert took her life. So I'm struggling to comprehend why a man of your means wouldn't rush to provide the necessary security to stop the bloodshed happening again."

He narrows his eyes on mine. "Who was murdered?"

"Abi." Penny steps forward, demanding his attention. "I don't care what was reported. She never would've killed herself. It had to be Robert. Or someone working with him."

Sharp glances dart through the room. Sarah to Hunter. Keira to her brother. All of them returning to Penny, silently questioning her theory.

"Abi didn't kill herself?" Torian repeats. "She was murdered?"

"Yes." Penny nods. "Without a doubt."

"And Robert is responsible?" There's an edge to his tone, an aggressive, barely leashed skepticism.

She keeps nodding. "He has to be."

"Right… So let me get this straight, because I'm starting to see a pattern." He pushes to his feet and rounds the desk to lean his ass against the front edge. "The police and news outlets reported Abi's death as a suicide. But you claim otherwise because…?"

"Because I know her."

"Of course." He inclines his head and crosses his arms over his chest. "And even though Luca and I assured you Robert is dead,

181

you also think that's a lie due to a grainy, undistinguishable image?"

"Don't be an ass," I snarl. "Give her the benefit of the doubt."

"I need to get the facts straight. Here I was thinking I was dealing with a one-off situation where she truly believed Robert was alive. But this is just panic gone wild, isn't it?"

"*No.*" Penny balks. "It's not. That photo is Robert. I know it is."

"And Abi was murdered, despite the police having labeled it an open-and-shut case?"

"Cole, stop messing with her," Keira pleads. "Let it go."

"Unfortunately, I can't. Because now she's got me thinking." He pushes from the desk, slowly stalking toward her. "Do you know how many people were aware of her location? How many were trusted with the knowledge of her return?"

She keeps her shoulders rigid, not backing down. "I don't know."

"One," he growls. "I kept everything under wraps for this exact reason. Nobody was updated on where her parents lived. Nobody knew what town or suburb. Not even me. There was only one person who knew those whereabouts. Only one person who could be held responsible for what happened if what you're claiming is true."

Shit.

That one person is Benji.

"Back off." I move in front of Penny, blocking her from the man now livid from her accusations. "She's still mourning the loss. It's only natural to question what happened."

"What she's questioning is my family. *Your* brother."

"She didn't kill herself." Penny raises her voice. "I *know* she didn't."

Fuck.

I turn to face her. "You need to stop. This isn't the time or place, okay?"

"Then when?" she pleads. "When's the time and place for me to get answers? When can I be heard?" Mindlessness enters her tone and her eyes. "You don't even believe me. I can see it on your face."

She's losing her shit.

Derailing.

"Get out of here." I jerk my head toward the hall. "Go take a warm shower. Calm down. Breathe."

"I'm not leaving." She stands her ground. "Not until I have answers."

And those answers will only come from scrutinizing my brother. By throwing him under the fucking bus.

"Penny, I understand what you're going through, but you've gotta chill the fuck out." I lightly grab the crook of her arm and start for the door. "Come on, I'll run you a bath."

"No."

I tighten my grip as she attempts to break my hold.

"Please, Luca."

I ignore her pleas as I tug her across the room. I'm almost prepared to haul her over my shoulder when I reach the threshold to the sound of thunderous footfalls barreling down the hall.

Decker greets us on the other side of the doorway.

He takes one look at me, his sister, then my grip on her arm and turns livid. "Get your fucking hands off her."

He doesn't wait for my compliance. He launches. Fist first.

20

PENNY

Luca releases my arm, ducks, but doesn't miss the impact. My brother's fist pounds into the side of his face, the crack of flesh on flesh sickening.

He's knocked sideways, his head hitting the wall with a heavy thwack.

He falls to the tile at the same time the apple rolls from my numb hand. I'm too stunned to move. The office erupts. Hunter and Sarah barrel past me. Keira curses.

I don't know what to do.

Luca is on the floor, glaring at my brother, and I'm unsure whose side I should be on.

"What the absolute fuck, Decker?" Hunter shoves Sebastian down the hall, out of view.

"Why the hell did you do that?" Sarah yells.

I remain silent. Keira does the same behind me, her wordless judgment scratching at the back of my neck.

"This is just one of the many reasons people don't run their mouth around here." Cole's tone is glib. "Making false statements only leads to trouble."

I glance over my shoulder, meeting his soulless eyes.

"Opinions have no place here. Only facts." He returns to his desk chair, seeming unfazed by Luca on the floor or the snarled aggression coming from Sebastian. "It's in your best interest to remember that."

He doesn't scare me. He's nothing in comparison to his father. What concerns me is his connection to Luca. They're family. Just like Benji, who I'm beginning to believe is a far more sinister man.

I drag myself to the hall, ignoring the underlying threat as Hunter shoves my brother again, over and over, pushing him farther away.

"Are you okay?" Sarah holds out a hand to Luca, his cheek dark pink and swelling, blood dripping from his nose.

"Fucking perfect." He ignores her offering and shoves to his feet, using the wall as leverage.

He doesn't look at me. Doesn't even acknowledge my existence as he leans against the plaster to massage his temples.

"How much does it hurt?" I reach for him, not sure what else to do, my fingers grazing his shoulder. I've seen that look on his face before—when he had a concussion, and migraines for days.

"It's nothing." He scoffs. "That asshole can't punch for shit."

My remorse builds, morphing and expanding, as his expression tightens with obvious agony.

I want to help him. To fix what I caused. But I also can't bring myself to apologize for attempting to clear up the misconceptions surrounding Abi's death. They need to know.

Everyone needs to know.

She deserves the truth.

"That punch is only a taste of what I'm going to do to you," Sebastian yells. "You're a fucking piece of shit, Luca."

"Shut your trap." Hunt pushes him again. "The shit you just pulled was a low blow."

"The shit *he's* pulling with my sister is lower. I can't believe you all stood there and watched him manhandle her."

Hunter gives a harder shove, pushing my brother into the living room. The barrage of abuse doesn't end once they're out of view. Sebastian keeps yelling. Keeps threatening.

The only thing that changes is the awkwardness settling around me. I stand before Sarah, her judgmental gaze fixed on me as Luca works his jaw from side to side.

"Can I get you anything?" I ask. "Ice maybe?"

"I'll get some Advil." Sarah turns on her heel and strides after her fiancé.

The air around me thickens. The weight of obligation to my

sisters wages war with my remorse. These people don't understand me.

They don't see things the way I do.

They'll never realize the intuition that comes from living around evil men and constant tragedy. Either that, or they simply don't care about Abi. They don't want to hear about her at all.

"You can stop staring at me. I'm fine." Luca pushes from the wall and staggers toward our bedroom.

I follow like a chastised puppy, walking a few steps behind until I pass the threshold where he stands in wait.

He closes the door behind us, the sound of the clasping lock a definitive, isolating click.

"Is that necessary?" I whisper.

"You didn't have to follow me in here." He continues to the bed, his feet dragging as he turns to sit on the mattress.

"I'm sorry he hit you."

"I don't give a shit about that," he mutters under his breath. "What I want to understand is why you're throwing my brother under the bus."

"That's not what I'm doing. I only wanted everyone to know Abi didn't kill herself. I want someone else to care; is that too much to ask?"

"What have I ever done to give you the impression I don't fucking care?" he asks. "I care, Penny. About you. About Abi. About Tobias and your whole fucking posse. But there's a way to have your voice heard and this isn't it."

The disappointment in his eyes is a staggering punishment. I hate it so much.

"I won't apologize for what I said, Luc. I have all the evidence I need."

His gaze narrows. "So you're telling me you think my brother is responsible? You think Benji played a part?"

My throat tightens. "I don't know."

"Are you serious?" He jerks back. "You're trying to pin Abi's death on my brother?"

"No, I'm pinning it on *Robert*. I didn't consider anything about your brother until Cole brought him up."

"And still you continued with the accusations. You realize

speculation like this can get Benji killed, right? The mere possibility of betrayal could be enough for Torian to end his life."

I close my mouth. Swallow.

"Answer me." He keeps his voice low. "Explain what the hell is going on in that mind of yours."

"I don't know." I shake my head.

There's too much noise. Too many voices. Some of them tell me I'm right—Abi didn't kill herself. Robert is responsible. Others suffocate me, laying blame at my feet, telling me I'm wrong, wrong, wrong. "I can't explain how I feel. All I know is that I'm certain Robert killed her."

There's more. So much more, but I don't know how to tell him.

"You don't get it. If Robert killed her, it means Benji is involved. Or he fucked up." He shoves his hands into his hair. "You heard Torian. Nobody else knew where she was. Not one single person had any idea where those women were."

"It's not his fault if Robert followed them."

"From where? The airport? After they were hurried onto a private jet from Greece?" He shakes his head and winces with the movement. "You think Luther preempted his own death, arranged for a jet, and had Robert waiting here in Portland?"

"Maybe Abi called someone. She could've told anyone she was going home."

"Benji wouldn't have risked it. There's no way he would've let that information get out."

"Then I don't know." I throw my arms up at my sides. "Maybe someone found them. Maybe some random person suspected something when they went for food, or gas, or whatever. Maybe Luther had a database of all the women he stole."

I'm clutching at straws. Scrambling.

Luca grins, the tweak of lips unkind. "You think Luther had a database? You seriously think he documented his crimes for someone to find?"

"No," I admit. "He was too paranoid, but—"

"*You're* too paranoid," he counters. "You're losing your shit, Pen. You need to pull yourself together."

"And you're complacent and dismissive. There are things you don't know, Luca. Things I haven't told you."

His eyes narrow. "What things?"

I don't want to say. Not now. Not after his heartfelt admission earlier.

"Penny?" He shoves from the bed. "What things?"

I lick my lips to ease the painful dryness. "I don't want to cause more trouble between us." I need to keep this to myself. Even Tobias knew not to announce his suspicions until he whispered them in my ear.

"There's no trouble between us, shorty. That's not what this is."

"Then what is it?"

"A learning curve." He eats up the distance between us, the tight pull of his brows announcing the pain continuing to pummel him. "No matter what happens, I'm still protecting you with my life. Nothing changes that. There's not one damn thing you could tell me to cause trouble."

"I could test that theory." I could... but I don't want to.

"Let me prove myself to you."

I shake my head, unable to voice my deeper suspicions.

"Come on, Pen. You know you can trust me."

I stare at him. At the conviction. The plea for understanding.

The problem is, I believe him. I believe everything he says yet he can't give me the same in return. "I recognize his voice, Luc."

"Whose?" He scrutinizes me.

My heart thunders, each beat rampant. "Benji's." I swallow again, unable to get enough moisture as Luca frowns at me. "I heard him on the phone the day Abi died. At first, I thought he sounded familiar because his tone is a lot like yours. But that's not it. I didn't realize until Tobias said something that his voice was familiar because I'd heard him speaking to Luther."

"What did Tobias say?"

"That the voice of Layla's husband sounded like one of the men his baba spoke to all the time. That he hadn't met your brother yet, but was worried he was a bad man."

He stiffens, his shoulders snapping rigid. "What conversations did you hear? What was discussed?"

"I can't remember." I wrap my arms around my waist. "Tobias didn't say, either. And I admit, I didn't sense a bad vibe when I first heard him in Portland, but now things are getting messed up and I don't know what to think."

Incrementally, his tension lessens. The rigidity fades as he cups my cheeks. "Do you hear what you're saying? You have no basis for these accusations. Your head is filled with stress from trauma."

I pull away. "No. That's not it."

His arms fall to his sides. "*Yes*, it is. Of course they spoke on the phone. Luther was his father-in-law. They were family. Benji is the parent to that asshole's only granddaughter. It's only natural you and Toby recognize his voice."

My breathing falters. "I knew that."

I knew, yet it slipped my mind. I knew, and still it didn't make me back away from speculation.

"You're grasping at straws, shorty. And the worst part is that you don't realize the trouble rumors like this can cause."

"No." I'm not being irrational. This can't be paranoia. "I never heard Luther talking to Layla or Keira. Only Benji."

"Luther was a man's man. He had little time for the females in his family. Ask Torian's sisters and they'll tell you the same thing. Their father never cared to speak to them."

I continue to shake my head. "That might explain the voice recognition, but it doesn't change Abi's death."

Luca gives a sad smile. A placating, condescending curve of lips. "I get that you don't want to believe she killed herself, even despite what she went through. But accusing people without plausible reason will only cause more bloodshed. I need you to trust me. I need you to understand that just like you know your sisters, I know my brother better than I know myself. He wouldn't be involved in this. Not after what we lived through growing up. You have to start telling yourself Abi's death was an accident."

"No."

"Someone has to be wrong, Pen. It's either me, Abi's parents, the police, and the medics. Or you, on your own, without proof."

The approach of footsteps carries from the hall and Luca turns away, knitting his hands behind his head as a light tap sounds against the wood.

"I've got the Advil," Sarah says. "Want me to leave it at the door?"

"Yeah." Luca begins to pace. "Thanks."

There's the rattle of a pill bottle, retreating footsteps, then silence.

Pained, punishing silence.

I don't like us being on different wavelengths. I hate the emotional distance resembling a chasm between us.

"I know you think I'm crazy." I clear the restriction from my throat. "Believe me, I'm sure I'd think the same if we switched places. But I can't change the way I feel. It's an instinct I refuse to ignore."

He sucks in a breath, letting it out slowly. "Then I'll talk to him. I'll get the answers you need to put your mind to rest." His hands fall to his sides. "But in return, I need you to promise you won't blurt shit out in front of Torian again. Words aren't just words here. They're ammunition. Next time you've got something eating at you, I need you to tell me privately, okay? Nobody else."

"Okay." I grab his hand and entwine our fingers, yearning for the warm connection that comes when we touch. Even though he's annoyed with me, the strength I gain from his presence is unmistakable. He's like a shot of stability. "I'm sorry, Luc."

"Don't be." His thumb rubs in circles around my palm. "I just have to know these things. I can't fix what I don't know."

More footsteps trek down the hall.

Another knock sounds.

"Time's up, fuckers." Hunter's voice carries from the other side of the door. "Big brother is about to go postal if you two don't show your faces."

"We'll be out in a minute." Luca slowly tugs me forward, making me stumble into him. Within a bated breath his lips are on mine, the exquisite softness feeling like an apology.

"It's best if you don't come with me," he murmurs against my mouth. "Spend the time with Toby. Try to relax."

I attempt to retreat, hurt by the exclusion.

"Don't pull away from me." He tightens his grip on my hand. "Let me fight this battle for you."

"There's more than one."

"I can handle them." He growls, oh, so protective and dominant. It's hard not to believe him. "I know exactly what you want."

"I bet you don't." I tangle my hands in his shirt.

What I want is more of this. The clear-headedness that only

comes when we're body to body. Chest to chest. Everything else fades when he's close. The guilt. The pain. The sorrow. He wouldn't have a clue of my desperation for more.

He chuckles. "Believe me. I know exactly what you want, and it's fucking hard to walk away."

He deepens the kiss, the vibrating rumble in his chest sinking into me.

I cling to him. His fingers. His shirt.

When we're like this the rest of the world doesn't matter.

There's no looming threat. No potential danger.

There's only me and him. Only protection and safety.

"We'll finish this another day." He diverts his mouth to my jaw. My neck.

I whimper as his lips brush the sensitive column of my throat. So soft. So sweet.

Then all too soon, he steps back.

That expression of pain still wrinkles his forehead. The swelling on his cheek has darkened.

I sweep my fingers along the damage and hold his gaze to gauge his reaction. "Does your head hurt as much as it did in Greece?"

"It's just a headache. I'll get over it."

"Would you tell me if it was more?"

He smirks. "Would you overreact and panic?"

Probably.

Definitely.

He scoffs out another chuckle. "I promise I'll tell you if there's something to worry about."

I nod, inching in to steal one last kiss. One last taste of clarity. I don't want to let him go. I need a few more strengthening seconds.

"It's okay, shorty. I'm not going far. You call and I'll come running."

"I'll call and you'll come stumbling."

"Either way, I'll still be there." He sweeps his mouth over mine. Once. Twice. "I'll find Robert and figure out what happened with Abi."

The reminder siphons my warmth. "And what if your brother—"

"Forget my brother." This time there's a warning in his tone. "Nothing is going to come between us. Not while I'm still breathing."

He makes for the door, each step of distance filling me with isolation. The loneliness only increases when he walks from view. There's the rattle of a pill bottle, muttered conversation in the distance, then the click of a closing door from another room.

I'm left an outsider, forced to follow on silent footsteps to stop outside the now closed office as the meeting continues without me.

I rest against the wall and listen to my brother bark threats at Luca. One argument follows the next, strategy seeming to come in second place to the aggression born from my existence.

Luca fights for me. For my sisters. He makes demands about their protection, offers to pay for their security, and finally convinces Cole to contact Benji after the meeting to obtain Nina and Lilly's whereabouts.

It doesn't seem enough though.

Nothing does.

I want them here. Yet, that will never happen.

They've only kept me around because of Sebastian. I have a plausible reason for being in Portland, while my sisters are loose threads to tie Cole to his father's crimes.

But I could prepare them. Warn them.

My pulse increases at the thought of reaching out. Then my confidence waivers.

I'd destroy any sense of happiness they had with the news. I'd steal their optimism for the future all because of an instinct. A hunch.

I slide to the floor, my legs bent before me, my elbows resting on my knees.

Do I have the right to ruin their freedom without proof? Because what if Luca is right? What if my thoughts are paranoia? If I'm losing my mind, I'll take Lilly and Nina down with me.

Padded footsteps from the living area break my focus. I glance to my side and see Layla approach.

"Hi," she whispers.

"Hi." Apprehension skitters along my arms. I know this lady least of all and yet she's been the one looking after Tobias. "Am I breaking the rules by being here?"

"Not at all. Have they said anything interesting?" She moves closer to the office, cocking her head.

"I'm not really listening..." I lie. "I just didn't want to stay in the bedroom and wasn't sure where else to go."

"That's okay." She smiles, kind and genuine. "If Cole was concerned about you snooping, I'd know about it. He also wouldn't hold a meeting in a place where you could overhear. So don't worry, because I'm not." She holds out a hand for me to shake. "I'm Layla, by the way. Stella's mom."

I glance at the offering, unsure if I can take her hand. We both know she's not just Stella's mom.

"Yes, I'm also Cole's sister and Luther's eldest daughter." Her arm falls to her side. "I'm sorry for everything you've been through."

I cringe and rest my head back against the wall, still unsure how to take apologies when they come from the blood of my tormentor. "You're also Benji's wife—am I right?"

She nods. "And Luca's sister-in-law. I wear many hats."

I drag my attention to the office door, wishing Luc was here with me. I could do with some of his strengthening stability. "I haven't met your husband yet. Is he anything like his brother?"

I'm fishing, hoping to catch a trail that leads to confirmation of my suspicions. One clue to wipe away my insanity would be enough.

"He's a good man. And an even better father." She leans against the plaster beside me, looming close. "I can't count how many times he's put his life on the line for me and my family."

I wince. This isn't the information I want.

"I miss him," she continues. "Even more now that the stakes are rising. But he always has to be in the thick of everything, trying to save the world."

"He sounds a lot like Luc." I lower my head, hiding my remorse. She's making me question myself even more.

"He is. But don't get me wrong—he has his days."

"What does that mean?" I shoot her a glance.

"He's great, but in the end he's still a man." She shrugs. "Sometimes he leaves the toilet seat up or doesn't listen to a word I say. Or he'll tell Stella she can have ice cream when I've already told her she can't. Nobody is perfect. What's important is that

193

we're good together, which says a lot when we're usually in each other's pockets, at home and with the family business."

"The family business… I haven't been told what that involves exactly."

She falls quiet, the seconds stretching until she releases a sigh. "It's complicated. I want you to know it's nothing like what my father was doing, though, if that's what you're asking."

I feign indifference. "No, it wasn't. I was only curious. Luca hasn't said much about his brother. He hasn't heard from him either. I think he's worried."

"Nobody has heard much from Benji lately. Not even me. Apart from being in and out of phone range, he's needed space." She crosses the hall to look at me head-on. "He hasn't told me as much, but I think he holds himself responsible for what happened to you and the other women. He feels guilty for not figuring out what my father was up to. I do, too."

I wince with renewed remorse. Her husband sounds honorable, despite how relative that term can be in this world. If only I could quit questioning Abi's death. "I'm sure it's a heavy burden to bear."

"Sorry." She cringes. "I don't mean to be insensitive if that's how it came across."

"Not at all." I offer a half-hearted smile. "I appreciate you trying to make conversation."

"I've been trying to figure out how to approach you for hours." She lets out a whisper of a chuckle. "This situation isn't easy."

I nod, no longer capable of words. Every kindness she utters makes me question my theory about Abi's suicide. I don't want to lose faith in my sister. I refuse. The Torian family are still my enemy.

"Why don't you come cook with me and the kids?" Layla waves for me to get up. "I've been left in charge of making lunch, and it may not be edible if I don't get an extra set of hands to keep Stella and Tobias under control. I still have no idea when the nanny will show up."

My heart stutters. Not only at the kind offer, but the carefree image of Toby she inspires. I want to see that side of him again. I yearn to be involved. "You wouldn't mind?"

"Not at all. It will give me an opportunity to get to know you."

Yes. And it will give me the ability to shed my weakness and dig deeper on her husband.

21

LUCA

I'm relegated to a private room at the back of the house with my MacBook, given a burner phone, and told to substantiate Penny's claims.

It's my job to prove Robert is alive.

I'm also left to establish whether Abi's death was murder or suicide, and I don't know which conclusion is preferred when I can't get hold of my fucking brother.

Penny has gotten into my head. Those instinctive feelings of hers are wearing me down. She's making me question everything —Robert's execution, the protection I've provided, and worst of all, Benji.

I haven't doubted him before.

His sanity, maybe. His loyalty? Never.

I can't quit scrutinizing Robert's actions as I scour hours of video surveillance. I fast forward and rewind unending vision from the gas station, trying to get a better view of the man who stole the money. Or his fucking car. I watch different angles of the same timespan over and over, attempting to catch a glimpse of familiarity until my headache builds into a migraine. And still, all I think about is my brother.

Something isn't right. Benji isn't usually distant. He keeps me updated to the point of annoyance. Yet today, alone, he's already left ten of my calls unanswered and hasn't responded to a single text.

He's gotta be in trouble. *Big* trouble. And I'm having a fucking painful time digesting the possibilities.

It isn't until mid-afternoon that I'm disturbed from the isolated hell of my thoughts by a light rap on the door. But the prospect of company isn't welcomed. For the first time in weeks, I'm not excited at the possibility of seeing Penny. Not when I don't have answers.

"Come in." I remain on the spare bed, my back against the headboard, the Mac on my thighs.

There's a rattle of cutlery, then the door creeps open.

It's not Penny who stands on the other side. It's Tobias, his tiny frame leaning over to lift a wooden tray of food off the floor, his shoulders taut as he marches inside.

"Do you need help, little man?" I slide my Mac to the mattress.

"No. I can do this." He keeps his gaze firmly affixed to the rattling glass of juice and the plate of sandwiches, his footsteps cautious until he reaches the bed to dump it at my feet. "It's a late lunch."

"I can see that." I smirk. "Thanks. Did you make it yourself?"

"I helped." He steps back, crossing his kiddie arms over his tiny chest. "Layla did most of it."

"Well, thank her for me, okay?"

He keeps his gaze downcast. "Yeah… okay."

This isn't the running, giggling kid from this morning. The boy standing in front of me is defensive, with his shoulders pulled back and his brows pinched.

"Is everything all right, Toby?"

His gaze snaps to mine, his eyes set in an exaggerated glare. "Everything's fine."

"You sure? You seem agitated."

He huffs. "I'm just fine."

I raise my brows and incline my head. "Okay. How about the others? Are they all fine, too?"

His lip curls.

This kid, who's apparently fine, looks like a fight dog about to attack.

"They're fine, too," he grates.

Yeah. Right.

"How 'bout you?" He glares at the swollen side of my face, despising my injury. "Are you *fine*?"

"I got sucker punched."

He puffs out his chest, as if pleased. "I know."

"Decker and I got into a bit of an argument."

"I know that, too."

"You saw?"

"No, I *heard*. Decker punched you because you were hurting Penny."

I push from the bed and the kid scampers backward, his arms falling to his sides, his aggressive expression transforming to fear.

I raise my hands in peace. "Calm down, little guy. I would never hurt you. Or her."

"You already did. That's why Decker hit you." He stands taller, his face filled with defiance as fear enters his eyes. "You're just like my father."

"*No*. I'm not. I'm nothing like that piece of shit."

"You lie," he snarls. "You brought her somewhere she doesn't want to be to make her do things she doesn't want to do. Just like him."

I jerk back, blindsided. Is that what he thinks happened? Is that his justification for us being here? "That's not what this is, Toby. This isn't like Greece."

"It's *exactly* like Greece. She's scared and you hurt her. She doesn't want to be here and you're forcing her."

"It's not like that." I keep my hands raised. "I'm trying to protect her. She's here so we can keep her safe."

"Safe from what? I thought we were here for family time."

Fuck. He's got me there.

"Luca?" He tilts his chin as if victorious. "They told me we were here so I could get to know everyone." His words drip with saccharin sarcasm.

He knows.

He probably always knew.

I shouldn't have expected anything less from the son of a sex trafficker.

I sit back on the bed and exhale a heavy breath. "What do you want to know, little man?"

He stares at me, his head still high. He takes his time, giving himself long moments to ponder whatever is going on in that brain of his before he asks, "Why did you hurt her?"

I guess I should be thankful that through all this—after the death of his father and being dragged from his home—his top priority is Penny.

"She was getting in trouble with Torian. I needed to get her out of his office before he snapped."

"Cole wouldn't hurt her."

"You're right; he wouldn't," I lie. "But he was angry, and sometimes when people are angry they say mean things they can't take back. All I wanted to do was get her out of there. So I grabbed her arm to lead her from the room. And yes, I know I shouldn't have touched her, but I thought I was doing the right thing."

He frowns. "You grabbed her arm?"

"Yeah."

The frown deepens. "Then Decker hit you?"

I nod, the movement throwing lighter fluid on the smoldering flames of my headache. "He doesn't like me very much right now."

"Because you grabbed her arm?"

"That, and other things. Mainly because he's worried about Penny, and I'm the perfect outlet for his concern."

He falls quiet again, his gaze fixed on me for long moments. "Why are we really here? In this house?"

It's my turn to take a mental breather. Kids aren't my thing. "Why do you think we're here?" I act like a fucking shrink, buying myself time.

"I know it's because something is wrong. Stella said she never stays at her uncle's house unless bad things are happening."

Great. Two snooping kids. Just what I need.

"That's something you should ask Cole. I've given out my quota of information."

"No. Please." His annoyance vanishes, a pity party taking its place. Big blue eyes blink up at me, begging. "Is it about Robert?"

I fight not to flinch at his direct hit. Where the hell is this kid getting information from? He's a miniature fucking spy master. "Why would you ask about him? What do you know?"

He doesn't answer—just keeps blinking those puppy-dog eyes.

"Tobias? What the hell do you know?"

He shakes his head. "Nothing. I just heard…"

"You seem to hear a lot."

He straightens. "Baba taught me how to listen."

"He taught you how to snoop," I correct, and he nods. "Tell me what you heard."

"It's nothing, I swear. His name has been mentioned a few times. That's all. I guessed he's the reason we're here… I'm right, aren't I?"

I contemplate my options. This kid could be useful. He could also be a huge pain in the ass if he rats on me. "I don't know." The paper copy of the bank surveillance image burns a hole in my pocket. If anyone could confirm the man in the photo is Robert, it's Toby, but I don't want to get my brains blown out for involving a minor.

"Yeah, you do," he snaps. "You know. You just don't want to tell me."

"Because you don't need to worry about things like this. We're taking care of it."

"*Tell me.*" He turns savage. Fisted hands. Red face. A true fucking Torian. "Is Robert here? Has he come back for her?"

I attempt to ignore the icy chill shuddering through me, but it hits hard. The assumption that Robert would be back for Penny… The instinctive response…

"We don't know." I retrieve the paper from my pocket and unfold the image for him to see. "Do you know who this is?"

Recognition sparks in his eyes.

"Who is it, Tobias?"

"It's him." He stares, transfixed or maybe frightened. "It's Robert. He grows his beard like that sometimes." He points to the blurred mouth of the man in the photo. "See the patch of missing hair right below his lip? It's from a scar. It always made him look stupid."

I don't know whether to be relieved or livid at the confirmation that the fucker is here. On one hand, I'll have the opportunity to kill him like he deserves. On the other, the news will only spike Penny's fear.

"Thanks. I appreciate the help." I refold the paper and shove it back into my pocket. "Can you do me a favor and keep this between me and you for now? I don't want Pen getting upset."

"She doesn't know?"

"I don't think she's one hundred percent certain, which is allowing her to sleep at night. If she knows for sure—"

"She'll be scared," he cuts me off. "He did horrible things to her. He hurt—"

"I know." I clench my teeth against the knowledge. "And I want to save her from the fear for as long as possible. That's why I asked."

He pauses a long while as he swallows. "Will you find him?"

"Yes." I fucking vow it.

"Will you hurt him?"

This time I'm not as quick to reply. Like Luther, Robert meant something to this boy. He was raised to look up to his father's right-hand man.

"Luca, will you hurt him?"

"Yes." I keep my teeth clenched. "I'll fucking hurt him. Because of what he did to Penny and all the other women. I'll kill him for what he's done."

Heartbeats of silence follow where I question giving him more details. He doesn't move. Doesn't speak. I bet he's one breath away from squealing like a pig when he gives a succinct nod.

"I won't tell… if you don't tell on me."

I frown. "What would I tell on you for?"

His attention turns to the tray of food. "I don't think lunch is very nice today."

I follow his gaze, narrowing my attention to the tiny pieces of fluff and hair sticking out from the side of one of the sandwiches.

He backtracks. "Maybe you shouldn't eat it." He shrugs and continues his retreat to the door. "And I don't think the orange juice is any good either."

I hold in a laugh and lean forward, looking into the glass to find tiny white bubbles in the sea of orange.

The little shit corrupted my lunch and spat in my OJ. "I guess I'll hold out for dinner."

He nods and turns for the door.

"Hold up, Toby. I'm not finished with you yet."

He freezes, like a criminal caught in the act.

"Penny mentioned you recognized Benji's voice." I lean back

201

against the bedhead. Calm. Casual. "Have you been able to remember any conversations you might have overheard?"

He glances over his shoulder at me, fear clear in his eyes. "She told you?"

"She trusts me, and you can, too. I want to make sure you both feel safe here."

He swivels slowly, returning to face me. "But he's your brother."

"He is." I incline my head. "Does that worry you?"

"Baba always said a man should never turn his back on family."

Luther may have said it. Didn't mean that fucker lived by it. He continuously threw his children under the bus. "I agree with the sentiment, but that doesn't mean family don't get punished for doing the wrong thing. If you think Benji is involved in something he shouldn't be, I need to know, okay? And I need you to tell me first so I can protect everyone. You and Penny most of all."

His eyes narrow, almost imperceptibly.

Fuck. I pushed too far.

He shakes his head. "I don't remember anything."

And I don't believe him. Not when his discomfort is increasing.

"That's okay." I give a half-hearted smile. "I just want you to know I'll protect you no matter what happens. I've got your back."

He nods, but there's no belief. He's entirely untrusting.

"Okay, kiddo. You can go play. If you find Penny can you tell her I'd like to see her?"

"She's not allowed. Torian said she has to leave you to work in peace."

"Right." Now Tobias' visit makes more sense. "That sounds like something he would say. Can you give her a message for me instead?"

He nods.

"Tell her I miss her, and that I'm working as fast as I can to get back to her."

It's sappy as fuck, but it's for the kid's benefit. I'll earn his trust through Penny, no matter the cost.

He smiles, nods again, and dashes for the hall, leaving the door open to allow the mumble of distant chatter to enter the room.

I wait a while, attempting to decipher the garbled conversation as I picture Penny out there, surrounded by people she doubts. Her discomfort encourages me to get back on the phone in search of answers. My paranoia over Benji keeps me working for hours without so much as a snack break.

I reach out to people who know people, who know more people. I try to get my hands on Abi's preliminary coroner's report, along with more surveillance images from the businesses surrounding the gas station.

I dial my brother's number over and over again, leaving innumerable messages, sending additional texts.

The more he ignores me, the more my gut protests.

I'm almost convinced he's fucked up again. That he's dragging me into a mess bigger than ever before.

I thought he'd settled down after becoming a husband. A father. He made me believe this new life with a crime-riddled family had been the right decision. That these circumstances weren't the best, but at least *he* was.

I've seen it with my own eyes. I've noticed the positive change.

He rarely drinks anymore. He has a purpose.

Problem is, all the positive changes don't mean dick if he's stuck in old habits. If anything, Benji's good fortune could be more reason for him to fuck up. He doesn't know how to be happy. It's a foreign concept. Self-sabotage may be the only routine he knows.

I fucking stew on those thoughts as I work. All I get in return for my hard hours are a few snapshots of a green sedan I think Robert was in. No plates. No make or model. And then there's the vague promise that the coroner's report might come through if my contact at the hospital can pull a few strings.

I don't drag my ass from the bedroom until after sundown when my stomach can't take the lack of food any longer.

Penny's the first to see me walk into the living area. She pushes up from the sofa, relief brightening her expression as she walks up to me, her hand reaching for mine. "Any luck?"

There's a wealth of hope in her eyes. So much fucking dependence, too.

I've let her down. All I have is confirmation of Robert's existence from a kid she'd resent me for involving. "I'm still working on it. Has anyone heard news on Benji? I thought he'd be back by now."

"No." She sinks into my chest, her face nuzzling my neck as if she was born to mold against me. "Nobody has told me anything."

At least Tobias didn't spill his guts. That's a bonus.

"Luca," she whispers against my throat, "What happens if I recognize him?"

I fight against the need to tense. "Recognize him from where?"

"Greece. Or from here."

Icy dread slithers through me. She means from being a rapist. From being part of the sex-trafficking operation.

"What if he was one of the men who helped lure me away?" she asks.

My brain regains its agonizing throb. The *thump, thump, thump* of my pulse is incessant against my temples. "Is that what you've been thinking about all day?"

"Not all day." She pulls back to meet my gaze. "It's just that Layla spoke highly of him. As a father and a husband. But I can't stop questioning him. I keep thinking—what if? And then it gets worse because I start thinking I'm going to lose you, too."

"I'm not going anywhere. I love my brother, Pen. I'd do anything for him. But if he's capable of doing the things you're talking about then he's not the brother I know. He's not my blood at all."

Hollowness gnaws at me. Not because I'm lying. Because it's the God's honest truth.

I'd disown him for that betrayal.

Fucking kill him.

The other guys return to the house for dinner soon after. The mass of people scatter around the living room, some at the dining table, the kids on stools at the kitchen counter, while a young female nanny keeps watch. Hunt and Sarah are on the sofa. Penny remains by my side while Decker glares at me from his standing position in front of the sink.

That fucker wants to hit me again. Or worse. *Definitely* worse.

"Has anyone heard from Benji?" I shove a wedge of pizza in my mouth and pretend I'm not fully invested in the answer.

"Not today." Layla sips from a wine glass. "He probably didn't charge his cell again."

"He's got sketchy reception," Torian offers around a mouth full of food. "I'm sure he'll be here soon."

The two hours that pass prove him wrong.

I help clean up after dinner and watch the nanny wrangle the kids to bathe, then later, put them to bed. The whole time my patience keeps levelling up. I'm left to dig through surveillance recordings on the sofa while Hunt and Decker head out to talk to more people, and Torian retires to his office. Penny doesn't leave my side, the twitch of her fingers becoming more fidgety as she pretends to watch whatever movie plays on the big-screen TV.

"Why don't you have a shower and get some rest?" I take a break from staring at the computer screen and run my hand through her hair. "I'll wake you when he gets here."

"I wouldn't be able to sleep anyway."

She still thinks a monster is going to walk through the door in the form of my brother. The more time that passes makes me believe it, too.

One by one, Sarah, Layla, and Keira retire to bed, leaving the two of us alone in the silent house.

I keep failing to get in contact with Benji and start praying he was in a minor car accident, for his sake, because unless he's physically incapable of dialing my number, I'll break his face for not returning my calls.

It's past eleven when Torian walks back into the living room, his cell in his hand, his hair mussed as if he's dragged his hands through it a million times. "He's here." He jerks his chin toward the front of the house. "I just let him through the gate."

Penny straightens from her leaned position against my shoulder, her eyes blinking away exhaustion.

"About fucking time." I close my Mac and place it beside me on the sofa. "Where was he driving from, Mexico?"

"Ask him yourself. I already told you I don't know where he's been." Torian continues to stare at his phone as he stalks away. "But give him my regards. Some business has come up that I'm going to have to deal with. I'll be in my office if anyone needs me."

Penny pushes to her feet in a flourish, her tired face turning pale.

"It's going to be okay." I reach for her, pulling her between my legs. "You trust me, right?"

She doesn't respond. Doesn't even act as if I've spoken.

"Penny?" I shove from the sofa to stand against her, dragging my hand over her hip. "You trust me." This time it's a statement. She *does* trust me. We both know it. I just need her to remember. "Whatever happens, I'll take care of you."

Her breathing labors. Her fingers fidget at her sides. When the front door opens and footsteps approach, she turns rigid under my touch.

"Breathe," I whisper. "Just breathe."

She nods, her attention on the entry to the hall behind me.

I don't turn to watch my brother walk in. I keep my eagle eyes on her. Scrutinizing. If she knows him, I want to see it for myself. I need to catch the first sign of panic so I can react accordingly.

"Hey, Luc," Benji greets. "Long time no see."

Her stiffness doesn't dissipate. She doesn't flinch as he approaches, neither confirming nor denying her fears.

She gives me nothing to go on. No hints. No leads.

Fuck.

"Hey yourself, big brother." I give her a reassuring smile and turn to the man who's a little shorter and leaner than me, despite his older age. "I've been calling."

"No shit." He continues toward me, dumping his suitcase at my feet before grabbing me in a bear hug. "I thought you'd get the hint I wasn't in the mood to talk."

"And I thought you'd get the hint it was important. You should've answered."

"Well, I'm here now." He retreats, his attention shifting to Penny as his arms fall to his sides. "You must be the woman I've heard so much about. You're Decker's sister, right?"

"Penny." I reach for her, dragging her into my side to place a protective arm around her waist. There's still no change in her expression. No clues. "Shorty, this is my brother, Benji."

She doesn't move. Doesn't speak. The only change in her appearance is the slight raise to her chin.

I can't tell what she's thinking. Not when she's back in warrior mode. Everything is tightly bottled, her thoughts barricaded from view.

"The others told me about you," Benji continues. "You sound like quite a woman."

"Your wife told me all about you, too." Penny clears her throat, adding strength to her tone. "But I already recognized your voice."

The hairs on the back of my neck raise. Every nerve is on edge.

"I've heard you before." Her tone is level, no hint of emotion. "Many times."

Benji's brows tighten as he shoots me a look. "What's she talkin' about?"

Now *that's* an expression I can work with. He's defensive

"She overheard conversations between you and Luther while she was in Greece." I rub my thumb along her side in a vain offer of support. "Turns out you spoke to your father-in-law more often than most."

He nods. "Yeah. He was always dialing my number. What did you overhear?"

She stands taller, taking a few seconds before she says, "I don't remember specifics. Not yet, anyway."

"Lucky you." Benji huffs out a laugh. "I remember vividly. How does that saying go? You can pick your wife, but you can't choose your in-laws."

"Yeah, it's something like that." I slide my hand from Penny's waist and grab her hand instead. I need a sign to point me in the right direction when it comes to her emotions. I've got no fucking idea if I should be relaxing or preparing for war.

"Did you ever travel to Greece?" she asks.

"No." He scoffs. "*Fuck* no. I was smart enough to keep my distance. Luther only used me to keep tabs on his daughters. Apart from that, he kept contact to a minimum."

"But you two spoke a lot," she counters. "I remember—"

"You remember what?" Benji's tone thickens with warning. "Is this an interrogation? Because if it is, I'm too fucking tired to deal right now." He grabs his suitcase handle, the veins at his temples pulsing.

"It's not an interrogation." I raise a hand in placation. "Let's just chill and bench this conversation until tomorrow."

"Fuck tomorrow and fuck this conversation." He glares at me. "I don't need to put up with this shit."

"I didn't mean to sound accusatory." Penny backtracks, moving out of reach. "I just…"

There's a pause of awkward-as-fuck silence while Benji holds my gaze, his eyes remaining narrowed for long seconds before he huffs out a breath.

"Forget it. Times are tough," he mutters. "We're all dealing with shit we don't need. And by the look of the swelling on Luca's face, he's handling more than most." His shoulders loosen slightly while he clings to the suitcase. "Did you get in a fight?"

"Decker took a cheap shot."

He huffs a laugh. "What about my girls? How are they? It feels like forever since I've seen them."

"Both are good. They went to bed a while ago." I hike a thumb to the far hall. "They're down that way somewhere. I don't know which room."

"Speaking of bed…" Penny gives a fake smile. "I'll leave you two to talk in private."

"You don't need to go." I grab her wrist before she can walk away and she gasps on impact. "Are you okay?"

She chuckles. Again, it's fake. "I'm fine. You surprised me, that's all."

"You sure?" I lean in to whisper in her ear, "You're not thinking of running, are you?"

"No. I learned my lesson last time."

I keep watching her, looking for a tell as I release her wrist. "I'll follow you soon."

She inclines her head and places a kiss on my cheek. "Good night."

"Night." I keep quiet as she pads to the hall, all the while wishing I was alongside her. I want to know what she's thinking. What she's feeling. Specifically about my brother.

"So, tell me why you didn't return my calls, Benj." It's time to drop the shit. Like he said, we're both too tired for this. "You've been ghosting me for weeks."

"I've been ghosting everyone for weeks. If you're not aware, I've been stuck looking after crazy-ass women, twenty-four-seven. You've got no idea how fucked up they are. Lucid one minute. Psychotic the next. It was PMS on acid. I'm surprised only one of them took the easy way out."

"Don't joke about that," I grate. "Don't *ever* joke about Abi in front of me again."

He laughs off my aggression. "Chill, Luc. I'm just saying they're messed up. That's all."

"You also told me they were doing good."

"Jesus Christ, that was a relative term. What's gotten into you? And not that I should have to mention it, but *you* judging *me* for the way I handle those women is fucking rich when you've got your hands all over one of the damaged."

One of the damaged?

I step back, because if I don't, I'll launch right through him, my headache be damned. "Did you really just say that?" I clench my fists, tighter and tighter, trying to squeeze away the need to strike.

"Are you kidding?" He focuses on my hands and scoffs. "You're going to hit me?"

I want to. What I wouldn't give to lay him flat for running his mouth. "Tell me why you were dodging my calls," I snarl. "Tell me what the fuck is going on with you."

He steps closer, getting in my face. "I already did. I had a lot of shit going on. Excuse me for not wanting my judgmental brother breathing down my neck after that woman decided to slash her wrists on my watch."

"Bullshit." He's lying. I don't know why. But that feeling Penny was talking about has taken over my gut. It's in my fucking head, poking, poking, poking me to dig deeper.

"Don't look at me that way," he seethes. "I bet you haven't spared a thought as to what I'm going through. Have you wondered what it's like knowing your innocent daughter has spent hours alone with a rapist? A fucking pedophile? Do you have any idea what it's like to try to console a wife whose father is a monster? To have to contemplate telling your daughter why all the photos of her grandfather are being removed from the house? Have you got any idea, Luc?"

No, I don't.

But cluelessness doesn't stop my anger toward his newfound attitude.

"You're only proving my point." I release my fists and spread my fingers, forcing myself out of the aggressive stance. "You always lay your problems on the line with me. Why have I been kept in the dark?"

"Maybe I quit wanting you to fight my battles. It's about time I grew up."

"You grew up earlier than any kid I know. You had to. We both did."

"Don't start that shit. Not everything is about our childhood."

"Isn't it?" I lean against the side of the sofa, feigning calm despite my throbbing pulse. "That's why we're here, isn't it? Why you chose to drag us down this path instead of a normal life."

He scoffs out a hate-filled laugh. "I never asked you to follow, Luc. It was your decision to be here." He retreats, dragging his suitcase toward the far hall. "Thanks for the warm welcome, though. It's always good to know you've got my back."

22

LUCA

I don't bother going to bed. There's no point.

I'm too invested in trying to work out Benji's role in all this.

I sit on the sofa armrest and stare at my reflection in the wall of glass leading outside. I go over everything, from the moment I thought Robert died till now. I try to figure out what Benji could be involved in, and when I don't come up with anything easily digestible I go in search of Torian's liquor cupboard and help myself to a bottle of scotch.

The alcohol goes down too easily. One mouthful after another, the burn helping to smother the panic as time ticks by.

"You're still awake?" Torian strides into the room, his suit jacket discarded, his tie loosened. "It's late."

"Yeah." I take a gulp of liquor and close my eyes with the swallow. The buzz has already hit me. My head swims in the small amount of alcohol.

He grabs a glass from the kitchen and continues toward me. "Do you plan on sharing?"

I pour him a generous finger and return my attention to my reflection, not wanting a distraction from my thoughts.

"Did you come up with any new information tonight?" he asks. "Any images? Leads? Answers?"

I clench my teeth, hating the reminder. "No. I've only got the few blurred side images of the suspected car."

"But you still believe Penny is right about Robert?"

"Yes. Now more than ever."

He studies me. "Why?"

Because your tiny half-brother backed her up.

"Call it intuition." I keep staring at my reflection, keep wishing for a better outlook to appear. I can't *not* believe her. I won't let my faith in her be anything other than one hundred percent.

"Well, you made the right decision," he mutters.

My gaze snaps to his, my brain taking a few seconds to catch up. "Meaning?"

"Meaning, there's been another incident."

I push from the armrest, the liquor sloshing in my glass. "What kind of incident?"

"With one of the rescued women. There was a break and enter. Masked men. Ski masks. Guns. They took nothing but shot the place up pretty good."

I keep my responses to myself. The guilt. The intense anger.

Penny predicted this. She fucking knew it.

"Didn't you have men on her? You said you were going to arrange security."

"I said I would get in contact with Benji to get their location. But he didn't answer my calls."

Fucking Benji.

"Nobody died," he continues. "Not yet, anyway. But time will tell. Apparently, the woman took a few bullets and lost a lot of blood. She's currently in ICU."

"*Jesus fucking Christ.*" I throw back the remainder of the scotch and pace.

I can't ask the questions hammering into me. I can't speculate. Because if Torian is anything like me, he'll turn the spotlight of blame firmly on my brother.

"Robert must have worked over one of my assets," he says around a gulp of liquor. "Maybe someone at the airport put a tracker on Ben's car. Or accessed bank records to get location receipts."

It's a long shot. Too fucking long for Torian to be aiming at.

"You think so?" I plant my feet and scrub a hand over my mouth, my neck.

"No." He narrows his eyes on me, waiting, tormenting. "I don't know how he's finding them." He shrugs, losing the hint of suspicion. "But the resources of my father and his men no longer surprise me. The one thing I *do* know is that we need to shut this down, and quick."

I keep rubbing my neck, attempting to relieve the tension building at the base of my skull. "What about those women? When are you going to start protecting them?"

"It's done. Benji gave me the details when he called for me to open the gate. Men are on their way now."

On their way to where?

I want to know those details. I need to find out if Benji took so long to get here because he was one of the shooters. "You don't want me to go for a drive and bring them back to Portland?"

"No. I don't want them any closer than they already are. I need to remain distanced from my father's mistakes. For now, they're safe." He places his empty glass on the coffee table. "You should get some rest. Tomorrow is going to be a big day."

I nod, not turning from my tormented reflection in the glass as he walks from the room.

My headache returns full force. My stomach wants to revolt.

I need answers, goddamnit.

I have to know if Benji is involved. If he has anything to do with Abi's death or this afternoon's shooting.

I have to fucking know.

The longer I stand here without a clue, without fucking grounding, the more I picture my brother doing stupid, unforgivable shit.

"Jesus fucking Christ." I snarl. "*Jesus. Fucking. Christ.*"

I cock my fist, needing to punch something. Anything.

I need answers. Not in the morning. Not when Benji's ready.

Fucking now.

I slam my glass down on the coffee table and stalk for the far hall. I open door after door, finding Tobias sleeping, then spare room after spare room before hitting the jackpot.

I don't have to see my brother through the darkness to know he's here. The familiar stuttered snore says it all and Layla's quiet breaths are an unwelcomed accompaniment, as I pad forward to stop beside the bed.

He's barely visible. There's only the red glow from the bedside clock to give the faint perception of where he is. But it's him. I know this man almost better than I know myself. At least, I thought I did.

The pound of my chest increases as I watch him sleep. He's saved my life a million times. He's all I've ever had. And now he could be everything that brings me undone.

He's unsettled while he rests.

Twitchy.

Something's playing on his mind, and I'm certain it could get us both killed.

He grunts. Groans. Snores some more. The restlessness adds fuel to my paranoia, ratchets my pulse, and feeds the pain in my temples.

All my adult life I've attempted to make up for needing his protection as a child. I've tried to repay him for the beatings he took on my behalf. I gave up income and a career and grounding.

But if he's helping Robert... If he's assisting in the murder of innocent women...

I pull the gun from the back of my jeans, my hand trembling as I guide the barrel to rest against the side of his throat.

He's guilty. Of what I'm not sure. But he's guilty of something.

I press the barrel harder, digging it into his neck.

His breathing shudders.

Chokes.

He stiffens. His eyes open.

"It's me," I growl, keeping my voice low. "It's time to start talking."

"Jesus," he hisses. "Are you insane? You'll wake—"

"If your snoring didn't wake her, this won't either. So, start talking, otherwise Torian is going to get involved, and I have the distinct impression you're not going to want that to happen."

He falls quiet, confirming my suspicions, fucking nailing them to the wall.

"Did you kill her?" I squeeze the gun in my sweating palm. "Did you kill Abi?"

"No," he snarls.

It's fucking bullshit.

"What about the woman attacked today? Were you involved?"

"What woman? What fucking attack?"

214

I scoff a breathy laugh. "Don't play dumb. I swear to God, it's only out of loyalty and your marriage to his sister that Torian isn't all over your ass right now. He'll see through the blinders soon enough."

"Get that fucking gun away from me, Luca."

I dig the barrel harder. "*Then fucking talk*."

There's a rustle of bedsheets. A squeak of mattress springs. A murmured, "Daddy?"

My stomach dives.

Stella is in here. In the bed. Near the pointed gun of a man influenced by alcohol.

"It's okay, baby," Benji whispers. "Go back to sleep."

I lower to my knees, sinking into the darkness as my gun remains in place.

For long moments, there's no movement. No noise. Then the slightest whimper of sleep breaches the air, the sound feminine and young.

"Get out of here," he seethes. "We'll talk in the morning."

"No. We do this now."

"Jesus, Luc." There's a tremble in his voice. "I didn't hurt those women."

I don't believe him. I fucking don't.

God knows I want to. I'd give anything to build a life here with Penny. To settle down and find some sort of normal. But every time I gain footing, he pulls the rug out from beneath me. "You've got two seconds to start—"

"I'm cheating on her," he whispers.

I snap rigid, mindlessly blinking for long moments. I don't understand. What he confessed doesn't make sense. "What did you say?"

"I'm cheating on Layla. There's another woman. *That's* what I've been keeping from you. *That's* why I've been distant."

No.

He wouldn't be that stupid.

He *couldn't*.

Cheating on Torian's sister is a death sentence. He knows that. Hell, everyone in a hundred-mile radius is well aware without anyone needing to write the fucking memo.

"I didn't plan for it to happen," he continues. "It was meant to

215

be a one-time thing. I was a wreck with this goddamn Luther mess. I just needed an outlet."

I fall on my ass, the news hitting hard.

If this gets out Stella will lose her father. Layla will bury a husband. I'll have no family left.

I shake my head and lower the gun, unable to hold it steady. "Who? Where? How long?" I can't stop the questions.

"It doesn't matter. It won't change anything."

I hang my head, my legs bent before me, the darkness consuming everything. Inside and out. "If Torian finds out—"

"I know."

"If anyone finds—"

"*I know*," he grates. "And I'll fix it. I just need you to buy me some time."

"Me? How could you be so fucking stupid?"

He doesn't answer. He doesn't have to.

If the past is any indication, he's already consumed with guilt. He always is. But it never stops him causing more destruction. The remorse doesn't starve his need to self-sabotage.

I push to my feet and shove my gun into the back of my waistband before I'm tempted to do something I'll regret. "I swear to God, Benji. Find a way to keep this quiet or I'll kill you myself."

23

PENNY

I stare at the darkened ceiling, unable to sleep.

I don't know where Luca is or how long he'll be gone. The only thing I'm certain of is the discomfort of not having him near.

I'm nothing without him. All my happiness and comfort is woven with each of his breaths. And when he's close, I'm okay with that dependence.

It's far better than keeping the company of hopelessness.

I try to picture what a future between us would look like. I shut my eyes, imagining normalcy and routine. What I wouldn't give for those things.

It isn't until sleep brushes me with gentle strokes that the bedroom door squeaks. Open, then closed. I tense, instinctively assuming a threat draws near. But my frantic heartbeat quickly fades at the measured footsteps making their way to the bathroom, the door clicking shut before the light flicks on to cast a slight glow over the room.

My stomach warms as the shower starts. The thought of Luca relaxed beneath the water makes me smile.

I slide from bed, needing to be closer to him, my oversized T-shirt billowing at my thighs as I pad to the bathroom. I shouldn't disturb his privacy. He'd never do the same with mine. But I can't help testing the door handle, and when I find it unlocked, I have no restraint to remain distanced.

I blink rapidly against the bright light and enter the room to lean against the vanity.

His head is bowed under the shower spray, his hair shrouding his eyes as his arms stretch to the wall before him as if it takes all his strength to hold himself upright.

He's not the picture of relaxation I envisaged. He seems defeated. Exhausted.

I don't think he even knows I'm here as he remains immobile, the rivulets of water coursing over the rugged lines of his shoulders and the angry scars along his back.

He's gorgeous.

Physically. Mentally. Probably spiritually, too, if I'd taken the time to learn more about him instead of being stuck in my own head.

I never could've imagined looking at a male's naked body without feeling anything but fear. Yet that icy chill doesn't brush my senses. Instead, warmth increases, and it's not from the steam filling the small space around us.

"What are you doing in here, shorty?" He keeps his hands on the tile, his head dropping lower.

"I couldn't sleep." I don't let my gaze dip below waist-height, not willing to face that challenge just yet. "I wanted to see you."

His tension doesn't lessen as he shuts off the taps and opens the shower door, the faintest wrinkle settled between his brows. He grabs a towel from the rail and gently scrubs the water from his hair, unfazed by his nudity while he wipes himself dry and tucks the plush material around his waist.

"Does your head still hurt?" I ask.

"Yeah." He steps onto the bathmat, his chest peppered with water droplets. "Turns out your brother can pack a punch after all."

"Do you need to see a doctor?"

He walks toward me, frowning. "Stop worrying about me. I'll sleep it off."

I can't. I am worried.

His pain seems deeper than normal. And the distinct scent of alcohol on his breath only heightens my concern.

"Where have you been?" I push from the vanity and raise a

hand, sliding a palm over his cheek, stroking his prickly stubble with my thumb.

He tilts his face into my touch. "You trying to keep tabs on me already?"

"No. I—"

"It doesn't matter where I was, shorty. I'm here now."

I ignore the twinge of rejection.

He doesn't want me clued in, and I have to be okay with that.

I won't demand his secrets again. For once, it seems my savior needs saving and I want to take that role. "You're exhausted. It's my turn to look after you."

His grin is subtle. Half-hearted, yet so unbelievably handsome.

I inch closer, placing my lips to his, facing another fear as I taste the liquor on his tongue.

He groans into the connection, his hands tangling into the shirt at my hips before he pulls back. "I should sleep in another room."

"Why?" My hand falls to my side.

"I can't do this tonight, Pen."

My heart tears. Fractures. "Do what? Be around me?"

He cringes. "The world is fucking crumbling, and I can't think clearly. I've got no restraint. I shouldn't have started drinking."

"You're not a monster, Luca. You don't need restraint."

"No. You—"

"*No.*" I counter, more adamant. "This shouldn't be one-sided. You can't be the strong one all the time. I need you to need me. I need you to want me."

He closes his eyes and rests his head against mine. "I've always fucking wanted you."

I feel those words, the agonizing admission sinking into my marrow. I can't stop myself from sliding my hands around his waist to pull him farther into me. Body to body. Hip to hip.

I freeze as the hard length of his shaft presses against my pubic bone. I clasp my lips tight, holding the gasp inside my throat.

I shouldn't be shocked… but I am.

I shouldn't be scared… yet there's some of that, too.

"It kills me every time you tense at my touch," he murmurs. "That's why I don't like doing it. I fucking hate hurting you."

"It's muscle memory. Or habit." I slide my hands over his chest to his face. "It won't last forever."

"Maybe not, but I'd prefer to give you space until it's gone." He attempts to pull away again, but I hold tight, clamping his jaw in my hands.

"You need to stop seeing intimacy as my biggest hurdle when being like this is my greatest reward. This isn't comparable to what I went through with Luther. What he did was vicious and cruel. But this…" I shake my head, frantically searching for the words to explain. "This is hope and optimism. It's kindness and consideration. It bears no resemblance to my nightmares."

"I get it—"

"No, let me finish." I implore him with my eyes. "Trying new things might bring up bad memories, but *you* don't. *You* wipe it all away. You're my prize, Luca. Please let me enjoy it."

He huffs out a laugh, the sound lacking happiness.

"You don't believe me?" I grab his hands and guide them to my hips. "Why is it so hard for you to understand that with each touch, each kiss, you help to make me feel normal?"

"Because you'll never be normal, shorty. *Never*. You're too remarkable to be mainstream."

My heart clenches. Hard. Tight. Punishing.

He keeps strengthening me. Over and over. Constantly making me a little more emboldened with every roughly grated compliment.

"Have I told you how happy I am that you found me?" I run my arms around his neck and brush my mouth over his.

A rumble emanates from his throat, his fingertips tightening on my hips. He kisses me. Gentle. Soulful.

But all too soon he breaks the spell, pulling away to rest his forehead against mine. "There's something you should know."

I lean back, seeing the emotion in his eyes differently than I had before. I was wrong. It isn't exhaustion. It's sorrow.

My heart clogs my throat. "Something else has happened, hasn't it?"

He nods. "Torian told me—"

"Wait." I place a finger to his lips. "Are Tobias and Sebastian safe?"

He winces. "Yeah, they are, but—"

"No. Don't say it," I beg. "Whatever it is, don't tell me. Not tonight. Don't steal me away from being here with you." I hold his gaze as I swallow over the lump in my throat. "Please just let me have this moment."

He remains rigid, his muscles locked tight.

"*Please.*" I shuffle closer, not sure how else to convince him not to ruin this.

I know I'm being selfish. I can't help it.

I'm needy when it comes to Luca.

I long for his compliments and even his desire. I want everything he has to give and I won't stand for those moments being marred by inevitable hardships. For once, darkness can wait until tomorrow.

"Please, Luca." I tug him forward by the edge of his towel.

He releases an agonizing groan, his restraint increasing my pulse.

That's the part of him I enjoy the most—his discipline.

He's much more of a man than I've ever experienced. So much so that I find myself lowering, about to fall to my knees to perform an act I've never willingly given before.

"What the fuck?" His hands lash out, one grabbing my upper arm to keep me from sinking farther, the other grasping my chin.

"I want to do this for you." It's the truth. I'm curious. And maybe a little sadistic, too. Or even self-sabotaging, waiting for him to disappoint me. But at least I'm doing this of my own free will. It's *my* choice. Nobody else's.

"Like hell." His nostrils flare as he glares. "Get off your fucking knees. *Now.*"

His vehemence shocks me, his grip unflinching until I rise to stand before him.

"You will never kneel before a man ever again." His breathing increases, his chest rapidly rising and falling. "Do you hear me?"

I open my mouth, but words fail me.

"Never," he growls. "From now on, Pen, you take your fucking place on a pedestal. There's no servitude. No fucking selflessness."

"But what if I want—"

"Then you find another fucking way. Do you understand? As long as I live, no man will ever look down on you like that again."

He renders me speechless and grabs my hips, lifting me to sit on the vanity.

I'm stripped bare of response as he falls to his knees before me, his rough hands sliding along my thighs to grip the side of my ass still covered in the bulking T-shirt.

"What are you doing?" I can't stop the stupid question escaping my lips. I blame it on the adrenaline rushing through me. The complete madness filling me with power. He elevates me to some sort of godly status, the reversal of our positions making my belly flip and tumble.

I've always been the servant. The slave.

Now I'm his master, growing more empowered by the leashed hunger in his eyes.

"Tell me you want this." He gently parts my legs, slowly inching forward, placing one gentle kiss after another along the flaming-hot skin of my inner thighs. "Or tell me to stop."

I can't imagine wanting anything else. For a moment, I'm so caught up in needing to be closer that I wonder if this was what it was like for Luther all along.

Did he crave me this way?

Was his desire for me as uncontrollable as mine for Luca?

Did his heart pound and throat tighten? Did his palms sweat and limbs shake? Is that why he stole me—because he was compelled?

"Don't go back there," Luca murmurs against my skin. "Stay with me."

I lick my lips, trying to wipe away the dryness. "I'm trying."

"What's stopping you?" He pauses the gentle kisses and pulls back an inch.

"Oh, God. I'm beginning to second guess if this is natural. Maybe there's something wrong with me."

His eyes narrow. "Whatever you feel is natural. If you want to keep going. If you want to stop. Even if you change your mind every five seconds. It's all normal."

He's right. It's natural. I guess I asked the wrong question. "What I meant is, is this healthy? Do I want you like this because I'm sick?"

He doesn't speak for long moments, the silence making my pulse beat faster. Is he about to give evidence to my growing instability?

Those lips press back against my inner thigh, his gaze remaining locked on mine as he says, "I wondered the same thing after what happened last night. But you said it yourself—this is nothing like what you experienced. It's the exact opposite. And after everything you've been through, I can't think of anything that's healthier, or that shows more strength, or trust, or more commitment to healing, than a woman wanting to gain pleasure from a man who adores her."

An ache builds behind my sternum. There's so much pain.

Good pain.

Restorative pain.

I drag in a breath, filling my lungs to capacity. "I love you, Luc."

His eyes flare, shock bleeding across his features before he bows his head into my legs, not saying a word.

"Luca?" The agony builds. "I'm sorry, I…"

"Don't be sorry." He raises his face again, staring back at me with ferocity. "You know I love you, too, shorty. I'd fucking kill for you."

"You already have."

He inclines his head. "And I'd do it again. Every single day for the rest of my fucking life. Without pause or doubt."

I burn—eyes, throat, heart. The heat overwhelms me, leaving beautifully wistful memories to soothe my scars.

"Now spread those thighs," he demands. "I want to make you feel good."

24

LUCA

THE SCENT OF HER DRUGS ME.

The heat of her consumes me.

But those eyes... those fucking eyes enslave me, leaving me powerless.

Everything inside me screams to dive farther between her legs, to lunge forward and take what's readily offered. Instead, I battle temptation, moving agonizingly slowly, my stubble grazing her inner thighs.

Each inch of devoured space intoxicates me more. Makes me burn. Pushes my restraint further.

All I want is to sate my need. But more importantly, I want to feed hers.

I stop a breath away from her pussy and close my eyes against the allure.

My mouth waters at her scent—sweet soap and heavy arousal. I can already taste her; the juices make my tongue swell in anticipation.

But still, I don't take.

I withstand the temptation. Teasing myself. Testing.

I need to know the mindlessness she inspires can be tamed because I won't hurt her. Not like this. Not ever. If I did, I'd—

"Luca," she begs. "I can't take the anticipation any longer." She shudders with an inhale. "I feel like there's a constant stream of electricity coursing through me... I'm trembling."

"Tell me what you need."

She whimpers. "I have no clue. This is new to me. But I trust you to know what you're doing."

I've got no fucking idea. Not with her. Not with someone I'm petrified of hurting.

Yet the compulsion to provide and protect latches its claws deep. I won't leave her wanting.

I nestle farther between her legs, placing my mouth right before her core.

Her breath catches with every inhale. Her tongue snakes out to nervously swipe her lower lip.

She's so fucking beautiful.

There's never been a prettier sight.

"Don't keep anything from me," I demand. "Not your fear or your pain. At the first sign of hesitation, you make sure you tell me to stop."

"I will."

I bridge the space to her pussy, my hands digging into her thighs. I never quit watching her as I take my first taste, the slick heat of her arousal coating my tongue.

She gasps. Jolts.

Her surprise fucking moves me. Soul deep.

I lick again and again, slow strokes, tender touches, until those jolts lessen and she settles into the sensation, her hands finding my hair.

At first, she's hesitant. Gentle touches. Gliding fingers.

But I need more. I want her to share this obsession. This compulsion.

I delve deeper. Lashing her pussy with longer swipes and teasing flicks against her clit.

The jolts return with each new movement, and it takes too fucking long to realize it must be because the sensations are foreign. She's never had this. Never had a man pay homage to her perfection.

The insight makes me work harder to please her.

I suck her clit, earning a throaty moan and a tightening of those gorgeous thighs around my head.

My dick pulses with need. From base to tip. Balls included.

I fucking throb for her, the urgency making me mindless. The torture of my headache is the saving grace stopping me from blowing my load in the towel.

I yank her closer to me, holding her on the edge of the vanity, her heels coming to rest against my back as one of her hands grips the counter. It's the perfect view, the landscape before me filled with smooth waist and perky tits covered under the thin layer of her shirt.

She doesn't quit watching as I devour her, nuzzling against her pubic bone, lashing her with harder strokes.

Her teeth dig into her bottom lip, her brows furrow, and that breathing, *fuck*, her breathing is so short and sharp I ache to claim her mouth.

"Come up here," she pants. "I want you."

No. I'm not fucking her.

The last thing she deserves is some pussy-starved, threadbare man rutting into her.

"Please, Luca."

I hold tighter to her thighs, lapping, sucking.

She whimpers. Wiggles. "*Please.*"

I don't listen. I keep devouring, every last drop of arousal sliding down the back of my throat.

"Luca, stop," she begs.

I freeze, instantly, and lean back on my haunches. "You okay?"

She nods, straightens, then reaches forward to grab my jaw, guiding me to stand with such exquisite confidence. "Drop the towel."

"Penny, we're not—"

"Please, Luc, just drop the towel."

I growl. "We're not having sex."

"I didn't ask for sex." She blinks up at me, all innocent and meek. "I only want to see you."

I'll give her anything she asks for when she looks at me that way. My towel. My sanity. My life. I tug at the material around my waist and release it to fall to the floor. But she doesn't take what she requested. It's the same as when I was in the shower; her gaze doesn't lower.

"What is it?" My dick remains hard, not bothered by her lack of attention. "What's wrong?"

226

She stares at my chest, her breathing remaining heavy. "I'm nervous. I've never seen a man naked without feeling threatened."

I tense. "And do you feel threatened now?"

"No."

"Then look at me."

Her brow furrows, those dark eyes wincing.

"Shorty, just because I'm hard doesn't mean I'll ever take something that isn't offered. You never need to feel vulnerable around me."

The wince deepens, her struggle intensifying. "I know."

"Then look."

She nods, her brows pinched as she lowers her gaze from my chest, to my gut, slowly descending all the way to the apex of my thighs.

I've never been self-conscious a day in my fucking life. Not about my body or my dick. But she makes me doubt my worth. I'm not good enough for her—never have been—and that's more apparent than ever as her innocent eyes survey my junk.

For long moments she remains quiet, her attention taking me in. "I never thought I'd find that part of a man tempting." She swallows. "It's funny how you always have a way of surprising me."

I don't know if it's pride, arrogance, or fucking relief filling my chest. Maybe it's a mix of all three that make me stand taller.

She returns her gaze to mine, raises her hand to lick her palm, then grasps my dick without a word.

I hiss with the brutally tempting restriction, the pleasure engulfing me. "*Jesus*."

"You'll never hurt me," she states as fact.

I nod. "I'll never hurt you."

She strokes my length, the smooth slide of skin gliding up and down my shaft.

I grind my teeth against the thrill... the consuming need for release... She feels so fucking good. "Can I touch you?"

She drags her teeth over her lower lip, still stroking, still tormenting. "Always."

I slam my mouth against hers, shoving a hand into her hair.

I rock my hips with her strokes, hungry for more as I lower my free hand between her thighs to penetrate her dripping pussy with two fingers. Her core clamps around me, soaking my palm as she grinds into the touch, her grip lethally tightening around my cock.

"Jesus. Fuck." I kiss her harder, faster, eating up her moans and needy whimpers.

I can't get enough. Not in taste or touch or sound. The pain in my head lessens, the agony meaningless when pitted against her perfection.

I want more. So much fucking more that I become mindless with need.

I twist my fingers inside her, flick her clit with my thumb. The pace of her stroke quickens, her attention remaining at the sensitive head of my shaft.

"Penny," I growl into her mouth. "I'm close."

She bites my lip. Bats those sultry lashes. Grinds harder.

I can't hold back.

I fucking come, my seed pulsing from me in waves to lash her thigh as I groan my pleasure. Over and over, the rivulets of milky liquid mark her skin.

I buck. I growl. I kiss.

And when I'm finally done, I fall to my knees, spread her legs, and this time, I fucking dive for her pussy.

I lick and lap and suck. I flick and graze and bite.

I add my finger to the mix, penetrating her slit and teasing her ass until those bated breaths become panted entreaties.

When we're like this it's hard to remember where she's come from. It's almost impossible to contemplate what she's been through.

Penny isn't damaged when she's lost in pleasure. There's no sadness or scarring. There's nothing but beautiful vibrancy, and I'm so fucking greedy for more.

Her fingers return to my hair, this time tearing, tugging, making my dick twitch all over again.

"Luca." She pulls harder. "*Luca.*"

She rips the shit out of my scalp and I grin as her walls spasm around my fingers.

I keep sucking. Keep licking.

I don't stop as she trembles around me, crying my name while she comes.

It isn't until her fingers lose their grip and she quits quivering that I pull back, falling onto my ass to stare up at her with pride.

I'm entirely spent. Physically. Emotionally.

She siphoned me of strength, but something else has taken its place. Something committed and lifelong.

This woman is everything. My priority. My goal. My future.

I don't want to be without her. Not for a week, or a day, or a minute.

She's mine. And not in the way she's used to. There will be no unwilling possession, because I'm equally hers for as long as she'll have me.

"Let's get you washed up." I push to my feet and grab her hand, helping her from the vanity to lead her to the shower.

She's quiet beside me as I turn on the water, and I hope that means she's peacefully content. I could watch her like this forever —her face flushed, eyes bright as she stares blindly ahead.

I smirk. "Need help taking off your shirt?"

The corners of her mouth rise with the hint of a smile. "No, I can do it on my own."

She reaches for the hem, and I do the same, my fingers brushing hers. We drag the material above her stomach, over her shoulders.

I'm hard again by the time I drop the shirt to the tile. Any man would be.

She's breathtaking. Mouthwatering.

I can't stop dragging my gaze over her, the lush curves of her hips, the smooth stomach, the perfect breasts. But the pièce de résistance is my seed sliding down her thigh.

"Like what you see?" she drawls.

"Without a doubt."

She lets out a breathy chuckle, the sound heaven to my ears.

I want this more often. The laughter and smiles. The subtle happiness that increases her beauty tenfold.

I lead her into the shower and close the door behind us. She moves under the water first and tugs me along with her, her arms raised between our chests, her head resting on my shoulder.

We stand in silence.

In contentment.

I kiss her forehead. Her cheek.

I can't stop pressing my lips to her delicate skin, tasting the salt, drowning in the warmth while she remains snuggled into me.

"You're quiet." I place my mouth on her temple and force my libido to tap the brakes.

"I'm happy."

I return my lips to her forehead, holding them there for long moments. "You sure?"

Despite being on cloud nine, I know this can't be easy for her.

"I think so. It's hard to explain."

I hold her tighter. "Try."

She's quiet for a while as she peppers slow kisses against my neck. "My stomach is giddy. It's all fluttery and warm." Her arms snake down to her sides, then wrap around my waist. "Good sensations have been foreign to me for so long that there's a sense of guilt that comes with them. Or maybe it's not guilt. Maybe it's the fear of this all being taken away."

"It won't get taken."

She sucks in a long breath and releases it slowly. "You can't know for certain. Nobody can predict what will happen tomorrow. Or the next day. Or the day after that. So there's this giddy, tingling part of me that I love, then there's this nagging, opposing side that chooses to be a constant reminder of how quickly life can change for the worse."

I get it.

I know she doesn't think I do, but I lived my entire early childhood in that zone. Every time I caught my parents laughing or smiling, the childish optimism in me would think they'd finally figured out how to be happy without causing pain.

It never stuck though.

And I can't oppose her way of thinking when I still have bad news to tell her. I'm worried I'll lose her trust and break her heart with the information of another attack. Then if she finds out I involved Tobias... *fuck.*

Maybe she's right. Maybe this will all be taken away, but she'll be the one doing the taking.

I tighten my hold on her, my migraine returning with the fear. "I'll always protect you. I promise I'll never stop."

"I know." She pulls back to look up at me with heart melting eyes. "But who will protect you?"

230

25

PENNY

I wake to the sound of the neighbor's dog barking incessantly, the slight glow seeping around the curtains announcing early morning.

The house is quiet. No voices. No kiddie giggles.

There are only me and the memories of last night to make me smile. I roll onto my side and stare at the man sleeping peacefully next to me. I'd fallen into slumber with his arms wrapped around my middle, his chest warm against my back.

I can't remember succumbing to pleasant dreams so easily.

There'd been no fear. No panic.

Only a building sense of hope with the protective embrace.

My love for him is scary. I think it's always been there, in the security and trust, but now it's also in the flutter of my stomach and the tightness of my throat whenever I look at him.

It carries through every inch of my body.

A rhythmic *pop, pop, pop* startles me, the familiar muted gunfire stealing a bite of my happiness. I slump back into the mattress. Sebastian must have headed straight for the shooting range as soon as he woke up.

I hate that he despises the man I adore. It makes me sick thinking of his anger.

I want to fix it.

Fix *them*.

If I'm going to reclaim my life, I need them both. No aggression. No threats. Just support and guidance.

I may have very little control over anything else right now, but I can make Sebastian listen to me. All I need is to be strong enough to face him, and I think Luca has already ensured I am.

I slowly inch from the bed and tiptoe to the dresser to pull on the pants and oversized sweater I left there the night before.

"Where are you going?" Luca grumbles, his face plastered into the pillow.

"I can't sleep with that dog barking. I'm going to get coffee."

He groans. "Do you want me to come with you?"

My heart swells as I bridge the space between us to place a kiss on his unmarred cheek. "Thank you. But I'm okay."

He grabs my hand and squeezes. "I'll be up soon."

"Don't. You need the rest." I reluctantly walk for the hall to head toward the continued gunfire at the other end of the house.

I drag my bare feet past the empty living area, then farther along the far hall, not stopping until I reach the door where the muted pops escape from.

I grab the handle, the gentle vibrations from the other side making my hand tremble, my pulse stutter. I want to back out already but I don't. I inch open a door, finding soundproofing on the walls and an ominous staircase leading down into fluorescent light.

More pops assail my ears, these ones harsh and biting. I quickly scoot inside, not wanting to wake anyone else, and clasp the door shut behind me.

It's cooler down here, the polished cement freezing my toes. I will myself to descend. One step after another. One punishing heartbeat after the next until I'm at the bottom landing, staring at a bulking man who isn't my brother.

Hunter wields the gun, his cannon arms pointing toward the far end of the long, expansive basement.

He stands before a professional shooting station, protective headphones covering his ears. It's not a downscaled DIY set down here. It's like I've seen in movies as a kid. Three individual stations. Paper targets hanging from the roof.

Another *pop* sounds, the blast ricocheting off the walls to make me flinch and gasp. He glances over his shoulder, his weapon lowering as his narrowed eyes pin me in place.

"Sorry." I wince. "I thought you were Sebastian."

He glares, then returns his attention to the target, raising his gun. He hates me. And why wouldn't he? He had a nice set of wheels before I got my hands on them.

"I'm also sorry about your car," I add. "I didn't plan for that to happen."

He lowers the headphones. "When you fly by the seat of your pants, you don't hold back, do you?" His tone is gruff, making it hard for me to tell if he's angry or attempting to make light of the situation.

"Is it fixable?"

He shrugs. "It's just a car."

"I know, but I'm sure it was expensive."

"It's just a car," he growls the statement with such venom I grip the staircase banister in preparation to flee.

"It's just a car. It's just a car. It's just a fucking car." He lazily circles his finger in the air with each repetition. "Sarah told me to keep repeating the mantra in the hopes it will stop me from putting a bullet in your head."

All the air leaves my lungs on a heave.

"Calm down." He rolls his eyes. "I'm joking."

"Right…" I force out a laugh. "Hilarious."

He turns his back to me, raising his headphones, then his gun to take aim at the target. "If you're going to stay down here, you need to get yourself a set of ear plugs."

I don't move, not sure if the muttered request is an invitation to stay or a demand to leave.

"The door or the plugs, Penny." He jerks his head toward the wall behind me, the mass of shelves displaying a myriad of equipment. "Hurry up. I've got bullets to waste."

I nod and hustle to the shelves to grab a set of plugs, shoving them into my ears as another set of *pop, pop, pops* erupt. This time, the sound reverberates through my chest, the vibration rattling my bones. It brings a slight buzz to my system. A building awakening. It's the power. The threat. I want it for myself.

I walk toward him, stopping a foot behind to watch as he aims and fires, the paper target dancing with the direct hit in the head.

Pop, pop, pop.

In a flurry of finesse he releases the magazine, loads another, then takes aim. *Pop, pop, pop.*

Pop, pop, pop.

He's brilliantly lethal. Mesmerizingly intimidating.

When he stops firing, I raise my voice. "Would you teach me?"

"Teach you what?" He pauses, arms still straight in aim. "To shoot?"

"Yeah. I've never done it before."

"Where's Luca? I'm not the sort of teacher you want."

"He's asleep. And I don't think the noise is something he's going to want to be around for a while after he received another hit to the head."

He shoots me a scowl. "Then what about your brother or Sarah? Even Keira would be a better option."

"Nobody is awake." I shrug, feigning indifference while my pulse hammers, waiting for him to lose patience with me. "And we're both already here…"

Just like I want to fix the rift between Luca and Sebastian, I also need to mend the damage I've caused with Hunter. The less enemies I have, the stronger I'll be.

"Fine." He pins me with that scowl. "You're going to have to move closer."

I inch toward him, my pulse ramping higher as I stand beside his bulky frame.

"Here." He grabs my wrist and smacks the gun in my hand, the casing warm from his hold. "You're going to want to—"

A throat clears behind us and I swing around to see Sebastian, his eyes wary, chin high as he stands at the foot of the stairs. "Am I interrupting?"

"Fuck no." Hunter snatches the weapon from my grip. "I was praying for a savior." He maneuvers around me, all strength and thumping footsteps as he yanks off his earphones and throws them at my brother. "Godspeed."

I'm left stunned silent as Hunter storms up the stairs, slamming the door behind him.

For moments, Sebastian and I just stare at each other. Sister to brother. Victim to criminal.

I think this is the first time we've been alone since Luther stole me. *Truly* alone. Without weighty emotion or people hovering close. And now that we're here, I'm not sure what to say.

"I didn't mean to interrupt." He shifts his focus over my shoulder, no longer meeting my gaze. "Was he teaching you how to shoot?"

I nod, finding it hard to come up with a response when he looks entirely defeated. I'm the one who broke him. Me and my feelings for Luca. "But he wasn't overly enthusiastic about talking to me, let alone handing over his gun. He told me he wouldn't be a good teacher."

Sebastian huffs out a laugh. "I don't know why. He would've killed more people than you went to school with."

My mouth falls open. I hadn't been oblivious to Hunter being a murderer, but those numbers aren't what I'd pictured.

"It was a joke," he drawls. "I'm sure the number hasn't reached triple digits."

It's my turn to breathe out an awkward laugh. "You all have really inappropriate humor."

"It comes with the work environment."

The criminal environment, I mentally correct. The death and destruction.

Silence returns. The awkwardness, too.

"Want me to leave you alone?" he asks.

I want to say yes. It still hurts to see him. To remember our childhood and the familiar bond we had. The yearning for the past is excruciating. But I have to think about him. And Luca. I have to concentrate on the future. "No. I actually came down here looking for you."

"Is that right?" He raises a brow, the slightest hint of hope entering his eyes.

"I thought it was time we talked."

He straightens, broadening his shoulders. "What do you want to talk about?"

I swallow over the adamant pulse in my throat and drag in a steadying breath. "I wanted to apologize for the way I've treated you, am treating you, and will probably continue to treat you."

"Okay..." He winces. "So this hatred of me is a lifelong commitment?"

"No, it's not. And I don't hate you, I just..." My chest tightens,

235

painfully squeezing. "I'm trying to protect myself the only way I know how."

"And you think you need protection from me?"

"Not *from you*, no. I need protection from the possibility of losing you. Everything else has been taken from me, Sebastian. Too many sisters in Greece were murdered. And anyone who defies Luther always disappears... Maybe if you weren't a part of this—" I wave a hand to encompass the room. The house. Everything. "—my return would be different. But it feels like loss has followed me here."

"I'm not going anywhere." He starts toward me. "No way in hell would I leave you."

"I know it wouldn't be by choice. But your job... And Robert." I wrap my arms around my waist, trying to hold in the building hollowness. "You didn't choose a vocation that's overly generous when it comes to lifespan."

"Robert can go fuck himself." He stops before me, his face pinched. "He's one man attempting to start a war with an army. He doesn't have a hope in hell of surviving. And yes, I admit working for Torian has its downfalls, but I'm more of a tech guy. I hide behind a computer most of the time. I'm not on the frontlines like Hunt or *Luca*," he snarls the name, adding to my emptiness.

"He's a good man." I let my eyes do the pleading. "I wouldn't be here right now, standing before you, if it weren't for him. And it's not just because he physically saved me in Greece. It's so much more than that. He rescued me mentally, too. Emotionally. He's the reason I'm whole, Seb. It's all him."

He presses his lips tight, his nostrils flaring.

"Why is it so hard for you to understand?" I ask.

"It's not hard to understand," he grates. "It's hard to digest. He shouldn't be touching you."

"Well, rest assured he feels the same way. But I like him touching me. After everything I've been through, he brings me comfort. Can't you see how monumental that is?"

"No, it only reeks of manipulation to me."

"You don't think I know all about manipulation? I spent a lifetime in hell getting to know every single facet of deceit. And it's not what Luca is doing."

Sebastian's jaw ticks. He doesn't believe me. There's no faith.

236

I squeeze my arms tighter around myself, creating courage. "I love him. More than myself. More than air. More than life. He's become the reason I get up in the morning. He's my hope for the future. And the balm to my past. I know you don't want to hear it, but right now, he's everything to me. He's the reason I breathe."

"And what happens when he's not? Where does it leave you mentally and fucking emotionally when he walks out?"

A sharp dagger stabs through my heart, piercing skin and bone. "Hopefully by then I'll be strong enough to stand on my own two feet." I drop my hands to my sides. "He's not obligated to a lifelong commitment, and he never should be. But while he's inspiring happiness, I want to cling to him. Surely I deserve that much, don't I?"

He cringes. "This isn't about what you deserve. It's about—"

"I know exactly what you think it's about. What I need you to comprehend is that I would've ended my life many times over if it wasn't for him. He's the only reason I stand before you. The *only reason*, Sebastian. I know that's hard for you to hear. It's even harder for me to admit. But it's the truth. And I think he deserves your gratitude for that. At the very least, you should stop threatening him."

His mouth snaps shut again, his jaw ticking.

"Please, Seb."

He looks away.

"*Please.*"

"I'll work on it," he growls and turns for the stairs.

Before I know what I'm doing, I reach for him, my fingers tentative against his wrist.

He stops. Stiffens.

My heart is a frantic butterfly in my throat as I walk to stand before him, not pausing for contemplation before I sink into his chest.

He stiffens further, every muscle cinched tight. He remains statuesque while I tremble, fighting hard against the burn in my eyes.

The contact is awkward. No warmth. No comfort.

He doesn't say a word.

I'm about to pull away in heartbreak when he releases a deep breath and drags me harder into his chest. His body relaxes into mine as his arms encircle my back, his mouth softly pressing against my forehead in a brotherly kiss.

The heat in my eyes increases, the threat of tears so close before I desperately blink them away. "Please forgive him."

He sighs. "I'll try."

"I need you to do more than that," I whisper. "I need this feud between you two to be over."

"How 'bout I start by not killing him and see where that leads?"

I huff out a laugh. "You all seriously have a warped sense of humor."

"Yeah... I was totally joking," he drawls.

I nudge him in the ribs and step back "Promise me you'll play nice."

"Fine." His arms drop to his sides. "I promise."

It feels strange to be having a conversation with my brother again. To argue and beg like I did as a child. It brings an overwhelming sense of home and the brief taste makes me want more. "Thank you."

He gives a sad smile. "All bets are off if he makes you cry, though. You know that, right?"

"Yeah, I know." I start for the stairs, Sebastian following close behind.

I hold the door open to the hall and we walk in comfortable silence toward the voices coming from the living area. Everyone is there—Hunter and Sarah at the dining table, Cole and Keira in the kitchen cooking, Layla, Benji, the nanny, and the kids on the sofa in front of the television. It's Luca who steals my attention, his hip cocked against the island counter, his stance casual even though I can read the tension in his eyes as he glances between me and my brother.

"It's about time you two got up here." Cole pulls plates from a cupboard. "Breakfast is almost ready."

"Perfect timing." Sebastian squeezes my shoulder and strides ahead, taking the furthest route from Luca as possible.

They eye each other, the evil stares not amounting to anything other than tension.

I guess the lack of verbal threat is a starting point.

Luca pushes from the counter, flicking me a glance as he stalks for the glass doors leading outside. I follow, my toes protesting the bitter chill while I breathe in the icy morning air.

"Morning." I don't stop until I'm in front of him, my bare feet brushing his boots as I lean into his chest.

"Morning, shorty." He engulfs me in a lazy hug, the familiar scent of his aftershave soothing me.

"I gather from the damp hair and fresh clothes that you didn't fall back asleep."

He stares across the courtyard, the towering mansion next door looming right beside the brick fence as the neighbor's dog continues to bark. "I got out of bed as soon as you left the room. I wanted to make sure I was close by if you needed me."

A grateful smile curves my lips. "I always need you."

He tightens his hold around me for a brief moment, then sighs. "Is everything okay between you and Decker?"

"It's better than it was."

"I'm glad to hear it." He strokes my hair. "How about the poison? Is that sinking in yet?"

"Poison?" I pull back, taking in his faint smirk.

"Has Sebastian turned you against me?" He appears calm on the surface, but I see the underlying fear in the tight set of his jaw. He's joking on the outside. On the inside he's worried.

"No, and he never will. You're stuck with me."

The smirk fades as he returns his attention to the neighboring building. "There's something I need to tell you."

I square my shoulders, preparing for the worst. "Is this what you wanted to tell me last night?"

He nods. "It's not good news, Pen."

I already gathered as much when he brought it up yesterday. I just hadn't been willing to face it. And if the news hadn't been about Tobias and Sebastian, that only left my sisters. "He killed one of them, didn't he? Robert found Lilly or Nina."

His chin hitches almost imperceptibly. It's all the answer I need for a wave of grief to take hold. I steel myself against the onslaught, straightening my shoulders in anticipation.

"Not dead, shorty. But Nina is hurt pretty bad. She's in hospital."

Relief doesn't come. It's as if the sorrow is merely placed on the back burner, waiting for the follow-through. "Will she make it?"

239

"I hope so. They're not sure at this point. The only good news is that Torian now believes you."

Again, my relief is non-existent. I'm left to drown in guilt. I should never have let them leave Greece without me. We should've stayed together.

"This isn't your fault," he murmurs. "I should've made sure they were protected. And when I found out, instead of telling you, I focused on getting my rocks off."

"No, you didn't. I knew. I may not have had the specifics, but I knew." I graze my fingers over his jaw. "We both needed the distraction."

He scoffs. "That doesn't stop me from feeling like a prick."

The glass door slides open. The dog bursts into more aggressive barking as I glance over my shoulder to see Keira poking her head outside. "Sorry to interrupt but breakfast is ready and Cole wants us all together to talk about what's happening."

Luca jerks his chin in acknowledgement. "We'll be there in a minute."

She smiles and sneaks back inside, closing the door behind her.

"I'm going to have to get out of here today." He drags me into his chest, his arms locking around me. "I can't sit on my ass while that fucker is out there."

I nod, already feeling the distance that will come between us. The exposure. The fear.

"Will you be okay without me?" he asks.

"No. But I'll manage, as long as you promise to stay safe."

"I can do that."

There's little conviction in his tone. There's definitely not assurance. I tilt my head to meet his gaze and stare into those harshly intense eyes, wordlessly begging for a more confident affirmation.

"I need you to return to me," I whisper. "You have no idea how much I need it."

His lips lift in a half-hearted smile. "Yeah, I do, shorty. Because I feel the same way."

26

PENNY

We sit at the two remaining seats at the dining table. Benji is slouched in the chair to Luca's left, his wife at his side. Sebastian is strung tight at my right beside Keira, while Sarah and Hunt sit across the table from us as Cole claims the head chair.

The kids are no longer around, their laughter and occasional shouts carrying from a far corner of the house.

"Penny, I've got something for you." Sarah slides what looks like a black leather wrist cuff across the table, a shiny metal design on the front. "I thought it might be a nice start to your arsenal."

"My arsenal?" I reach for the offering, running a lone finger over the metal.

"What is it?" Luca asks.

"A blade," Hunter mutters. "I bought it for her a while back, but apparently my gifts aren't appreciated."

Sarah grins, saccharine sweet. "I appreciated it on merit. What I didn't approve of was the hidden GPS tracker you told me nothing about." She holds my gaze with a cautionary stare. "Just a word of warning, these guys tend to trample over privacy and personal boundaries. Make sure you remember that if Luca ever buys you jewelry."

"It's the thought that counts, right?" Cole smirks. "It's the little things we do to keep you protected."

Sarah ignores him, keeping her attention on me. "The metal

part is a retractable blade. I can teach you a few tricks with it later if you're interested."

"I'd love that." I place the cuff on my wrist, then turn my arm to clip it in place as the rest of the table eat their breakfast. "I'd appreciate anything you're willing to show me."

"Are you two finished now?" Cole asks around a bite of bacon. "We've got a lot to discuss."

He isn't lying.

He spends the next half hour relaying a mass of information that steals my appetite.

He explains how Nina was attacked by masked men in her parents' home, taking two bullets—one in the chest, the other in her thigh.

Luca squeezes my leg as I'm told of her precarious situation in ICU. I think I'm supposed to be appeased, or even thankful, when Cole tells me men have now been assigned to keep an eye on her, along with Lilly, but I'm not placated in the slightest.

"We're nailing this fucker to the wall as soon as possible." Cole turns his gaze on me, his dark stare narrowing.

With one look, I understand why he's feared by grown men. There's no soul behind those eyes. No warmth. Or fear.

"I assure you those women are taken care of." He enunciates the words slowly, the bitter grate to his tone making the reassurance more of a threat. "The men assigned to their protection are ex-military. They know what they're doing."

He goes on to vaguely mention the informants, authorities, and members of his outer circles who are currently searching the state for the man of the hour and his unknown sidekick. Luca adds details of a green sedan. Hunter stops eating to mention a potential lead who left a voicemail in the early hours of the morning, while my brother remains quiet, holding Keira's hand on the top of the table for all to see.

Then the rules start.

The kids won't be attending school. Us women aren't allowed to leave the house without an escort. And everybody is to advise Cole of their whereabouts at all times.

"I know I'm stretching the limits of our task list, but can we add the death of your neighbor's dog to our daily chores?" Hunter asks. "That fucker kept me up all night."

"It wasn't just the dog." Sarah's attention turns to Luca. "Don't forget about the people fucking in the bathroom beside ours."

My cheeks flame. Red-hot. And I try to ignore the way Sebastian's fingers clench tighter around Keira's.

"I've said it before, and I'll say it again," Luca snarls. "We're not fucking."

"Yeah, whatever." Hunter waves him away, his focus on Cole. "Can we kill that dog or not?"

"Talk to the old lady who lives there." Cole pushes from the table, taking his dirty plate with him. "But make sure you're prepared before you knock on her door. She's a typical Italian mother. You won't leave her house with an empty stomach."

"Speaking of mothers." Keira turns pained eyes to my brother. "We need to cancel tonight. It isn't safe."

Sebastian inclines his head. "I'll make the call."

"Cancel what?" Cole continues to the kitchen, placing his plate in the sink before he returns. "What isn't safe?"

"It's nothing." My brother sits taller. "We'll postpone."

"Postpone what?" Cole pins his focus on Keira. "If Robert is stopping you from your usual plans, I want to know what they are."

Sebastian scoffs. "You just confined the women to the house. How is that any different?"

"It's okay." Keira remains calm. "We were going out for dinner, that's all."

"With who?"

"It doesn't matter."

Cole smirks, the expression becoming unkind. "*Who*?"

"My parents," Sebastian snaps, pushing from his chair.

Luca's hand presses harder into my thigh, offering adamant support.

"They're here?" My voice is high-pitched with apprehension. "In Portland?"

"This had nothing to do with you, Pen. We made plans weeks ago for Keira to meet them. They weren't going to come anywhere near you. And we sure as hell weren't going to mention anything that's happened." Sebastian shoves his chair back into place. "It was just meant to be dinner and drinks. A laid-back welcome to the family."

I tense, keeping all the threatening panic low in my belly. The thought of Mom and Dad being near is overwhelming. They're in the same state as I am. The very same city.

"You're not cancelling." Cole returns to his position at the head of the table. "We don't hide."

"Despite all of us having to relocate to your mega mansion?" Sebastian bites out a vicious laugh. "I'm pretty sure this is the definition of hiding."

"This is *protection*. It's fucking *strategy*."

"Call it whatever you want. But I'm not dragging my parents into the line of fire. Not for you. Not for fucking anybody."

Cole raises his brows. "Not even your sister?"

"Torian," Luca warns.

"No." I swallow to ease the dryness taking over my throat. "This has nothing to do with me. I don't want them dragged—"

"You're not cancelling." Cole pulls his cell from inside his suit jacket and frowns as he taps the screen. "This is the perfect opportunity to draw Robert from the shadows. We'll make it a joint family event. We'll invite everyone. I'll even host at the restaurant and pick up the tab."

"No." I slide my chair back only to be stopped from making a dramatic outburst by Luca's hand grasping mine. He demands my attention with the squeeze of my fingers, his determined eyes attempting to assure me.

"It's okay," he soothes. "We need to talk this out."

"I don't think it requires much talking." Keira glares. "It's heartless to bring more people into this."

Cole slaps his cell down on the table. "How do you not understand that they're already fucking involved? *Anyone* Penny cares for is a target. Maybe not right now, but certainly in the future if this drags on. What the hell do you think is going to happen when Robert can't get his hands on her?" He stares at me. "He's been successful in finding your friends. How long do you think it will take for him to start coming after us? He already shot at you once."

"We don't know it was him." Hunter stabs a hand through his hair. "It still could've been someone looking for me."

"Bullshit. You don't believe that. He came after Penny, and soon he'll come after us all. And not just everyone at this table, but

244

Decker's parents, and our fucking kids. We need to think about Stella and Tobias."

"I'm not risking them," Sebastian seethes.

"There is no risk. We'll have the neighborhood surrounded. I'll place guards on the door. We'll have men scanning the surveillance recordings and on street corners and rooftops for blocks. He won't get near the party. We only need him to get close enough for someone to take him out."

"Right…" Sarah glances around everyone at the table. "And you can arrange all that before tonight?"

"Watch me."

I shake my head, my stomach twisting in knots. I can't let him do this. I can't.

"How do you even know he's nearby?" Hunt asks. "You said he was responsible for the attack yesterday. He's probably still driving around the countryside with his dick in his hand."

"Because of this." Cole unlocks his cell and slides it across the table. "He took more money from Luther's bank account this morning."

"You couldn't have led with that information?" Luca snatches the phone and shows me the email.

"Look at the time stamp, asshole. I only just got the notification."

"Fuck." Sebastian slumps back into his chair, his elbows on the table, his head in his hands. "You're asking us to use our parents as bait."

"No, I'm asking you to have dinner with them in a controlled environment," Cole corrects. "After the last shooting, the restaurant windows are bulletproof. I'll ensure the security is second to none. They'll be safe."

I keep shaking my head, but Sebastian doesn't react.

He's caving.

How is he caving?

"No." Blood surges in my veins, fueling me. "I won't let you." The weight of everyone's attention presses on my shoulders, my chest. It's hard to breathe. "Please, Luca." I turn to face him, my knees brushing his thigh. "Don't let him do this."

"He doesn't have a choice." Cole reaches out a hand, wordlessly requesting his phone. "This needs to happen."

245

"Not necessarily. If we find him today there won't be any risk tonight." Luca shoves to his feet and stares down at my brother. "What time are you meeting your parents for dinner?"

There's a beat of hope-filled silence before Sebastian raises his head to glance over his shoulder. "Seven. Why? What are you thinking?"

Luca focuses on his watch. "I'm thinking we've got twelve hours to find this fucker. And I don't plan on wasting a single minute. So let's get our asses moving."

27

LUCA

I STALK BACK TO OUR ROOM, PENNY HUSTLING TO KEEP UP AT MY SIDE despite knowing she's going to be stuck here all day. I head straight for the duffels in the corner, pulling my Mac from the bag as she escapes to the bathroom and turns on the shower.

I'm still hunched on the floor when someone else enters the doorway behind me.

I don't need to look to see who it is. His resentment already thickens the air.

"If you're going to kill me, make it quick. Otherwise I've got shit to do." I push to my feet and start for the bed as the shower door grates from the adjoining room. I dump my ass on the mattress and open my computer, scrolling to my home-surveillance software. I looked over a million hours of recordings yesterday, but none of them were mine.

"If I kill you, I promise it won't be quick." Decker leans against the doorframe, wishing the life from my lungs with his narrowed stare. "What are you doing?"

"Checking my security feed from the other night. If it was Robert who shot at Penny I might have recorded his car. And if I've got his car, I might have his plates, which means we've got something to track."

He pushes from the doorframe and moves to the end of the bed, continuing to glare down at me as I play the feed from the night Penny ran.

I watch in double time as Hunter's car pulls into the drive, another vehicle following moments later. I hit pause, rewind, and watch it again.

It's that green fucking sedan with what looks to be a blurred hooded man behind the wheel.

I hit rewind again. Pause. "You got a pen?"

"No," Decker grates.

"I need to figure out these plates." I look up at him from my lowered vision. "You want to help your sister, don't you?"

"I'd do anything for my sister. *You*, on the other hand—"

"Quit the bullshit. Either take down the details or fuck off."

He remains in place, pulling his cell from the back pocket of his jeans. "Well, what the fuck are the details, you perverted fuck?"

I grind my molars as I skip the video back and forth, trying to get a clear view. I relay letters and numbers through clenched teeth, and hope they're the right ones, before pressing play on the video.

I scrutinize every aspect of the pixelated car. The busted headlight. The dents and scratches. Every detail counts.

"Jesus Christ." I hit the slow-motion button and watch the replay of Hunter and Sarah walking across the lawn to the front of the house. "Jesus fucking Christ."

"What is it?" Decker moves to my side, staring down at my Mac. The car creeps onto screen at the same time as Hunt knocks on my front door.

"They were right there. *Right fucking there.* All they needed to do was look over their shoulder and none of this would've happened."

"If you want to see it that way, you could also say this never would've happened if you didn't cozy up with my sister and take her back to your house in the first fucking place."

I ignore the throb reigniting in my head.

I count to ten.

Breathe.

I do whatever calming voodoo I can muster to keep my ass on the bed instead of launching my knuckles into Decker's face.

"Does it show him following Penny after she left?" he mutters.

I keep every muscle clenched while the video continues.

My fingers twitch as I watch the desolate street, not a single vehicle passing before Penny runs from the house. She's frantic, and I have to fight a wince at the pain in her features. The pain *I* caused.

She scrambles into the black Suburban in my drive and doesn't stop when Hunter and Sarah come rushing after her.

The seconds after she speeds away make me furious. As my friends reach for their phones and pace my front lawn, the green sedan drives by, following less than a minute behind. He must have circled the block and been watching the house.

"He was *right there*." I jab a finger at the screen. "If Hunt was paying attent—"

"It's not Hunt's fault."

I scoff. "No, it's mine, right?" I shove from the bed, my brain screaming in protest at the sudden movement. "This is all on me."

"I didn't say that." Decker relaxes, settling into calm superiority. "But it sounds like you think so."

Fuck him.

Not only for the judgment and the threats. Fuck him for nailing exactly how I feel.

It's my fault for not realizing Robert had found her. It's my fucking fault for not confirming he was dead in the first place.

I should've been all over this. I should've fucking known.

"Do you really blame yourself?" He shakes his head and scoffs. "Do you seriously think you could've stopped this from happening?"

Without a doubt, if I'd been on the top of my game. If my focus had been aligned.

But instead of protecting Penny I endangered her. Became distracted by her. And even now, with one of her friends dead and another injured, I don't think I can regret falling for her.

"You couldn't have seen this coming. Torian told me Robert was dead. That *all* Luther's men were taken care of. Get your head out of your ass and realize you're no better than anyone else. You couldn't have predicted this. You're just as helpless as the rest of us."

"It was my job."

"Yeah, well, it was my job to find her in the first place. She's *my* sister. So quit the pity party."

249

Is that it? Is all this macho hostility because I found her instead of him?

"And while you're at it," he snarls, "quit fucking her, too."

"Don't push me, Decker." I grind my teeth to the point of pain. "I've told you I'm *not* fucking her."

He scoffs and looks away, his jaw ticking.

The need to fight this out is reciprocated. There's only one reason we aren't, and she's a few feet away, behind that bathroom door.

"Look." I huff. "I care about her. And whether you approve or not, I'm going to keep protecting her."

"With your dick?"

"Enough," I warn. "We don't have time for this."

He straightens, his vicious eyes meeting mine. "Fine. But we also don't have time for you bitching about how you let her down. So powder your fucking vagina and make up for your mistakes."

My ears keep deceiving me. Through the threats, his demands sound similar to thinly veiled approval.

I breathe out a laugh. "She got to you this morning, didn't she? Whatever she told you in the basement has you second-guessing putting a bullet between my eyes."

"Hardly. I'm still trigger-happy, motherfucker. Keep pushing me and you'll see how close I am."

There's little intimidation in his tone. Penny must've dug deep under his skin, and a whole heap of pride accompanies that knowledge.

She's healing.

Slowly, but surely.

The water cuts off in the shower, then the screen door clatters open.

"She's going to be out here in a minute." I clap my Mac shut and sidestep Decker to grab my wallet and car fob from the bedside table.

"Where are we going?"

I pause. "We?"

There's a beat of silence as I turn to face him.

"Yeah, *we*. The two of us are all she's got. And I'm not going to put my family in harm's way because of my hatred for you. I want to find this fucker, and it needs to be before tonight."

The bathroom door opens and Penny pads into the room, her loose hair damp around her shoulders, her skin flushed, her T-shirt and jeans still incredibly baggy. As soon as she notices I've got company, she stops, her eyes growing wide. She glances between me and her brother. "What's going on?"

"Nothing." I walk for the duffle to dump my Mac inside. "Deck and I are getting out of here."

Her gaze turns frantic. "The two of you?"

"It's all good, Pen." Decker jerks his chin at her. "We're setting our differences aside. For now."

She pins me with a stare. "Is he serious?"

"Quit eying me like that. You heard the guy; we've become best buddies." I wink at her. "But we need to make a move. We've got a lot to do."

She continues with the visual tennis match as she slowly nods. "Okay. What should I do? I need to help."

"Nothing," Decker answers for me. "Relax. Read a book. There isn't anything you can do."

The moron has no idea she's incapable of relaxation. She needs a distraction.

"You said you remember Luther talking to Benji." I walk to her, gliding my hands over her upper arms. "It would help if you started recalling anyone else he might have spoken to. I need names and specifics. Come up with as many details as you can. No matter how big or small." I run my fingers over her chin and lean in for a kiss. "Robert's working with someone, and the more information we have, the easier it will be to find him."

She nods into me. "I can do that."

Decker mutters something under his breath and trudges to the hall.

I take a second to breathe her in. To remain close before I have to leave. I kiss her again, deeper, and my dick appreciates the proximity.

"I like this." I skim a hand down her arm to the leather cuff firmly affixed to her wrist. "It looks good on you."

"It's the only weapon I have, which means I'll never take it off. All I need now is to learn how to use it."

I lean back, already regretting the distance I'm about to place between us. "I'll teach you as soon as I can, okay? And I'm sure Sarah would be happy to show you a trick or two."

"Okay."

I step away, retreating toward the door. "I'll have my phone on me all day. Do you still have the cell I bought you?"

Her eyes widen. "I didn't bring it."

"It's no big deal. I'll be back as soon as I can. But if you want me for any reason, just ask one of the others for a phone. They've all got my number."

She bites into her bottom lip, her teeth digging deep. "Please stay safe."

I smirk. "Always."

She attempts a smile. "I mean it. I need you to come back. And I need you to look after him." She glances toward the hall and lowers her voice. "Please don't let anything happen to Sebastian."

"I will." I cross a finger over my heart. "I promise."

I just hope I'm capable of fulfilling the vow.

28

PENNY

I STARTED ON THE LIST AS SOON AS THEY LEFT. IT TOOK A WHILE, MY unwanted memories unwilling to come forward after I've spent weeks attempting to suppress them.

When I'd finished, Keira texted the information to Luca.

She didn't seem surprised by the names I came up with. Nothing triggered her interest—at least not from what I could tell. Her disregard only made me strive to focus harder on my past in the hopes of coming up with something pivotal.

Even after she sent the message, I relived my time in Greece like a rolodex, flicking over one memory to the next, trying to recall the details of Luther's conversations only to gain tiny snippets that seemed inconsequential. There was too much static to think clearly. Too much debilitating anger that blocked the finer details of the past.

By mid-morning, I was frantic with the need for a distraction without Luca by my side.

There were no updates on his progress as I watched Tobias and Stella play with the nanny. I surrounded myself in their laughter because each passing hour made my apprehension grow.

The other women spent their time making calls and dinner plans. I overheard Layla cancelling reservations people had already booked at Cole's restaurant, while Keira contacted extended family to invite them to the special occasion.

None of the men came home for lunch.

Neither Luca nor Sebastian interrupted the afternoon "Female Empowerment" session Sarah made me attend in the basement.

I both appreciated and cursed every minute that ticked by as I held a gun in my hands and learned how to aim and shoot. And although I adore the leather cuff strapped to my wrist, I much would've preferred Luca to be here giving me good news instead of having Sarah instruct me on how to slice someone's carotid with lethal efficiency.

"They're going to find him," were the only soothing words offered to me from Layla while us four women sat outside in the afternoon sun, the neighborhood now sickly quiet without the barking dog.

It wasn't until later in the day when the sun began to set and Keira excused herself from another chat session around mugs of tea in the kitchen that my confidence in Luca's promises faded.

She didn't give an excuse for leaving my side, but it was clear she needed to get ready for the evening with my parents. They all did. Which meant I was left to sit on the sofa by myself, drowning in fear.

I hadn't let myself believe Luca and Sebastian would return empty-handed.

But they have. I can feel it.

When the front door opens not long after and heavy steps down the hall bring Luca into view, the sight of him only confirms my despair.

Even though he stands tall, head high, shoulders straight, his expression speaks of failure. Those usually intense eyes now beg for forgiveness.

I swallow over the tightening in my throat and look away, my hands clutching the sofa beside my thighs.

"We tried everything," he says in greeting as he walks my way. "We looked everywhere. Spoke to everyone. We fucking interrogated and threatened and threw our weight around, but nobody knows a damn thing."

He stops before me, his red and swollen knuckles clenched at my eye level.

I fight against the need to blame him. To yell and scream even though it's not his fault.

"Where's Sebastian?" I keep my gaze lowered. "Did he come home with you?"

"Yeah. He's getting ready."

A sharp stab enters my heart, penetrating deep. "So, that's it? There's nothing more that can be done? I just have to sit back while my parents are used as bait?"

"They're safe. Nobody is going to get to them. Torian has men set up everywhere. There's not an inch of space in a three-block radius that won't be watched."

Yet again, I'm defenseless against the demands of powerful men.

Everything is always out of my control.

"Your list helped." He strokes a hand through my hair. "Just not enough to find anything concrete."

I jerk my head away and push from the sofa. Antsy. Angry.

"I tried, Pen," he murmurs. "I fucking tried."

I know. That's what makes this worse.

I don't want him to exude defeat and wordlessly beg for forgiveness. It only increases my suffering.

"I'm hoping he's left Portland," he continues. "We've got so many eyes on this city, someone would've had information if he was still here."

I nod, but there's no belief to accompany the gesture. I'm well aware Robert is in control inside his perfect hiding place.

He's preparing.

Scheming.

And I refuse to let him win.

"So, what now?" I suck in a deep breath, forcing strength. "What am I supposed to do?"

"We wait it out. If someone catches sight of him tonight, then Hunt and Sarah will handle it. If not, we try again tomorrow."

"Right… We wait…" I scoff at the ridiculousness. My parents are lambs at the mercy of hungry wolves, and I'm expected to kick back and watch television as if their lives aren't on the line.

"There are things I hate about this, too, Pen. I want to be the one to find him—to fucking slaughter him. I don't want to be stuck here all night either."

"Then don't. I'm not stopping you."

His eyes narrow. "I get that you're angry. But don't pull this shit with me. You know you're my priority."

I can't help it. My rage grows and my helplessness along with it.

"Come here." He grabs my wrist and tugs me into him, wrapping his arms around my back. "This will all be over soon. And your parents won't even know they were a part of it."

"I hope you're right."

Slowly, his confidence seeps into me, strengthening my resolve. When he releases me, I'm no longer clinging to anger.

"I need to take a shower. Come with me."

"Not this time." I slump onto the sofa. "I need to clear my head."

"You sure?"

"Positive." I want space. Even if only for a few minutes.

"Okay." He reaches for the television remote on the coffee table and hands it to me. "I won't be long. Find a movie to watch, and I'll order dinner once I come back."

I nod.

"You know I'm proud of you, right?" He gives a sad smile. "You're taking this like a warrior."

"It doesn't feel that way. I'm so angry I could kill someone."

He chuckles, soft and low, then leans in to place a quick kiss on my forehead. "Aren't we all?" He retreats, heading toward the hall. "I'll be back soon."

I scoot farther back on the sofa and stare into space.

While he's gone, the others return to the mansion to prepare for the party. Chatter echoes through the halls. The kids' laughter carries from different rooms. Doors slam, and hinges squeak with the flurry of movement.

Then one by one, they leave while Luca and I eat Chinese out of cardboard boxes and pretend this might not be the worst night of my rescued life.

The only people left behind are us, the children, and the nanny, the sudden quiet of the once bustling house leaving me numb.

It doesn't take long for anger to return. Then jealousy.

Everyone else is meeting my parents.

My mother.

My father.

And I'm here, watching as the nanny herds Tobias and Stella down the hall to shower and dress for bed.

"I'm not sure if you want to hear this, but Torian sent me a text." Luca tilts his cell screen my way from his position beside me on the sofa.

I've doubled the security on the house. If you go somewhere, take a tail with you.

"Why would we go somewhere?" I ask. "Do you plan on leaving?"

"Not at all." He gives a subtle shake of his head, his expression turning sympathetic. "But it's not too late if you want to see your parents."

"No." My answer is immediate.

I'm not ready.

Maybe soon. But not now.

"I don't mean face-to-face." He pockets his cell. "We could drive by the restaurant. You should be able to see them without leaving the car."

I open my mouth to repeat my protest, only the words don't come. Yearning clogs my throat instead. It's a painful, agonizing hunger for closure.

I'd kill to see them. Even if just a glimpse.

The thought of my mother's smile... the remembered sound of my father's laugh...

The slightest glimmer would mean the world to me.

"What about Robert?"

He shrugs. "Like Torian said, we wouldn't leave without protection. I'd make sure we were covered."

I swallow over the anticipation tingling like wildfire in my stomach. The pounding of my pulse becomes thunderous.

I want this.

With every pain-filled heartbeat, I really, truly want this.

"Okay." I nod. "But only if you think it's safe."

He gives a half-hearted grin. "Let's get you in the car."

I scoot from the sofa. "Hold up. Let me get changed first. Can you tell the nanny?"

He inclines his head and then I run for the hall, yanking off my baggy sweater to throw it to the bed.

I pull on jeans, a comfy suede jacket, and a pair of Sketchers before meeting Luca at the front door.

"I've arranged the escort." He releases the deadlock and pulls the door wide. "One of the guards from the gate will lead the way to the restaurant."

"Good." I follow Luca to his Suburban, my hands shaking by the time we reach the doors and climb inside.

"You should lie down." He winces in apology. "We don't know who's watching."

"Not this time, please. I'll stay on alert. I promise."

He sighs and starts the engine, not answering my plea.

We drive from the property in silence, following a silver sedan slowly through the streets.

"You look nice..." Luca keeps his attention on the road. "For someone who has no intention of leaving the car."

My cheeks heat, stupidity warming my face. "It's silly, I know." He doesn't answer, the quiet compelling me to fill the silent void. "Even though they're not going to see me, I want to look presentable."

"It makes sense." He grabs my hand and entwines our fingers. "But you don't need to explain."

I ignore the world gliding by around us and focus on him—the one who continues to devote his life to making mine better. But the increasing happiness doesn't detract from the rampant beat of my heart as we drive closer to my parents.

My palms grow slick with sweat. My throat dries.

"You're going to be fine," he murmurs. "It'll do you good to see them."

I know.

I really do.

It's the gravity of the situation. The vulnerability I've always feared.

"When you finally do stand face-to-face with them, what will you say?"

I balk at his question. "I don't know. I have no idea."

His lips curve in a thoughtful smile. "You're going to cry like a baby."

I know that, too. My tears well just thinking about it.

"It's going to be beautiful, Pen." He shoots me a glance.

"Seeing you happy. Smiling. Even through the tears. It's going to be so fucking beautiful."

I'm lost for words. For thoughts.

His care for me is unlike anything I've experienced. Even from my adoring parents.

I love him. God, how I love him.

"What?" He scrunches his nose before returning his focus to the road. "What's that funny look for?"

"Nothing." I swallow and turn to face the windshield, unwilling to let emotion get the better of me.

"We're almost there."

My breath catches as the silver sedan's brake lights flash. I dig my teeth into my lower lip. Sit straighter. Scan the sidewalk.

"See those men on the corner?" Luca jerks his head at the two casually dressed guys leaning against a brick wall, their attention on their cell screens. "They work for us." He tilts his chin to the other side of the road. "Those three, too."

I trek my attention to the small group chatting out the front of a bar.

"There are men all over the streets. In parked cars. Inside buildings. On top of roofs. All armed and ready at a moment's notice."

I nod, no longer concerned about cover when my pulse feels capable of instigating a heart attack. I can sense my parents nearby. It's as if their hum fills the air; my belly, too.

The sedan pulls into a parking space on the side of the road up ahead, allowing Luca to overtake and glide into the next available spot. I scan my surroundings, looking along the shopfronts to my left.

"Over here." Luca focuses out his window. "That's Torian's restaurant right there."

I scoot forward in my seat, transfixed by the bright glow coming from the wall of glass. The interior of the building is filled with a mass of mingling people, all of them standing and drinking from champagne flutes and pints.

I search the guests, my nervousness building with each unfamiliar face.

"I can't see them." I scoot farther along the seat, my ass hovering on the edge. "I can't even see Sebastian."

259

"He's in there somewhere." He points a lazy finger from the steering wheel. "There's Hunt and Sarah."

I nod, not caring about those two. Or Benji. Or any of the Torian family. I need to see my parents. After allowing hope to build, I'm now frantic to lay eyes on my mom and dad.

"Want me to drive past?"

"Yes." I nod. "Please."

He pulls onto the street, the creep of the car slow as we approach the restaurant with the front door guarded by two hulking men, another situated at the far end of the building.

I scour the crowd of smiling faces in a frenzy, my attention moving from one person, to the next, to the next. "Where are they?" My stomach churns. Nausea takes over. "I still can't see them."

"Do you want to take a closer look?"

"From where?"

Luca glances at me, his apprehension visible as he frowns. "I can take you around back and sneak you in through the kitchen."

"No." Although I appreciate the suggestion, disappointment overwhelms me. "It's too risky."

"We'll take our time." He continues driving down the street, past the restaurant, and turns at the corner.

"It's okay." I peer over my shoulder, confirming the silver sedan is following us before I sink into my seat. "It wasn't meant to happen tonight."

He turns again, taking a side street behind the back of the buildings. We pass small staff parking lots until Luca pulls into one filled with vehicles, Torian's Porsche parked closest to the few steps leading into the restaurant.

"What are you doing?" I ask.

He stops the Suburban in the last available parking space and cuts the engine. "We're going to sit here for a while, in case you change your mind."

"I—" I cut my sentence short, already second-guessing myself.

If only I could see them. Just a glimpse.

Time passes as my indecision intensifies, the clawing temptation making it difficult to think while Luca watches me. Each minute spent under his gaze is a million heartbeats filled with anxiety and hesitation.

I'm not ready to speak to them... I can't face their questions and tears... I'm not prepared to explain my past...

But I'd give anything to see them.

Anything.

"Are you sure I won't be seen?" I release my belt. "How will this work?"

"I'll go in before you. Then you can follow when the coast is clear."

He's out of the car and opening my door before I can move. He leads me through the parking lot, my breath frosting the air.

The night is still. Behind us there's nothing but silence while up ahead is street noise and the sound of people laughing and chatting.

I pause. "Maybe we should go back to the car."

"I won't let them see you."

I sneak a glimpse over my shoulder, the hair at the back of my neck standing on end. The silver sedan is waiting in the shadows on the side street. The darkened face of the man sitting inside stares straight at me.

"He's keeping an eye on anybody that approaches. And he's not the only one."

I nod, only slightly appeased, and continue after him, one slow step after another until Luca is reaching for the back door, pulling it open with a squeak to poke his head inside.

He blocks my view of the interior for pained heartbeats before he sidesteps and allows me entry into a bustling stainless-steel kitchen.

"Come on." He holds out a hand and drags me inside.

The new noises are overwhelming. The sizzle of hot plates. The clink of saucepans. There are barked orders from a man wearing a chef's uniform as he scans the four workers situated at different cooking stations.

None of them pay us attention as Luca leads me across the room, this time stopping at a swinging door with a circular peephole.

"Here." He peers through the opening. "They're over the far right of the room. Talking to your brother."

My insides squeeze.

Heart. Chest. Stomach.

I can't move.

After years of trying to forget the love and support of my parents due to the weakness it brought, I struggle to take the final step.

"Pen?" Luca tugs on my hand. "Come on."

I stare into those eyes, the noise increasing, my pulse deafening.

He lessens the panic. There's the strong hold of his hand, the unfaltering focus, the confident tilt of his chin. Everything about him makes me want to be bold.

I can do this.

After everything I've been through, I can do this one simple thing.

I inch forward, stealing my hand from his to place my palms against the door for grounding. At first, the view is the same as outside. People are everywhere, the faces unrecognizable.

Then I spy Sebastian in his suit with Keira wearing a floral flowing dress and cream jacket nestled close at his side.

I hold my breath as my gaze drifts over the people in front of him. The shorter height. The greying hair.

My eyes blaze as I stare at the back of my parents' heads.

That's all there is through the crowd. Their familiar hairstyles. The recognizable frames.

But it's them.

My heart.

My home.

Overwhelming gratitude consumes me. I stare at them for a lifetime, the noise disappearing, the outside world evaporating.

"You're smiling." There's pride in Luca's voice. "Really smiling."

I sniff through my tingling nose. "It may only be the back of their heads, but I'm currently seeing the most beautiful picture right now."

"Yeah." He pauses. "Me, too."

The emotions intensify and I tremble with thanks as I turn my attention to Luca, ensnared in his pride-filled eyes.

"Go on." He jerks his chin at the peephole. "Keep lookin'. I'm going to steal something to eat and stop distracting you." He winks and walks away, aiming for the kitchen staff preparing hors d'oeuvres.

"Thank you." It takes a moment for me to drag my gaze back to the party. I watch. Listen. Pretend I'm part of the festivities.

I let the laughter from the people inside the restaurant sink into me, the happiness, the calm, and attempt to read Sebastian's lips as he continues to talk to our parents.

I don't move as waitstaff walk in and out of the kitchen, the whoosh of the door beside me bringing clearer insight to nearby conversations. I hear names and punchlines. Drink orders and compliments.

Then horror.

Every ounce of my joy evaporates when a male voice asks, "Hey, Dodge, how have you been?"

That's all it takes. One question. One name.

Dodge.

Ice enters my veins. My breathing labors.

I can't see who the speaker is. I can't even determine who they're talking to, but that name brings crystal clarity.

My memory hadn't triggered this morning when I wrote that list, but it does now.

Dodge was a man who supplied Luther with information. A spy of sorts. A traitor to Cole.

I inch back from my peephole and try to get my memories to cycle while attempting to hear the respondent at the same time.

I fail at both.

I remember thinking Dodge was a snake. A slimy, manipulative piece of shit, but I can't pinpoint specific references, only the repeated farewells Luther often spoke.

Keep digging for me, Dodge.

Don't let me down, Dodge.

"What's going on?" Luca comes up behind me, hovering close. "Did they see you?"

I shake my head, still trying to tear pieces of information from a brain that refuses to release them. I need proof. It took too long for me to be believed about Robert.

"Pen?" Luca grabs my shoulders and turns me to face him. "Talk to me."

I try to find answers in his eyes. Still, nothing comes. There are only repeated farewells and snide compliments.

You're invaluable, Dodge.

Luther rarely gave out compliments. Not to his sons, or his right-hand men. It was only to those he manipulated to further his goals. Only to pawns caught in his web.

And now one of those conniving puppets is in the same room as my parents. Within threatening distance of those I love.

"I recognize a name from someone in there." I watch Luca's expression, searching for support. "A name of someone who previously conspired against Cole."

Luca stands taller, shooting a glance out the peephole before returning his attention to me.

He transforms before my eyes. From calm and in control to a strung-tight, laser-focused soldier in a heartbeat.

"Tell me the name," he demands.

29

LUCA

"Dodge," she whispers. "The person's nickname is Dodge."

I hold myself in check, not reacting as my stomach bottoms. But she notices the freefall, her attention narrowing in concern.

"This is bad, isn't it?" she asks in a rush. "Do you think he's here for me? Or my parents? Could he be working with Robert?"

"No. It's okay." I rub her arms and paste on a fucking painful smile. "I've had my suspicions, that's all. And I know how close he is to Torian."

How unbelievably, fucking close.

Breaths escape her lips in panted panic. "What about my parents?"

"They'll be fine. Nobody is stupid enough to risk anything tonight. But I need you to do something for me, okay?" I guide her away from the door, my hand on the low of her back as I lead her to the storeroom. "Wait in here for a while. Just until I handle this."

She plants her feet, her frantic gaze searching my face. "Handle it? What does that mean?" She leans closer, whispering, "Are you going to kill someone? Please, Luca, I want to get my parents out of—"

"They're fine." I open the storeroom, flick on the light, and place pressure on her back to encourage her inside. "I'm only asking for ten minutes. Don't leave this room."

I don't wait for a protest. I shut her inside, the sight of her fear-filled expression haunting me as I stalk for the dining room, past the swinging doors, and into the crowd of guests.

I pass Torian's relatives, friends, and trusted informants as my fury builds. I stalk by women whose husbands have worked with the crime family for years while a tick forms under my right eye. Then I stop before Dodge and look that motherfucker in the eye, knowing on instinct Penny is right about him. Knowing that whoever referenced his nickname tonight is one of the few old-school elders who stood by Luther's side from the beginning of his crime-riddled reign, because they're the only people who have ever called my brother by that name.

The sight of him infuriates me. Fucking sickens me.

I ignore the older man flanking his side, and grab the front of Benji's shirt, bringing an abrupt halt to their conversation.

"Outside," I snarl. "*Now.*"

His eyes flare wide. A flash of fear and guilt hits him before quickly being smothered under anger. "What the—"

I yank his shirt, making him stumble, then release him to storm for the kitchen, not stopping until after I've shoved open the back door and jumped down the stairs to the loose asphalt.

He's slow to follow, descending to ground level with stiff hesitance. "Luca, whatever it is—"

"Save it." I launch my fist at his face, my knuckles colliding with bone.

He jolts backward, stumbling, but I hold him on his feet with an unyielding grip around his throat. "You fucking snitch." I keep my voice low, too fucking aware of the watchful eyes lurking in the shadows. I shove him, over and over until he's up against the brick wall. "You were working with Luther."

He doesn't fight me. Doesn't even protest my grip as his face turns red. All he does is hold my gaze, wordlessly spewing guilt in my direction.

"You fucking piece of shit." I drag him forward and slam him back again. "You stupid, fucking piece of shit. How could you be so reckless?"

"You weren't here when Luther was around."

All the air leaves my lungs on a heave. Despite how things were adding up—even though evidence was mounting—I still hadn't believed.

266

Not entirely.

Not until now.

I release his throat and stumble backward.

He's dead.

Benji is as good as buried. No trial. No second chances.

"Jesus goddamn Christ." I shove my hands into my hair, pulling at the strands to try to make the mania stop.

"You've got no idea what it was like." He straightens from the wall. "You wouldn't understand."

I can't deal. Can't even fucking fathom his level of stupidity.

Problem is, if I don't take this to Torian, I'll be dead alongside Benji. And if I rat out my own blood, the admission probably wouldn't absolve me anyway.

There's no way out of the mess he's created. There's no possible way I can fix this shit.

"Why?" My question is barely audible. "Why the fuck would you even…" I can't finish the sentence through the bile thickening at the back of my throat. "How did this all start? You had to have known what he was doing. There's no way you weren't aware of those women."

His shoulders slump, and he throws his hands up at his sides. "He—"

The back door to the restaurant opens, quickly dragging my attention to Layla whose mouth gapes at the sight of us.

"What's going on?" She slams the door shut and scrambles down the stairs.

"Get out of here, Layla." I glare at her. "This is a private matter."

"No," she pleads. "It's not. He's my husband. This includes me, too."

I scoff. "You've got no idea—"

"Yes, I do." She rushes in front of Benji, acting like a shield to my rage. "I know exactly what this is about. *Please,* Luca. We've been waiting for the news to get out for years. We never thought our actions would cause this much trouble."

Our actions

I'm blindsided. *Again.* Completely and utterly dumb-fucked.

"It was my idea for Benji to tell you there was another woman," she pleads. "I'd hoped it would stop you from digging further. We

267

just needed a little more time. Once Robert was taken care of this all would've blown over."

"Blown over?" I seethe. "How the fuck do you think this would've blown over? Your husband was ratting on your brother."

"Layla," Benji warns. "Let me deal with this." He grabs her arms, attempting to drive her away. "Go back inside."

"I can't." Tears form in her eyes. "This is because of me. *I* started this."

"Layla," Benji snaps. "*Get back inside.*"

She reaches for me as she's pushed to the side. "Luca, please let me explain."

My nostrils flare. My fucking head threatens to explode.

I don't want to hear from her.

The only explanation I need will come from Benji. But that asshole isn't as open to being a Chatty Cathy like his wife.

"I was a horrible person when I first met your brother," she says in a rush. "I was materialistic and petty. Like everyone in my family, I craved money, but I wanted some for myself. Some that was my own. *Our* own," she clarifies.

"I wanted to have financial security because Dad kept telling me Cole would never succeed in taking over the business, and the thought of being poor scared the hell out of me. I was the one who put pressure on Ben to do something about it. Something above and beyond the work he did for my brother." She blinks those long lashes at me, her tears building. "When Dad offered to pay us to keep tabs on Cole, I didn't think it would be a big deal. It was only a father wanting to be updated on his son. At least, that's how it started."

"Layla," Benji grates. "That's enough."

"Shut the fuck up." I clench my fist, preparing to silence him. "At least she has the balls to talk."

"Fuck you. I can talk fine on my own." He tugs down his shirt, righting the crinkles as he speaks under his breath. "It was only meant to be brief updates on business dealings. I'd be financially compensated if I kept Luther in the loop. That's all. We thought we were setting Stella up for the rest of her life in case things went south under Torian's leadership. But before we knew it, the demands got bigger and the threats started. It went from being harmless information to phone taps and spy software."

Fuck. "Phone taps and spy software?"

Layla hangs her head, but Benji lacks the same remorse. He holds my gaze, unblinking.

"He was like a father to me," he mutters. "A *proper* father. He saved me. *Guided* me. He gave me the chance to have a family, for once in my life. To have money and power and pride. I was a fucking man, no longer needing you and your white knight routine to save me from myself."

I scoff. "Well, there's no fucking white knight to save you now, is there? Nothing can help you this time."

"You don't need to." Layla lunges forward, reaching for me, her fingers gripping my jacket as those eyes continue to beg. "Cole doesn't need to know."

I huff out a laugh. "And I guess Penny doesn't deserve to find out either? She doesn't get to learn how Abi really died."

Neither one of them speak. Both remain silent while I compound their crimes.

"That's how your scheme got fucked up, right? Robert got involved? You gave him information," I sneer at my brother, all vicious teeth and seething hatred. "Tell me you gave him insight on Penny. Tell me and I'll end this now."

He doesn't answer, and I don't pause in my response. I nudge Layla out of the way with my shoulder and swing a fist, my knuckle pounding into Benji's gut.

He hunches, coughing, spitting.

Layla wails, her ragged breaths pathetic when coupled with her corruption.

I lean close to my brother's ear as he clasps his hands on his knees, trying to catch his breath. "Tell me."

"Fuck you," he chokes. "I didn't tell him jack shit about her."

"You're a liar." I see red. I *feel* it. There's only heat and rage and mindlessness as I raise my fist again.

"Stop, Luca," Layla cries. "Please. He didn't give any information to Robert. It wasn't him. *I* did it. *I* told Robert where they were."

My brother pauses his recovery, the shock on his raising face seeming genuine as he looks at his wife. "No, you didn't." He shakes his head. "You wouldn't."

"I didn't have a choice. He threatened to tell Cole everything.

And you kept refusing to give him information. You thought you could handle it on your own. You were going to get yourself killed."

"She's lying." Benji looks at me. "She had no idea where I was. Nobody did. But it's true about that fucker threatening us. He's going to tell everyone. That's why I was late yesterday. I was trying to find him and fix this myself."

I glance between them, having no clue which one is bluffing. "I swear to God, if I don't get the full story, without contradictory bullshit, I'm going to lose my shit."

"I already told you." Layla's tear-soaked eyes plead with me. "I had Benji's location on my phone. I always do."

"Like hell," he spits. "I was using a burner."

"Yes, but you had your main cell with you. In your bag or the car. I don't know where exactly, but it was with you, Benji. I'm not lying." The first tear escapes as her lips tremble. "I did this. I'm responsible for that woman's death. And for the attack yesterday. It's my fault."

I stare at her. At the beautiful face that hid those sinister actions.

"Why didn't you tell me?" Benji collapses against the wall. "Why the fuck—"

"Because you wouldn't have given him what he wanted. You were more likely to come clean to Cole," she sobs. "I had no choice. I did it to protect Stella."

"You did it to protect yourself," I snap. "To protect your perfect fucking life in your perfect fucking house—"

Benji straightens, shoving from the wall to pull Layla into his side. "What's it matter? The damage is done now. We need to move on. We can bury this."

"Bury it?" My head fucking throbs. "And then what? Wait for Robert to come after Penny?"

He scoffs. "You barely know her."

I gnash my teeth to the point of pain. Clench my fists until my knuckles burn. I could kill him. Right now. In this moment. I could retrieve the gun from my waistband and shoot him for his blatant disregard for her life.

"This is my *family*, Luc. My daughter."

"If you tell her, it's one more loose end," Layla pleads. "If Cole

270

finds out, he won't hold me accountable. He'll blame everything on Benji. He won't care that it was my fault."

"That's because your husband is a grown-ass man who never should've done this in the first place. Now tell me what else you told that son of a bitch."

The back door swings open and Hunt and Sarah step outside, their curiosity switching between the three of us.

"What are you doing here?" Hunt directs at me. "Aren't you meant to be at Torian's with the klepto?"

I ignore the taunt as they continue down the stairs, the door banging shut behind them.

"Who died?" Sarah asks.

"Nobody," I sneer. "I'm just trying to have a conversation with my brother."

"Must be a serious conversation." She plasters her hands on her hips, all smug and superior. "I'm sensing a wealth of hostility."

The door squeaks opens again, and I curse under my breath at the added audience. It isn't until I glance up to see who it is that my world drops.

Penny.

Her gaze treks over me, from my clenched fists and intimidating stance to the stupid asshole in front of me who bears the brunt of my anger.

It takes a brief second for her expression to change. From curiosity to horror, the color draining from her features.

"It was him," she whispers, still holding the door as if unsure whether to flee back inside. "It was your brother."

Benji's gaze bores into the side of my face as her eyes beg for answers.

I don't know what to say. I don't know how to fix this.

My brother has dragged us into a mess I can't even comprehend, and all I want to do is get her out of it.

"Shorty, I need you to go back inside for a few more…"

My words drift off as Torian comes up behind her, still wearing the mask of hospitable exuberance he always radiates at these functions. He shows no shock at the gathering. No surprise at all at his sister's tears.

"Why did the party move to the parking lot?" He reaches over Penny's shoulder, opening the door wide to get out.

Decker follows a few steps behind. "What the hell are you doing here, Pen?"

Nobody speaks. Nobody moves.

"Don't look at me." Hunt raises his hands. "Sarah and I came out here to fuck."

Torian stops at my side. "Do I need to ask again? Why is my sister upset?

"It's been a long week, Cole." Layla sniffs. "I'm overemotional. That's all."

I fight the need to glare at her as Penny cautiously descends the stairs. Her approach is slow, but her head is high, her shoulders straight. She's preparing for battle.

I start toward her, needing—more than anything—to get her out of here. "We came for a drive to see if we could catch a glimpse of Penny's parents. We're leaving now."

"You're not going anywhere until I have answers," Torian's tone is calm as he lashes out to grab my arm in a white-knuckle grip. "Tell me why my sister is crying."

My pulse detonates.

His hand on me is enough to push my rage beyond my control.

My lip curls with the restriction. The hair on the back of my neck rises.

"Just drop it." Layla wipes her nose with the side of her hand. "I had a fight with my husband. That's all. It's none of your business."

Torian ignores her, and my brother, too. Instead, he pins me with his narrowed stare, wordlessly siphoning the truth.

"Get your fucking hand off me." I yank my arm from his hold and reach into my pocket, retrieving my car fob. "Sarah, I need you to take Penny back to the house. I don't want her parents seeing her before she's—"

"No." Penny shakes her head. "I'm not going anywhere."

I walk to her, not stopping until we're toe to toe. Chest to chest. I wrap my arms around her and pull her so damn close my mouth is a breath from her ear as I whisper, "I need you to do this for me. Trust me."

She stiffens and draws back until those frantic eyes meet mine.

A myriad of thoughts dance in those dark depths. There are

questions. Accusations. Fears. I can hear them all, the volume deafening.

"I'll follow soon." I mark the lie with a quick kiss.

God only knows if I'm going to get out of this to see her again. And from her gasped exhale, I think she knows it, too.

"I don't have all fucking night," Torian seethes. "We have guests to return to. Get her the hell out of here, Sarah."

Penny's eyes widen as she shakes her head. "Please, Luca."

"*Go*. Everything will be okay." It's another lie. After weeks of priding myself on telling her the truth, I'm now tainting this thing we have between us. "Make sure the car on the side street follows you."

"I'll take care of it." Sarah comes up behind her, wrapping an arm around her shoulders to lead her away.

Penny's first step is fumbled, her feet stumbling before she sucks in a deep breath and continues on her own. Everything in her expression speaks of sorrow, the pain marrow deep, but I remain quiet, stiff, my focus returning to the group as the two women climb into my car and slam the doors.

"Someone better start talking," Torian warns. "I want to know what the fuck is going on."

"Color me curious, too," Hunt drawls. "The suspense is killing me."

Benji keeps his mouth shut as Sarah drives from the parking lot, the purr of the second car starting moments later.

It's Layla who crumples as she turns to face her brother. "It was a misunderstanding. I thought he was cheating on me."

Jesus.

Fuck.

Not this bullshit again.

I fight a telling reaction. I force myself not to close my eyes at the compounding lies. I use all my strength to hold back a sneer. But the weight of Decker's gaze bores into me from the top of the steps. He's reading me, his narrowed stare demanding the truth.

"I've set her straight." Benji wraps an arm around his wife's waist. "She was paranoid with me being away too long."

"Is that right?" Torian straightens to his full height, all regal and superior. "Why do I have a feeling you're lying?"

"I swear on my life, I'm not cheating on her." Benji holds up a hand in surrender. "I never would."

I mentally scoff. His life isn't worth dick. Cheating or not.

"Layla," Torian warns. "Tell me the truth."

"I am." Her throat works over a heavy swallow, her guilt clear for everyone to see. "He's not cheating."

"Shit. This is serious." Hunt inches closer. "What's going on? And why wasn't I involved?"

"Stay out of this," I warn. "The last thing this night needs is your commentary."

"Touchy much?"

"Quit the shit." Torian raises his voice. "You realize this neighborhood is being watched, right? I told you all I'd have men everywhere. Did you think about that when you were having your domestic argument out in the open air?"

He's bluffing.

"Do you want to know the updates texted to me while I was inside trying to entertain our guests?" he continues. "Want me to show you?"

They're lies.

We kept our voices down. The guard in the silver sedan would've only seen the fight. Nobody would've heard us. But *fuck*. I wouldn't stake my life on it.

Everyone falls silent as I struggle to come up with a plan. I need to get Benji out of here. We only need a head start.

"You look tense, Luc." Torian's tone is threatening. "Want me to take a guess at why?"

"I fucked up." Benji speaks before I get the chance. "Luca's not involved."

"Shut your mouth," I warn.

"It's true." He straightens, raising his chin. "I need to take responsibility."

"I said, shut the fuck up, Ben." I glare at him.

"Please, Benji." Layla grabs his wrist. "We'll talk about this at home."

"No, you'll talk about it here." Torian steps closer to my brother. "*Now*."

"He stole money," I mutter. "He stole money from *me* and I'm pissed. That's all this is—a family matter. It's nobody else's business."

"No, fuck that." Benji holds Torian's stare. "I betrayed you. I went behind your back and—"

Before the sentence is finished, Cole pulls a gun from his waistband and places the barrel to my brother's forehead.

I don't move, not an inch, as Layla screams, the piercing shriek slicing through my throbbing skull.

"Keep talking," Torian sneers.

"I was a rat for your father."

"*No*." Layla falls to her knees, her manic sobs increasing. "It was *me. I* did this. *I* made this mess."

Torian's aim doesn't waiver from Benji's head as I take in my potential opponents—Hunter with his chest puffed out, his fingers twitching at his sides, and Decker whose face is emotionless, not a hint of anger.

"I need everyone to calm down." I step closer to Benji only to have Hunter's attention snap to me.

"Back off." He points a finger at me in warning. "Stay out of this."

"I can't." I shake my head. "He's my brother—"

"He's going to be your dead brother if he doesn't start talking a lot faster." Torian jabs the gun barrel into Benji. "Spill it all, you son of a bitch."

"It was *me*." Layla tugs on his trousers. "*I* caused this. I begged him to do it. Dad made me believe—"

"Don't worry. I already assumed Luther convinced you I was worthless," Torian snarls. "You had no faith in me."

"It was a long time ago." She slowly drags herself to her feet, tentatively reaching for the gun, only to be shoved away.

"Get inside. I'll deal with you later."

"Cole, *please listen*."

"So help me God, Layla, if you don't walk back into that restaurant and pretend this never happened, I will make you regret bringing a daughter into this world."

She gasps, her tear-streaked face losing color. "What does that—"

"*Now*."

"Do what he says." Benji jerks his chin at her. "Go."

"No." She shakes her head, frenzied. "This was *my* fault. *My* decision. I did this, Cole. Not him."

"Either get inside or watch your husband die."

Fuck.

I reach for my gun, prepared to aim at Torian, when Hunter makes the same move. I turn my attention to him instead, both of us staring down the barrel of the other.

"Fucking hell." Decker jumps down the stairs. "Why don't we all take a breath and get the story straight before we start turning on each other?"

Torian ignores him. "On your knees," he demands of Benji.

"I said, get the story straight first." Decker pulls out his gun, placing it to the back of Torian's head.

Holy fucking shit. It's a Mexican standoff.

No winners. All losers.

Layla stumbles backward, shaking, sobbing, her hand raising to cover her mouth.

"What the hell are you doing, Deck?" Hunt snaps. "Lower your fucking gun."

"I can't." He shrugs. "Cole's protecting his family, and I'm protecting mine."

"How the fuck do you figure that?"

"If Benji dies, Luca could be next by association. And unfortunately, my sister has caught feelings for that asshole, which means he's as good as family to me. I can't stand by and let this happen. Not until the full story is heard."

30

PENNY

I stare into the distance, my body heavy as I struggle not to throw up.

I know what I saw back there.

Luca had been blindsided. By his brother.

I feel it in my gut; Benji is Dodge. I just can't bring myself to believe it. That truth would have major consequences and I don't want to contemplate any of them.

"Want to talk about it?" Sarah gives me a sympathetic look from behind the wheel as we turn and head down a street I'm unfamiliar with.

"No." I glance over my shoulder, checking to make sure the silver sedan is behind us.

"Don't worry; he's following. He won't leave us." Sarah gives another one of those pitying looks. "I'm just taking a more populated route home instead of the fastest."

I nod and settle into my seat, not seeing anything but the scene back in the parking lot as we pass block after block.

I can't get Luca's stricken face out of my head. The anger. The agony. I want to be there with him. By his side. Learning the truth.

"Your parents are nice," Sarah murmurs. "Quiet, but doting. They seemed to have had a great time driving around the country in their RV."

I don't answer. Not only because the inane chitchat is life-draining, but because I can't add thoughts of my parents to the washing machine of turmoil building inside me.

I want her to take me to Luca. I need to know what's going on.

I'm about to ask her to turn around when a car horn blares behind us, the flashing lights of high beams illuminating the interior.

I rise in my seat, blinded by the car behind us as a white truck speeds past on the wrong side of the road. I panic, bracing for an attack when it turns down the next street, practically on two tires.

"It's okay." Sarah gives me a half-hearted smile. "Just another asshole who doesn't know how to drive."

No, it's an omen. A stark sign I'm heading in the wrong direction.

"I have to go back." I clear my throat as we approach an intersection, still able to hear the screeching truck in the distance. "I need to talk to Luca."

"Take my phone." She grabs her cell from her jeans pocket and hands it over. "Call him."

"I don't want to call him. I need to see him."

She ignores me, pulling to a stop at a red light. The longer she remains silent, the more I hear the taunting sounds of that truck, the squeak of rubber, the rev of the engine.

The noise adds to my urgency, pushing me to hurry up and get to Luca. "Please, Sarah. Turn us around."

The light changes to green and she accelerates.

"*Sarah*, I want—"

Tires shriek.

A horn blasts behind us.

We reach the middle of the juncture, my focus moving from Sarah to the beaming lights barreling toward us from her side window. "*Sarah*," I scream. "*The truck*."

I brace for impact, my hands white-knuckling the seat. But it's not enough to stop the force slamming through me.

My airbag deploys, knocking the oxygen from my lungs, belting me in the face.

Darkness steals my vision. I gasp for breath and blink rapidly, attempting to dislodge the inky black as my ears ring.

"Sarah?" I blindly reach for her. "Are you okay?"

She groans as my sight shifts from dark, to grey, to an almost decipherable blur.

I hear things. A rapid mass of noise. The hiss of something mechanical. A car door slams in the distance. Screams. Then gunfire—rapid, bone-chilling gunfire.

I scramble to undo my belt around the inflated airbag. "Sarah, wake up. You need to wake up."

The shots ring louder. From different directions, the closest approaching.

My hands shake in my search for the goddamn buckle, my fingers trembling as I finally release the clasp.

"Sarah." I reach for her again, this time seeing the crimson blood staining the airbag beside where her forehead rests. "*Sarah.*"

Everything quietens. The outside world becomes still as my heartbeat intensifies.

She's hurt. Bad. The color once brightening her face is gone.

"Please, Sarah."

She groans again, filling me with rampant hope.

The familiar tap against my window that steals it away.

I stop breathing.

Swallow.

Tap, tap, tap.

I remain frozen, caught between the need to scream and hide. Fight and surrender.

I know who's at my door. I know without doubt before I turn and come eye-to-eye with Robert, his face now clean-shaven, his hair in a buzz cut as his gleaming smile bears down on me.

The instinct to flee is overwhelming; the necessity wails inside my skull. It takes all my will to shut it down.

What takes its place is a maniacal huff of laughter. I knew I'd never escape. Not from him. Not from the nightmares in Greece.

I could scramble into the back of the car and run from the other side, but he'd catch me.

I could yell for help, yet all I'd achieve is a bigger tally to the dead bodies lying on the ground outside.

The bad guys always win. Always.

He quirks a brow in question and shifts the aim of his gun from me to Sarah.

"*No.*" I push open my door. "Stop."

He smirks and lunges for me, pulling me from the Suburban by my hair. I struggle not to cry out from the pain and scramble to find my footing while he pats me down with an aggressive hand, his gun still trained on Sarah.

"She's dead," I lie.

"Then shooting her isn't going to matter, is it?"

"No, Robert, please." I clasp my palms in prayer. "I'll go with you. I'll go willingly. Just leave her alone."

He smiles, a true, genuine smile that may have had the potential to be handsome if he wasn't a monster. "You missed me, didn't you?"

I press my lips tight against the need to defy him, to spit in his face and wipe the smug satisfaction from his expression.

"Don't worry." He winks. "It'll be just you and me before you know it."

"Let her go," a man yells in the distance.

Oh, God.

"*No*," I scream as Robert swings me around, not pausing a beat before he shoots in the direction of the demand, hitting a man in the chest.

The shock on the stranger's face, along with the sickening jolt of his body, shoves me straight into the horror of my past. All of it comes rushing back—the helplessness, the torture. It suffocates me. It's impossible to breathe.

"*You piece of shit.*" I lash out, smacking and punching as his grip tightens in my hair. "*You fucking monster.*"

"There's my pretty Penny," he taunts. "It's good to see you've still got fight left in you, because all Abi did was cry like a little bitch."

I scream, pummeling his chest, scratching at his face until he reefs me along beside him, storming for the silver sedan behind us, the hood and windshield peppered with bullets.

People scramble to safety in the distance. Some frantically talk on their cells. Others flee the scene.

There are so many witnesses. So many potential casualties to my demise.

"Quit fighting." Robert tugs me harder, making me stumble. "It's time to get out of here."

I don't stop punching at him as he drags me toward the car and over the driver's dead body lying on the asphalt, a gaping head wound sending bile rocketing up my throat.

I gag. Choke.

Robert doesn't care. He continues to yank me along at his side before reaching into the driver's side of the vehicle to pop the trunk.

Oh, God, no.

I increase my struggle, clawing and scratching like an animal. Hitting. Kicking.

People call out from their hiding places, pointlessly threatening him to stop.

"The police are on the way."

"I've got a gun. Let her go or I'll shoot."

They won't take him down. And the police won't get here in time.

I'm going to die at the hands of a rapist. Just like I knew I always would.

"Get in." He releases my hair when we reach the back of the car, and pulls the trunk open. "Hurry up. I don't want to have to damage that pretty face any more than it already is."

The sight before me makes me wither. I stare down at my new prison, the dirty carpeted interior seeming more of a sanctuary since it will be away from his touch. But it's only the start. The deceptive prelude.

"Come on, pretty Penny." He leans close, his breath making me shudder as he whispers, "It's my turn to have you now. Didn't I tell you you'd be mine?"

Yes, he did. And I'd believed him.

With everything inside me I knew it was true.

It was Luca who made me forget. He temporarily distracted me from my future. From my fate.

"Get in." Robert shoves me with force. "Protesting won't save you, but it will permanently destroy your beautiful face."

"Fuck you." I stand my ground.

"Have it your way." He lunges for my legs, hauling me off the ground to topple me into the trunk.

Metal collides with my hip, sending shooting pain around my waist, and I cry out as my head hits the dirty interior. Neither impact stops me from scrambling to my hands and knees.

"Don't even try it." Robert pulls his gun on me and I freeze. "That's a good girl." He looms over me with a leering smile. "You wouldn't believe how easy it was to get to you. How fucking simple when I had someone on the inside. And I can't wait to tell you my plans for the future, but for now, enjoy the ride." He shoots me a wink and reaches to close the trunk.

I quickly duck, missing another impact to the head as he locks me inside the darkened space.

As soon as his footsteps recede, I scramble to get a textural hold on my surroundings, panic overwhelming me.

I slide my palms over everything, searching for an end in the carpet to pull upward in the hopes of finding something beneath. But I can't lift the floor when my weight already rests on top of it. I can't even slide my fingers into the cavity below to search for a jack or any sort of tool.

A door slams. The engine growls to life.

I fight tears as the car moves forward, the pace increasing. Sirens wail in the distance and I set my gliding hands in search of the tail lights. I rip at the upholstery, tugging and tugging until my fingers scream in protest.

The more I rip and yank, the faster the car accelerates, sliding me around the trunk with each of Robert's sharp turns.

I begin to pray for a vehicle collision. That this psychotic asshole will wrap us around a pole, because death by his hands would be better than a life under his fists, but then the red illumination of the tail lights seeps through, the glimpse of light in the darkness giving me hope.

I squeeze my fist into the opening. Tug at the wires. Thump at the warm metal at the back of the light. I thump and thump and thump as I'm thrown around the small space like a doll. I swear I'm about to break through, and that the anticipation has increased the static in my ear to drown out the sirens. Until I realize I can still hear the rumble of tires against gravel. The low hum of the radio.

Oh, God.

The wail of cop cars trails in the distance. Robert must have lost them.

I'm on my own.

I fight back panic as the vehicle turns and turns again, then slows… stops… The grumble of a garage door grates from right outside my spacious coffin.

Wherever we are is still in Portland. Maybe even suburbia. But far from the police that previously gave me hope. Now there's only resignation as I slide back into the woman I once was. The victim. The slave.

From hell to salvation and back again. All in the blink of an eye.

I'd been so happy this morning. Despite the trials and tribulations, I'd breathed freely, yet I took it for granted for too long. I hadn't embraced the gift of reclaimed life. I'd refused to grasp it in both hands.

Maybe that's why this has happened.

Maybe my lack of gratitude has brought me full circle.

I shouldn't have held back in telling Luca how I felt. He deserved to know he was everything to me. Not just a savior or a protector. He was my hope. My future. My life.

The trunk opens and Robert greets me with his smirk still firmly in place.

"We're here, milady." He reclaims my hair, making me scramble as he drags me out of the car to my feet.

I don't let a hint of fear escape. Not one glimmer of sadness or anger.

I lock everything inside, taking on the painful build of adrenaline.

He wants me to be scared of him, so I won't.

He wants me to feel helpless, so I refuse.

"Where are we?" I take in everything within the limited restriction of my view as he continues to grasp my hair.

The three-car garage is empty apart from the vehicle he stole. It's pristine, too—the floors polished, the storage shelves in perfect order. Either the owner of this house has OCD, or they have cleaning staff.

"This is a temporary pitstop." He drags me toward a door across the far side of the room. "I've got a few things to take care of before we can return home."

Home.

The word chokes through me.

"You can't be serious." I stumble as he tugs me harder, opening the door with a harsh kick. "Greece will be the first place they look for me."

"They?" He laughs. "There won't be anyone left behind to look." His hand pinches tighter as he drags me down a darkened hall, the inside of the house smelling like death. It's putrid, the vile scent bringing a gag-inducing taste to my mouth.

"You'll get used to it." He yanks me harder, past art on the walls, beneath high ceilings, along plush carpet.

I attempt to cover my nose and mouth as I stumble, only to have my arm fall to my side at the sight of a woman lying face down on the carpet.

"Watch out for the old girl. She's resting." Robert keeps pulling me. "Her dog is, too."

Up ahead, a large Golden Retriever blocks the path, its limbs stiff.

I can't hold the bile in any longer. I retch, the meagre contents of my stomach falling a few feet from the dead bodies.

"You need to toughen up, pretty Penny. You never used to be this weak."

He gives my hair one long, hard yank then shoves me away as he flicks on a light, exposing a gleaming white foyer with a staircase bordering both walls. The picture-perfect scene brings a whiplashed contrast from the darkened death and destruction.

"Go on." He jerks the barrel of his gun at me. "Get upstairs."

I can't move. Can't think.

Back in Greece, Robert was a monster. He tortured my sisters, raped them, and tormented me. But he was leashed. Luther held him in check.

Now he's a free agent. Willing and capable to cause unimaginable horror. And I don't know how to effectively fight against it.

"Don't worry about Mavis, my love." He jabs me in the shoulder blade with the gun. "You wouldn't have liked the old bitch."

All the air shudders from my lungs.

I know where I am. With heartbreaking dread, I know exactly who the elderly woman is.

"You just figured it out, didn't you?" He snickers. "Surprise. I've been watching you." He jabs the gun again, this time into my stomach, making me grunt. "Now you're going to watch me."

I backtrack, heading toward the staircase. "Watch you do what?"

"Kill everyone who betrayed Luther."

Blinding panic overcomes me as I walk without thought. I'm too focused on trying to force myself to think, but nothing comes.

I can't run. Can't hide.

I need to fight. I just don't know how.

We reach the top of the staircase and he shoves me left into a darkened bedroom with the moonlight spilling through the open curtains.

"Take a look at the view," he taunts. "It's spectacular."

I don't move. I don't want to see.

"*Look,*" he demands, digging the gun into the back of my skull.

He won't kill me, not yet. But I comply regardless, not wanting the little strength I have left to be beaten from my body.

I approach the window to stare down at Cole's yard.

Even though I anticipated the sight, the reality stabs through my chest like jagged glass.

The illuminated empty living room is right there. The place where I spoke to Luca outside this morning is in clear view.

Robert approaches, settling in behind me, his arm wrapping around my waist. "I watched you with another man," he growls in my ear. "I saw him place his hands on something that's mine. Do you understand how that made me feel?"

I close my eyes and force myself to remember that moment. The bliss. The warmth.

Luca is always the light in the darkness. The protection in the face of my fears. I can't forget the strength he's given me.

"I got a front row seat to the way you looked at him," he snarls. "That's why it's important you watch what comes next."

"You won't kill him," I whisper. "He's smarter than you."

"Really? You don't think I've taken the time to prepared to take down your SEAL? I killed Abi and got away with it. You should've seen her, all meek and vulnerable in her childhood bed. With her parents close by, she didn't dare to raise her voice to me. It was all tears and whispered pleas as I slit her wrists. She made it so fucking easy to creep out of there unnoticed. I would've done the same with Nina, but I needed a little more excitement. I decided to shoot that bitch instead."

I sink my teeth into my lower lip, battling the need to release the screaming voices inside my head. To kick. To attack. I bite until I taste blood and bile. I clench my fists until I've gained enough control to turn in his grip and face him.

"But you failed." I hold his gaze, his nose bare inches from mine. "You didn't kill Nina and now she's more protected than ever."

His eyes narrow. "Bullshit."

I smile through the hatred. "Luther would be disappointed in you."

There's a second of hesitation. A small bite of stillness before he lashes out, grabbing my throat in a choking grip.

I grasp at his wrist, attempting to break the hold as I struggle for air. I can't remember what to do. There's no memory of what Luca taught me before I'm shoved backward into the window.

"Don't worry, Pen. I'll fix my mistake. I might even make you join in."

I gasp for breath as footsteps creep down the hall, alerting me to another threat. I tilt my head, trying to get a gauge on this second enemy that lurks in the darkness.

"That's right. I'm not alone." He grins. "And I have the best leverage to take down everyone responsible for ruining my life."

"You're wrong. I'm not a big enough draw card to pull anyone into a trap."

"I agree. You're worthless." He bridges the space between us, pulling me close to kiss my jaw, my cheek, making my skin crawl. "That's why I made sure I had something far greater than a whore to make them fall to their knees."

"Like what?"

"You'll find out." There's confidence in his gaze, a gleaming assurance capable of sending a shiver down my spine. "For now, let's get you down to the kitchen."

He clasps a hand around my wrist, his grip directly above the leather cuff I'd completely forgotten.

I release a sob at my failure.

After everything Luca taught me, I couldn't break from a choke hold, and didn't even remember my weapon. Nothing has changed. I'm just as careless and ignorant as when I was first taken.

The only difference is that I now refuse to give up. I won't let him win when he plans to hurt Luca.

I'd give my life for the man who saved me.

My soul.

"Come on." He tugs me toward the door. "I have a fresh length of rope that's going to look perfect against your skin."

31

LUCA

Torian keeps his weapon trained between Benji's eyes. "I can stay like this for however long necessary. We all know as soon as one of the guards watching this block stumbles upon the asshole with a gun to my head, they'll take you out."

He's right. I've been lucky so far but that luck will soon run out. "He's my brother. He's yours, too."

"He's no brother of mine."

Benji raises his hands in surrender. "There's no excuse for what I've done. But let me explain. Let me tell you why."

"I know why. *Money*. For fucking pieces of paper, you greedy shit."

"Torian, I've had enough. I'm done here." Hunter lowers his weapon and walks to Benji's side. "We can't do this. Not out in the open. We have to move this somewhere else."

Torian doesn't budge.

"I'm serious," Hunter growls. "You're angry. And for good reason. But whatever's going on in that head of yours can't happen in a public place. You also need to give him a fair hearing. If Layla—"

"Leave her out of this," he snaps.

Layla lets out another sob. "I'll never forgive you, Cole."

"*You'll never forgive me*?" he roars. "Are you kidding?"

She flinches, then hikes her chin and straightens her shoulders. "Stella will never forgive you. Keira will never forgive you." She adds strength to her tone. "Luca and Hunter and Decker *will never forgive you.*"

He doesn't respond. He just stands there. Weapon pointed. Finger on the trigger.

"I'm lowering my gun, too." Decker points his barrel to the sky as it descends. "We can discuss this with civility. Stella deserves that much."

Still, there's no movement from Torian. Not a flinch or loosening of his posture.

I keep my aim on the back of his head, the weight of this situation becoming heavier through the quiet.

I'll never get away with killing him. I wouldn't want to anyway.

One bullet would steal everything I have.

I built a life with these assholes. I found a semblance of home.

"I'm lowering my weapon." I stare at Benji, hoping these aren't our last moments together. "We're going to do this the right way."

Torian scoffs. "You trust I won't kill your brother, then shoot you, too?"

No, I don't. This could be suicide. But I have to put faith in everything we've been through. I have to trust I've earned enough of his respect to grant Benji a hearing.

"We're family. And families fuck up sometimes." I lower my gun, my heart pounding at the vulnerability as I place it back in my waistband. "You can't expect any of us to be perfect."

Torian swings around, removing the threat from my brother to place the barrel against my chest. "I can expect whatever the fuck I want."

I hold his gaze, glare for glare. "You're a smart man, but you're not thinking straight. Don't let a knee-jerk reaction destroy your family."

His lip curls, his weapon digging further into me.

"I risked my life for you in Greece," I add. "And I'd do it again. You know me. You know Benji. He fucked up; that's all."

Torian breathes out a laugh. "This is just a fuck-up?"

"He'll pay a price. A heavy one, I'm sure. But you can't kill Stella's father. You can't kill your own brother."

He steps close, snarling. "I ensured the death of my own father. This piece of shit will mean nothing in comparison."

I don't bite. Not when he's begging for me to engage.

He wants a fight, and I won't give it to him.

"Come on." Hunt steps close. "Go back inside. We'll take care of this later."

Torian smiles, slow and brutal. "We're not done here." He places his gun inside his suit jacket. "As soon as the party is over I'm dealing with this." He levels Hunter with a stare. "Keep an eye on Benji." He doesn't wait for a response before stalking for the stairs, pulling the door wide to disappear inside.

There's a collective sigh of relief. A sniffle from Layla. A curse from Decker.

"Well, that's definitely not what I expected when I set out to fuck my fiancée in the parking lot," Hunt drawls.

I ignore him, bridging the distance to my brother to grab his arm and drag him out of earshot of the others. "What's your plan? Are you going to run?"

"I'm not a coward," he snips. "And I won't leave my daughter."

I keep my mouth shut, unwilling to point out the alternative might mean dying as a traitor.

"This is my mess, Luc. I'll fix it for once." He walks to Layla, grabbing her hand as he calls over his shoulder, "Maybe it's time for you to focus on your own issues."

He's talking about Penny. And she's far from a fucking issue. But he's right about me needing to focus on her. I jog toward them as they start for the steps, blocking their path.

"What did you tell him about Penny?" I sneer under my breath. "Does he know about the party?"

She lowers her gaze, her guilt clear.

"Is she in danger? Did you risk her fucking life?"

"No," she pleads. "I made sure the event was safe. I told him everything would be heavily guarded, and said he wouldn't get within three blocks of the restaurant. Along with the extra security at Cole's front gate. He knows he can't do anything tonight."

"Either that or he knows what to fucking prepare for."

"Leave her alone." Benji walks into me, shouldering me out of the way. "Torian will deal with this. It's not your job."

I clench my teeth as they walk inside, and pull out my phone to dial Sarah's number.

"What are you doing?" Hunt attempts to snatch the device. "Put the cell down and tell us what the fuck is going on. Was Layla talking about Robert? Has she been running her mouth to him?"

"Give me a minute." I turn my back to him. "I need to make sure Penny got home." I listen to the ringtone, each unanswered trill poking my pulse back into agitated territory. When she doesn't answer, I try again.

"Who you callin'?"

"Sarah. And she's ignoring me." I start for the cars, only to remember she took my fucking Suburban. "I need some wheels." I swing around to face the two enforcers now staring at me with raised brows.

"What the fuck is going on?" Hunt demands.

"Nothing." I huff out the congealed air thickening in my lungs. "Can I borrow a car or not?"

"Don't look at me, fucker," he grates. "She trashed mine, remember? And besides, we have to talk about what the hell just happened first."

"Not now. I need to get to Penny." I switch my attention to Decker. "How about yours?"

He eyes me for long moments, his narrowed focus judgmental as he reaches into his pocket, then lobs his key fob at me. "I'm coming with you."

"Why?" I catch the offering and start backward toward his truck. "Your parents are still inside."

"I don't like the look on your face. You seem to know a lot more about what's going on than I do, and I have a feeling Penny's involved."

"All I know is that Sarah isn't answering her phone. They should be settled at Torian's by now."

Deck flicks a glance to Hunt. "Call her."

I keep trekking backward, unwilling to wait as the big guy huffs and pulls out his cell to dial.

I'm beside Decker's truck when Hunter lowers the phone. "She's not answering me either. I bet she's already in the shower."

"Tell Torian I think something is wrong." I yank the driver's door open. "And get in contact with the lookouts. Make sure nothing is on the radar."

Decker races toward the passenger side of the car. He's barely in his seat when I gun the engine and slam my foot down, sending us screaming backward out of the parking space before shoving into drive.

"Keep trying to call her." I clench the steering wheel as I increase my speed through the streets, taking the back roads, cutting corners and flying through amber lights.

"Jesus Christ." Decker grabs the side of his seat in one hand and the rail above his head with the other. "I'm sure they're okay. Sarah's smart."

Props from the glorified tech guy don't mean much when pitted against the sinking feeling in my stomach. I never should've let Penny out of my sight. I never should've brought her to the restaurant in the first place. It was her curiosity—her fucking hope —that made the risk seem insignificant.

"Is she still wearing that wrist cuff?" Deck reclaims his phone.

"Yeah, why?"

"I'll check the GPS. Saves you wrapping us around a pole if they're at Torian's."

I lean over, briefly focusing on his device. "You've got access to the tracker?"

"Who do you think installed it? Hunt doesn't know dick about tech." He falls quiet for a moment, pressing buttons repeatedly until he flashes the screen my way. "See? There's nothing to worry about. They're at the house."

I squint at the red dot in the middle of a map, the tiny writing indicating Torian's street.

"Now maybe think about laying off the gas," he drawls. "I don't appreciate you setting a time trial while I'm in the car."

I ease off the accelerator and relax into my seat, but the twist doesn't leave my gut. If anything, it intensifies.

"Like Hunt said, Sarah's probably taking a shower."

"Yeah. Maybe." I don't buy it. The raised hair on the back of my neck tells me otherwise. But paranoia isn't uncommon when I think about Penny. "Once we get to the house, you should drive back to the party to keep an eye on your folks. Robert's still out there somewhere."

He nods, remaining focused on his cell as I turn onto Torian's street.

"How are they anyway?"

He ignores me, raising the device closer to his face.

"Deck? I asked about your parents."

"Slow down." He sits straighter and shoots a glance out his window. "I need to check something."

"What is it?" I ease off the gas. "What's going on?"

"The GPS isn't syncing." He glides his finger over the screen. "Now that we're closer, it's saying she's next door."

"Why wouldn't it be syncing? How accurate is this thing?"

"Accurate. It's previously pinpointed Sarah to within a few feet. It shouldn't be out by an entire house." He keeps pressing buttons. "But even if it's up to date, it's no big deal, right?" His voice is edgy. "She's only next door. Maybe they went to speak to the old lady about the barking dog."

Like hell they would. Neither one of those women are stupid enough to be walking around the streets at night. Not even to the neighbor's house.

"Hold up." He raises a hand as we reach the ostentatious white, double-story building beside Torian's, with its open front yard, billowing trees and thick bushes. "Should we check it out?"

I stop before the driveway, placing the car in park. "Call Sarah again."

He complies, the muted ringing uninterrupted until voicemail cuts in.

"Would Penny have taken the cuff off?" He shoots me a panicked glance. "Then, I dunno, thrown it over the fence or something?"

I wipe a hand over my mouth, not buying that story either. "I'm hoping your app is a piece of shit."

"It's not. I've been tracking a long list of people with this for months."

I cut the ignition to climb outside. I stare at the darkened house, the only illumination coming from the window in the very middle of the lower level, the light seeping through the sheer curtains from a distant room.

For a house earlier consumed with high-decibel dog barking, it's now eerily quiet. The canine doesn't even yap when Decker follows me outside and slams his door shut.

"Something doesn't feel right." I rest my arms against the top of the car. "We need to keep moving."

"Wait a minute." He takes a step toward the gutter. "There's someone in the upstairs window. Third from the right."

I trek my gaze to where he's looking and squint at the darkened curtain.

After what I just went through with Benji, I'm hoping it's another dose of paranoia that has me imagining a gun barrel pointing in our direction. I blink to dislodge the mirage, only it doesn't budge. Instead a red dot appears, the glaring gun laser gliding toward Decker.

"Get down." I jump onto the hood, and dive over the car to tackle him to the ground. We land in a heap, my shoulder colliding with asphalt. *"Move. Move. Move."* I grab his jacket, dragging him to his feet. "Find cover." I run for the bushes, hunched over, and pull my weapon from the back of my pants.

Decker follows a heartbeat behind, but the gunfire I anticipate doesn't rain down. There's nothing. Only panted breathing and the fucking chirp of crickets.

"Tell me I wasn't the only one to see that." I peek through branches, my gaze levelled at the window that no longer has any sign of life.

"You weren't."

"Then we're in some heavy shit." I keep low and creep closer to the house. "Message Hunt. Tell him to get his ass here asap."

"Do you think Penny's in there?"

I can't talk about her. One nudge of that trigger and fear will take over my decision making instead of logic. I hunch, running as close to the ground as possible toward a nearby hedge.

Decker remains in my shadow, pulling out his phone and tapping at the screen. "Are you going to answer me? What the fuck are we doing?"

"You wanted to stop. So we stopped." I glare. "Now, I need to know what the fuck is going on."

"You think she's in there." It's a statement this time, one laced with panic.

"What I think is that a gun laser was pointed directly at your skull. So either the old lady living here quit taking her meds, or someone else is in there attempting to start a war."

"Fuck." He pockets his cell, palms his Glock, and checks the magazine. "What do you want me to do?"

"Keep quiet and follow me." I scramble from one bush to the next, moving toward the farthest corner of the front yard.

The chances of gaining any advantage are dick to none. They know we're here. I can only attempt to find the fuse box and shut off the power, which might leave our enemy scrambling long enough for us to get inside unnoticed.

"I hope you're good with dogs." I run for the head-high sandstone wall blocking us from the back of the house and scale it with a few well-placed footholds.

My boots hit the ground and I tense, waiting for the scramble of canine feet that never eventuate.

The only change to the night is the brighter glow coming from around the rear of the house more than fifty yards ahead.

Decker lands beside me with a heavy thud. "Where's that fucking dog?"

"No idea. But I'm not hanging around to find out."

I haul ass along the side fence, noting the lack of ground-level windows along this part of the house. Only small rectangles for the basement and large squares on the upper level. Or there's the too obvious option of the side door.

"We'll make our way in through the basement." I jerk my chin toward the first small window. "That way we can start clearing rooms from top to bottom."

"But?"

"I don't see any screens or sliding partitions to be able to dislodge. If we break glass we're going to be heard."

"What about the door?" He inches closer. "I've got a bump key. I could get it open in seconds."

"They'll expect it. We need an edge." I scan every inch of the side of the building and yard. "I can't see any cameras; can you?"

There's nothing. Not even the fuse box.

"I can't see shit," he mutters.

"Then we're going in without cutting the power." I run for the house, keeping a low profile as I make my way to one of the lower windows. I fall to my knees and skim my fingers over the glass edges, looking for a weak point, shoving it with the heel of my palm, thumping it with my elbow.

"Let me try the door." Decker backtracks.

"Leave the fucking door—"

A scream carries from inside, the guttural cry filled with fear.

My heart stops. My fucking world tilts.

"That's Penny." Decker sprints for the door. "To hell with being stealth."

I shove from the cement, scrambling to stop him from doing something stupid. But he's already pulled a key from his pocket to jam in the lock by the time I reach his side, his jacket swept off to wrap around it. With a few quick taps of the butt of his gun, he jiggles the handle, then twists.

"Like I said, it's easy as shit." He shoves his arms back into the jacket.

"Keep your mouth shut." I nudge him out of the way, staying low, my weapon ready as I creep inside.

It's shadowed in this part of the house.

Quiet.

There's no fucking sound apart from the barely audible squeak as Decker closes the door.

I visually sweep the laundry, making sure each dark corner doesn't hold a threat before I continue to the open doorway.

Footsteps tread lightly from another room.

"I know you're close," a familiar voice taunts from nearby. "I can hear you."

"Luca?" This time it's Penny, her call stabbing through me as I remain quiet. *"There's only two of them,"* she screams. *"They're not—"*

Her words are cut short with a wail.

Decker makes to rush past me. I'm forced to block his path, shoving him backward before holding a silencing finger to my mouth. "Think," I warn under my breath. "Don't react."

I'm fighting with every fucking breath to run for her myself.

I can barely think through the instinct to get to her as fast as possible. But that shit isn't smart. We need to do this right. I'd knock Decker out before I'd ever risk him endangering her further.

I inch toward the doorway, and glance along the hall. To the left there's nothing but shadow. To the right there's a soft glow coming from the far end of the house.

She's down there, and if there's only two of them, that could make for easy work.

It's getting from here to there without being noticed that's the problem.

I indicate with a finger motion that we're moving forward and take the first silenced steps into the hall. Decker stays on my ass, his exhales breathing down my fucking neck.

A twinge of sound carries behind us. A footstep, then a snicker.

I swing around, about to take aim when something rolls along the floor toward us, the cylindrical device looking like a grenade in the low light.

"*Move.*" I lunge for the closest door, grabbing Decker by the shoulder, to launch us both into the room. We fall, but it's not onto carpet—it's down a fucking staircase.

My head hits a sharp corner directly against my healing bullet wound.

Fuck.

I tumble, flipping through the air like a son of a bitch.

The pain and vertigo are nothing in comparison to the burst of blinding light and the accompanying thunderous sound exploding in my ears.

A fucking flash-bang.

The noise is deafening. The resulting shriek inside my skull is torture.

I land in a heap at the foot of the stairs as Decker fumbles beside me.

I can't see.

Can't think.

Can't stand.

I'm on my hands and knees, my stomach revolting with nausea, my nose wet with an accompanying scent of blood, my brain squeezed in a life-threatening vise.

There's nothing but static and agony as I fail numerous attempts to get onto my feet only to land on my ass when something hard presses into my skull through the darkness.

"Long time, no see, Luca," Robert greets. "Now, tell me, which one of you wants to die first?"

32

PENNY

I scream, rattling the chair I'm bound to, yanking my arms against the rope knotted behind me.

The blast had rocked the house, the loud boom hitting me in the chest while a bright burst of light exploded down the hall. I'd initially thought it was an attack strategy from Luca, but Robert's henchman standing guard at the door to the kitchen didn't show any shock at the eruption.

In fact, he's smiling, pleased with himself.

I scream again, longer and louder, using the noise to disguise the grind of my cuff blade against the rope.

"Shut up and quit struggling," he shouts. "Or I'll hit you again."

I ignore him, letting out another throat-piercing shriek as I pull and tug and slash.

"Nobody's coming to save you now, bitch. We came prepared." He points his gun toward me, shooting another glance down the hall. "Things are about to get wild."

He's young. Probably my age. Mid-twenties, with a thirst for blood if the excitement in his eyes is any indication.

"You expect me to listen to you?" I spit. "You're nothing. Nobody." I saw at the ropes, making my hand cramp from exertion, until the restriction at my wrist begins to loosen. I push harder, cut faster, then scream again, this time in pain when the blade slices through skin.

The warmth of blood trickles over my palm as the asshole storms toward me to slap a meaty palm across my cheek. "Shut. The fuck. Up."

My head flings to the side, the impact blazing across my face, reawakening the throbbing injuries from earlier. The violent jerk of my shoulders frees my right wrist, the blade still tightly clutched in my palm.

I gasp. Not in pain.

It's energy. *Electricity*.

I snatch for the ends of the rope, making sure they don't fall to the floor and expose my partial freedom as I return my attention to my tormentor. "Fuck you, you weak piece of shit."

He smirks, levelling his gun on my chest. "Fuck me?"

Air congeals in my lungs, the pressure building. I can already anticipate the impact of the bullet. It's right there, demanding me to keep my mouth shut.

The need to distract him pushes me to take the risk. I refuse to let Luca jeopardize his life to save me again.

"You won't shoot. You *can't*," I correct. "If you kill me, Robert will do the same to you."

"I'm getting to a point where I'm willing to find out." He leans closer, getting in my face. "So either shut your fucking mouth or I'm putting a bullet in your head."

I drop the rope. Swing my free arm. Aim the blade for his throat.

The metal nicks skin, the contact barely penetrating before he lashes out, pushing me away to send me toppling backward in the chair. I hit the tile hard, the blade escaping my grasp, my left arm painfully restricted behind me.

I scramble with my free hand for my weapon, fumbling it between my stretched fingers as I tug to loosen my trapped wrist. I raise the blade in defense, but I'm not under attack. Robert's thug backtracks, a hand clamped over his throat while his other trembles with the pointed gun.

He stares at me in shock, lips parted, eyes wide as blood seeps between the fingers on his neck, the drops of crimson falling one by one onto his white shirt.

I roll from the chair, my wrist still trapped in rope, and

frantically saw at the binding. My heart hammers. My breathing stutters. He's going to shoot me.

"You're losing a lot of blood." I tug and tug at the chair. "You need to get to a hospital."

"Sh-shut up." He releases his throat to inspect his hand, sending a deluge of gore down his neck.

I gasp. It's bad. That small nick must have hit his carotid because the amount of liquid is extensive. That motherfucker is going to die. Fast.

I huff out a breath, the thrill of victory giving me a vibrating sense of hope.

"Fuck you." He jabs the gun in my direction as I keep sawing. "You stupid c-cunt." He stumbles into the kitchen counter, the weapon tumbling from his hand, his legs collapsing beneath him.

I tug at my bindings, the final length of rope loosening enough for me to yank my arm free. I'm on my feet in an instant and running for his gun. I fall to my knees and slide, snatching the barrel. But he doesn't fight back. He spreads out on the floor, blinking sightlessly at me, his mouth moving without words.

Holy shit. He's done for, the pool of blood building around him.

I point the barrel at his head, my finger twitching against the trigger.

"B-bitch," he chokes, his grip uncurling around his throat. "F-fuck you."

I watch the life seep from him as I sheath my blade in the cuff. I wait precious moments, making sure he doesn't experience a resurgence of energy before I make for the hall, ignoring the putrid smell to stop at an open door leading into darkness.

Grunts and groans carry from inside. Indecipherable muttered words, too.

"Shed some fucking light, Greg," Robert snaps. "I can't see dick down here."

I freeze, caught like a deer in headlights.

"Ahh, so it's not Greg," he muses. "Is that you, my pretty Penny?"

He's in control, the excitement in his voice fueling my fear.

"I think you're going to want to see this," Robert drawls. "The switch is right near the door."

"Penny, run."

Sebastian? He's here?

My knees weaken.

"*Now*, Penny," Robert snarls. "Before I lose patience."

There's a groan of pain, then another growled demand to, "Just run."

My vision blurs under the burn of tears. My heart squeezes. "Luca, are you here?"

"*Run.*" He answers me, the word grated in agony. "Get out of here, shorty."

I can't.

I won't.

Oh, God.

He never left me to fend for myself. I would rather die than turn my back on him and the gun trembling in my hand could change everything. I could kill Robert. I could save Luca.

My limbs shake as I reach inside, sliding my hand along the wall to flick on the light. I quickly slip back out of view, careful to remain hidden as I glimpse down at the staircase illuminated before me and a vacant corner of the room below.

I can't see them. Not any of them.

There's only the sense of horror lurking close.

"Come join us," Robert coos. "You already know you're safe. It's your loved ones who may not last the night."

I plaster myself against the wall, unsure what to do.

I don't have a phone. And I can't risk leaving them, even momentarily, to search for help.

I steel myself against what I'm about to see and descend the stairs, the gun raised.

The room comes into view gradually.

I notice Sebastian first, his tense frame facing me. Then there's Robert a few feet behind, a weapon held in both hands, with another down the front of his pants. He has one barrel trained on the back of Sebastian's head, the other arm pointed farther away.

"What did he do to you?" my brother snarls. "What the fuck did he do?"

"Don't worry." Adrenaline has masked my pain. "I'm okay."

I take another step, my heart lodging in my throat at the sight

301

of Luca on his knees a yard behind, his face pale, his eyes filling with regret.

"Get out of here, Pen." He can barely keep his head up. "I need you to run."

"Drop the gun." Robert advances on my brother.

"No." I aim it at my enemy's head, the weapon shaking in my fragile grip.

"You can't kill me, baby. I've told you before I've got the sweetest fucking leverage known to man. You're gonna want to know what it is before you pull the trigger."

"Then tell me."

He laughs. "In time. Now don't make me count. I'm growing impatient." He cocks a brow, waiting one tense second, then another. "Fine, have it your way." He lowers the barrel, aiming at Sebastian's thigh, then pulls the trigger.

The gunshot blasts the air, ripping a scream from my throat.

Sebastian roars, falling to the floor and curling onto his side, desperately clutching at his right thigh. Luca falls, too, clasping his head, his face burying into the carpet.

I choke on a sob, the sight of their suffering far more punishing than any horror Luther ever inflicted.

"Penny, get the hell out of here. *Now.*" Sebastian struggles to get back up. "Run."

"Fucking *run.*" Luca lashes out, the futile swipe of his arm knocking him off balance.

"Or you could drop the gun." Robert smirks. "You already know you're not going anywhere."

He's right.

My heart is in this room.

Slowly, I place the weapon on the step at my feet, my eyes blazing.

"Good girl. Now come down here and join us."

"Don't do it." Luca pushes onto his hands and knees. "Please, Penny."

I don't think I've heard his desperation before.

He's scared, and I can't stand his fear. It rips me apart in the most agonizing torture.

"It's okay." I suck in a breath, blink away the threat of tears, and descend the stairs. "Robert doesn't want to kill me."

"Don't." Sebastian battles to get to his feet, hissing and wincing as he grabs at his injured leg. His black suit pants cling around the bullet wound, the blood seeping onto his boot, then the floor. "Get out of here."

No. This is my domain. I know this monster better than they do. Neither of them stand a chance without me, and I refuse to live in a world without them. So we're in this together.

Live or die.

"She was never going to leave," Robert taunts. "She can't walk away from those in need. She wants to be the savior, but like always, she's the cause of the bloodshed. She was responsible for the death of hundreds of women through my pure frustration. Weren't you, my sweet?"

I fight against the penetrating words, refusing to let them sink in as I reach the bottom of the stairs.

"If you would've stopped manipulating Luther and become like every other slave, many lives would've been saved," he continues. "But you had to be better than everyone, didn't you?

"They still would've been used and discarded," I whisper. "The only difference is that I would've joined them."

I return my attention to Luca, a knife twisting in my gut at the sight of his ashen skin. He's hurting, badly, but I can't see an injury. "What did he do to you?"

"Forget about me." He sits back on his haunches. "Save yourself."

"It's time to hurry this along, pretty Penny. We don't have all night." Robert inches closer, his guns trained on the back of Luca and Sebastian's heads. "We're going to play a game. One where you get to choose which one of them lives and which one dies."

More sobs clog my throat, the building sorrow tattooing my heart. "You'll kill them both no matter what I do."

"I promise I won't. You know why?"

I shake my head.

He smirks. "Because watching you live with the guilt for the rest of your life will be fucking bliss."

This time the torment escapes, the agony parting my lips. I sob, believing him. He's sick enough to follow through.

"Decide," he taunts. "The brother or the lover."

My lips tremble. Everything does. I can barely think over the shuddering rack of my body.

"It's okay, shorty." Luca hunches over, his hands on his knees, his forgiving eyes on mine. "You know the right choice. You need him more than me."

"Don't pull that bullshit," Sebastian mutters.

"How honorable." Robert jams his gun into the back of Luca's head. "Make your choice or I'll do it for you."

"Wait. *Stop*," I beg. "I'll decide. Just give me a minute."

I need more time. I can't do this.

"Don't leave me hanging," he growls. "Fucking tell me."

I glance from my brother to Luca, knowing there's only one choice.

It hurts. Oh, God, how it hurts but there's no other way.

Someone has to die.

"Penny," Robert growls.

My pulse becomes a staccato, the thunder pounding in my ears. "I choose…" I can't say it. Can't get the words out.

He snickers, loving every moment of my struggle.

"*Run, Penny*," Luca roars. "Just fucking *run*."

I raise my chin, strengthened by the reminder of his salvation. He's always been my shield. My lifeline.

No matter how much this hurts, I'm indebted to return the favor.

I turn my attention to Sebastian, hoping he understands my heartache—the gut-wrenching agony—as I cement my choice. He smiles at me in return. A pained, yet comforting smile forever etched in my mind.

Then I divert my gaze to the monster, swallowing over the agonizing dryness of my throat as I start toward him. "I choose me."

33

LUCA

My heart drops as she breaks into a run.

I can barely hold my head up, even struggle to see, but she's clear before me, her determination obvious as she sprints to take her own life.

I pivot on my toes, swaying with the movement and lunge, diving for Robert's legs. Gunfire pummels my ears, the double shots striking fear in my veins as I take the motherfucker to the ground.

Penny screams. It's all I hear, the high pitch, the terror.

I climb on top of my blurred opponent, swinging my fists at the darkening obscurity of his body, sometimes connecting with hardened flesh, other times with empty air.

More screams ring out. Pain lashes at my face. My head fills with pandemonium. The only notable thought I'm capable of holding revolves around Penny's safety as knuckles punch into my cheek, my jaw.

She can't be taken. Can't die.

Not by him.

Decker yells something about a gun, but I struggle to make out the words. I don't care anymore. Not about my life or my pain. Nothing matters except Penny's safety as I search blindly for this fucker's throat, latching on with both hands to squeeze with all my strength.

The impacts to my face increase. My consciousness fades.

I close my eyes against the vertigo.

Clutch harder.

Pray.

I roar with the effort of staying alive, fingers clawing at my skin, Robert bucking beneath me.

"I said, I've got a fucking gun," Decker yells.

I don't let go.

One more burst of gunfire and I'm as good as dead anyway. My brain can't take anymore. I keep squeezing, harder and harder, until the punches lose their strength and the bucking stops. It's then that I open my eyes, the double vision making it hard to distinguish if the fight-less asshole beneath me is dead or bluffing.

I squint. Lean forward. Blink and blink.

He wheezes, still dragging in breath.

I'm about to swing a heavy punch at his face when Penny dives to her knees beside me, shouting a war cry as she stabs a blade into his throat. She doesn't pause after one attempt. She repeats the severity over and over, continuing to yell her lungs out with every puncture of skin.

I slide off of him, falling onto my ass like a pile of garbage.

Despite the horror, the clarity of her is a fucking sight to behold.

She's fierce.

Strong.

So fucking beautiful.

My head continues to swim as I struggle to my feet, my body swaying. I attempt to right the sudden lurch of movement, stumbling backward, but it's no use. I'm completely fucked, unable to stand straight.

"Luca?" Decker's voice calls over the static. "Luc?"

I blink and blink, getting obscure snapshots of him grabbing Penny's arm to drag her away from mindless destruction.

He'll protect her.

He'll do what's right.

I bump into something. A desk. A box. I don't fucking know, but it sends shit scattering around my feet.

"Luca?" Her voice is pained as she turns to me.

I want to be strong for her, but there's no fucking strength anymore. I can barely keep my head up as I plant my feet, willing my sea legs away.

She rushes forward, those dark eyes taking over my vision. "You need to get to a hospital." She cups my cheeks, the warmth of gentle hands slowing the world's spin just a little.

"We don't do hospitals." I kiss her forehead. "You be strong, okay? Don't take shit from anyone."

"Why are you telling me this?" Her face turns stark, the brief glimpses of clarity cutting me to my core.

"Take care of yourself."

"Stop it." She increases the pressure of her palms. "Look at me."

I'm trying. But everything is heavy. My head. My hands. My feet.

"Focus," she pleads. "Look at me."

Decker comes up beside her, his frame no more than a sickening blur. "How bad is your head?"

I huff out a laugh, my sardonic humor only making the sway worse. "It's nothin'." My words are slurred, my tongue thick.

"Come on." Decker limps close, sliding an arm around my back. "We'll get you to the car."

He's got no hope. Even without a bullet in his leg he wouldn't be able to budge me. And it sure as shit doesn't help when my face starts diving for the floor.

It's a smooth glide, like I'm flying in slow motion, gentle and welcoming against the snatch of Decker's hands as he fails to hold on to me.

Penny's cry fills my ears and I want to tell her it's okay. I want to tell her so many things. But my face hits the floor and my world ends.

34

PENNY

I stare at Luca on the hospital gurney, his bulky body dwarfing the bedframe. He's still. Almost lifeless. And after hours spent sitting here in silence I can't bear the sight, yet I refuse to look away.

His face is battered. The bruise from my brother mars his cheek and the fight with Robert is evident from the swelling and scratches everywhere else.

But the internal injuries make my stomach churn in fear.

"He'll wake soon." A woman speaks from behind me. "I promise."

I glance over my shoulder at the nurse standing in the doorway and wish I had her optimism. I want Luca to recover more than anything. I want him to wake without complications.

I need him to still be mine even though he's been battling a bleed on the brain, probably since Greece, the severity of his injury having the ability to alter his decision-making.

"He's a tough cookie," she continues. "How long ago did you say he sustained the initial impact to his head?"

I hesitate, unsure what I told her earlier. "A few weeks, I guess."

When Sebastian dropped us off outside the ER, he told me to keep my mouth shut. And I have, to an extent. As far as the hospital staff are concerned, we had a car accident. The only complication came when their scans outlined evidence of a brain injury sustained prior to tonight.

"As far as subdural hematomas go, his is relatively minor."

"But the doctor said it could have caused personality changes, right? His decisions over the past few weeks might not have been his own."

She shrugs. "It's possible. Why? Had he been acting irrational or unlike himself?"

That's the thing—I don't know.

I'd barely spent a few moments with him before he risked his life to gain the initial head injury. Everything we shared after could've been a side effect.

"I'm not sure." I wrap my arms around my middle, holding myself tight. "Maybe."

She steps into the room, her eyes kind as they trek over me. "And how are you feeling? I'd still like to take a look at your injuries whenever you're willing."

"I'm fine." I drag my jacket sleeves farther down my hands, not wanting her prying eyes to notice the blood or rope burns. "The impact with the airbag was the worst of it."

"Those can be a bitch." She smiles, the building silence uncomfortable for long moments before she inches back toward the hall. "Please trust me when I say there's no need to worry about him. He's a lucky man."

"She doesn't know the half of it." The graveled murmur from the bed stops my heart.

I keep staring at the nurse, as those words repeat in my ears. I don't drag my attention from her until she glances at the bed, her smile widening.

"I think your man is awake." She grins at me then turns her attention to Luca. "I'm going to quickly page the doctor. You've got two minutes of privacy before I come back to check your vitals."

I nod, my vision blurring.

I'm not going to cry.

I am not going to cry.

The nurse walks away, leaving me to rein in the rampant beat of my heart and the building shake in my fingers.

"You're not talking to me anymore, shorty?" he whispers.

That voice. *Oh, God,* that voice.

I drag my gaze from the door and meet the gorgeous eyes of the man laid out before me. With one glance he warms me. Makes me whole.

But he's still pale. Entirely fragile beneath the muscle-man persona.

"They didn't know when you'd wake up…" I grab his hand. "I wasn't sure if you would."

"Pessimism?" He grins. "From you? No way."

I squeeze his fingers, both loving and hating his sarcasm. "It wasn't pessimism. It was fear. I could barely breathe through the thought of losing you."

"I'm not going anywhere."

My heart pounds. Squeezes. Wrenches so tight. "Do you promise?"

"You know I'm a sucker for giving you anything you want."

Yes, I know.

But his face sobers and for a moment there's only silence and contemplation before he says, "I can't remember everything. You need to bring me up to speed. What happened? What's going on?"

"I don't know." My lips lift in an apologetic smile. "I wish I had answers, but I haven't heard from anyone. When you collapsed, Sebastian wouldn't let me call an ambulance. Instead, we dragged you into his truck and drove you here. I haven't seen or heard from anyone since. Not my brother. Or Cole. There's been no police to question what happened either."

He sits, wincing as he repositions himself against the pillows. "What did you tell hospital staff?"

"Not much." I reach for my chair, dragging it closer to the bed, not once releasing his hand. "I told them we had a car accident."

"Good." He nods. Cringes. Groans. "My head is fucking killing me."

"You've got a bleed on the brain. They think you've had it since Greece."

He raises a brow. "That would explain the headaches."

"It could explain a lot of things."

"Meaning?" He frowns. "What's wrong? You look upset."

I *am* upset. So damn upset at the thought of our future

uncertainty. "The doctor asked if you've been acting differently because it's common an injury like yours could cause a change in behavior."

"And?" His brows pull tighter. "You're going to have to dumb it down. I'm still not catching on to what's worrying you."

"We barely spoke before you hit your head in Greece. Now we're…" I wave a lazy hand between us. "I don't know. I just thought maybe this thing with us is the change in behavior they were referring to."

He grins, the curve of lips announcing a complete lack of seriousness. "You think the way I feel about you is due to brain damage?"

"Please don't joke. It's not unlikely—"

"Pen, if being with you is a side effect, then I give you permission to give me a love tap to the head every once in a while to keep the momentum going. I'll even buy you your own bat." He drags my fingers to his lips for a quick kiss. "I'll take an ass whoopin' every week if that's what it takes."

"That's not funny, Luca. I'm seriously scared."

He breathes out a chuckle. "You should be more scared about being stuck with me. 'Cause I ain't letting you go."

My chest burns under the weight of his promise, the heat increasing when his expression turns serious.

"You're everything, Pen. You always have been. What I feel for you isn't fake."

"I'm not saying it's fake…"

He squeezes my hand. "I know what you're saying, and it's not true. I fell hard for you the first moment we met. I was done for before I even hit my head."

I smile. Nod. It's all I can do against the build of hope. "I'm glad you feel that way."

"What else is bothering you?" His fingers retreat from my grip to delicately sweep over mine. Back and forth. Over and under. Gently coaxing. "Is there something I don't know?"

"Not really. I'm just unsure of what's happening with everyone else. Sebastian was shot. Sarah was hurt, too. And I keep expecting the police to walk in here and demand answers." I lower my voice. "I killed a man, Luca. I watched him bleed out."

"Don't think about it. The cops aren't coming. Your brother

311

didn't call an ambulance because he planned to go back to the house and clean up. We'll hear from someone once all the loose ends are tied."

"But it's been hours. And he was—"

"I'm sure he's fine. And tidying loose ends takes time. All hands would be on deck to sweep that shit under the rug."

I'm not convinced, but I try to believe him. I need to stop listening to the fear that shackled me for so long and learn to trust in him wholeheartedly.

Robert is dead.

Luca is alive.

My family is safe.

It's time to be free.

Except... "What about your brother?" I hold his gaze, hating the cringe he gives me. "He was working with Robert."

"Torian will deal with Benji."

"What does that mean?"

He shrugs. "I honestly don't know. But no matter what happens, I'll make sure you're safe."

"*We're* safe," I correct. "There's no me without you."

He huffs out a half-hearted chuckle. "And vice versa, shorty. I don't want to be here without you."

I bow my head into our hands, shielding my face due to the building tears. His fingers find my hair, his touch drifting through the strands.

"I love you, Pen," he whispers. "When I found out Robert had you, I..."

"He's gone." I add strength to my voice as I return my gaze to his. "You saved me again."

"Like hell I did. I don't remember much, but I can still see you running for him. Don't ever do something like that again."

I would. I'd do it now if I had to.

This world needs Luca. The good guy disguised as a villain.

"Your face is bruised." His fingers stop their delicate caress, his eyes narrowing slightly. "Did he hurt you? Before I got to you, did he—"

"No. I'm good. Robert rammed his truck into Sarah's car. The worst of my injuries are from the deployed airbag."

I don't want to concern him with the intricate details of my battle scars. None of that matters now.

He sinks farther into the pillows, his shoulders losing their tension. "Then tell me what I need to do to make you happy. I want to see that gorgeous smile."

My stomach does a swooping roll, tumbling and turning. This man is everything. All my hope. All my security.

He's my way home. I have to finally let go and allow him to guide me there.

"I am happy." I smile from deep in my heart, with all of the optimism I can muster. "You make me unbelievably happy."

He doesn't respond. Not in words. Just with the lazy grin that fills me with unending warmth.

"Sorry to interrupt." The nurse walks into the room, skirting the bed to stop before the heart monitors on the other side. "It's time to check the patient. And you—" She gives me a one-second glance. "—have a visitor."

"Me?"

She nods and turns her attention to the door.

I do the same, finding my brother standing there, face solemn, legs stiff.

"Oh, God, Sebastian." I shove from my chair and rush to him, gently engulfing him in a hug.

He tenses, taking two seconds to relax into the embrace before returning the gesture. "Hey, Pen. I'm glad to see you, too."

"Are you okay?" I inch away to look at him. "Have you seen Sarah?"

He eyes the nurse with suspicion. "She's recovering. It takes a lot to knock the wind out of her sails."

I step back, understanding his hint for subtlety.

"How's he doing?" He jerks his chin toward the bed. "Did they give him the lobotomy I hoped for?"

"Very funny," Luca growls.

The nurse chuckles. Sebastian gives a faint smirk. But something's not right. I see more than weary exhaustion in his features.

"How's your leg?"

"Flesh wound. It'll heal."

"Then there's something else. What's wrong?"

He shrugs. "Nothin'. I just, ahh…" He rubs the back of his neck. "I thought with your enforcer laid flat you might want some additional support."

I nod. "Thank you. I'm glad you're here."

He cringes, meeting my gaze. "Pen, I wasn't talking about me."

"Then what do you mean?" I lower my voice. "What's going on?"

He pauses, the silence growing tense. My heart beats double time, drawing out the quiet. It isn't until his nose crinkles in apology that I understand. Without words or action, I know exactly what he's done before he says, "Mom and Dad are waiting at the entrance to the ward."

I hold my breath against the arrhythmia.

"Jesus Christ, Decker," Luca snarls. "Are you a fucking idiot? You can't dump this on—"

"It's all right." I shoot him a forced smile. "I'm okay."

I am.

Really.

I can handle this. I can face my parents.

I'll walk right up to them and say hello. We'll hug… and cry… and…

Oh, God. I can't do this. I can't see them without losing myself. Without releasing my thin grip on stability.

"Sir, you need to rest," the nurse demands. "Sir, please."

I blink out of my panic to see Luca flinging back the covers in an attempt to climb from the bed.

"Stop," I beg. "*Please*. I can do this."

It's a lie.

I can't do this. I don't know how.

"I'm coming with you," he growls.

"No. I should do this on my own."

It's another lie.

I need him. I'll *always* need him.

But there's no escaping this reunion. And I owe it to my parents to have it take place in relative privacy.

"Trust me." I give him a genuine smile. "It's time."

His hand clutches tight to the bedsheet, the intensity in his features never wavering. "You sure?"

I nod.

"I love you," he vows. "And I'm right here if you need me."

The swooping roll of my insides returns. "I love you, too. With everything I am, I love you."

Sebastian clears his throat, the sound awkward as he rubs my arm. "You don't have to do this now. As far as Mom and Dad are concerned, they're here because I needed to see someone about this pulled muscle in my thigh." He winks. "They're not expecting you. They still don't know."

The chance of escape brings relief. Temporary, misguided relief. I can't put this off forever.

"I'm doing this." I nod to convince myself. "Take me to them."

My pulse beats erratically in my throat, the rhythm and severity increasing as Sebastian leads me from the room and into the hall.

The ward is quiet, the early morning hour making my surroundings desolate.

"Do they know what happened last night?" I ask.

"No. Once I left the party, Keira took them to their hotel. They're just as clueless as they've ever been. But your car accident is starting to hit the news. I caught sight of a sketchy video on the television an hour ago."

My legs grow heavy with each step, the building throb in my veins becoming too much.

Then I see him—my dad.

He stands on the other side of the open ward doors, his attention focused on something out of view, the glow of the sunrise highlighting his face.

My feet stop of their own accord. I can't move any farther.

"It's okay," Sebastian whispers. "It's all going to be okay."

It doesn't feel that way. My body is in overdrive, my thoughts and fears colliding into a mass of hysteria.

I'm about to turn and hide when my dad looks our way. His face brightens at the sight of his son, then completely falls when he sees me.

He stares in horror. Wide eyes. Gaping mouth.

"What is it?" my mother asks, her arm reaching into view. "What's wrong?"

He doesn't answer. He's frozen.

Sebastian continues without me, walking to our father's side while my mother stands.

I want to run.

To them. *Away* from them. But I can't move.

I blink the blur from my vision as my mom turns to face me, her hand immediately raising to cover her mouth.

All I feel is panic and pain.

All I see is heartache and loss.

"Penny?" My mother glances from me, to my father, to my brother, and back again, her confusion unwavering.

"Pen, is that you?" my dad asks.

I tremble. Arms. Legs. Heart.

The eight feet of distance between us is so close, yet unbelievably far. No matter what I do, I can't get my feet to move, my voice to speak.

"It's her." Sebastian starts toward me. "It's really her."

My chest restricts. My heart and lungs are ripped from me.

My mother takes a step, a sob breaching her lips. "Penny..." She runs, the pace hobbled, her face stricken. "My baby girl."

I break, my tears rushing free, the heated trails searing my cheeks as air heaves from my lungs.

I'm engulfed in restricting arms, my mother's love circling me even tighter. I close my eyes against the emotional onslaught, sucking in breath after hiccupped breath, not wanting the love to weaken me, and not being able to deny it at the same time.

"I don't understand." My dad's voice approaches. "How did this happen?"

More arms engulf me. The scent of my father's aftershave sinks deep into my lungs.

There are sobs and laughter and sniffles.

Hugs and questions and comfort. So much soul-shaking comfort.

I let it wash over me. Consume me.

I sway with the waves of emotion, taking in all the sensations of home as I squeeze my eyes tighter in an attempt to stem the unending blubbering.

"Everything is going to be all right, baby girl," my mother soothes. "Everything is going to be just fine."

After years spent denying my suffering, I give in.

I succumb to the pain. I let my grief break free.

I cry until the tears clean away the heartache, all my memories purged from the deepest, darkest depths of my soul. And when my sobs finally subside, I begin to breathe again, knowing I'm finally ready to start healing.

35

LUCA

I scowl as the nurse flashes a light in my eyes.

"You don't need to look at me like that." She lowers the mini flashlight and grabs my hand. "I get that you're not happy being here. I'm just doing my job, and apparently, looking after you is a top priority, so grip my hand and show me how macho you are."

I clench her fingers, my scowl remaining in place. "Who says I'm a top priority?"

"My supervisor. I was told to make sure Mr. John Doe was taken care of and that he receives everything he asks for." She holds my gaze, raising a brow.

I chuckle. "Feel free to call me John."

"How kind of you." She drops my hand and grabs the other. "Want to tell me what happened to your head, John?"

"I have no idea."

She rolls her eyes and steps away, removing a blood pressure cuff from the monitoring equipment near the head of the bed.

While she's wrenching my arm into submission, I cock my ear toward the door, trying to catch a hint of Penny's voice.

This shit with Robert might be over, but the battles she has to face are only just beginning. And I want to be by her side for every single one of them.

"Your blood pressure is a little high."

"No shit." My girl is in the hall, facing one of the most

monumental moments of her life, and I'm laid flat, unable to help her. "Give me some aspirin and a ticket out of here. I'll be fine."

"With all due respect, *John*, you've got a subdural hematoma. Which means you're not leaving anytime soon. You need to be under observation to ensure the bleeding doesn't increase."

I revert back to glaring, not appreciating her calm superiority as Decker limps into the room. He moves to stand against the far wall, watching silently as the nurse takes my temperature like I'm a five-year-old with the flu.

He doesn't talk. Doesn't change his masked expression of exhaustion. He doesn't give one hint as to what's going on with Penny or why he's left her out there on her own.

"What the fuck are you doing?" I growl.

He answers by cocking a lazy brow.

It's the nurse who stiffens and meets my gaze. "Do you need me to leave?"

"Is that an option?"

She sighs. "Like I said, I was told to give you everything you asked for, which includes privacy if it's requested."

"It's requested," Decker murmurs.

"Definitely requested," I grate.

She huffs out a breath and places the thermometer back into the stand near the head of the bed. "I'll give you five minutes. Then I have to come back and finish my obs." She makes for the door, giving a quick glance at me over her shoulder before leaving the room.

Still, Decker doesn't speak. He remains against the wall, exhaustion heavy in his slumped shoulders, expression indecipherable.

"Where is she?" I ask. "*How* is she?"

"In the hall. And you'd be a better judge of how she's feeling than I would. All I know is that her tears don't fill me with giddy optimism."

"Tears were inevitable."

"Yeah, I know. I just don't appreciate seeing her like that after everything she's been through." He leans forward to massage his thigh with a wince. "Do you two have plans?"

What the fuck sort of question is that? "Plans for what? Today? This week? The next ten years?"

His expression doesn't change. He just eyes me with disinterest. "All of the above."

I sit, readjusting myself against the pillows, and eye my clothes on the bedside table. I need to get out of here. "That's her decision."

"Don't dodge the question. I'm asking if you plan to stick around. Is this thing between you two temporary or long-haul?"

"I'm not dodging anything. I have every intention of staying by her side. Thick and thin. Good times and bad."

Still, there's no reaction. No protective brotherly response. No encouragement or threat. He either lost a lot of blood from that bullet or something is going on. Something that will require me getting my ass out of here, consequences be damned.

I tug out my cannula and grab my clothes from the side table. "Do you have more questions?" I slide from the bed, my vision darkening with the movement. "Or are you just going to stand there and admire me all day?"

He pushes from the wall and shuffles forward, stopping to grab the wooden board at the foot of the bed with both hands.

I jerk on my jeans, impatiently waiting for whatever brotherly threat he has up his sleeve. "You preparing to hit me again? Is that it?"

"No, I'm done with that. You've proven yourself."

I yank up my zipper and clasp the button. "Well, fan-fucking-tastic. Sounds like all my dreams have come true." I tug off the gown and throw it to the bed. "All I've ever wanted is to prove myself to you."

He scowls.

That's all he does. There's no snarky retaliation. No threat of violence.

I'm prepping him to fight and he's giving me nothing. Something is seriously wrong. "What the hell is going on? Where is she?"

"Penny's fine. She's in the hall. I thought I'd give her a few seconds alone with our parents."

"And my brother?" I clench my jaw, tight, hoping like hell I'm not about to be given a death notice.

He shrugs. "He's still alive. For now."

"Then what the fuck is this really about?" I grab my shirt from the mattress and tug it on. "I know you're not in here to welcome me to the family."

"You're right. I'm not." His voice is low as he narrows his eyes on me. "I'm trying to determine how fucked up your head is."

I pause in the middle of straightening my shirt. "Why? Because you think I can't look after your sister?"

"No. Because there's shit that needs to be done, and I'm not sure you're capable."

"What shit?" The question comes with hesitance. "Robert's dead, right? My memory is foggy, but I could've sworn—"

"He's dead." His face hardens as he glances toward the door, then returns his attention to me. "Problem is, he wasn't jerkin' our chain when he said he had leverage."

Adrenaline floods my system, the panic overriding the dull throb in my head to bring some semblance of clarity. "What leverage?"

He sucks in a breath and straightens. "He took the kids." His face turns pained, the fear and desperation finally seeping through. "He kidnapped Tobias and Stella, and we've got no fucking idea where they are."

I hope you enjoyed Luca. The next book in the Hunting Her world is Cole.

I fell for the enemy. A man whose actions resembled the devil so closely it was sickening. But I learned from my mistakes.

At least I thought I had. Until I'm tempted back into his life with a case I can't refuse.

Cole Torian needs my help. And I'm unable to deny him.

Please consider leaving a review on your book retailer
website or Goodreads

Titles in the Hunting Her World

Hunter

Decker

Torian

Savior

Luca

Cole

Seeking Vengeance

Ruthless Redemption

Bishop

**Information on Eden's other books can be found at
www.edensummers.com**

ABOUT THE AUTHOR

Eden Summers is a bestselling author of contemporary romance with a side of sizzle and sarcasm.

She lives in Australia with a young family who are well aware she's circling the drain of insanity.
Eden can't resist alpha dominance, dark features and sarcasm in her fictional heroes and loves a strong heroine who knows when to bite her tongue but also serves retribution with a feminine smile on her face.

If you'd like access to exclusive information and giveaways, join Eden Summers' newsletter via the link on her website - www.edensummers.com

For more information:
www.edensummers.com
eden@edensummers.com

Printed in the USA
CPSIA information can be obtained
at www.ICGtesting.com
LVHW041639160124
769024LV00025B/206